THE SENTINEL'S SONG

A RETELLING OF ST. GEORGE AND THE DRAGON

THE CLASSICAL KINGDOMS COLLECTION
BOOK TEN

BRITTANY FICHTER

WANT FREE STORIES?

Sign up for a free no-spam newsletter and free short stories, exclusive secret chapters, and sneak peeks at books before they're published . . . all for free.

Details at the end of this book.

To Kaitlin (Fairest)

I still smile every time I look at one of the many moments you captured for our family. The beauty that you bring to light with film brings glory to God as it emphasizes the beauty He's placed down here on earth. As much as I miss your pictures, though, I miss you even more. One of these days, I'll get to hug your face off once again.

PROLOGUE

S abra, keep up."

Sabra snapped her attention back to her cousin and urged her horse to catch up with his. She wasn't worried about getting left behind. Their eight guards would sooner eat fire than let her get out of sight. She did, however, believe her cousin's threat that if she couldn't keep up, he would make her wait another two years before bringing her to the trade talks again. Sabra was ten now. She'd already waited too long for this adventure to be left behind.

Their ride was pleasant. The morning was golden against the cone-shaped rocks that pierced the sky at the foot of the nearby hill. Chimneys, Demir called them. A strange name, as they had nothing to do with a kitchen. Demir said they were carved by the strong winds and rains, wearing away the softer rock on the outside with only the harder rock remaining, their tops pointing like arrows toward the sky. Behind the stone chimneys ran yellowish brown stone hills, riddled with holes that Demir said were the entrances of hundreds of caves, also carved out by wind and water.

And no, Demir said, they didn't have time to cross the ancient volcanic valley between and explore. Even if the very existence of such a fantastical place had been teasing Sabra since they'd set out yesterday.

The sky was a mix of yellow and blue, and after the night's storm, the air smelled of rain and soil. It hadn't made for a particularly restful night in the tents that Demir and the guards had put up, but now Sabra relished the way the world felt fresh and new. Especially as they made their way toward the city gate.

"Time to see how well you've been listening," Demir said, looking back from his horse at Sabra with a smirk. "What's the city's name?"

She smirked back. "Kappadona."

"And to what kingdom does it belong?"

"Kappadona is its own kingdom, just like Segzein," she fired back. Then she turned to her favorite bodyguard, Shakirat. The imposing man never smiled. He was trained not to, according to Demir. But she was sure she saw the corner of his mouth turn up when she was particularly saucy. "It's like he doesn't even know me," she told Shakirat. "When is he going to learn that I'm always listening to his never-ending lessons?"

Shakirat kept his eyes on the market as they entered the city, but sure enough, she was sure the corner of his mouth lifted.

Demir arched a dark eyebrow and smiled. "And what are such kingdoms called?"

She huffed. "City-states." Then, before he could ask another question, she pulled her horse up beside his. "Now I have a question for you."

"Of course you do."

"Since Father's not here—"

"Sabra," he turned and gave her a look. "Just because your father isn't here doesn't mean we can run around doing as we wish."

She sat taller. "I happen to know that we're outside of Segzeinian jurisdiction."

He rolled his eyes. "Nice try."

"But you promised to tell me about the Dune Pirates!"

"I said I'd tell you when you're older."

"I am older!" She flipped her hair like some of the court ladies did. "That's why you're taking me on this journey!"

Demir cast her a smug sideways glance, which annoyed her even more. "Yes, but I also said you would get married when you're older. And ten isn't old enough for either."

Sabra huffed. "Well, then, could you at least tell me about the Blue Bands?"

Demir let his head fall back and groaned. "Sabra, you're going to be the death of me. How about you sit quietly and enjoy the ride?"

"And if I don't?"

He closed his eyes. "If you don't, I'm going to lose my sanity."

"Very well." Sabra sulked. Demir was her favorite person in the whole world. There were times, however, where he gave a little more deference to her father than Sabra would have preferred.

The market was lively and full, however, with so many interesting things to do that Sabra couldn't stay annoyed for long. Especially when something shiny caught her eye.

"Demir," she called, "what is that man doing?"

"Which one?" He turned in his saddle.

"Over there. The one hitting the hot metal with another piece of metal."

"He's a smith. He's making a horseshoe." He glanced at her. "We have smiths at home. You know what those are."

"Not that one." Sabra waved impatiently. "The one to his left. It looks like he's making..." She squinted in the harsh morning light. "A sword?" Sabra was sure Segzein didn't have any smiths like *that*.

Demir shielded his eyes. "He's a swordsmith."

"A swordsmith." Sabra studied the man as they passed his stall.

The man's beard and hair were gray, but through his shirt, which stuck to him with sweat, Sabra could see strong, muscled arms, unusual on someone his age. Her father's arms were half their width. Although, she supposed one would have to be strong to hit metal with a hammer all day.

"Can I have one?" she piped.

"A swordsmith? No, your mother would not think that an acceptable pet."

Sabra pulled her horse up to her cousin's and gave his shin a small kick. "You *know* I don't mean the man. I want a sword!"

"First of all, don't kick when you're on a horse. You could spook him. Second," Demir gave her the smallest hint of a smile, the one he always had when he was about to tease, "what in the sands would you do with a sword?"

"Learn to use it!"

"I'm already teaching you staff," her cousin held up a hand as she opened her mouth to protest, "much to your mother's dismay. I think she'd use the thing to behead me if I let you come home with one."

Sabra rolled her eyes, but Demir was right. Her mother was more than understanding with many of Sabra's "odd" interests, as she phrased it. But a sword fighting princess was most likely far beyond the limits of her patience.

"Out of curiosity, why do you want a sword?" Demir asked as they made their way down the center of the crowded marketplace. Some people stopped and stared up at their traveling party, but most seemed to find them uninteresting. Probably because, while this was Sabra's first time at the trade talks, Demir was here in their neighboring city state of Kappadona at least once a year.

"Aside from fighting?"

He gave her a wry smile, and she grinned and shrugged. "I don't know. It reminds me of my stories, I suppose."

Demir snorted. "Those stories are going to get you into trouble someday."

"Perhaps. But not today. Is this it?" They were nearing a large olive tree encircled by a low wall covered in brightly tiled mosaics. At least a dozen men and women sat on the wall, and a few more sat on blankets in the tree's shade. Some were chatting. Others were eating. But as Sabra's party approached, most eyes turned to them.

"Who is this, Demir?" a woman who looked to be in her fourth decade asked, nodding at Sabra.

"This is my cousin," Demir said, hopping off his horse. Then he turned and helped Sabra down from hers. "I promised her that she could come and listen to our trade talks this year."

"We keep no nannies here." One of the men scoffed, and the woman who had first spoken nodded and pursed her lips.

"Sabra," Demir said, standing taller, authority ringing in his voice, "is ten years of age. She is also the future queen of Segzein."

A low murmur passed through the group, and many of the people turned to whisper to one another. Finally, the first woman, who Sabra guessed to have some sort of authority in the group, nodded and patted her blanket and scooted over. Careful to mimic Demir's every move, Sabra followed him to the blanket and sat beside him. This was one of her first public appearances outside of her own kingdom, and, as her father had told her before they'd left, this would be the first impression she would make on outside allies. She might be young, but she was still the future queen.

And Sabra tried to focus on the trade talks. She really did. But there were so many people talking and so many names and places that soon it was hard to pay attention at all. And instead of listening as she should have, Sabra found herself staring at the swordsmith's stall over and over again, until her cousin's voice took her by surprise and made her jump.

"We're pausing the talks for the midday meal." He gave her a kind smile. "Go over to that fountain and eat there if you'd like to. I know these talks are long, and they'll only get longer."

Sabra gave him a grateful look as he pressed a little sack of food into her hands. First impressions or none, she didn't think she could stand to hear about tariffs or taxes one more time without going crazy.

The fountain was even larger than the olive tree, and so was its shadow. People of all ages were gathered around it and reclined on the three steps that encircled it. Sabra took her lunch there and found an empty place where she was hidden from the sun and could watch the swordsmith. Her guards stationed themselves a little distance away on each side of her, where they would wait until Demir called her back.

Sabra couldn't really tell why she found the swordsmith so interesting. Perhaps it was the way he was able to hit the weapon on the same spot every time without missing. Or maybe it was how the blade was shaped like no sword Sabra had ever seen. There was something incredibly soothing about watching the constant, methodical work.

"That's my grandfather."

Sabra jumped as a boy sat on the step beside her. He looked to be about her age, his hair thick with large, dark brown curls and his eyes steel gray. His skin was swarthy, as though it might be olive, except for the fact that he spent too much time in the sun.

"The man you've been staring at," he said, nodding back at the swordsmith. "He's my grandfather." The boy grinned. "He'll not bite, you know."

"I never thought he would." Sabra was not used to being at a loss for words. She turned back to the man. "I've just never seen someone work so fast and so well with metal."

The boy sat taller, and his chest puffed out a bit, as though this last bit of praise brought him pride. "Nobody works as fast as he does. Or makes weapons quite as well."

That was a lot of boasting for a boy who couldn't be more than eleven or twelve years in age. But Sabra didn't move to correct him, as she could admit to never seeing the like. Instead, she turned to him.

"I'm Sabra."

He pushed a piece of dark hair out of his face. "I'm George."

"How long have you lived here?" she asked.

"My whole life. What about you? You must be new in town if those are yours." He motioned to her guards.

Sabra laughed. "I don't live here. I'm only visiting with my cousin." She pointed back to the olive tree, where Demir was eating and talking quietly with some of the merchants.

George considered them thoughtfully. "Is your cousin a statesman then?"

She looked at him and studied him again. "How did you know?"

He shrugged. "That's where all the important meetings take place. Now, if he were king or a prince, he would have passed our village and visited one of the larger cities, where the kaftans dwell. Statesmen, however, like to deal with our merchants directly."

"You sure know a lot about politics for being the son of a tradesman."

He scowled at her. "What's what supposed to mean?"

"It's not an insult." She turned to look back at the busy street. "Most tradesmen don't care for the intricacies of state work. Mine don't, at least."

He sat forward. "*Your* tradesmen? What are you a princess or something?"

Sabra beamed and straightened her shoulders. "Actually, I am."

The boy blinked at her several times, which made Sabra laugh even more. Finally, when he spoke, he was slightly less cavalier. "Which kingdom are you princess of?"

"Segzein. And I wish you wouldn't do that."

"Do what?" he asked, glancing nervously at Shakirat.

"You're talking to me all funny now. Talk like we were before."

"Talk like what?" His eyes grew even wider.

"Like we're friends."

"Um..." He glanced again at the guards. "Are we friends?"

"Of course we are." She paused. "Unless you don't want to be."

"What I mean is...I don't have to call you Your Highness or anything like that?"

Sabra glared at him. "I'll smack you if you do."

He studied her for a long moment. But just as she was about to walk away and give up on the whole thing, he finally grinned. "All right, then. Friends. But only if you let me show you around the market." He stood and held out his hand. Sabra took it and let him help her up. When they were standing, she was surprised to find that he was a whole head taller than she was.

"Have you ever eaten a honey prat?" he asked, his eyes suddenly bright.

She snorted. "Of course. Who hasn't?" Honey prats were one of the region's most famous treats, dozens of layers of crispy paper-thin sweet bread, all stuck together by the honey in the center. Even the poorest children in Segzein had tasted honey prats.

"Not like this, you haven't." He took her hand and pulled her toward one of the stalls, and Sabra giggled. Her guards trailed them, and she could feel Demir's watchful eye from where she sat. No one sought to intervene, however, so she let the boy tow her across the busy street. She might not learn all the intricacies of Demir's dealings with foreign merchants this year, but that was more than all right. Today, she was having fun.

CHAPTER 1

FRIENDS

12 YEARS LATER...

Sabra feinted to the left and then back into a ready stance and waited for Demir to make his next move. But as she expected, he merely twirled his staff and gave her a patient smile as he slowly circled the center of the mat.

The padding of their bare feet was the only sound in the room. Another reason Sabra loved staff practice days with her cousin. No one was allowed to intrude and watch. It was a refreshing break from having everyone and their mother privy to her conversations. Also, it was the only place that she was allowed to wear her bright pink pantaloons. Of course, most women wore trousers beneath their dresses. Sabra wore them nearly every day. But the matching dress for this outfit was cut scandalously (in Sabra's mother's words) short. For ease of movement, Sabra had assured her, to make staff practice easier. It'd also made her mother nearly faint the first time she'd walked out of her room wearing it.

As he held back, Sabra tightened her grip on her own staff and grinned back. She could be patient, too.

"Tell me," he said as they continued to circle, "Which clan was the last to join Segzein prior to becoming a kingdom?"

Sabra stuck her tongue out at her cousin. "Can we go one full hour without you interrogating me?"

11

"You turn twenty-two in two weeks." He quirked an eyebrow. "Do you want to go before the Assembly unprepared?"

"I would be unprepared if we hadn't been preparing for this for my entire life." Sabra laughed, exasperated. "You're thirty-three. Why don't we quiz you for a while?" She gave him a wicked grin. "I could ask you endless questions about why you haven't yet found a wife."

"If you're so ready, then tell me why I had to negotiate a trade deal between the Sowens and the Woodsmen last year."

Sabra made a false move to the right, but he didn't take the bait. So they returned to circling. "The Sowens needed new wheat cribs for their harvest, but the Woodsmen insisted on payment in gold rather than allowing them to pay in harvest as is traditionally done." He opened his mouth, but she continued, knowing exactly where this was going. "You mediated and brought about an agreement that allowed the Sowens to pay for the wheat cribs in incremental payments that would allow them to bring in the harvest before the full payment was due."

"Good." He moved in with a spinning strike, but she dodged and was able to land a small blow to his side as she maneuvered out of the way.

"See?" She wiggled her eyebrows at him. "Contrary to what you think, I've been paying attention."

"Very well, brilliant one. Tell me this. If your father were to die now, who would inherit the throne?"

"With the Assembly's approval, I would." She considered a way to bridge the gap between them. His reach was much longer than hers.

"And then?" he asked. "If you weren't approved?"

"You would be considered."

He nodded. "But what if I failed as well?"

Her breath caught in her throat, and she stumbled slightly before regaining her control. Had he actually posed a question she didn't know the answer to? That hadn't happened in...well, for a very long time. "There isn't one?" she asked hesitantly.

He smirked as if he'd known she wasn't sure. "I know you guessed, but you're right. It *would* have been my second cousin on my mother's side. But since he died last year, the Assembly hasn't yet designated a third-level heir."

Sabra snorted delicately. "So I was right after all."

His movement was so fast that Sabra was barely able to get her staff up in time to block him. Then he was there, inches from her face, looking down at her with sweat dripping down his chin. "You hesitated."

"Have you come to practice, or simply to steal my one escape from everything Inquest?"

Then his smile disappeared, and he moved back into circling. "Actually—" he began hesitantly.

"Here we go. I knew you hadn't joined to have fun with me."

"*Actually*," he gave her a look. When he spoke again, his voice was low. "I thought you might want to know that Semih relinquished his position on the Assembly last night. Mahzar is being installed today as the new Justine head."

Sabra's steps slowed, but she did her best to look unperturbed. "I suppose we shouldn't be surprised."

"No," her cousin agreed. She could feel him watching her closely. "But I find it interesting that such an exchange should take place two weeks before your Inquest."

In spite of their slow practice, Sabra suddenly felt slightly breathless. "You don't think he'll cause trouble, do you?" she asked in a lower voice.

"I hope not. I can't see why he would. But you know him. He's done nothing but nose his way into other people's business since he was younger than you." Demir's frown deepened. "I just hope he'll mind himself." He paused and looked back up at her. "And you need to mind yourself, too."

"I have no idea what you're talking about."

"You say what you're thinking and don't care who you offend."

Sabra sniffed. "I see no reason why I should."

"Queen or not, politics are like a dance, Sabra. Refuse too many partners, and soon you'll have no one to dance with when a crisis arises."

"People need strong leaders. After all, you can't always compromise."

"People want leaders who get things done. And trying to stomp all over someone like Mahzar won't get you anywhere. Even if you are right."

Before Sabra could come up with a reply, the sound of the door drew both their attention, and Sabra looked up to find her mother studying them with pursed lips.

"Hello, Mother." Sabra smiled impishly, knowing full well what *that* look meant.

"Every time I think I've got you turned into a perfect lady, I find you in here."

"No one's perfect, Auntie," Demir gave her a boyish grin, all signs of stress gone.

Sabra's mother scowled, but under it, Sabra could see affection. Though Demir was Sabra's first cousin on her father's side, being orphaned at age eleven had made him as dear to her mother as any son would have been.

"Well, if I can't keep you out of those things," she said as she glared at Sabra's pantaloons, "I can at least tell you to change out of them now. You've got suitors here who wish to wait on you, and I won't have them seeing you like this."

"How many?" Sabra didn't even bother trying to hide her apprehension. There were many things about being the official crown princess that she was looking forward to after she passed her Inquest.

Choosing a suitor was not one of them.

Her mother raised her eyebrows. "Three."

Still, knowing better than to argue with her mother, Sabra groaned and handed her staff to her cousin. He gently poked her in the back with it as she trudged toward her waiting mother. "Make sure you tell me all the details," he called after her. "I want to know if you see the one with the snowy white beard or the one who refers to you as 'Child.'"

Sabra turned to scowl at her cousin. "For taking my Inquest so seriously, you seem to think my husband candidates hilarious."

He shrugged unapologetically. "A man's got to laugh sometimes."

Unfortunately, Sabra thought as she followed her mother to her room to change, he was right. If Sabra hadn't been the one who was being forced into matrimony, her suitors would have been comical.

"At least someone's enjoying my pain," Sabra said as they walked.

"Sabra," her mother hissed. But Sabra didn't miss the slight upturn of Shakirat's mouth when she turned to glance back at him. She grinned to herself. Make that two who were enjoying the show. Once they reached the privacy of her quarters, she changed clothes and surrendered herself to her servants.

The least offensive of the group vying for her hand was only a few years older than herself, and if she was honest, he wasn't completely loathsome. But when they were together, he acted as though he were already king, and as though he were doing Sabra a favor by entertaining her. He talked endlessly of mundane policies that Sabra couldn't have cared less about, and by the end of each talk, Sabra was sure the female Assembly members had only allowed him as a contestant because of how pretty he was.

Sabra winced as one of the servants pinned her hair a little too tightly.

"Sorry, Your Highness," the servant muttered, her mouth full of pins.

Sabra tried to smile back, but it felt more like a grimace as the woman jabbed another pin into her skull.

The suitor that Demir found most humorous was older than Sabra's father. He had a snowy white beard and a belly like he'd swallowed a melon, and when he walked too fast, as she'd learned the first time he'd come to court her, he began to wheeze and had to return to his carriage.

She'd insisted they take a walk every time after that.

There were at least eight others, each as objectionable as the last, who had begun to cast regular shadows upon the palace steps. And Sabra dreaded them all. But today, after her mother was satisfied with her clothes and hair, she whispered in Sabra's ear.

"I don't think you'll mind so much today. We've got a new one. I think his parents are from the south."

Sabra stood taller and looked at her mother. "New? I've never seen him before?"

Her mother shook her head, obviously pleased to be the bearer of such news. "And he's rather handsome, if I do say so myself." And with a wink, she ushered Sabra into a parlor where three men sat on the sofa. The one with the unfamiliar face had darker skin than most of those in the region, which was probably why her mother guessed his family was from the south. He was tall, and his eyes were a clear brown, almost golden in the beam of sunlight where he sat. His shoulders were broad, and his hands looked as though they were used to a good day's work. His jaw was sharp, and his gaze steady.

Yes, Sabra could look at him very easily for the rest of her life.

But, of course, the other competitors were not about to let their intended prize be carried off by some smooth southerner. Grandpa, as Sabra had secretly named the man with the snowy white beard, and Jitters, as she called the nervous man closer to her age, looked most displeased at this new addition. Grandpa was openly glaring at the man while Jitters bounced his knee up and down, staring blankly at the wall with a furrowed brow.

All three stood as she swept into the room, making sure to use every bit of poise and grace her mother had hammered into her throughout her nearly twenty-two years. Her mother settled into a chair in the corner, looking rather smug.

"Your Highness," Grandpa said as all three men bowed low. Hopefully, they wouldn't have more who decided to join them. Sabra had purposefully set only certain times and days when she would entertain suitors, as she couldn't handle having them constantly pop in, begging for her attention. The goal had been to prevent a constant ring of hopefuls at all hours of the day. She'd been successful, as there were now only two days a week when she had to dread the courting, but those days had quickly become unprecedented torture as more and more men sought her hand.

Sabra smiled as graciously as possible at all three men, but for a moment, felt frozen in panic. So often had she called the two by their nicknames in her head that she had momentarily forgotten their names. So instead, she gave herself a mental shake and merely nodded at each.

"Gentlemen," she said. Then she looked at her newest possibility, and her heart thumped a little unevenly.

He took her hand and bowed over it. "Your Highness," he said, his accent thick and crisp, and his voice deep and melodious.

Sabra could listen to him for the rest of her life as well. This was getting more and more promising.

"I thank you for allowing me the hope of perhaps claiming your hand," he said, his golden brown eyes meeting hers as he stood again. "You are even lovelier up close than from afar." A smile played at his lips. "And I suspect a good deal stronger-willed than you let on."

Sabra tried to duck her head to hide her grin, but it was too late. Her mother had already heard and was pursing her lips. Sabra's will of iron was not on her mother's list of commendable wife qualities.

"I'm curious as to how you should know that," she said with a little laugh.

"Your eyes," he said, his own smile widening. "They are like a spark to kindling."

"And what is your name?" she asked.

"Abasi, Your Highness."

"How about we go for a walk, Abasi?" Sabra wound her arm through his. "I would like to hear more about you." She could feel the resentment rolling off of Grandpa and Jitters in waves, but she didn't feel too badly. They'd had their chances to bore her.

Arms linked, they stepped out onto the palace wall. The wall was nearly twenty feet thick, laid with cobblestones that ran like a street around the entire palace. Justine guards were stationed at various points, where they kept watch on the activity below. The sun was turning golden as the temperature began to drop, which was a relief, as it was unusually warm for spring.

Another reason Sabra loved to walk the palace wall, other than to peel Grandpa from her side, was for the view. So when her suitors were particularly...attentive, she could gaze out over the kingdom she loved. Today, the reflection of the pink saline lake just south of the city was so bright it was nearly blinding. The valley beside the lake was barren, with the exception of small grasses, flowers, and bushes, their various shades of thin green at a sharp contrast with the lake's vibrant pink. Surrounding the lake were low rounded hills pocked with caves that from a distance looked like holes in a honeycomb.

The city itself was beautiful, too. The glass windows in the library complex sparkled in the sun, and so did the mosaic tiles in the larger buildings that peppered the city. Further out, the buildings grew smaller and less impressive, but everything was neat and orderly. And it all moved and ran like a well-trained team of horses.

"Princess?"

Sabra turned. Fantastic. Her first decent catch in months, and she got caught daydreaming. "I'm sorry," she laughed. "What was that?"

"Looking at your city?" he asked with a knowing smile.

She smiled back, her cheeks warming slightly. "I was."

He nodded out at the lake. "In all my travels, I've never seen its like." He tilted his head to the side.

"So you've traveled," she said with a nod. Her heart twisted slightly in her chest, the smallest hint of jealousy echoing inside of her. "What is your clan?"

"I must confess, I don't live in Segzein," he said, matching his pace to her own, and Sabra's heart fell into her stomach. Well, so much for this beautiful face. She had thought at first that he must be the child of some of those who had come to Segzein from the south. But if he wasn't from Segzein, this was all for naught. The basniins allowed her to choose her own husband, but they were quite insistent that while Sabra could marry anyone who wasn't in clan leadership, she *must* marry a Segzeinian citizen. No outsiders. Even if she chose him, they would never allow the marriage to take place.

"I am from the kingdom of Chimmambe," he continued, oblivious to Sabra's unfortunate revelation. "My brother was passing through here and saw you and asked someone who you were. When he learned that the princess was searching for a husband, he said to me, 'Why don't you go and seek your fortune? You are young and handsome, and you would make a fine king.'" He beamed and shrugged, as though this recommendation should make Sabra's day. Sabra smiled politely, but as she did, she suppressed a sigh. Grandpa and Jitters would be ecstatic.

"What is your trade?" she asked in an attempt to keep the conversation going, trying not to let her disappointment be too apparent. The poor man had come all the way to the palace. The least she could do was given him the rest of the walk. If nothing else, his presence here was keeping her from having to spend more time with Grandpa and Jitters, not to mention her other enthusiastic followers.

"I catch pests."

"Pests?"

"When a house or village is having rodent problems," he said proudly, "I come and set traps and poison for the pests."

"That's a useful calling. I suppose the people you help are grateful."

He shrugged, then his eyes lit up. "Yes, but the most satisfying part of it for me is the crack of death as their bones snap."

Perhaps a long walk was a bad idea after all.

Unfortunately, Abasi was all too happy to regale her with stories of his pests. Many, many stories.

She would just have to pray for the Maker to bring the right man to the palace steps.

"Sometimes, I sit for a whole day until I hear the rat scratching its way inside. Then I set the traps..."

She would pray hard.

CHAPTER 2

STRANGER

Sabra got up early the next morning, refreshed and ready to work. She'd pleaded a headache the night before and gone to bed uncharacteristically early. It wasn't a lie, for she truly had gotten a raging headache after the evening spent having to listen to Jitters mumble away after Abasi had gone.

Determined not to repeat the disaster that had been the day before, Sabra meticulously planned out her day so that she was busy from morning until night, on the chance that her mother decided she ought to entertain suitors two days in a row.

"It's going to be a good day today, Nisa," Sabra told her hand-maiden as they exited the palace gates, Shakirat trailing them faithfully from a distance. "I'm feeling productive and impertinent." She glanced back just in time to see the slightest hint of a smile escape the corners of Nisa's lips, and Sabra felt her own grin grow. It *was* going to be a good day.

"What do we have on the agenda today, Princess?" Nisa asked as they made their way into the crowd.

Sabra drew in a deep lungful of fresh morning air and smiled. Despite the early hour, as the sun hadn't yet risen, the streets were bustling with horses and foot traffic and vendors. Old men and women paused to chat leisurely with one another while children chased and teased. The smell of the early summer day mixed with the scents of lamb cooking over spits in the market and freshly picked sprigs of mint and thyme.

"I think we'll start with the Physics' spoke and make our way around from there."

Nisa nodded, and they set off to the east, where the healers lived. "And what do you wish to see there?"

"I heard that Elif's son purchased a large quantity of aloe plants the last time he traveled and brought them home. I want to see how successful she's been in maintaining those, and if she thinks they might be a good product to grow in large quantities. Oh, good morning!" Sabra grinned to a little girl who darted out of her family's home to wave. She turned to Nisa. "Wait for me here, will you?"

Nisa narrowed her eyes slightly. "Your Highness—"

"I'll be back!" she called cheerfully over her shoulder, ignoring the disapproving look her handmaiden was sending her.

The house was one of the few in the square that wasn't as well kept as the others. The few times Sabra had seen the girl's parents, they looked thin and sickly. So whenever she planned to go this way, she brought a few extra sweets with her.

The little girl took the treat and threw a hug around her legs, then ran away giggling. Sabra had tried to bring more food before, but long ago, she'd learned that the girl's parents wanted no charity. They would hardly speak to her, simply refusing the gift in polite protestations and then locking themselves in their home.

Thankfully, the girl was not so difficult to please. Today, however, as the girl looked back to thank her, the girl's mother called for the child to return home. Her eyes were wide as she stared at Sabra, and she scrambled to hurry the child inside. As she did, her sleeve on her left arm fell down over her shoulder, revealing the blue band tattooed there. The woman let out a small cry as she tried to cover her shoulder up before locking both herself and the child in the house.

Sabra sighed.

"You won't change her mind."

Sabra looked down to see the speaker.

He was sitting cross-legged there in a threadbare stall. His service, not one needed on a daily basis, was to stitch up wounds, and when he wasn't stitching up wounds, he was sewing bandages to sell as well. Sabra knew this, of course, because she'd asked him.

"I don't suppose you'll tell me why," she said, coming to stand beside him.

He grinned up at her. "No, I won't. But I will happily sell you a bandage."

She raised an eyebrow. "If I buy one, will you tell me about your tattoo?"

He laughed. "You're a wily one, Princess." His voice grew lower and gentler. "You know your father wouldn't appreciate this conversation."

She huffed. "I was hoping this would change your mind." She pulled an herbed roll from her pocket.

He laughed. "No more than the sweet roll you brought me yesterday. Or the wedge of cheese last week."

"I'll find out somehow," she said with a wry smile.

"Princess!"

Sabra turned to see Nisa glaring at her. "If your father finds out—"

"I'm coming, I'm coming."

Sabra handed him the roll. "See you later."

He laughed. "I'm sure you will."

"Your Highness!" Nisa scolded her in a whisper as Sabra returned to her side. "Your father was very angry the last time you were seen speaking to one of them!"

"And do you mind very much when I get in trouble?" Sabra tossed her hair out of her face.

Nisa frowned. "I worry for you. And the Blue Bands you speak with. They get in trouble as much as you do."

Sabra closed her eyes for a moment before rubbing her face. "You're right. I'm not trying to get them in trouble." She grimaced back at the rundown house that was now behind them. "I just wish I could understand."

"Back to what we were doing," Nisa looked at her parchment. "When you have your recommendations about the aloe, would you like me to send your recommendation to the head Physic?"

Sabra had once told Nisa that she could leave her ever-present lists at home to give her arms a break, but the girl had only smiled politely before taking them right out with her again. In the year since Nisa had come to serve Sabra, Sabra had hoped to teach her to have a little fun sometimes, but as of yet, none of those subtle instructions had seemed to stick.

"Yes, please," Sabra said. "He's actually the one who asked me about it. After this, I want to hear from the Sowens about their new load of seeds, so we'll visit their spoke once we're finished here. Then I'd like to visit the Sophians, the Tradesmen, and finally…" She paused to think. "The Justines."

Nisa's pen stopped moving. "The Justines?"

Sabra nodded. "I've heard the clan has a new head. I thought I would congratulate him." And possibly clarify that she was not to be trifled with. But she kept that part to herself.

"I apologize, Princess, but if I'd known we were headed to their spoke, I would have worn a different set of shoes." She scrunched her nose at her own shoes. "They disliked it the last time I wore these into their meeting house. They said they were too dusty."

"No need." Sabra smiled back at her. "Look in that sack I handed you. I brought an extra pair of slippers."

"Thank you, Your Highness." Nisa nodded and scribbled on her parchment.

They made their way to the central market in the Physics' spoke on the eastern side of the city. As Sabra had expected, Elif, one of the clan's more respected members, was more than happy to show off her new aloe plants. They were doing better than Sabra had expected. She'd anticipated the plants would be shriveled and discolored from Segzein's semi-arid climate. There was a reason the Physics bought many of their healing herbs from the traveling caravans that came from farther north, where the wind wasn't so dry and the rain came more often. But old Elif was proud to bursting when she showed Sabra the three dozen little green spiky plants.

"This variety is even more potent in healing burns than the old stuff we used to buy from the caravans." She smiled smugly. "And it grows fast. Within a few years, we should be able to stop buying it completely."

"That's fantastic." Sabra beamed. "What would you say if I brought someone over from the Sowens? If we could get them enough plants to grow their own, do you think that together you could harvest them sooner on a larger scale?"

Elif gave Sabra a shrewd look, one that canvased Sabra's entire person several times. Not that such an appraisal bothered Sabra. She had come to expect skepticism from the older citizens. It wasn't personal. They simply didn't know what to expect from a princess of twenty and one years. She would simply need to prove herself to them.

And Sabra was more than ready to do that.

"Why not let me raise them on my own?" Elif finally leaned back in her chair and raised a practiced brow at Sabra. "I'd make more money than if I let the Sowens in on the crop. And if they got in, then the Tradesmen would want in, too. Why not keep the cuttings for myself and sell what I have?"

Sabra considered this. "You could," she said slowly. "But if you did that, you would have to supply everything yourself, and from what I know of your lands, you don't have enough to meet the demand that would come." She paused.

"What if the Sowens and Tradesmen were required to pay you a stipend for every plant they sold? The plants would propagate faster that way, as there would be more people to care for them with more land, and you'd receive payments for whatever length of time you agreed to." She paused and thought for a moment. "You could also continue to grow your own on the side. You could easily bottle it up into your own salves and sell the salves directly to merchants passing through. Merchants would be far more willing to pay a higher price than anyone here. And you could sell as much as you want without worrying about selling what your patients might need because the sowens would supply that." She nodded to Nisa to take note. "The Sophians made a similar contract with the Justines last week regarding parchment production."

Elif studied her for another moment before breaking into a grin. "Your father wasn't wrong when he said you had a good head. I would be happy to speak with the others."

Sabra smiled. "Wonderful. I'll send you word as soon as I've talked with them."

"I wish you favor," the old woman called as Sabra waved good-bye. "And may your Inquest be blessed."

The sun was bright by the time Sabra and Nisa left the old woman's home, and it matched the glow that filled Sabra's heart. "Two weeks," she whispered to herself. Two weeks until her Inquest. And then she would no longer simply be the princess. She would be the queen-to-be. An excited shiver ran down her shoulders and arms. She was so close.

The morning continued on the fine note it had begun on. Sabra's meetings in the Sowens' and Sophians' spokes went just as smoothly as her talk with Elif had, and she was in the middle of searching for a mid-morning snack in the Tradesmen's spoke when someone cast a shadow over the crate of dates she was examining. Annoyed, she looked up to see a stranger.

A very handsome stranger.

He would have looked annoyed as well, except that his mouth was twitching as though he were trying to suppress a smile.

"Working hard today, are we?" he asked.

Having no idea who this man was but enjoying the spark of good banter, Sabra grabbed a few dates and paid for them before turning to face him and raising her chin defiantly. "Always." She popped one in her mouth.

His smile grew. Who in the sands was this man? Did he know who he was addressing in such a casual manner? Had he mistaken her for someone else?

The stranger was at least a hand taller than Demir. His shoulders were wide, and his chest was broad. He was possibly even larger than Shakirat, who was now staring him down. His dark brown hair looked like it might have been curly, except that it was cut close to his head. His face had sharp angles, and his Adam's apple stuck out noticeably. He stood a foot above the crowd, and many, even in their hurry, were giving him a wide berth. Sabra was absolutely certain she had never seen this man in her life. She would have remembered if she had. And yet, there was something familiar about him... She squinted, trying to imagine him without the stubble that covered most of his face.

"And what exactly does today's work have to do with dates?" he asked, not bothering to hide his grin now.

She shoved one more in her mouth and arched an eyebrow at him as she chewed it, careful not to bite into the long pit. "Starvation. And princesses. They don't work well together."

"Ah. Can't have that now, can we?" He was looking at her now with an odd mix of humor and affection. He must truly have confused her for someone else.

Nisa stood to Sabra's right, just a little way back, but Sabra could feel her bristling at the audacity of the stranger as though she wanted to bore a hole through his head. Sharkirat, who usually appeared bored, had his hand on his sword's hilt, and looked as though he'd like to set the stranger on fire for merely existing too close to Sabra.

Sabra rolled her eyes but couldn't help chuckling. "And what would a man such as yourself want to know all that for?"

This time, he tilted his head thoughtfully. "You really don't know who I am?"

She studied him again. There was definitely something familiar about him. If only she knew why.

"Sabra," he said gently. "Look."

Nisa made a choking sound, as did many of the people around them. Not that Sabra minded. Her title wasn't a point of pride. But it was a bold move on his part. She couldn't remember the last time anyone had called her by her given name who wasn't related by blood. It just wasn't done.

Then it hit her, and she was throwing herself into his arms like one of her father's overly affectionate dogs.

"George!"

The way his arms wrapped around her in return made her already speeding heart accelerate.

Sabra wasn't sure how long the hug lasted. It wasn't long. It really wasn't. But long enough for her to feel the stares of everyone around them. George seemed to feel it, too, because he pulled back but kept hold of her hands, laughing as he looked her over from her head to her feet. It wasn't a leering, invasive kind of stare that one or two of her suitors had dared. Rather, he looked the same way she felt inside. In complete disbelief.

Her own expression probably mirrored his. The way his hands felt, however, rubbing her fingers as he held them, made it hard to focus long enough to decide. His eyes, which had first caught her attention, were that old familiar steely gray. And now that she was staring into them, she recalled how unusual their color was for the southern part of the world.

She was also vaguely aware that they were causing a scene. But she wasn't too worried. The princess's enthusiasm wasn't a secret. Sabra never did anything halfway. Of course, she thought wryly, that didn't mean everyone had to like it.

"I was hoping I would see you here." He laughed again, almost nervously, and looked her up and down again. "You're not a little girl anymore!"

Sabra slapped him on the arm, which was surprisingly thick and hard. "You're one to talk. The last time I saw you, you were sixteen!"

"You dare call the princess by her given name?" Nisa's words were clipped, impressive in their indignance for a girl of such small stature. She seemed to have recovered from her shock, and her sharp tongue was now free.

George's face, which had been the picture of unbridled joy a moment before, melted into one of horror as he looked around them, probably realizing how many rules he'd just broken.

"Of—of course." He bowed his head, and to Sabra's chagrin, let go of her hands. His gaze slipped to the ground. "I'm so sorry, Your Highness. I just..." He swallowed convulsively and looked back at Sabra, alarm thick in his eyes.

Sabra rolled her own eyes and turned to her handmaiden. "George, this is my handmaiden, Nisa."

George nodded, his olive face slightly paler than usual. "Miss," he bowed his head again. "Please forgive—"

"There's nothing to forgive." Sabra glared at her servant, who was still giving George the death stare. "George is a childhood friend. I would be offended if he called me anything else." She wound her arms through his and whirled them around.

It took much of her self-control not to shiver with delight as she did.

What was wrong with her? She glanced back up at the hulking man beside her and shivered anyway. George was what was wrong with her. And all of his enormous self that hadn't been there the last time they'd met.

And he wasn't distracting at all.

Nisa followed behind with slow, indignant steps, but she knew better than to contradict the princess.

"What are you doing here?" Sabra grinned. "And why didn't you come sooner?" Then, before letting him answer, she tugged on his arm and began to move. "Come on. Let's walk, and you can tell me everything that's happened in the last seven years."

George chuckled. "Well, if you *have* to know, I'm actually not supposed to be here." He gave her one of the lopsided grins she'd missed so much. "My grandparents prefer that I stay close to home. But my master sent me to one of the libraries here for some information."

"Your master?" Sabra asked.

"I'm apprenticing with a scholar in Kappadona."

"Huh." Sabra pulled them into the shade of an olive tree and studied him.

His eyes widened slightly. "You disapprove?"

"No." She shook her head and continued to study him, as though that might reveal something new she'd missed. "I just always saw you as taking over your grandfather's smithing."

"I can smith." He rubbed his neck and grimaced slightly. "But for some reason, they wanted me to take another occupation."

Sabra frowned. That didn't make any sense. The last time she'd been to Kappadona for the trade talks, she'd been fourteen, and he'd been sixteen, and his grandfather had given him so much work that she'd spent the whole afternoon watching him work in the little dirty tent. Not that she'd minded, of course. Now that she thought back to that day, she remembered staring at very little but his arms sticking out from beneath his rolled-up sleeves. But before she could ask, he looked at the world around them.

"I have to admit," he said, "your city confuses me." He looked back at her. "And why is your lake pink?"

Sabra laughed, and they resumed walking. "You're not alone. But once you understand, it's much easier. Probably easier, actually, than other cities." She stopped and pointed to the palace walls, pristine and white against the high desert. They were near those walls now, which were lined by a single circle of olive trees like the one they'd been standing beneath.

"The lake is pink because it's filled with salt. And it's so shallow it's barely taller than you are in the center. But that's not important. What is important is that the palace stands at the center of the city." She gestured to her home, largely hidden behind the great wall that circled all the palace grounds. "We have seven clans that make up our kingdom. If you walk around the palace, you'll see that it's at the center of the city. The city is divided into wedges that jut out from the palace in every direction, much like wheel spokes. All spokes start with a central market that faces the palace. From there, they move out to other buildings, places of business, homes, and fields, though most of the large fields belong to the Sowens."

"Will the knowledge I seek most likely be in one spoke more than the others?" he asked, squinting in the sunlight at the world around them.

Sabra nodded. "You'll probably find what you're looking for with the Sophians in that direction." She pointed. "Their job is to record and protect our knowledge. Everything from how the Sowens harvest their crops to the method of stitching up a wound to the history of the Justines' court rulings will be found there. Then there are the Physics." She pointed in the direction from which she'd first come that morning.

"The Physics are our healers," she continued. "The Sowens head our agriculture. The Tradesmen run the largest market in the city right here." Sabra indicated to the street they had just come from. "But they also manage basic trade regulation and settle disputes for other clans as well in their lesser markets and trading activities. Sophians, as I said, gather, guard, and sell knowledge. The Woodsmen are responsible for most of our infrastructure. Buildings and roads and such. The Justines handle the law. And of course," she stopped and curtsied dramatically, "that leaves the Capitans."

"Which are?" His smile was amused.

"Royalty, of course."

"So are you *over* all the other clans?"

Sabra tapped her chin before leading him over to a stall selling dried fruits. She examined their wares as she thought.

"Not over, exactly. Each clan has a head, a member of the Assembly. They are called basniins. The Capitan basniin, which would be the king or queen, often breaks ties. We're more in a managerial position, I suppose, acting as mediators for the other clans, and we do our best to understand the workings of the clans as a whole, rather than the little details they pay attention to."

"So your father's *not* the king?" He frowned.

"No, he *is* the king. And I will be queen." As long as she passed the Inquest. Not that failure was even a possibility. "But our authority isn't as...sovereign, I suppose, as it is for other monarchs around the world. There's often more room for negotiation."

He nodded slowly then purchased several small bags of dried fruits and offered one to Sabra. She took it and grinned, reminded of their many shared outdoor meals as children on the steps of the fountain.

"I only began my apprenticeship last year," he said slowly, "so I don't know many of the finer details. But if my research is correct, each clan runs nearly independently of the others. As in, they have their own markets, homes, and organization."

"Correct." Sabra nodded.

"But they're all dependent on one another, in that they can't survive on their own. And each has a certain amount of authority in their own sphere of influence."

Sabra grinned up at him. "Maybe you were cut out for reading all day after all."

"That makes the design of the city more understandable. And don't be a brat." He poked her and then glanced nervously back at Nisa. Sabra laughed, but at the mention of his apprenticeship, she once again had the urge to ask him why his grandfather had apprenticed him to someone else. She could tell, though, that was a conversation for someplace that was a little more private. As it was, they were drawing more than enough attention. Sabra was used to it, but George appeared not to be.

"I'll explain," Sabra said, coming to stand in front of a small fountain. "We've left the Tradesmen's market, in case you hadn't figured that out. We're now in the Sophian spoke."

"And Sophians do what again?"

"They're the ones you're looking for. They're responsible for recording and keeping our history and knowledge. They have a market of their own. But if you look around, it's not nearly as large as the Tradesmen's market. And most of their wares have to do with parchment, pens, books, and lessons."

"Lessons?" George raised his eyebrows.

Sabra stared at him for a moment, drinking in everything he'd become. She also marveled at how easy it was falling back into step with him again, as if seven years had never passed. As if they'd walked and talked like this every day.

She wished they had.

"Sabra?" He looked as though he was about to laugh.

"Oh, sorry." Sabra shook her head to clear it. She needed to quit acting like a smitten child. "Where were we?"

He grinned this time. He'd caught her staring at him, and they both knew it. "You were telling me about the lessons?"

Sabra nodded and, glad to divert the attention away from her, indicated an elderly woman sitting in front of a small tent, writing on a parchment. "That's Mistress Hatice. She's a master learner of grain, meaning she's studied wheat and how to plant, raise, harvest, and thresh it, as well as the history of different kinds of grain in Segzein. If you pay her a copper, she'll answer five of your questions. Pay her a silver, and she'll give you half a day to talk about anything you like."

George scratched his head. "But I thought the Sowens were in charge of agriculture."

"Oh, they are." Sabra flipped her long hair out of her face as a breeze came up. "But many don't know the history and wouldn't be able to tell you about the year the goat beetles came and ate the corn two centuries ago, and the entire city nearly starved. Of course, Mistress Hatice is not the only one. There are hundreds of master learners who learn about specific parts of our economy, history, practices, skills, and other aspects of our culture. Some are paid by groups of parents to educate their children. Others might visit a master to understand what's gone wrong with their trade."

"But doesn't that cause resentment between different spokes? I mean...clans? If they're competing for similar customers?"

Sabra smiled. "It could. But it also breeds competition, which is good. And if things ever get out of hand, which they do every now and then, the Justines are called, and they solve things quickly according to the law. Or the Capitans." She grinned and shrugged. "We're not too bad to have around either. And slightly more fun."

He stopped walking and turned to study her. Her face flushed slightly as she wondered what was going through his head.

"What?" she asked.

He chuckled and shook his head. "Nothing. It's just that you know so much. I've never heard of a statesman who was so familiar with the needs and names of their people."

Sabra's blush grew. He couldn't possibly understand how much that meant to her. Instead of elaborating, she merely waved her hand at the people surrounding them. "I love these people. They're mine, and I'm theirs. Why wouldn't I know them?"

"That all makes sense," he said as they continued to walk. "Would we have time to visit them all today?"

Sabra glanced down at his travel clothes. "Unfortunately, the Justines have strict rules in their clan about appearances. We would have to get you a change of clothes and shoes to enter their spoke, which we probably don't have time for today." She resumed walking, "But we can visit the others and cut across their market by skirting the palace wall. They don't like it, but they have to let us pass."

"A bit strict then?"

She laughed. "You have no idea. Word has it that their original clan was incredibly superstitious, but I think it's just an excuse to tell everyone else what to do."

George was quiet for a moment. "That makes me curious about something else."

"Which is?"

He stopped walking and pointed. "You have seven clans. But on your seal, you have eight spokes."

Sabra felt her smile freeze on her face as she looked up at him. "Yes, we do." She glanced back to see that Nisa was staring off into the distance, looking bored. Still, it would be better not to let anyone see how much that bothered her. Well, anyone but George.

"Why?" he asked.

Oh, if only he knew how often she'd asked that question herself. How she feared failing due to this strange hole in her knowledge, the mystery that sent her gentle father into fits of anger whenever she brought it up. But they were still in public, so she gave the answer she'd been fed more times than she could count.

"The kingdom left one of the spokes open for the housing of those who didn't have enough. Many of our poor live there. The houses are old, but they're better than nothing. Many of our migrants move out of the little houses once they can afford to. Most of them work in other spokes, choosing which clan they wish to integrate with."

She paused thoughtfully. A large number of the Blue Bands lived there as well, though, and many of them never moved on. She'd watched the spoke enough over the years to notice dozens of the tattoos the people so desperately tried to hide when in the other spokes.

As if reading her thoughts, he nodded at a stall not far from theirs. A thin man was stacking parchments at a table under the tent.

"What about him?"

"What do you mean?"

"Several times this morning I've seen people with a blue tattoo that wraps around their arms. He has one, too."

Sabra followed his gaze and hesitated before dropping her voice. "We call them the Blue Bands."

"Because of the tattoos?"

Sabra nodded.

He thought for a moment. "Why do they wear them?"

Sabra wanted both to rejoice and groan at this question. To rejoice because she knew she wasn't the only one asking about the Blue Bands or the seven clans. To groan because she knew the lecture she would receive if anyone overheard her conversation and reported it to her father or cousin. She could recite it by heart.

"I'm not sure," she finally said, giving him a look that she hoped he could understand. Then, for the sake of those around them, she forced a smile and pulled him down the road. "Now, let's find some lunch so you can chase down that master learner on a full stomach."

CHAPTER 3

ESCAPE

Sabra wished that afternoon could last forever. But eventually, after meandering all over the Sophians' spoke until there was nothing left unseen, both George and Sabra had to admit that it was time for him to do what he'd been sent to do.

An awkward silence settled over them as they came to stand in front of the master learner's tent. Sabra had hoped the man would be busy with another customer, but, of course, he was ready and waiting. So she turned to George and dredged up a smile.

"Will you be around tomorrow?" she asked with false optimism.

He gave her a less convincing smile. "Unfortunately, I have to leave as soon as I'm done here. I need to be home in time not to alarm my grandparents tomorrow."

She frowned. "You'll travel the highway at night?"

He shrugged. "I've got a horse and a sword. I'm not too worried."

Sabra pursed her lips but didn't argue further. He was certainly taller than the average man, and solidly built as well. Still, that wouldn't prevent highwaymen from using arrows or encircling him.

He laughed. "I'll be fine. Really." Then his eyes widened.

"What is it?" she asked.

"I just remembered. There's a medicinal tea here that my grandmother always buys from the caravans when they come. I wouldn't suppose you know of the..." He twisted his face up as he thought. "Blue leaf tea, I think it's called?"

Ah, that she could answer. Sabra pointed to the east. "That'll be Eser's mix. He's one of the Physics' most well-known sellers. You'll find him in their spoke, just across from the palace."

"Thank you." He paused and looked at the ground before looking back up to meet her eyes. "You amaze me, you know. You always have."

Sabra's breathing hitched, and she had to remind herself to breathe. Why couldn't she feel this way whenever her suitors praised her? Because praise her they did. They praised her until she wanted to throw up. But never had it carried so much weight.

Why did she even care so much about his praise, this man she hadn't seen in seven years?

"Well, um, I should go." He reached out as though he might touch her. Then he glanced at the master learner, who was watching them with unveiled interest, and his hand fell back down to his side. Regret immediately crashed down inside her. What had he been about to do?

"Would it..." He took a deep breath, his gray eyes boring into hers. "Would it be all right if I wrote you a letter? When you didn't come that first year, I was afraid something had happened to you..." His voice trailed off, and shame burned inside her.

"I'm sorry. I wanted to tell you that the trade talks had been moved here, but when I wrote a letter and sent it to the city, it was returned. All three times."

Understanding and relief lit his eyes. "Ah, that would be it. See, we don't actually live in the city. My grandparents live a little ways out on their own land." He took two steps toward the master learner then looked back once more. "A letter then?"

She grinned back. "I'd love one. And in your letter, tell me where I might send one of my own."

He grinned. "Of course." Then he took a deep breath and blew it out. "Well, here I go."

She watched him address the master learner, who glanced at her once before nodding and leading George into the tent.

Suppressing a sigh, Sabra turned to go home.

"Are we still going to visit the Justines?" Sabra jumped as Nisa's bubbly voice came from behind her, sounding happier than she had since Sabra had hired her. Sabra had completely forgotten she was there.

"We're late as it is." Sabra grimaced at the sun. "I think we'd better head home for now." Still, her feet dragged as they made their way back, and for possibly the first time in her life, the brightly colored baubles and delicious smells of the markets held little draw. All she wanted to do was go home. Unfortunately, the palace was quite large, and a full trip around the walls alone could take an hour.

The palace lamps had been lit by the time she got back, and Sabra's heart jumped slightly as she realized how long she'd been gone. Her pace quickened as she moved through the gates and up to her room in the southeastern tower.

"I'm going to rest for now," Sabra told Nisa when they finally stood outside her door. "You can do what you want with the rest of the evening."

Nisa frowned. "I thought you might need help preparing for supper."

Sabra forced a smile. The girl was diligent, to say the least, but she could be really bad at taking a hint. "I'm perfectly capable of getting myself ready for dinner. Thank you, though."

"At least let me send someone up to draw a bath."

Sabra hesitated. A bath would be nice. She'd walked a lot that day, even for her. "Very well, thank you. Then you may go."

Once the door was shut and safely locked, Sabra turned and leaned her back against it. Her whole body felt heavy and sluggish. For once, she had no interest in supper. She opened her eyes and looked around her room, hoping for a distraction. Anything to keep her from thinking about what George was doing right now. When would he leave? Would he linger in the city for any reason? If he waited for too long, the tea seller would close his tent, and his grand-mother wouldn't get any tea.

A knock startled her, and Sabra took a second to gather herself before calling, "Who is it?" through the door.

"We've brought hot water, Your Highness."

Sabra stepped back and unlocked the door. Nisa hurried the two menservants into the room and bossed them around until they'd filled the tub in the corner exactly to her specifications. Once they were all gone again, Sabra undressed and sank into the steaming water, slowly relaxing her muscles one by one and inhaling the scent of lavender that Nisa had so diligently sprinkled in.

Still, even after her bath, Sabra couldn't shake the heavy feeling from her mind or her muscles.

It wasn't just that George was leaving. At least, not completely. It was the questions he'd raised during their conversation that day. All of her problems always returned to those same questions. The ones her father and cousin refused to address, and the servants and citizens pretended to know nothing about. Now, at least, she knew she wasn't crazy. George had asked, too, and he'd been in the city for less than a day.

What was everyone hiding?

Sabra was dressed and drying her hair with a towel when another knock sounded at the door. She opened it to find a dirty boy in clothes that were too big for him standing outside. He had warm brown skin and brown eyes that were always just a little too bright. His sharp little chin stuck out defiantly and would have been adorable if his mere presence didn't promise trouble.

"Princess," he said, folding his arms and looking up at her.

She folded her arms in return. "Serkan, what are you supposed to be doing right now?"

"Running a message to Basniin Yasin."

"Then why are you here?"

He gave her a rebellious smile. "I have something for you."

"And I have a thrashing for you unless you hand it over and go about your duties." She held her hand out.

He gave her a look of horror. "You'd strike me?"

"Considering you nearly managed to steal two of my necklaces last time you came to deliver something to me, yes."

When his look of faux horror didn't move her, he rolled his eyes and scoffed. "You caught me. I made sure you did."

"What do you have for me, Serkan?"

He thrust a piece of folded paper at her. "Fine. You have a letter."

She took it but kept her eyes on him. "You read it, didn't you."

"I can't read, and you know that."

She cracked a grin. "But you tried."

He shrugged, unrepentant. "A man gave it to me. Who was he?"

She chuckled in spite of herself. "How am I supposed to know that?"

"Well," he said a little too nonchalantly, "word has it that everyone saw you kissing a man in the square today—"

"Goodbye, Serkan." Sabra shut her door.

"I knew it!" he called through the door, his voice muffled. "You did kiss him!"

Sabra went back to her bed and laid down to read her letter. Her heart thumped a little unevenly as she unfolded the page again. And it wasn't because of Serkan's propensity for gossip.

Inside, written in large, square script, was her letter.

Princess Sabra,

First of all, please don't hit me for using your full title. That greeting is to prevent my capture and torture should any of your indignant servants receive and read this first. I didn't want to say it aloud today for fear she might hear, but your handmaiden frightens me. I'm rather sure she was plotting my demise as we talked. She glared at me the entire time we were together.

But threats against my life aside, I wanted to thank you again for today. I've thought of you often over the last seven years, and though it might sound strange, I've missed you. Is that odd, considering we only saw each other once a year for five years?

I'll admit I feel as though I'm breaking some law, calling a princess by name and teasing her as if we're children again. Writing you this letter, short as it is, seems criminal. I couldn't help myself, though, when I saw the inkwell and parchment ready and waiting by the master learner's door when we were finished. For a half-copper, he was kind enough to let me pen this note so I could give it to a servant before I left.

But I needed to know you a little more. I'm not sure when my master will send me again, and as my grandparents wish me to remain close to home, I don't know when I'll be able to return.

So if you're in the mood to humor an audacious commoner, I'd love to know what you've been doing these last few years. I might as well admit that I'm terribly focused on my apprenticeship and grandparents, so I have few friends my age. Today was like a gust of cool wind on my face, reminding me of what it felt like to enjoy myself with a companion for just a little while. And though we spent hours together, I feel as though we barely had time to say hello and goodbye. So, to keep me from going completely mad from the tedium, I adjure you to tell me more about yourself.

Before you think me incapable of remembering manners, particularly with a royal, I'm under no impression that you'll be able to write much, or even at all. I heard today that you'll be choosing a husband after your Inquest, and as soon as you have an intended, I'll cease writing so as not to bring about any sort of impropriety. But for now, if you're ever bored enough, I wish to learn everything I can about you, if for no other reason than to make up for lost time.

I must go now. The sky is growing dim, and I need to purchase that tea before I return to the road. In the case you wish to write back, I've drawn a rough map on the bottom of the parchment with directions to my master's shop, in case you send someone to deliver it.

Your friend,
George

Sabra knew she should be practicing for her Inquest or reading a history book or talking politics with whichever Assemblymen were hanging about the palace. But for once, she didn't feel like making progress. Instead, she tucked her letter carefully in her desk. Then she pulled out a stack of worn parchments and began to arrange them on her bed. Maps, histories, random notes, and written questions that she began to order carefully so they would make sense. Many of the papers had been folded so many times that their ink had nearly disappeared, and some of the parchments felt more like floppy cloth than paper. She'd done this a thousand times, it seemed. And yet, as always, no new insights appeared.

Four little fleshy paws landed on one of her corner maps, and Sabra swept her cat up into her arms and nuzzled its warm, pink neck.

"Hello, Thing," she said as the animal purred. "Did you miss me?"

The cat seemed to glare at her, as if to rebuke her for even considering such a possibility. Missing a human was below his dignity, and she knew it. But every once in a while, she hoped.

"What is everyone hiding?" she murmured into the cat's neck as she stared down at the mess. "I just don't understand it, Thing. Whatever happened couldn't have happened that long ago. There has to be someone in the kingdom who doesn't know about my father's edict. Or doesn't care, at least."

Not that there was an official edict. At least, not that she was aware of. But there had to be, as everyone seemed to cower in fear at the very mention of this mysterious past whenever she asked questions. The only Blue Bands who dared speak to her were children. And the old man in the Physics' spoke. But even his was always playful banter. She didn't even know his name. The rest cowered and ran away from her as though she were some terrible tyrant.

Supper was fast approaching, and she would need to leave to join her parents soon. But determined not to lose this precious bit of privacy, she put away her papers, pulled out a new parchment, and began to write.

Dear George,

I suppose you shall be forgiven for using my title, just this once. You were absolutely right when you said Nisa wanted to kill you, but that's because she's a good and loyal servant and would chop her own finger off if my father told her it would protect me.

Sabra paused. She wanted greatly to confide in him about the mysteries they'd discussed that day. But she refrained. If anyone were to find her letter, she would be in more trouble than she'd ever been in before, upcoming Inquest or none. So instead, she decided to fill him in on what she'd done for the last few years.

You asked today that I tell you all about me. I'm afraid it's not incredibly interesting. I spend most of my time with my cousin and father as they prepare me for the Inquest. Even most of my free days are spent studying history and interacting with my people in their various spokes. I want to get to know them and see how their worlds work. That way, when I'm queen, I'll be intimately knowledgeable of everyone's needs and the deeper inner workings of the kingdom. Don't get me wrong. I enjoy it immensely. But there are moments, like today when I was walking with you, when I miss having more time to spend as I please.

How she desperately wanted to tell him of her quandary. How no one would answer her questions. How she was nearly eaten up with curiosity over whatever great event she was missing in her kingdom's history. How she had a hunch that the trade talks had been moved to Segzein for this reason, so her father and cousin could more closely monitor what was said by outsiders regarding the way things had once been. Sabra sighed.

I'm afraid I'll need to go soon. Supper will be served, and I can't be late, or my parents will suspect something. Most likely, they've already heard about their daughter's exploits in the markets today. Not that it would surprise them. But there's sure to be some sort of lecture, and I'd like not to give them reason for yet another one. Please write again when you have the chance.

    Yours truly,
    (Simply) Sabra

Sabra sealed her letter and directed it as George had instructed. Once it was sent off with a servant, she lay on her bed and pulled out a small book. Just for a moment, she promised herself. She only needed to clear her mind.

Her cousin would probably disapprove. He didn't find ancient legends and folklore nearly as useful as studying true history. But Demir wasn't here, and she was alone. She could afford to get lost alongside ancient knights and dangerous quests for just a few minutes. A short escape from reality wouldn't hurt anyone.

CHAPTER 4

SORRY

Sabra? Sabra."

Sabra's eyelids fluttered open to find her mother standing over her. Her hand was on Sabra's shoulder, gently shaking her awake. Her eyes, however, were fixed on the book, which had fallen open on the bed beside her.

"What time is it?" Sabra asked, sitting up and rubbing her eyes. She hadn't meant to fall asleep at all.

"Where did you get this book?" Her mother, ignoring her question, had picked up the book and was skimming its pages, her beautiful dark eyes wide. Thing moved further back in the bed, stepping with great precision, as if their actions offended him. Sabra wished she could get out of answering her mother's questions as easily as her cat.

"One of the Sophian libraries," Sabra said. At the tone of her mother's voice, she was suddenly awake and suspicious. "The master learner said he thought I would enjoy them. To escape from my studies for a bit." She paused. "Actually, I've had it since I was very young."

Her mother pursed her lips and glared at the offending book once more, as though its faded blue leather cover offended her. "Just don't let your father see it."

Sabra's first instinct was to ask why, but she kept her mouth shut. This book had been one of her most constant companions since she was a child. For all she knew, it was a simple storybook with knights and wars and good and evil. She'd spent countless hours wondering what it would be like if Segzein had such noble deliverers. Not that Seigzen was at war much. Still, the stories had given her someplace to escape from the sandstorm of royal life.

But if her father wouldn't want her to see it...

Sabra could only think of one reason why.

She gave a quick nod and shoved it beneath her mattress before joining her mother at her vanity. This was a new development she hadn't considered before. But here it was, practically dropped in her lap by accident. She would simply be grateful in the moment and mull over the ramifications later.

"You've slept through half of supper," her mother said, working her runaway hair and smudged makeup back in place. "I thought perhaps you'd taken ill."

Sabra smiled. "No, just tired."

Her mother placed a kiss on top of her head. "Well, then. Let's not keep everyone waiting."

Sabra stood and followed her mother to her parents' chambers. There was an official dining hall, of course. Several, in fact. But most nights, her family liked their little personal gatherings, and Sabra was happy that way. It was one of the few times during the day that she got to see her parents together, and practically the only time she was allowed to speak freely with them without servants or courtiers listening in. Even Shakirat stayed outside the door.

"She fell asleep," her mother announced with a smile as they both joined the men at the low table in her parents' chambers. Sabra sat in her usual chair, between her parents and across from her cousin.

"You must have been tired," her father said as he cut his meat.

"I was." Sabra began to fill her plate. "I don't think I've ever walked about the markets as much as I did today."

"Yes," Demir said, narrowing his eyes. "It must have been exhausting."

Brat.

Sabra kicked him beneath the table. He met her gaze, and she held it for a moment, silently reminding him with one slowly arched eye about the time she'd caught him kissing some foreign princess at a ball.

Sabra's parents watched the exchange, looking back and forth several times.

"Is there something we should know about this?" Sabra's father asked, his eyes crinkling the way they always did when he found something humorous.

Demir must have decided not to call her bluff because he shook his head. But just as Sabra was sure she'd gotten off easy, her father cleared his throat.

"That's interesting," he said, chewing slowly, "because I heard today that you were spotted kissing a stranger in the market." This time, he let his smile slip before schooling his face again under the weight of her mother's frown.

Sabra let her head roll back and groaned. "I don't know who started that rumor, but they need to leave before I have them exiled. For the last time, I didn't kiss anyone today."

"But you were with a stranger?" Sabra's mother asked.

Sabra drew in a deep breath. "George isn't a stranger. I've known him for years. I used to play with him every time we went to the trade talks, before they were moved here. You can ask Demir." She waved her spoon at him. "I haven't seen him in seven years, and I was happy he was visiting." Were they going to make this as hard as possible?

"But why are people saying you kissed him?" her mother pressed.

Apparently, they were.

"I gave him a hug. There was absolutely no kissing involved." She cut her lamb with a renewed energy.

Not that she would have minded a kiss.

She mentally shook herself. George was an outsider and lived in another kingdom, so marriage would be next to impossible. Even contemplating such outcomes in her few spare, secret moments would be foolish, for she was practical enough to know that *those* kinds of dreams would lead straight to heartache.

"Don't be too hard on her." Sabra's father grinned at her mother. "If I remember right, you shared a few sweet moments with several fellows."

Sabra nearly choked on the olive she'd just put in her mouth, and Demir laughed aloud.

"Auntie!"

"That was before you asked me to marry you." Her mother gave her father a warning look, which only made everyone laugh harder. "And I was *not* trying to pass the Inquest."

For a long moment, Sabra's parents held each other's gaze. Sabra always wondered how they did that, speaking without actually talking. Whatever her mother told her father, however, had him suddenly clearing his throat and looking at his food once again.

"You know that if you pass the Inquest," he said, sounding official, the way he did when he was reading out an edict, "you'll be choosing a husband immediately after."

"I am aware of that," Sabra said coolly.

"What your father means to say," her mother picked up the conversation, "is that perhaps it would be wiser if you began to curb some of your enthusiasm. At least around men you're not entertaining as a possible husband."

Sabra wanted to retort that that would be easier if some of the men presenting themselves were the least bit desirable. But that would only distress her parents, and she had no desire to make them uncomfortable. "Of course," she said demurely. But inside, she was secretly relishing the way it had felt to be held in George's arms, even if only for those few fleeting seconds. And judging by the look Demir was giving her now, he knew exactly where her rebellious thoughts had strayed.

"How are you feeling about the Inquest?" her father asked,

cheerful once again. But Sabra was glad for the change in topic.

"Good." She nodded at her plate. "I feel like I've really gained an understanding of all the different economies, and Demir and I have been going through the questions each Assemblyman is most likely to pose. Only..." Her mind strayed back to the unanswered questions.

"Only what?" her mother asked.

"I know you don't want to hear it," Sabra said softly. "But if I'm going to run the kingdom, I need to know."

Demir's jaw tightened, and he glanced at her father. "Sabra—"

Something inside of her snapped.

"No." Her hand came down on the table, louder than she meant it to. "I'm not a child anymore. In two weeks, I'm going to be faced with questions as to what's best for this kingdom. I'm going to be asked about civics and history and how to plan for the future, and I can't do any of that properly unless I know what happened." What she was doing was incredibly stupid. Her father had threatened all sorts of punishment in the past whenever she brought up even one inconsistency. But now, she was going in with all of them. George's own questions today had made her bold, and the pressing nearness of her Inquest was suddenly looming. She was most likely on her way to being queen, and she deserved answers.

"I don't know what you're talking about." Her father's face, which had been round and cheery, soft and full of affection only moments before, turned to stone.

"I know that you're hiding something from me." Sabra refused to look away. "Even strangers are asking questions. Every time I ask anyone to tell me what's being kept hidden, they run away like scared mice. And the Blue Bands. Those people with the blue tattoos—"

"How do you know about them?" her father glowered.

"I'm not blind, Father. And I can see that—"

"Sabra, we've talked about this," her father growled, his black and white bushy eyebrows pushing together.

"There are eight spaces in the royal crest's octagon," Sabra said in a rush, "but only seven clans. Why give two spaces to the Justines on our seal while leaving a whole spoke of our physical land empty? And don't tell me that it's because we wanted somewhere to put the poor people. There are poor people all over the city, and only a portion of them live in the spoke. And most of them are Blue Bands. Even newcomers choose a clan when they move here. They work. They improve themselves. They leave. But the Blue Bands stay. And not only that, the libraries are missing entire years of written histories—"

"No one will ask you anything about that during the Inquest," Demir said, his face slightly pale.

"Please," her mother said with a pained expression, "just let it go."

Demir kicked her under the table again. *Compromise*, he mouthed.

"If I'm going to be queen, I should know!" Sabra cried, looking back and forth between her parents. "I *need* to know!"

"And I will tell you what you need to know when you need it!" her father exploded.

"What if something happens to you?" Sabra met his glare. "What then?"

"Then Demir can tell you." He stood, pushing his robe out of the way. "And I don't want to hear about this ever again."

"You ask me to carry the world on my shoulders," Sabra snapped. "But you won't actually hand it over for me to try."

Her father's dark eyes met and burned into hers. "You are intelligent and quick-witted, Sabra. But arrogance doesn't become you. And if you refuse to listen to your elders, I might as well have made Demir my heir." He turned and stalked into her parents' sleeping chamber.

Sabra's mother took a deep breath and shook her head to herself before standing. Briefly, she placed a cool hand on Sabra's cheek.

"He didn't mean it," she said softly. "You know how he gets when he's feeling pressured. I'll talk to him." Then she followed her husband into the bedroom.

Sabra stood and went to the door, unshed tears stinging her

eyes.

"Sabra."

Sabra stopped, her fingers on the door handle. She didn't turn, though, as Demir came up behind her. He ignored this, however, and pulled her into a hug.

"Your mother's right," he said into her hair. "He didn't mean it. He always regrets the things he says in the morning." He pulled back and gave her a smile. "You know just how to discomfit him. That's the problem. He's used to getting his way, and his little girl throws all that out the window."

"I've always wanted him to be proud of me." Sabra wiped her nose on the back of her hand. "But he won't give me the chance to show him what I can really do."

"You'll get there." He chucked her gently on the chin. "I promise. Just give it time."

"What about you?" Sabra sniffed and looked up into her cousin's deep brown eyes. "Do you agree with him? About keeping the truth from me, I mean?"

Demir's smile disappeared, and he frowned at the ground. "I don't know."

Sabra gave her cousin another hug and left her parents' chambers for her own, her tears making her tired once again. As she dressed herself for bed, though, Demir's words ran circles around in her head.

I don't know.

What in the world could be so terrible that they would gamble not telling Segzein's next ruler? Had they done something horribly immoral? Had something awful been done to them? Would it put the kingdom at risk if too many people knew? As if she would tell anyone such a secret.

"Sabra."

Sabra had just pulled out her nightdress and was staring at it when her father's muffled voice came through the door. Anger flared in her chest again, and she opened the door and stiffly curtsied. "Your Majesty."

He winced briefly and rubbed his hand over his eyes. "Come with me," he said gently. "There's something I need to tell you."

Ten minutes later, Sabra and her father climbed into the lookout point, one of the highest points in the palace. When they were at war, it was used to watch enemy troops, but now the night was peaceful. The moonlight danced over the pink waters of the lake to their southwest. The ancient cave-riddled stone hills with natural arrow-top chimneys surrounding them stood to the east and north. To the west were hills too distant to make out anything more than their existence. Surrounding the city walls, like a buffer between it all, were large, green fields full of sprouting crops. The pink lake retained just enough of its color in the moonlight to give it an eerie glow.

Sabra sat on the bench on the west side of the tower and wrapped her arms around herself as well as she could. It was cooler than she'd expected it to be. Without a word, her father took off his cloak and laid it over her shoulders. Then he sat beside her and sighed.

"I'm sorry."

Sabra's throat grew thick, but she leaned against his shoulder, and in turn, he wrapped a large arm around her and drew her close to his side. They sat like that for a long time. Sabra had so much she wanted to say, but now after her outburst at supper, she felt as though she'd used up all of her available words.

"Do you know why we chose you?"

Sabra turned and faced her father. "At the orphanage?"

He pulled her close, and she snuggled in. "Your mother and I realized that we most likely wouldn't be able to have any children. And while Demir was next in line for the throne, your mother wanted a child." He kissed her forehead. "We both did. So we went to the orphanage and met the children there. There were several who seemed to be good choices from a logistical perspective. Several boys who would be good playmates for Demir, a little closer to his age than you were. A few girls who had come from renowned families in the Capitans but had been orphaned in the attacks by the Dune Pirates." His eyes tightened briefly. Then he glanced down at her again, and they softened.

"We were about to leave and discuss our choices. Then you toddled up." He tightened the arm that was holding her. "No one knew which clan you were from or even knew your name. You had been there a few months, and they had taken to calling you the tiger cub."

"Why?" Sabra laughed. It was a strange feeling on the heels of the anger.

"You had the brightest eyes I'd ever seen. And you were intelligent. You must have been watching the other children because as soon as we were finished talking with the last child of those they'd lined up for us, you came forward and presented yourself as though you'd been summoned." He let out a booming guffaw. "You put your little hands on our knees and tilted your head like a small cat." He took a deep breath and looked back down at Sabra. "I knew as soon as I looked into your eyes that you were special."

Sabra sobered and looked out over the nightscape. "How so?" She hadn't felt very special tonight at supper.

Her father paused. "Some people are given gifts of power. The Fortiers and their blue fire. The queens of Hedjet with their healing powers. But some people are gifted with abilities of the mind." He pulled away and took Sabra's shoulders in his hands. "Sabra, I could tell from the moment you set eyes on us that you could lead a kingdom. Your mother could see it, too. And we have never doubted our decision to bring you home." He pulled her into a big hug. Sabra leaned against him as she had when she was a little girl. "Not ever," he whispered into her hair.

Sabra drew in a shaky breath. "Then why are you hiding so much from me?"

"There are..." he said slowly, "pieces of our past that we need to move on from. Things we suffered. And the people who are alive now still remember that pain." He frowned slightly. "People like your cousin."

Did he mean Demir? What was Demir trying to forget?

"The more we can point them toward the future," he continued, "the more we can leave that past behind." He kissed her head again. "Now, go to bed. I'm sure you have a dozen things to do before breakfast, knowing you."

Sabra hugged her father once more and then did as he said, only remembering that she had his cloak when she got back to her room. Oh well. She would give it back tomorrow.

He had been right when he'd guessed that she would be busy. And yet, as much as she wanted to listen and let matters be, Sabra knew in her heart of hearts that she couldn't do that. If she was going to be responsible for these people, she needed to know what they had been through. And based on what her father had said that night, kind as it was, it sounded almost like he didn't plan to tell her at all. Still, she had to hope.

Thirteen days, she thought to herself as she blew her lamp out. Thirteen days until she was tested by the kingdom's most powerful men and women. And while Demir might not be certain whether or not her ignorance would be addressed, Sabra knew she wasn't willing to wait any longer. She rolled over and felt something hard. After feeling its rough, leathery surface, she realized that it was her book, still there from where she'd shoved it under the mattress that evening.

She pulled out the book and decided she needed a better place to hide it. She'd need to hide her research papers as well.

Sabra might not know the truth. But she knew now that this book was more than just a fairy tale, as evidenced by her mother's unease. She also wondered if its giver had meant something more as well.

I'm sorry, Father, she thought sadly as she climbed into bed. Tomorrow, she was going to the library.

CHAPTER 5
MISSING

Sabra was up before the sun again the next morning. This time, however, she left a note for Nisa to let her know that she could spend the day as she chose, as Sabra wouldn't be needing any help this morning. This would frustrate Nisa, of course, but there were simply some things that couldn't be done with a handmaiden in tow.

Instead of meandering through the various spokes as she had the day before, Sabra went straight to the Sophians' spoke. She passed the smaller tents where master learners were just getting their doors open and their little fires lit to ward off the coolness of the early morning and headed straight for one of the largest structures in the city, second only to the palace.

The library was the pride and joy of the Sophians, and with good reason. Though they had countless buildings dedicated to the preservation of historical documents and materials, the towering library soared into the sky. The complex was nearly impossible to look at when the sun was high, its rays reflecting off of the tiled, domed roofs. There was one large central dome with twelve more scattered around it. Three arches heralded entrance to the largest dome, the arch in the middle at least four stories tall.

Inside was no less spectacular. The stone tiles, which covered the walls, had been painted with scenes from Segzein's most prominent moments in history. The main room was six stories high, slightly shorter than the palace throne room. Where the dome ended at the top the vertical walls began, each filled with recessed slots into which books and scrolls were placed, two or three to a slot. Several spiral staircases graced the room, if it could be called that in all its enormity, allowing one to cross back and forth between the five levels of stairs and walkways that had been built against each wall. This way, no space was lost, the walkway allowing anyone who could climb that high to search its scrolls and books without hindrance.

The domed ceiling was one giant mural. Sabra had once been told that the Woodsmen's best artists had been hired to paint it, and the whole project had taken two years, as the paint, which reflected light, was rare and had to be purchased from one of the eastern kingdoms. The mural featured the kingdom's eight spokes, the same as the seal. But in each spoke was a person doing some sort of work that reflected his clan. As with all of the other paintings and images of the spokes, however, the eighth character was missing, and the Justines' character, a man who was stretching his arm out over the eighth spoke, a scale in his hand, seemed off to Sabra. It was as though the painting had been altered. Even the colors were slightly off.

"Your Highness?"

Sabra turned to see a young woman looking at her expectantly. She wore the yellow robe of a learner apprentice, no doubt training for her future place as a master learner in her own right.

Sabra smiled. "I'm looking for Master Mirac."

"Of course." The young woman bowed. "I'll let him know you're here."

Sabra considered climbing to the highest level to see the ceiling better. She'd done so years ago, but she'd been younger then. Unfortunately, she wasn't kept waiting long enough to try now.

"Look who's returned," came a gravelly voice from her left. Sabra turned to see a tall man emerge from the shadows. His gray hair, as usual, looked as though it hadn't been combed for years, and his black robe, though clean, was rather rumpled.

"Master Mirac," Sabra replied, giving him the customary nod of respect. "Thank you for seeing me."

"I assume you need something, or you wouldn't be here." His face was hard and the quirk of his eye skeptical. If Sabra hadn't known him better, she would have missed the slightly amused curl of his lips.

"As a matter of fact, I do. Of course, I can ask for Master Leon if you're too busy to help me." She held his gaze and put a hand on her hip.

He snorted. "Do that, and you might as well have stayed home."

"Well then," she said with a wry grin as she pulled the little leather book from her bag, "I suppose you can tell me something about this and why you gave it to me."

All signs of sarcasm and humor disappeared as his eyes widened. In one swift move, he had the book out of her hand and hidden in his robes. With his other hand, he put a gentle but firm hand on her back and silently pressed her forward, his eyes sweeping the room around them.

"Come with me but stay silent," he whispered so quietly she nearly missed it.

Sabra obeyed, allowing him to lead her to the back of the library and through a nearly invisible door in the wall. From there, he led her through several more rooms, each with its own sets of scrolls and books, where they'd been placed lovingly in the open spaces within the walls.

They must be moving through some of the smaller domed parts of the building, Sabra realized, excitement growing within her. She'd never been in this part of the library. For several minutes, they continued on in silence, moving from room to room until they reached a room so small only three people could have been comfortably seated inside. There was a simple desk, several candles, a small hearth, and a window that opened up to a small flower garden outside. Two small chairs sat in front of the desk and one behind.

This room also had holes built into the walls for scrolls and books, and most of them were full.

Master Mirac locked the door behind him then strode to the window and glanced outside. After a moment of searching, he closed the curtain, darkening the room. Then he went to the small fireplace and lit it before retreating to the chair behind the desk, motioning for Sabra to sit as well.

She chose the chair farthest from the door, though she wasn't sure why.

"So," he said, leaning back in his seat. "What makes you think this book is special?" He pulled the little book out and put it on his desk.

"Other than you snatching it away before taking us into hiding? You gave it to me."

"When you were a child. Would it be wise to entrust something nearly priceless to a little hooligan like you?"

Nisa would have died if she heard the way Master Mirac addressed Sabra. But Master Mirac had known Sabra as long as she could remember. He'd kept an eye on her when she was small and Demir would come to browse the library for his own research. Master Mirac had taught her to love reading and learning, and as far as Sabra was concerned, he could call her whatever he liked.

Now she held his steady gaze. "It would be if you thought the prize was worth the gamble."

He studied her for a long moment, his jaw working thoughtfully as he did.

"Why ask me now?" he finally said. "I gave you the book years ago."

"Last night, my mother saw the book. She said my father wouldn't like it." Sabra sat up. "And my father loves nothing more than a good story."

Master Mirac froze. "Did your father see it?"

"No." Sabra leaned back. "You told me to keep it hidden from the servants so they wouldn't accidentally misplace it. I've kept it from everybody." In truth, Sabra really had guarded the book, but more from a place of possessiveness than even the fear she spoke of. Of course, the fear had been there when Master Mirac had warned her that the servants might try to put it away with the palace books instead. But for some reason, those stories of knights and valor had always felt like they were Sabra's and hers alone. And she'd had no desire to share. When everything in her life was considered that of the people, it was a welcome respite to have a place of her own to vanish to when no one else could see.

"Then how did your mother find it after all these years?"

Sabra looked down at her lap in shame. "I fell asleep reading it yesterday after a long day." Her heart squeezed slightly as she remembered her busy day. Where was George now? How far had he made it in the night?

"Ah. And her comment made you suspicious."

Sabra looked at him again. "I've always been suspicious. Just not about the right things, apparently."

For the first time, Master Mirac barked out a laugh. "Yes, I think you have." Then his smile was gone as soon as it had come. "So why did you come here?"

"Like I said. You gave me the book. And I think you gave it to me for a reason."

The hesitation that flashed through the master learner's eyes was so fast that Sabra nearly missed it.

"You do know something," she said softly, her heart beating so fast it made her dizzy. She gripped the edge of the chair. Was she about to get her answers? After all these years? Had the evidence been hiding right under her nose?

Master Mirac opened his mouth then paused. When he spoke, it was slow and deliberate. "By law, I know nothing of what you speak."

Ah. By law. Sabra had figured that had something to do with it.

"By law, are you allowed to give me any idea as to what happened?"

He shook his head then gestured at the wall of books beside his desk. "No. But I can tell you that master learners are required to keep our own histories throughout the duration of our lives. It's a tradition that's been kept for centuries. You can find mine over there."

Sabra stood and went to the wall he had indicated. There were leather-bound books there. They looked much like ledgers, but there were dozens. And on each binding was engraved a year.

"When did you begin keeping these?" she asked, going back to the beginning and moving forward from there.

"When I was initiated as a novice learner," he said. "I was twenty-five years when I began."

Sabra found his first book and began to count. It seemed as though there was traditionally one book per year, although, some years warranted two, it seemed. At first, nothing seemed amiss. But then, after skimming about half of the books' bindings, she stopped. Going back, she did the math.

"Two years are missing." She stood and looked at Master Mirac. "The year I was born and the one before that."

He stared up at her from beneath hooded eyes. "And?" Then he nodded back at the books. "Now, open one up from before the two missing years. Tell me what you see."

With trembling hands, Sabra took one of the books from five years prior to the first missing year and opened it up. She skimmed the first part but stopped quickly.

"Words have been blotted out." She frowned. Some were singular. Others were entire paragraphs. Then she sucked in a breath as she turned the pages. "Entire pages have been ripped out!"

"You said it. Not me." Master Mirac stared into the fire.

Sabra's knees felt weak, so she put the book back and made her way back to her chair before collapsing into it. "I was right," she whispered. Then she met his eyes. "But why?"

His thick eyebrows drew together, and he put his steepled fingers to his lips.

"According to the crown," he said slowly, "there are certain times and events that never happened. His eyebrows went up. "There was, however, a fire that took place not long after your parents took you in. It burned many of our books and records."

"Including," Sabra said just as slowly, "all records of those two years."

He nodded once.

"But," she looked back at the place where the two books should have been, "why didn't you tell me this before? I've been here countless times looking for answers."

"No offense, Princess," he said with a wry smile. "But adolescent girls aren't generally known for being highly secretive, whether the secrets are theirs or someone else's."

"So why now?"

"You're just weeks away from your Inquest. If you're about to take the crown, it's only fair that you know what you're accepting. Or at least," he paused, "as close to knowing as you can get."

"Tell me," Sabra whispered, going to his side and kneeling beside his chair like a small child begging for a story. "I swear, I won't breathe a word to a soul."

"And what if," he raised his eyebrows, "you find a truth so objectionable you can't be true to your conscience by staying silent?"

Sabra felt her blood go cold.

"That's what I thought," he said with a sad smile. Then he stood and went to the door. "I'm afraid, Princess, that if you want your questions answered, you'd better pass that Inquest after all."

CHAPTER 6
HELP

Sabra jumped and let out a squeal when something touched her side. She whirled around to find Demir laughing as he pulled back the staff he had poked her with.

"Lost?" he asked, his eyes gleaming. When he wasn't being annoying, he was what most women considered rather attractive. On the taller side, fit, with dark, curly hair and brown eyes that seemed to dance when he was in a good mood. It was honestly a mystery to Sabra as to why he wasn't married yet. Not that she would tell him that. It would only stroke his ego.

"I came out here to be alone." She gestured to the little flowered balcony. "When you're done annoying me, I can get back to studying." She scowled at him before looking back down at the book in front of her.

"Sabra, you've been studying for the last three days. Your mother was beyond aggravated when you didn't even show up to visit your suitors. I was only able to hold her off by reminding her that you would worry about such things after you passed the Inquest, but she wasn't very happy about it."

"Thank you." Sabra kept her eyes on her book.

"Oh, come on. You know that when *I* say that you're too focused, you're *really* too focused." He put his staff down and leaned against it. "What's going on?"

Sabra turned toward her cousin and studied him for a long moment. He was right. She'd never studied so hard in her life. But then, she'd never come so close to understanding the mystery of the eighth spoke in the seal either. Master Mirac, through his cryptic little hints, had thrown her world on its side three days ago. It was as though someone had put her in a barrel and rolled her down a hill, only to stop the thing and leave it tipped on its side. And now that she was closer, she wanted desperately to ask Demir why. Why such things were being hidden. If he wouldn't tell her, at least he could give her a reason. Master Mirac's foreboding words played in her head, never ceasing, even while she slept.

And what if you find a truth so objectionable you can't be true to your conscience by staying silent?

Those missing years had come from the time around Sabra's birth. Meaning her father had been king, and her cousin, though a child, would have been old enough to remember what happened during the time that didn't exist. And while her father could be a stubborn old bat, there wasn't a mean bone in his body.

Was there?

"Sabra," Demir said slowly, leaning toward her slightly. "Are you alive? Or should I send a healer?"

"I had something strange happen the other day," she said slowly, trying to come up with the most diplomatic way to phrase what she wanted to say. Something that wouldn't tip him off immediately as to what she was talking about. Better to make it look as though it were all a giant coincidence that the missing years coincided with the rest of the mystery.

"What was that?" he asked, his smile fading.

"I went to the large library to look for some information on the Justines."

"And?" he prompted.

Sabra hesitated. "There were two years of history missing."

His eyes widened for a second before his face went neutral. "Oh, you mean from the fire." He probably would have fooled a stranger into thinking him unruffled, but Sabra knew her cousin far too well.

"What fire?" she asked innocently.

"There was a fire just after you were born. The books and scrolls were organized differently then. By year instead of by subject. They were able to put the fire out before it took everything, but many records were lost."

"I see." Sabra held his gaze. She almost asked if the fire had blotted out all those words and torn individual pages out of the books as well, but he clearly wasn't going to budge. She was sure he had to say these things, probably dictated by her father. But he could at least give a sign of some sort, something to tell her that he wanted her to know the truth.

But as he stood before her now, he offered her nothing. So taking a deep breath, she fixed a smile on her face and nodded. If he was going to play the fool, so was she.

As soon as her cousin was gone, suddenly recalling a meeting he was to attend, Sabra readied herself to go out. Nisa would wash her hands of her mistress soon if Sabra didn't start taking her more places as was considered proper. But Nisa was too loyal to Sabra's father to be entrusted with the mission Sabra was about to embark on. So Sabra grabbed a fig bar and a date cake that remained on her plate from breakfast and wrapped them each in a linen cloth. She tucked one in her reticule and held the other in her hand.

Then she put on her best walking shoes and her simplest dress, which was a dull brown color with far fewer ruffles than any of her other dresses. She wrapped her face in a long scarf and pulled her long, dark hair into a coil beneath it. Those who knew her well would recognize her, and technically, nothing she wore was below her station. But for those who weren't her constant companions or over-seers, she would be invisible. Just another face in the crowd.

Hopefully.

Then she stood just outside her door and waited with the fig bar in hand.

She didn't have to wait long. She could hear Serkan's whistling from down the hall, and she glanced around once more to make sure they would be alone as soon as he appeared.

As soon as he rounded the corner, she grabbed his arm and dragged him into her room.

"Princess!" The boy gasped dramatically and then dusted himself off, as if she'd knocked him over. "What was that for?"

"I need you to distract everyone while I use the servants' door," she said.

He squinted up at her, and his smile grew calculating. "I think the princess is supposed to use the front doors."

Sabra rolled her eyes. "What do you want?"

"Two coppers. And a piece of that chocolate stuff the next time you get it at supper."

Sabra held up the food. "A fig bar it is."

"What? That's not what I—"

"Are you going to get a fig bar anywhere else?"

He huffed, but after a second of glaring held his hand out. Sabra smirked and motioned for him to lead the way as they went back out into the hall.

"If you decide to get tricky with me," Sabra leaned down and whispered in his ear, "I'll have you reassigned to the cook again. No more errand duty for you. I hear she needs a new helper."

Serkan stiffened and turned to look back at her in horror. "You wouldn't," he hissed.

Sabra let her smirk grow. "The kitchen garden gets hot this time of year."

Serkan gave her a murderous look, but she could tell from the set of his shoulders that she'd won. This round, at least. She'd need to check all her wine for toads for the next week.

True to his word, or perhaps his fear of being made to work for the headstrong cook, Serkan darted around the corner, and a second later, there was a crash. A few other servants in the hall ran to see what had happened, and Sabra used their diverted attention to silently make her escape.

She knew the servants' passages and secret passageways by

heart. As a child, she'd spent years exploring them until someone tattled to her mother, and she was then banned from playing there anymore. She rarely used them now, but every once in a while, when she wanted to lose the attention that always seemed to follow her, she would manage a scene to be caused somewhere in the palace that would allow her quick access to the palace exits.

The sun was higher than she expected when she finally got out. Carefully, she pulled the scarf more tightly around her face and made her way to the nearest gate. She knew who she wanted.

But doing that without being recognized would be a challenge. So she pulled the hood of her cloak farther over her face.

Once she was off the palace grounds, getting to the desired clan was easier. She walked to the northern side of the palace wall and set off to the Physics' market.

The walk to the market wasn't long, but Sabra was dismayed when she arrived to find the old Blue Band gone. His little ratty tent was up, but he was nowhere to be seen.

"Excuse me." Sabra approached the person in the tent beside his. "Do you know where the owner of this tent is?"

"He always goes home at midday," said the woman, a seller of fish oils.

"Do you know where he lives?"

"Unfortunately, I do." She pinched up her face. "He lives in the eighth spoke. Don't ask me how I know that. I just do."

Sabra thanked the woman and made her way to the eighth spoke.

It was an interesting spoke and the one that Sabra spent the least amount of time in. Most of the homes were small and run-down. There were no grand buildings or magnificent basniin mansions as there were in other spokes. Where there weren't homes built, the empty lots were mainly used as a place for homeless citizens and visitors to pitch their tents. Tents of all shapes and sizes were scattered over the wedge-shaped piece of land between the houses, with clotheslines strung up between each little tent or home.

She prayed that the people who noticed her wouldn't recognize her as she made her way to the edge. She already had the attention of several families who were sitting outside for the midday meal. Only then did it occur to her that she had no idea where she would find him. She didn't even know his name.

So she took a breath and began to search. Up and down rows, in and out of clumps.

She'd been to the spoke several times, but never with this much time to explore. It was really a strange layout, not at all thoughtful and organized like the rest of the city. The large plots of land where visitors and newcomers pitched their tents seemed to almost resemble building foundations, similar to those that stood in the other spokes. The parts of the spoke with proper houses were more orderly, the buildings set in lines and rows. But many were ramshackle, and the people who stood outside of them were often thinner and paler than those who were encamped temporarily around them.

And Sabra didn't miss the sightings of several of the swirled blue bands tattooed on arms here and there.

After an hour of searching, she nearly gave up, when she finally caught sight of him, sitting under a tree in front of one of the aging homes.

"Good morning," she said, nodding to the old man as she came to sit across from him.

The man was eating a piece of fruit. She sat down across from him, and he gave a small start when he saw her.

"You're a difficult man to find," she said in a low voice.

"Princess," he answered evenly. "You seem a determined person."

She removed the date cake from her reticule. "I was hoping to ask you a few questions." She tore the date cake in half and held a piece out. "Over breakfast, perhaps."

He smiled, as though she were an amusing child, but he accepted the cake piece with a nod. "You ask dangerous questions."

Guilt momentarily flared in her chest. Yes, her questions were that.

She would keep it fast.

He shoved the cake in his mouth then leaned back and removed a length of blue cloth from the bag beside him. Then he pulled a needle and thread out and began to embroider as he chewed. His hands were amazingly fast for his age. "Why not ask your father or that cousin of yours?" he asked, his needle moving in and out of the material in a blur.

"I believe my father has good intentions." Butterflies flitted around in her stomach, but she quickly smothered them.

He arched a graying eyebrow, though his hands never slowed. "But you don't trust him."

"It's not that." Sabra spoke slowly. "It's more that I don't agree with his decision."

The man glanced around. There were several of the others watching them now, men and women who mostly looked to be around this man's age. Everyone else had cleared away as though Sabra had the plague.

"And you would risk such open defiance to the crown in such a public place?" His voice was low.

Sabra glanced at them then back at the man. "I get the feeling that you all stand to lose little by telling me."

Again, he smiled as though this amused him. "Except our lives." He changed to another color and began embroidering again.

"That is true," Sabra said, feeling rather sick to her stomach.

"Why now?" he said in that same soft voice. "You've haunted my tent for years now. But never have you come this far for answers."

Sabra cleared her throat. "I feel as if my time is growing short. I'm determined not to take the crown in utter ignorance."

"Ah." He nodded and continued his work.

After a moment of debating whether or not she might risk staying a little longer, she leaned forward. "You're very skilled. Where did you learn?"

"My mother. She was a master seamstress."

"And what did your father do?" Sabra asked. He was hiding something. She was sure of it. Perhaps she could learn something about all those missing years, pages, and words by asking less direct questions.

"He was…" the man paused. This only piqued her curiosity more. Why would someone his age have to stop and consider what his father's trade had been? "A swordsman," he finally said.

Sabra blinked at him. Whatever response she'd been expecting, that wasn't it.

"I'm afraid, Princess, that I cannot answer your questions," he said, bowing his head. "I'm but a poor man, and I must attend to my daily work."

"Of course." Sabra did her best to smile as she got up.

The man put his hand out in a farewell gesture, but as he did, he knocked over the clay mug of tea he had sitting beside him. The drink went all over Sabra's dress.

"Oh, Your Highness, I'm so sorry!" He leaned forward and pressed the length of blue cloth into Sabra's hand. "Take this. Use it to dry your dress."

Sabra began to object, saying she was perfectly fine with letting it dry on the way back, but the man tightened his grip on her hand, pressing the cloth in harder. "I insist," he said. "It's only proper." His eyes narrowed.

An instinct, something deep inside her, fluttered in warning. "Very well," she said softly. "Thank you."

She turned to go, wiping at her wet dress for show, and hurried all the way back to the palace. With each step, she wanted to examine the cloth he was so determined to give her. But she wouldn't allow herself to look at it, for fear of drawing attention, until she was safe in her room again with the door locked. Then, on her bed, she stretched it out flat.

It was a sash. Sabra hadn't recognized its shape all rumpled the way the man had held it. And at its center was the embroidery he'd finished as she sat there.

The work was simple but masterful. The edges were sewn so finely that she had to look twice to see that they had been bordered with a delicate, nearly invisible design. What caught her attention most, however, was the emblem in the upper right corner. It was a sword, silver, with a light blue streak that danced around it delicately, almost like wind. A hand gripped the hilt of the sword. The entire picture was no larger than her thumb, and encircling it all was a ring of symbols. They looked like characters from another language, but it was no language Sabra had ever seen.

The language she might never have seen before, but the picture looked familiar.

Sabra frowned. Where had she seen this picture? It was from a book. She knew that. She could distinctly recall the blue ink, so it must have been a page she'd seen more than once. But most books had few to no pictures, or the pictures scattered randomly through the text were simply fancy letters. And most were in black and white. But this one was a bright indigo. Actually, the indigo had probably been what caught her eye in the first place. It was a special shade, one that wasn't common in most clothing or ink or even paint. If only she could remember…

Sabra froze.

Of course.

Master Mirac's book.

She scrambled to get off the bed so fast that she nearly fell off. Then she reached into the place she'd hidden it that morning to prevent the housekeepers from discovering it. She flipped through the pages so fast that she tore one in her haste. But it was worth it when she found what she was looking for.

The image on the kerchief was actually only a small part of a larger illustration. The knights had emerged victorious after slaying an evil witch disguised as a great monster, and the general, who was standing on the beast, had thrust his sword up into the air as his men below did the same.

Sabra lifted the kerchief again to examine it more closely. The resemblance was perfect, although only part of the picture had been captured in the embroidery. But those symbols. Where in the world was she to find them? She could visit Master Mirac again, but as her last visit to the library was so recent, she didn't want to raise suspicion by returning too soon.

She looked around her room, as though it might hold some secret answer. Then her gaze landed on the pile of letters she needed to sort and put away. Immediately, Sabra knew what she needed to do.

She ran to her desk and whipped out a pen and fresh parchment. But just as she started writing, a knock at the door startled her and made her blot her ink. Huffing, Sabra began again, this time faster.

"Your Highness?" Nisa called. "Your mother has asked that you join her. Your suitors are here for tea."

"I'll be there soon," Sabra called back, trying to keep the annoyance out of her voice. "I need to change first."

"I'll help." The door handle turned but caught on the lock.

"Actually," Sabra called back, racking her memory for some sort of chore that would please her mother and distract from her tardiness, "I'd like for you to run to the market and bring me some..." Some *what*? "Some olives," she said lamely. "Olives that are ripe, unripe, and overly ripe."

"Oh." She could hear Nisa's confusion even without seeing her face. "Um, very well. Where shall I bring them?"

"To the tea," Sabra called back, dipping her pen in ink once more. "I'll be using them to test my suitors." That sounded even more stupid and pointless. "To see whether they can tell the difference between the olives."

"Yes, Princess."

Sabra breathed a sigh of relief as she heard her servant's retreating steps. But there wasn't much time to celebrate her small victory. Now she had to pen a letter and get herself dressed for tea. Oh well. What she could do would have to be good enough.

Dear George,

 I apologize for this letter's brevity, but I need your help. As you're a scholar, I thought perhaps you might be able to find the translation

of these symbols for me. I have to go now, but this is of the utmost
importance. Thank you so much for your help.
    As always,
    Sabra

Sabra copied down the marks that made up the circle around the picture. It would take too long to copy the image, but the words would help more than the picture. She was sure of it. Then she melted a bit of wax and sealed the letter with her personal signet.

It was bold. If she or the runner got caught with such a letter, there would likely be consequences for both of them. Sabra dressed as quickly as she could and then risked a run down to the stables on her way to the tea.

The messengers, who were grooming the horses, stood upon her entrance.

"Princess!" the master stablekeeper exclaimed, tucking an escaped gray curl behind her ear. As if Sabra would care that the woman's hair wasn't perfect. "What a surprise!"

"I know." Sabra smiled. "I apologize for intruding, but I was on my way to tea and was hoping to send a message." She looked around and was relieved to find the face she was looking for. "With Yusuf."

The master stablekeeper looked at her in amazement, but had enough manners not to ask why Sabra was requesting one rider over another. "Of course." She motioned to the others. "Let the princess give Yusuf his work."

Sabra cast her the most grateful look she could as the stablekeeper cleared the room. Then she was left alone with Yusuf.

Yusuf wasn't a young rider. But he was from another kingdom and had only joined her father's ranks four or five years before. She prayed to the Maker now that she wasn't endangering him as she pressed four coins into his hand.

"Princess!" He gaped at the coins. "I'm already paid by the palace stew—"

"I know." She willed him to look her in the eye. "But this is a message of a personal nature, and it shall require you to possibly take rest and shelter if there's a storm." Unlikely, as George's town wasn't very far on horseback, but still possible. "Use what you need and keep the rest. But it is of the utmost importance that it reaches its destination. I want you to give it to no one but the man himself." She swallowed. "Can you do that?" In her head, she added, *without telling my father?*

This was more than a little dangerous. If she pushed her father too far, there would be consequences. He loved her, but he was also Segzein's king, answerable to more than just Sabra or her mother or even himself. If someone read this letter and word got back to her father or the Assembly, Sabra might not be allowed her Inquest.

But something foul was haunting Segzein. And if she didn't seek out this ghost and face it now, it might do more than haunt her in the future.

To her relief, Yusuf didn't even blink. Instead, he gave her an easy smile, the corners of his eyes crinkling good-naturedly. "Of course, Princess. It would be my privilege." He bowed and grabbed two of the traveling sacks that the couriers kept prepared with food, water, and blankets and loaded it all on one of the waiting horses. She gave him the directions, and two minutes later, he was gone.

CHAPTER 7

CAN I?

"Daughter."

Sabra looked up from her book. Not that she'd actually been reading it. "Sorry, what was that?"

Sabra's father smiled and shook his head. "Daydreaming about all those dashing suitors who have come to seek your hand?"

Sabra made a face. "I'm still not sure I believe you that Mother just appeared among your choices. I feel as though all the good, decent men go to work, and the rest show up here to torment me." She took a deep breath. "Sorry, what were we discussing?"

"The trade commission as proposed by the merchants in Kappadona. But I can see your mind is elsewhere." He sat down across the table from her.

In the week following her secret letter to George, the days continued like an itch Sabra just couldn't reach. With her Inquest fast approaching, she needed to study. But every time she opened her books or recited her lessons to her cousin, more questions seemed to bubble up inside. All those holes she'd discovered over the years swelled with each day, crowding each other out until she was no longer able to recite a paragraph without stumbling upon another realization that something was missing.

She watched for Yusuf, praying hourly that he might bring her an answer from George. But that, too, was a desire unfulfilled. She tried not to think about George or his silence too much. He was probably busy with his apprenticing or taking care of his grandparents. He might even have a woman, someone he gave all his spare time to, what little there was to offer. He hadn't mentioned anything about a girl, but then, they'd only been together for one day and exchanged one letter each since being reunited.

Why did that thought make her feel less than satisfied? Surely he would still attempt to help her. Wouldn't he?

Sabra's father let out a loud laugh this time. "You really are lost today, aren't you?" He smoothed down a piece of hair that the wind had blown over her head. "Do you want to tell me what's bothering you?"

Did she want to? Absolutely. Could she? Absolutely not. He'd proven that the week before. So she chose a safer thought to share instead.

"I guess," she said slowly, "I've wondered sometimes what my life would have been like had you and Mother not chosen me."

Her father's smile fell. "Why do you wonder that?" he asked softly.

George's face leaped to the forefront of her mind, and Sabra was very glad her father couldn't read her thoughts.

"How could one not think it?" She did her best to grin. Her father knew her well enough to usually sense when something was wrong. "So many what-ifs took place that day. What if you hadn't come on that day? What if someone else had chosen me first? What if I'd been sick, or..." She stopped and drew in another deep breath. "It just makes me wonder sometimes why it was me the Maker let you bring home."

The king put down his book and took her hands. They were large and warm, and he held her fists in his like he did when she was little.

"The what-ifs aren't important. What matters is that the Maker made you to be queen. You were meant to be here in this moment now." He looked at her until she met his eyes. "You will encounter difficult days. And in those days, I pray you remember that you were made for such times."

Sabra stared back at her father, and very nearly told him everything then and there. Only the strength of her desperate need to know kept her mouth shut. Instead, she got up and hugged his neck tightly, praying that soon she would pass her Inquest, and he would keep his word, and everything would be made clear. One day, she would have no more secrets. But today was not that day, she thought, as he bid her farewell.

Doing her best not to think about what her old friend was doing, the days continued to pass in a blur, and yet each moment and hour seemed to last a lifetime. She didn't even bother pretending to listen to her suitors anymore as they blathered on. Instead, she was running the mystery symbols through her head, comparing them to the languages she knew and those she'd seen on the carts of traveling merchants. She needed to find out more. And while Master Mirac had promised to tell her what she needed to know, she wasn't sure whether that would be after the Inquest, provided she passed, or after her coronation, which Sabra hoped was a long time away. Either way, she was more determined than ever to find the answers.

Because she knew her father was serious about staying away from her questions, Sabra knew she had to be careful. She was tired of fighting him, and it only made things worse. So she changed tactics. She challenged her father no more, and she no longer pestered Demir with questions about the gaps in her knowledge. But while she was out in the markets, she used her new information to quietly ask questions in ways she hadn't thought to ask before.

One day, a Justine woman dropped the basket she was carrying, and a load of scrolls fell out. Sabra had been there to speak with a master about a proposed law, but she stopped to help the woman clean it up.

"Thank you, Princess," the woman said with a friendly grin.

"You're welcome." Sabra watched the woman as she turned to go, then called after her. "Please, madame?"

The woman turned. "Yes, Princess?"

Sabra glanced at the palace. Of course, no one would be watching her. She came and went as she pleased. "I was wondering," Sabra said slowly, returning her gaze to the woman, "do you recognize this?" She pulled a parchment from her pocket and unfolded it. On the parchment was the picture from the sash that she'd copied with her calligraphy pens and colored inks.

The women froze. "Your father.." she whispered.

"I promise," Sabra replied in a low voice. "I don't even need to know your name. I just have so many questions."

"I can't." The woman turned away, but Sabra followed her.

"I need answers if I'm to rule well!" she whispered after her as loudly as she dared. "Please! Just...are you familiar with the symbol? Yes or no, that's all I'm asking."

The woman's small face clouded with apprehension, but she opened her mouth as though to speak.

She never did speak, though. Instead, she simply snapped it shut again and shook her head. "I'm sorry, Your Highness," she said, brushing past Sabra at twice the speed she'd been moving earlier. "I just couldn't say."

So that was a yes.

She tried several other times over the next few days. And every time she asked, the man or woman would deny having ever seen the picture, but their eyes and bodies would say differently.

Why would her father put so much effort into terrifying their people? Why would he burn historical documents and accounts? Her father, who had taught her to love and value history and to turn to those wiser than her for direction, had effectively ended her search before it began. The gentle man who kissed her forehead and wrapped his cloak around her shoulders had succeeded in driving fear into their people deeper than a tent stake. But why?

Finally, the night before her Inquest arrived, and Sabra was determined to put every bit of study and preparation out of her head. If she didn't know something after a lifetime of study, she wasn't going to learn it tonight. So she put away all of her books and maps and journals and locked her door. Then she pulled out her little book about the knights and settled in for an early bedtime. Tonight, she would lose herself in a world that wasn't her own.

"What's that book?"

Sabra let out a little shriek, and her book fell on the floor.

Serkan bent and picked it up then examined it. "Can I have this?"

"How did you get in my room?" Sabra snatched it out of his hands. She looked at the door, and sure enough, it was still locked.

"Crawled in through the window."

Sabra stared at him. "It's three stories up!"

He shrugged and gave her a smug grin. "I'm a good climber."

Sabra simply stared at him expectantly. It was a skill her mother had perfected over the years, one that Sabra had practiced often in the mirror to master on her own.

Serkan rolled his eyes. "Fine. They're doing repair work on the roof. I snuck up when they weren't looking and let myself down on a rope."

"By law, you could be hanged for this." Sabra glared at him. Of course, she would never hang a boy. But this was ridiculous. Parents or no parents, the child had to learn some manners, or he was going to lose his place in the palace by the time he was fifteen years. And it wouldn't be by her hand.

"You're not going to hang me." He wriggled his eyebrows at her. "You put up a good show, but you're soft as cream on the inside." As if to prove his point, he snatched an apricot from the bowl of fruit Nisa had left on Sabra's bedside table.

"So can I have it?" he asked again, mouth sticky with apricot juice. "You never answered me."

"No, you can't have it. Now get out of my room." She paused. "Besides, you can't read."

"You're right. I can't."

"Then why do you want it?"

He shrugged. "Because it has swords in it. What's it about?" He climbed up on her bed and sat on it, still munching away at the fruit.

Sabra considered kicking him out. That he had seen the book was bad enough. He was well-known throughout the palace as a horrible gossip. And yet, tonight, for some reason, Sabra found herself wanting to share the story with someone else. She'd vowed to avoid all politics and pretenses. All she wanted was to get lost in a world with villains and heroes who knew what to do with them.

Besides, tomorrow was her Inquest. If she failed, it wouldn't matter who knew because no one was going to tell her what she wanted to know. And if she passed? Well, she'd have a lot more to go on than a book of stories that, for all intents and purposes, was nothing more than fables.

"Please?" He gave her large, pleading eyes that she knew better than to trust. "The last time I got a story was when Jorgan got drunk."

"Fine." Sabra let out a long, exasperated breath. "But," she held her finger up and gave him a look that was meant to melt metal. "If you so much as breathe a word about this to anyone, I'll tell the steward that you snuck into my room. You'll be scrubbing dishes at night for weeks."

His eyes widened so much that Sabra nearly smiled. "So," she said smugly, "does that mean you still want to listen?"

He frowned slightly, and for possibly the first time in his life, stopped to think before answering. When he did, though, there was none of his usual smirk.

"I promise." His voice was soft and vulnerable and lonely, and in spite of her annoyance, moved something inside of her.

With a sigh, Sabra opened the book. She nearly ordered him onto the floor. But he looked so small and sleepy in the bed that she let him stay at her feet, where he had curled up like a little cat. This did not seem to impress Thing, who jumped off the bed to perch on the window ledge and glare with distaste. Sabra shook her head. She was probably spoiling him now to the point that he wouldn't want to do any work for weeks, but she decided to ignore that fact and simply enjoy sharing her secret with another soul, even if only for a little while.

"...and the warriors went forth, chasing the monsters into the evening sky, and the people were able to sleep peacefully once more, knowing they were safe for another night."

Sabra closed the book and let out a satisfied sigh.

Serkan sighed as well. Several times Sabra had thought he'd fallen asleep, but every time she'd turned to look, he'd simply lain there, his eyes distant and his hands folded beneath his head. Each time, it had struck her how young he looked. She could only imagine what kind of lecture she'd get from her father if he saw her fraternizing with a servant the night before the Inquest. But it felt wrong to chase the boy away, especially when he looked as lonely as she felt.

It was moments like this when Sabra felt the full weight of the crown she was seeking, and whispers echoed in her head, traitorous voices wondering if it really had to be like this. It was the same voice that, just as Sabra hovered between consciousness and sleep, wondered what it would be like to have George pursuing her rather than her petty suitors. It was the voice that whispered, *What if everything was different?*

But no. Sabra had a duty to fulfill. She'd been training to be queen her whole life. And no matter how much she might want some of the conveniences that came with a life outside of royalty, this was her calling. She was meant to be here.

"All right," she said, standing with a groan. "It's time for bed. We need to get you out of here before someone sees." She hadn't meant to read for quite so long, but the stories were just as magical as ever, and the boy's obvious enthrallment with them only encouraged her more.

To her surprise, he got up without protest and padded to the window. She took him by the shoulders and steered him back toward the door. "While I don't want anyone seeing you sneak out, how about we not risk your death as you climb out of my window in the dark?"

He paused before the door, a slight frown on his face. "I wish they were real."

"Who?" Sabra yawned.

"The knights." He gave her a half-smile. "It would be nice if there was someone who could ride in and fix everything."

Sabra returned his smile with a wistful one of her own. "Yes. Yes, it would."

CHAPTER 8
A BIT HARDER

The next morning, Sabra's wistfulness was gone, and determination had taken its place. After a quick run around the palace wall, Sabra went back to her room and bathed. Then she allowed Nisa to help her into the stiff, commanding gown her mother had ordered sewn for the event. It was a high-backed dress of red fabric covered in thin golden filigree that ran the full-length of the bodice, skirt, and sleeves. The skirt wasn't exceptionally full, but that's because it was meant to be practical. Sabra knew better than to mention it aloud, but silently, she decided that the dress would be a little more practical if it were slightly less pressed.

Once she was dressed, her mother took Sabra to her parents' chambers and sat Sabra in front of her own vanity. Then she proceeded to boss the servants to no end. Sabra's dark hair was pulled back and up on her head, and she wore simple gold bangles on her arms that jingled slightly when she moved them. Her slippers were made of delicate golden thread, and her ears were hung with simple golden hoops.

"Commanding and gracious." Her mother nodded to herself as she walked slowly in a circle around Sabra, examining every inch of the dress. "You're perfect."

"Of course it's perfect," her father laughed from the other side of the room. "You've had three fittings."

Sabra smiled at her father as her mother continued to fuss. Thankfully, he was in a good mood this morning. Generally, he was a pleasant person to be around. Sabra's challenge from the two weeks before, however, had made the air between them tense, as neither was willing to back down. Sabra's mother had once joked that she might as well have been their child by blood, for she and her father had wills to match.

"Wait." Her mother's head snapped up. "Have you eaten yet?"

Sabra shook her head. "I'm not that hungry this morning. I was just going to have a peach."

"Sabra—" her mother began, but her father cut them off.

"Just leave her alone, Melisa," he said, standing. "I didn't want to eat the morning of my Inquest either."

"But your makeup." Her mother frowned. "A peach will make you all sticky."

"We have these things called knives," her father laughed. He went over to the fruit bowl that was left over from his breakfast and picked up a peach. Picking up a small golden knife from behind the plate, he began to slice the peach. Then he put the slices on a clean plate and handed it to Sabra. She took them with a grateful look and began to eat carefully. As she did, her mother whispered something to her father. Instead of laughing and brushing whatever it was off, though, as he had done with most of her mother's fussing that morning, he frowned slightly as well. Then he nodded, and they turned to her.

"What is it?" she asked, reaching for another slice.

"Sabra," her mother said, the crease not leaving her forehead, "we want you to know that whatever happens today, we're proud of you, and we believe you deserve this more than anyone."

"Thank you?" Sabra looked at her father for an explanation.

"I learned this morning that there might be some...pushback among the Assembly," her father said slowly. "Nothing I would consider too concerning. We just don't want you to be caught by surprise and think it's your fault if the basniins' decision isn't unanimous."

"Why would it be a problem now if it hasn't been already? I've only been in line for the throne my entire life."

"This, if it's brought up, would have nothing to do with *you*," her mother said. "It would have solely to do with *our* decisions."

Sabra put her food down. "If this is supposed to help me, it's doing the exact opposite. Whatever you're going to say, please just say it."

Her father opened his mouth, but a knock at the door interrupted them. "The Assembly is ready, Your Majesty," a servant called through the door.

"Maker, protect her," Sabra's mother muttered as they made their way to the door.

The walk down the corridors to the throne room seemed short most days, but today, it dragged on and on, and Sabra was beginning to sweat by the time they neared their destination. As their little procession made their way down the halls, the servant at the head, followed by her parents and with Sabra at the rear, people paused and bowed, as though they were embarking on some great adventure, rather than visiting a room Sabra had inhabited at some point nearly every day of her life.

They paused on the threshold, and Demir joined them. He was looking handsome in his dark tunic and trousers. An embroidered purple sash draped neatly from his shoulder across his body to his waist on the other side, and his ceremonial boots went nearly to his knees. A thin saber hung at his side. He greeted her parents then put his hands on Sabra's shoulders.

"Remember, the Sowens will especially want to hear their irrigation rights mentioned in the more recent treaties, and the Woodsmen—"

"Demir." Sabra grinned. "I think my head is full."

He smiled and touched her cheek. "Yes, it probably is." Then he took a deep breath and nodded to her parents. The king nodded to the man at the door, and the doors swung wide open.

When Sabra had first been adopted, she was inseparable from her parents, and had spent a good deal of their meetings toddling barefooted across the throne room's gold-veined marble floors, looking up in awe at the murals painted on the distant ceiling. As the years had passed, she'd begun wearing shoes, but had continued growing, learning, and laughing within its walls. Now it seemed to have grown with her, no longer a place of play but a place of duty.

Men and women of the court from all the different clans were standing at the edges of the room, leaning against or standing between the thick columns that surrounded it. Even a number of commoners had been allowed in for the spectacle. This, her father had always said, was to let the people feel that they were a part of the process, so they wouldn't feel as though they were being excluded from the goings-on of the Assembly or the royal clan. Sabra knew most of the people in the room, and usually she would have visited them and struck up conversations as she went. But today, everyone was somber and silent. The fate of the kingdom rested on Sabra's performance this morning.

Three long tables had been set up in the shape of a horseshoe, and the Assembly members from each clan, or basniins, as they were individually called, were sitting in their respective places with their clerks standing behind them, prepared to fetch a new pen or more ink or parchment should the need arise. Everyone stood as Sabra's family entered the room. Her father and mother took their places at the head of the horseshoe, and Demir stood just behind them, but Sabra went to the open end opposite her parents.

"Present," the court crier called, his words echoing in the room, "are the honorable members of the Segzein Assembly. First, we honor the king and head of the Capitan Clan, His Majesty, Furkan Basniin Capitan, his honorable wife, Melisa Kralicenin Capitan, and their daughter and Inquestee, Sabra Erbasniin Capitan Hopeful. Present also are the basniins." As he announced their names and titles, each basniin stood and bowed.

"From the Sowen clan, we have Yasin Basniin Sowen." Sabra relaxed slightly when she heard his name. Yasnin was a lean man in his sixth decade, and his favorite topic of discussion was the growing of strawberries. Sabra liked strawberries.

"Next, I present Nazan Basniin Sophia." Sabra definitely liked her. She spent lots of time with Master Mirac in the library and had even personally recommended a number of books to Sabra for study once Sabra's date for her Inquest had been set.

"Esemeray Basniin Physic." Esemeray wasn't a bad woman. She wasn't a particularly interesting woman either, but Sabra had been able to get her rather excited once or twice while asking questions about the healing properties of lavender. Sabra felt safe with her on the Assembly.

"Baran Basniin Tradesman," the crier intoned on.

Baran was rather young for a basniin and noticeably nervous. He was bulky, as his father had been, but all his father's tenacity had seemed to skip a generation. Not that Sabra minded, for he loved to help and had been more than happy to answer her questions whenever she came to ask. In fact, his attention was always so rapt that Sabra suspected he probably would have tried for her hand had they not both been basniins.

"Ozge Basniin Woodsman." Sabra had absolutely no opinion on Ozge. The tall builder had never given her a chance to form one. To him, everything seemed to be one perpetual bore and more than enough reason to get back to finishing whatever building or road he was working on at the time.

"Finally, I present Mahzar Basniin Justine," the crier finally announced. "We welcome Mahzar, as it his first hearing in the Assembly since his predecessor appointed him."

Sabra and Demir exchanged a brief glance as everyone applauded the new statesman. They'd been expecting Mahzar, of course, but Sabra had been hoping that Old Semih might have come one last time for this particular event. If the Justine clan was strict regarding the law, Mahzar's interpretations of that law were formed with an iron fist. Even now, as the man smiled and nodded to those congratulating him, his sharp eyes flashed around furtively, roving every corner and line of the room and finally coming to rest on her. Sabra was not looking forward to his questions.

With all of the clan heads present, the holy man appeared and led the prayer, asking the Maker to grant the Assembly wisdom. Then her father stood to speak.

"My fellow basniins," he said in his deep, rolling voice. "I thank you for coming to consider my daughter for the position of queen. This is a sober matter, and our fathers, when they took their vows, knew that simple bloodlines weren't enough to ensure a wise, just leader."

Sabra stole a glance at the reactions of her judges. Everyone but Mahzar's eyes were on her father. The Justine's mouth was pinched up into a hard line, and he wrote something on his parchment, though Sabra couldn't see what it was. She was sure she would find out later.

"So," her father continued, "a precedent was established wherein the clan heads would gather to examine the Capitan Basniin Hopeful by asking pertinent questions and weighing the answers." He fixed his eyes on Sabra, and she felt herself smile as they filled with a familiar warmth. "I know that she is young, but I've never doubted her leadership abilities. I can promise you that her desire to serve her people has never wavered, and I believe you'll all agree when I say that her hunger for knowledge has served her well. I know that she has darkened the doorsteps of many of you in her search for answers to her never-ending questions."

Nazan, the Sophian head, chuckled, and several with her, and Sabra knew everyone was remembering the time Sabra, at the ripe old age of seven years, had followed Nazan for three days straight, asking her every question conceivable about frogs. It had been that week that Nazan had assigned Master Mirac as Sabra's personal guide whenever she visited the library.

"So, I will relinquish the room to Mahzar so he can begin our questioning. I trust that you will all keep your questions focused and appropriate."

For a moment, Sabra was sure the sudden ice in her father's voice was directed at her, warning her not to wander into forbidden territory. But she then realized that he was glaring at Mahzar instead.

"Thank you," Mahzar said to the king, bowing his head. Then he turned to Sabra, and energy, pure and fiery hot, shot through Sabra's veins. This was it. Everything she'd lived for would be decided on this floor. And yet, despite her sweaty palms and her rapidly beating heart, Sabra let the thrill of the moment carry her. She had studied her whole life for this. This was what she had been born to do.

Mahzar gave Sabra a polite smile. "I apologize because I don't know you as well as the other basniins. I hope to rectify that soon, though." He glanced down at the parchment he'd been scribbling on. "Please name for me the twelve statutes that define Justinian law."

Sabra nearly laughed. She'd known them since she was eight.

Slowly, slowly, as the other clan heads tossed her questions, and she answered every single one with confidence, Sabra began to relax. In fact, she even began to enjoy herself.

"How far does the diameter of Segzein stretch from east to west? What landmarks signify the boundaries of our lands?"

"Which southern tribe did Segzein refuse to trade with for two decades prior to the war that took place four hundred years ago?"

"When Basniin Ata of the Sowens accepted the marriage proposal of Basniin Balil, what positions did they fill after the marriage?" Ozge asked.

Sabra slowed and took a deep breath. "Basniin Balil maintained his position of basniin," she said slowly, "and Ata became the honorable wife of Balil."

"Why?" Mahzar pressed.

Sabra paused. "Because in the event of a marriage between two basniins, to maintain the independent sovereignty of the clans, the basniin who has lesser seniority or power maintains his or her position while the spouse of a higher position relinquishes all claims to his or her own seat. It preserves a distribution of power and prevents undue influence of a personal nature of one clan on another."

Mahzar gave her a long, strange look, as if he was turning her answer over in his head. Finally, he nodded. "Good."

Yasin picked up where he left off. "Who was the fourth monarch of our kingdom, and what atrocity was she put to death for?"

After about an hour, Nazan put down her pen and leaned back in her chair. She glanced at the other heads before addressing Sabra in a loud voice. "You've answered well. But enough of the child's play. Now I would like to ask you something a bit harder."

Sabra smiled. "I thought you'd never ask."

Two hours later, Sabra wanted to collapse into a chair. Her feet were killing her, and her knees seemed to lock up every time she forgot to move them. But she had answered to the best of her abilities. At least she could confidently say that.

"Well," Basniin Baran glanced at the other basniins nervously. He was the second newest basniin, and had only been installed the year before. He was also the youngest, only two years older than Sabra. "I think...I mean, can say that I had no doubt you would pass." His round cheeks flushed. "But I didn't expect your knowledge to be so thorough as even this." He looked at her and gave her a shy smile. "But I can say, Princess, that the Tradesmen clan will be happy to have you as queen."

"The Physics say likewise." Basniin Esemeray nodded. "You have our full support."

Sabra took a deep breath and allowed a small smile to touch her lips. Demir had warned her that sometimes, the clans preferred to pressure their Inquestees in order to test their stamina. That she already had two votes of confidence was encouraging. That was two fewer heads to impress further.

"I should like to speak with you further about the intricacies of our seed laws." Yasin, the Sowen basniin, put his pen down and frowned slightly. "But as we all know your willingness to learn, I think my people would be glad to see you on the throne."

Sabra nodded. She'd focused slightly more on trade deals than agricultural law during her questions from the Sowens, but if it made them happy, she was more than willing to speak with their leaders. That was the crown's duty after all.

Three down and four to go. She dared a glance at Demir, and his hint of a smile was enough to keep her cautious confidence afloat.

"I, too, should like to have the Princess spend more time with our builders," Ozge, the Woodsmen's basniin, grumbled. Then he huffed, as if the words were being torn from him. "But as Yasin said, it's likely that she will be able to learn our ways sufficiently by the time she takes the throne."

Sabra nearly let out a shout. Four out of the seven. She couldn't fail now, even if the others all objected. Still, she kept her joy contained out of respect for the remaining members. It wouldn't do to treat them as though they didn't matter.

"I have been convinced of your dedication since you were four and you refused to bring one of your father's books back to the library." Nazan gave Sabra a knowing smile. "My vote is yes."

Sabra threw the woman a grateful smile then turned to her father, who was beaming. "I always knew you were fit for the crown," he said, standing. "But you have surpassed even my expectations. Well done, daughter. Well done."

"Thank you, Father." Sabra's stomach warmed at the pride in his eyes, and his words made her blush. Her father wasn't the kind to be free with compliments. His was high praise indeed.

"Is she, though?" A man's voice rang through the hall.

Everyone turned to see Basniin Mahzar lean forward in his chair.

"What do you mean?" Sabra's father asked, frowning.

"As impressed as I am with your performance, Princess, for it was undeniably excellent, I'm afraid I've been struggling with the legality of your claim to the throne since learning that this Inquest was going to take place."

"And you waited until now to say something?" Nazan scowled.

"If you recall," Mahzar said in a patient tone, "I only joined the Assembly several weeks ago. It was not my place before that to speak. And since the Inquest was so close, I wanted to hear what she had to say first. I thought that perhaps I would be able to object on other grounds without bringing up such a...delicate subject." He gave Sabra an apologetic smile, his long, dark curls moving up and down with his shoulders as he shrugged. "I'm sorry, Princess. Your performance was superb. Which makes it even more difficult to discuss my doubts."

An aching, hollowing feeling started in Sabra's belly and radiated out to her limbs and even her face. She was flushing profusely, and it was all she could do to keep her voice steady.

"I am afraid," she said in slow, measured words, "that I am not sure what doubts you are referring to."

"Your bloodline, to put it simply."

"Do you mean my adoption?" she asked.

He nodded. "Your adoption was done well. Everything was perfectly legal, down to the last dot."

"Then why on earth are you intimidating the girl?" Yasin snapped.

Mahzar turned to face Yasin. "Because we don't know what her true bloodline really is."

"She was found in the Capitan spoke!" Her mother was glaring daggers at him. "Even if we don't know who her parents are, she was found among our own people."

"Do you really think it would be impossible for her true parents to cross the spoke boundaries and place her there?" Mahzar raised his eyebrows. "There would have been no physical walls to keep them out. Anyone could have put an infant by a fountain and run to tell the tale. She could be a foreigner for all we know."

Whispers went up from the crowd surrounding the tables, and Sabra threw a helpless look at Demir. But for the first time in her life, he looked as shaken as she felt.

"The adoption was legal," her father growled. "You said everything was done right."

"She's been raised and educated in every way as a Capitan," her mother added stiffly. "Even if she wasn't a Capitan, there would be no way to tell the difference. You couldn't have asked for a better performance."

"Which I acknowledged openly. There's no question as to the princess's aptitude."

"Then what is your problem?" Sabra's father asked in a low, dangerous voice, and Sabra had the ridiculous desire to run and hide behind him as she had when she was little. But she stood where she was, frozen. Never at the beginning of this day...or ever, for that matter, had she expected to perform so well at her Inquest and yet feel so utterly helpless.

"The fate of the kingdom is too precious to gamble on matters of bloodline. The clans were very clear in their vows when the kingdom was born. Each had a duty to fulfill, and they agreed to suffer the curse of broken vows if they deserted their bonds," Mahzar answered, his eyes narrowing at the king. "And we all know what happens when clans break their vows."

"Don't!" Sabra's father brought his fist down on the table so hard that the bang echoed through the room. All whispers ceased. "Don't," her father repeated, "go there."

Sabra looked back and forth between them as they waged some silent war. While she didn't know what they were saying with their glowers, she did know that it had something to do with her mystery. Mahzar had mentioned a broken vow. A clan's broken vow. A curse. If she hadn't been distraught over the situation, Sabra might have been able to piece her research together with this revelation. Whatever this mystery's answer was, she felt as though she were balanced on a precipice, and it was just out of reach.

"My apologies." Mahzar bowed his head, the image of penitence. "Forgive me." Then he fixed his eyes on the king again. "But I'm afraid that it is my duty to warn the Assembly and the kingdom that such an ascension to the throne cannot be permitted."

"Six of us have given her our votes." Nazan said in a frosty voice. "Yours cannot supersede them."

"I object because there is no precedent for you to even place a vote. She isn't legally eligible for you to vote for or against."

"You may be an expert in the law, but so am I." Nazan raised her chin. "My mastery is in legal history. And I can assure you and everyone here that there is nothing in our law that prevents an adopted child from taking his or her parents' occupation."

"You may have studied our history, but you are not a Justine." Mahzar's voice went flat. "And it is not your duty. It is, however, mine." He turned to the king, all traces of his smile gone. "King Furkan and members of the Assembly, I'm afraid I must, as head keeper and protector of the law, forbid the princess from receiving the crown."

"You *forbid?*" Sabra's father's voice was quiet and terrible.

"If I do not," Mahzar replied, "the Maker's retribution will do far worse." He looked at Nazan. "I'll issue a Challenge."

"Don't bother." Nazan tossed her pen on the table. "No one will accept it."

"You don't speak for all of us, Nazan," Ozge grumbled.

Nazan turned to glare at him. "It doesn't matter. The Challenge must be accepted by all uninvolved basniins before it can be official. And I am saying no."

"I, um, I vote no as well," Basan said, raising his hand halfway, glancing around him as he did. "I mean, to the Challenge. Not to her coronation." He blushed as he looked at Sabra. "Of course, I want her to have the throne."

"Then I'll count the Justine clan as voting in the negative," Sabra's father replied with a smirk. "And with a vote of six to one, the majority rules." He smiled at Sabra once more, tenderness in his gaze. "Child, you have done well. We welcome you to the fold." His voice dropped slightly, and if she wasn't mistaken, slightly quivered, and his eyes looked distant, a little sad even. "Your purity and goodness will bless our kingdom in the eyes of the Maker."

Sabra smiled, and the fear began to melt away as the sound of cheers and applause grew deafening. Mahzar stood quietly and exited the room, followed by his attendants. But Sabra chose not to focus on what she had lost.

Because she had gained her future.

CHAPTER 9
DRAGON

B e kind." Sabra's mother gave her a warning glance in the mirror as she straightened Sabra's crown. "I know none of them have proven themselves to be a knight out of your storybook, but you'll be spending the rest of your life with one of them. You might as well begin by not insulting the poor man."

Sabra sighed. The week since her Inquest had been a whirlwind. Gowns were commissioned, the documents were read, signed, and sealed, and most importantly, the ceremony to officially anoint Sabra as Crown Princess and to choose Sabra's future husband was prepared.

No one had yet told Sabra what she wanted to know most, but even Sabra had to admit that there simply wasn't time for deep, drawn-out conversations. There were simply too many changes to make as the kingdom prepared to officially welcome its new future queen. She was now an erbasniin, the ancient term for a future basniin or clan head. And while she wasn't queen yet, and wouldn't be until her father died or abdicated, as some monarchs did in their older years, there were a myriad of legal documents to prepare so that she could immediately step into her father's place when he was gone.

Soon, though. Soon her father would tell her. He'd promised.

Even the promise of having all her questions answered, however, couldn't cheer her. Not when her future husband was on the line.

"The pride of a queen is one matter," her mother continued as she smoothed her hair, "but the gentleness of a wife is another."

Sabra scoffed. "If only the men outside had done something to earn such merit and favor."

"You should be grateful. Many young monarchs don't get to choose their spouses. Their parents or the local counsel arrange their marriages. You have an exceptional opportunity here that few young rulers in your position can boast."

"I know." Sabra looked at her hands.

"Did you have a chance to look at the lists I had sent up the other night?"

Oh, Sabra had. There were currently twenty-two young men vying for the position of king. Technically, any Segzeinian was allowed to apply for the future ruler's hand. Whether he was a tailor, farmer, scholar, or lawyer, as long as the man wasn't a basniin or erbasniin, he could ask that his name be put into the selection pile for the princess's consideration.

Of course, that pile was vetted. Members of the Capitan clan were assigned to research each applicant. No vagabonds or criminals were accepted, nor were non-citizens, in order to prevent influence from other crowns. Names were also discarded for poor moral conduct or if the applicant was found to be a disreputable citizen. So every man who presented himself to her today out on that platform was, by human standards, an upstanding, productive citizen of Segzein. She ought to be happy. As her mother said, few rulers were ever given such a clean, clear set of choices.

And yet, after examining every name on the list, as well as the notes the researchers had written about them, Sabra had yet to be excited about any. In her ridiculously thick head, all she could imagine was finding someone like George.

It was funny. She hadn't seen him in years. And though he'd crossed her mind a number of times, she hadn't thought of him regularly until his visit. The moment she'd realized who he was, she'd immediately missed their friendship. It felt as if she'd been missing a piece of herself all those years. And that piece showed up just before she had to bid him farewell.

It wasn't fair.

"I didn't even want to be queen," her mother said, interrupting Sabra's thoughts. She wore a distant smile as she fussed with the cosmetics on Sabra's vanity. There was little left to do, but her mother moved around the little jars anyway. "I was furious with my mother for signing me up. I had other love interests, and the king, for all his pomp and circumstance, was not one of them. I'd only ever met him once, when he came to my parents' stall in the market."

Sabra watched her mother's face carefully as she listened. She'd never heard this story before.

"When your father chose me, I was livid. I was smart enough not to show it, of course. But it was a long time before I began to look at your father with any sort of affection."

"That's hard to believe," Sabra said. "Looking at you now, I mean."

Her mother smiled. "That's because your father hadn't gotten the chance to work his magic."

Sabra leaned back. "Is that something I really want to know about?"

Her mother laughed. "I mean his kindness. Your father knew I didn't want to be his wife. And yet, for some reason, he was certain I was the queen and wife he'd been looking for. So he showered me with kindness until one day, I looked at him and realized I couldn't imagine life any other way."

Sabra sat and considered her mother's words long after her mother was called away to see to a problem on the stage. Could she find love among the list of names she'd been given? Despite the applicants being vetted, Sabra felt a great deal of danger in the choice she was about to make. How was she supposed to know who was there for the right reasons? Sure, none of the men were known murderers or openly evil. But there was a great difference between not being a horrible person and being a good man.

Sabra was soon called to make her way to the stage that had been erected in front of the palace. The people were gathering to watch, and she needed to take her place. Panic fluttered in her stomach as she walked, and her hands sweated as she wondered what made her qualified for this kind of decision.

In general, Sabra lacked little in confidence. Rarely had she set her hand to a task that she did not master, and when she didn't immediately master it, she could always find someone to show her how. But there had been moments like this over the last week that had her wondering if maybe...just maybe she was an imposter. Perhaps Mahzar was right, and she didn't deserve this position. As she made her way down a set of stairs, Sabra felt very much like an ill-prepared child. Not only was she to be made crown princess today, but she was to choose her future husband. Very soon, she would be a wife, and probably not long after, a mother. That wasn't even considering what would take place if her father grew sick and had to leave his position.

Wife.

Mother.

Queen.

When had life become so hard?

For one traitorous moment, she wondered what life would be like if she weren't a princess, and she and George had a chance at a simple life. She had begun writing him one last letter this morning, but three sentences in, had crumpled the thing and thrown it in the fire. She had planned for it to be a letter of farewell. One more moment of freedom and fun for both of them to share in remembering what had been. But what was the use? If he sent a letter back, she didn't know if she would truly be able to keep herself from reading it and responding again. For once she was betrothed, which would happen today, correspondence with him would no longer be appropriate.

This made her sad.

Focus, Sabra.

Sabra walked out onto the back part of the platform. She was still hidden behind the curtain that separated her from the front of the stage, where one of the master learners was giving the crowd a historical account of how choosing the monarch's spouse came to be. She came to a stop at the back, staring at the curtain as she practiced breathing.

"Are you well?"

Sabra turned to see Demir. He was looking handsome, as always, with his dark hair pulled back into a knot on the back of his head, and a short, respectable beard that he had grown for the ceremony. He wore a dark brown tunic embroidered with flowers from their hills and tall brown boots beneath.

"I have no choice." Sabra forced a smile. "I must be well. It's my duty."

Demir frowned slightly as he put his hands on her shoulders. "Today is a choice, Sabra. No one is forcing you to become queen." He paused. "I hope I haven't ever made you feel that way, that this burden was yours to bear alone."

Sabra's smile felt more real this time. "Never. You've always been wonderful. And I want to be queen. I really do. I just..." She glanced back at the curtain. "All of this in one day. The crown. Choosing my husband." She shook her head. "It's just a lot. I thought I was ready, but..." No. She couldn't give in to the fear. She was ready. She had to be. "Never mind." Sabra straightened her shoulders. "I've let Mahzar's doubts in a little, I suppose. That's all. I'll be fine." Then she paused. The words were on her lips, ready to tumble out. It was a foolish question to ask, most likely. But here and now, before she took vows in front of all of her people, she needed to know.

"Did you ever..."

He straightened her crown. "Did I ever what?"

"Did you ever resent the fact that I was made my father's heir?" she blurted out. "I mean, since I was adopted, and you would have been next in line for the throne and—"

"Sabra, stop."

She did, but she watched her cousin closely, searching for any signs of hesitation on his part.

Demir gave her a knowing smile. "I had lost my family just before you were adopted. And I was grieving. You were like a bright light in a dark place, a star lit by the Maker Himself. You are good and kind and you put the rest of us to shame." His brows furrowed slightly. "But you're sure you want this?"

"Why do you ask?"

He pursed his lips. "You seem sad."

Did she? "I don't mean to be." Sabra drew in a deep breath. "I've hoped for this my entire life."

Still, Demir frowned slightly, searching her eyes for a moment longer before letting go of her shoulders. "Very well. But I do ask that you please come to me the moment you need something. Anything." He chucked her gently on the chin. "Please?"

She sighed but gave him a reticent grin. "Very well. I promise."

"Sabra."

Sabra turned to see her father gesture to her, pride lighting up his face.

"It's time."

"I'll be cheering for Grandpa." Demir winked and tapped her nose, laughing quietly at her scowl as she turned to follow her father.

Swallowing hard, Sabra lifted her chin and followed her father through the opening in the curtain. She kept her head high as she surveyed the hundreds of people squeezed in front of the stage. There were so many that they filled the streets between the stalls and buildings. So many faces gazing up at her, joy and hope reflected in their faces. She recognized many, and her courage grew as she smiled and nodded once. A cheer went up from the crowd.

"Come, Princess," her father called to her from the raised dais that had been built upon the stage. Sabra went to him and knelt before him. Behind him in a line stood the other clan heads, each wearing a similar ceremonial robe to the one she wore over her dress. They looked like a rainbow, as each clan had its own color.

"Fair heir, you have been tested and tried and have proven yourself worthy of this crown." Her father touched the slim golden crown that now rested on her brow. So it is with the blessing of the Capitans that you now receive the duty and burden of sight, watching over your people with the vigilance of a hawk." He held up a sparkling purple gem cut in the shape of a diamond. Gently, he pressed it into one of the raised spikes in her crown until it rested in its place. As he leaned back, he beamed at her, and in spite of her apprehension, Sabra knew the pride in her father's eyes was worth everything she would endure today.

This was what she'd been waiting for.

Basniin Nazan of the Sophians stepped up, a smile on her lined face as well. "And with the blessings of the Sophians, you now receive the duty and burden of knowledge." The gem she placed in Sabra's crown was yellow.

Basniin Yasin of the Sowens was next with a green gem. "And with the blessings of the Sowens, you now receive the duty and burden of sustainment."

The Tradesmen's stone was silver, and the Woodsmen's was orange. The Physic gem was blood red. After them were the Justines.

Sabra's heart beat faster when she realized it was Mahzar who would be adding on her final gems. An opal, if she remembered correctly in her dazed state, for purity in justice, and a shiny piece of obsidian, for the execution of that justice. But as Mahzar stepped closer, Sabra could see that he held no gems in his hands.

"Mahzar," Yasin hissed softly with a glance at the crowd. "What are you doing?"

Instead of answering, Mahzar turned to the crowd, his dark robes swishing. "I am here to offer myself as a suitable marriage partner for Sabra Kralicenina Capitan."

"What is the meaning of this?" Sabra's father bellowed. "You are a clan head. Basniins cannot be joined in matrimony. You, as a keeper of the law, should know this!"

"But she is not a basniin." Mahzar turned to her father with innocent eyes, then back to the crowd. "She would be, of course, if we could prove her lineage."

"We've been through this," Nazan snapped. "She was legally

adopted. There is nothing in the law that prevents any adopted child from inheriting his parents' legacies."

"But there is law," Mahzar replied evenly, "requiring each clan head to maintain a pure bloodline. No individual from one clan may rule as a basniin for another."

"You voiced your objection," Sabra's father growled. "And you were outnumbered. Let us proceed." He waved to the other basniins to continue, but Mahzar stepped forward.

"I promise," he called to Sabra. His voice was gentle but loud enough for the audience to hear. "If you marry me, I will step down as well. I'll treat you with respect and make sure that your every desire is met."

"My desire...my *duty* is to be queen," Sabra snapped.

"And would you bring down a curse upon your people?" His eyes darkened, and his voice hardened.

"What curse?" Sabra scoffed.

"Mahzar!" her father barked.

But Mahzar turned to their audience. "You remember the last time the clan treaty was broken!"

The crowd shifted uncomfortably, and many people looked at the ground.

"How did it fare for that clan? They brought down a curse upon themselves for breaking their solemn vow, and what happened then?"

Sabra watched in horror and fascination. Was this it? Was she about to get answers to the questions that had plagued her since childhood? And why here and now in front of the whole kingdom? The Justines were religious about their law-keeping. But it now seemed that Mahzar was blatantly throwing the rules of the land to the wind by speaking publicly of whatever had happened.

"Guards, take him to the throne room. Basniins, you come as well. Meet me there, and we'll discuss this. Everyone else, go home."

But the guards didn't move. They stood perfectly still at their posts.

"Guards!" the king shouted.

Still they waited. A sinkhole opened up in Sabra's stomach. The guards might serve her father, but they were Justinian. Which meant that whatever Mahzar was trying to do here, he wasn't alone. Every fighting force in the kingdom was his.

"Shakirat?" she whispered, staring at the one soul who had never left her side. Who had faithfully followed Sabra around since she could walk, who had once dived in front of her to save her from a poisonous serpent and been bitten himself.

His jaw twitched when she called to him, but his eyes stayed forward.

Meaning that everyone who wasn't Mahzar, including the crown, was powerless.

"Guards," Mahzar said in a calm voice. "Please move the people away from the stage. I wouldn't want anyone to be hurt."

"What are you doing?" Sabra cried.

"I suggest everyone leave the stage," Mahzar continued in that maddeningly calm voice. "Otherwise, this is going to hurt." Then he turned back to Sabra and bowed. "Before we begin, Princess, I humbly apologize." He met her gaze and held it, his voice so gentle he might as well have been speaking to a kitten. "I really didn't want this for you."

Sabra glanced at Shakirat, waiting for him to throw himself in front of her or grab her and drag her away. But he only stood there, his eyes trained on Mahzar.

Sabra looked back at Mahzar, and he shrugged. "Very well, then. Have it your way." He took two steps back so he was standing at the edge of the wooden stage, and put his fingers on the large oval clasp on his cloak. He rested them there for several seconds, during which he closed his eyes and scrunched them shut. His body tensed up, and his shoulders hunched. Almost as though he were anticipating—

He cried out as he punched the clasp back into his chest. His cry was cut short, though, by wheezing. Wheezing that deepened until he was groaning. Groans that turned to guttural growls. And finally, a roar.

The crowd screamed and tried to run, but the guards herded the people to stand against the walls and away from the stage rather than allowing them to leave. Closer and closer the crowd pressed in on one another, trying to get as far from Mahzar's seizing body as the guards would allow them.

As he roared, his head flew back, and his arms flew out. His warm, golden skin grew pale, the veins within them turning pink then white. His skin became rough, raised bumps protruding out so far they cast shadows on the bumps behind them. Then the bumps became so pronounced that they no longer resembled bumps but coins that lay down flat against his body.

Scales, Sabra realized with horror.

His eyes lengthened, their pupils stretching into horizontal slits. All the while, he was growing until he was three times the length of his original height, from head to...tail. He had a tail.

He let out another roar as wings tore themselves from his back and unfurled, nearly as long as he was tall. Spikes lifted from his now serpentine neck, and when he opened his mouth again to let out his unearthly scream, rows of needled teeth glimmered in the sun.

Sabra's knees nearly gave out as she recognized a creature she'd only ever seen in her little story book. But dragons weren't real.

Apparently, they were.

His wings beat as he rose into the sky, the setting sun glinting off his white, polished scales.

"Just remember," he said, his voice now like that of a bear crossed with a snake, "this was your choice, my people. I must return to the old form in order to protect the old ways. And so must you honor the vows, if we wish for our way of life to go on."

"There's nothing in the old ways that forbids—" Sabra's father shouted, but the dragon cut him off.

"You have three days to make your choice, Princess. Marry me, step down, or force my hand."

"You would do that to your own people?" Sabra cried over the wind his wings were creating.

"If I don't," he said, his serpentine voice oddly gentle. Almost a purr. "Your desolation will be heavier than anything I could inflict.

So to give you a taste of what evil is possible if you break your vow now…"

He looked around him, his wings beating furiously as he hovered over the crowd. "I'll begin by destroying this abomination." He opened his mouth wide and stretched his neck toward them. Fire engulfed the stage Sabra stood upon. The throne, the overhang, the platform, even the king's special chair, which had been brought out for the occasion. Screaming pierced the quickly falling eve as white flame lit up the darkening sky. Their guards, Shakirat included, were nowhere in sight.

Sabra stared stupidly at the beast until someone slammed into her. She looked up to see Demir's face close to hers.

"Run with me," he hissed.

"But I can't leave them!" Sabra looked out at her people.

"And what do you propose to do about it?" he snapped. "You can't fight him. And if you tried, he might do something far worse." He tugged on her arms. "Let's go."

Sabra glared at her cousin, but she knew he was right. She'd prepared herself for years in staff and wit, but a flaming, flying dragon was out of her realm. So she let her cousin drag her back to the palace. And for the first time since she could remember, Shakirat didn't follow. When she looked up, he was gone. As were all the other palace guards.

And though she should be grateful not to have a traitor following her, it made her angry.

Resolve began to harden in her chest.

She might be young. She might not be a warrior. But she was the one and future queen. And she determined then and there that she would never feel this helpless again.

CHAPTER 10
REAL

The throne room was pure chaos when Sabra arrived with Demir. People were running everywhere. Many were arguing, crying, demanding to know what had happened. And that was just the leadership. The courtyard outside the main doors was filling up, people shouting to be let in so they might hear an explanation from the king.

"There will be order!" Sabra's father shouted at the top of his lungs. No one listened, though. Only then did Sabra truly feel the absence of the Justines. With the room void of their white cloaks with gold edging. There was no one to enforce the king's word.

This was bad.

"It's like a den of animals," Demir muttered. He turned to Sabra and bent slightly to whisper in her ear. "Stay at my side. I don't want you out of my sight until we get this figured out."

Sabra nodded. She wasn't about to argue with that. Not that she feared Mahzar or his threats. Her anger was too hot for that. But she wasn't about to do something foolish so she could play into her enemy's hands.

In three long strides, Demir had made it to the side of the room. He snatched a vase with flowers from one of the spaces carved into the wall, dumped the flowers, and pushed his way through the crowd to the front of the room, Sabra on his heels. When he got to the front of the room, he held up the vase and slammed it down on the ground. The shattering glass caused the roar of voices to quiet as they all looked up.

"That's enough!" Demir roared. "Now, if you want to figure out what to do about this mess, then I suggest shutting up and having some order. Or you can take your hullabaloo outside, but I won't stand for it here!"

Many in the crowd looked, shamefaced, at the ground. Several glared, but most had the decency to press themselves closer to the walls as the king stood.

"I want the tables set up for counsel. Everyone else needs to leave."

Some began to yell out again in protest, but Demir drew his sword. "You heard the king."

Somehow, ten minutes later, the room was empty of all but the basniins and their assistants. Sabra sat at her father's right hand. Demir stood behind her, close enough that she could feel his presence. It was a comforting presence. If anyone would keep her safe, it would be him.

"Have any died?" Sabra's father asked when all the doors and windows were secured.

"No, Your Highness," the king's steward answered. "There were fourteen significant burns and several injured in the rush of the crowds, but no deaths." He paused. "But the Justines have taken control of all roads into and out of the city. They're also dispersed among the spokes. You cannot walk any distance without catching sight of two or more." He glanced nervously at the door behind him. "They're even out on the palace steps," he said in a slightly lower voice.

"They will not burst in right now, if that's what you're concerned about," Nazan said in a rather bored tone. "The Justines may be terrible, but if they gave us three days, they won't set foot anywhere near the princess for three days. Their honor will not allow them."

"Honor, my foot." Ozge snorted. "Those monsters are a suspicious, superstitious bunch. If they keep their word, it'll be only because they fear retribution from the Maker for violating their laws. Not because they feel any obligation toward us or the princess."

Sabra's father nodded, and she could see his chest fall as he released a deep breath of relief. "Well, if you're so certain, then that's one thing in our favor. Now, we need to face the truth." He steepled his fingers and leaned forward. "Our clan of law-keepers and enforcers has gone rogue and are now demanding that our crown princess marry their basniin and step down. We're cut off from all of our neighbors. We have no military or guard, and our enemy knows every detail of our defenses because they set them in place. So what do we do?"

The room was silent for far too long. Sabra fought the urge to shift uncomfortably.

"Well," Baran of the Tradesmen began, picking at the corner of his ceremonial robe nervously, "I suppose we ought to find out why they're doing this."

Nazan snorted. "He told us why he's doing this. He thinks we're breaking the law by allowing an adopted basniin to take the throne. The Justines believe any clan that breaks its sworn vow to keep the ancient laws will usher in a curse."

Sabra grabbed a pen and a piece of parchment from the stack that had been placed between herself and her father, and she began scribbling down the comments as they were made. This was making far too much sense to be an accident. She was finally seeing all those missing pieces of the puzzle. Now, if only she could figure out how to put them together.

"I knew allowing them two spokes was a mistake," Ozge grumbled.

"What was that?" her father glared at the Woodsmen's basniin.

"Exactly what I said." He returned the king's glare. "We allowed them to drive the Sentinels out, and now we're—"

"You swore never to utter that name again," the king growled. "I'd better not hear it again."

"I didn't swear anything. My predecessor did. I was against this from the start. And now see what we've done!"

"What have we done?" Sabra asked, looking back at Ozge. Usually, the grumpy Woodsman said little of interest, but he had her attention now. "What are you all talking about?"

Demir cleared his throat loudly behind Sabra, but she wasn't about to be dissuaded. That hole in her knowledge was gaping larger by the minute. There was no way her father could deny her such knowledge. Not while they were under attack. Still, perhaps she would get more information by listening than demanding. So she waited.

"Bygones being what they are," Esemeray of the Physics said, looking uneasily back and forth between Sabra's father and Ozge, "we need to know what to do *now*. We weren't able to stop what happened today. If they actually decided to harm us, rather than our courtyard, my people wouldn't be able to treat everyone. It just wouldn't be possible. We would be overwhelmed."

"We'll have to form militias," Ozge said grimly. "All able-bodied men would need to report to us, and we would have to do our best to arm them with what we have." He turned his hard gaze on Sabra's father again. "Do we have any weapons the Justines didn't take?"

"Militias wouldn't make a bit of difference." Yasin of the Sowens rubbed his hands as though he were cold. "None of them are trained. They'd fall like wheat in a famine."

"Nazan," the king said to the Sophian basniin, "what do you know of the creature? Do we have it in any of our histories?"

Nazan, whom Sabra had always thought to be a handsome, distinguished woman, looked down at her notes for a moment. "It depends on which version of history you wish to hear."

Sabra's breaths came in short, fast bursts. This was it. She was so close. Surely, her father would tell her now.

"And what do you mean by that?" the king snapped.

"Do I have permission to speak freely?" Nazan leaned back and folded her arms.

"Good grief, woman. We've just been attacked. Just tell me what I'm asking."

"There is record," she began slowly, "of a similar attack. But we have no way of knowing whether or not the attack was related. But that took place before Segzein was officially a kingdom." Nazan's sharp gaze cut from Sabra's father to Sabra. "The Justines had been invited by the other clans, though there were only five at the time, as two more joined later, to join the treaty. But they only joined after their people were attacked." She paused. "No one knows exactly what happened that night, but our annals show that *something* intervened to defend them. It came from the sky and breathed out fire."

Sabra was writing so fast her hands hurt. But she stopped at this and looked up. "Wait, you said the other *seven* tribes?" Her heart began to pound as she stared at the Sophian basniin. If there were seven tribes before the Justines had joined, that meant...

There must have been an eighth tribe.

"It's of no consequence," Sabra's father snapped. "Nazan, how about you keep your vow while you tell us about what I *actually* asked to hear."

"She's going to be queen," Nazan said, her brow still raised. "Why are you shielding her from what might make or break her rule?"

"I said to move *on!*" the king thundered.

"No." Sabra stood so fast her pen clattered to the floor, but she didn't pick it up. "I need to know this. Nazan is right, Father. You promised you would tell me what I need to know. And as this involves *my* crown and *my* marriage, I think I *need* to know."

"I will tell you what is and isn't necessary," Sabra's father spoke through gritted teeth. "Now sit down and show a little respect."

"The Sentinels are still out there," Nazan said, seeming unmoved by the king's anger. "We need to call them back. They can fulfill their oath, and we—"

"I mean it, Nazan!" Sabra's father threw his goblet. It hit the ground so hard that it broke a chunk of stone from the floor.

"No." Sabra shook her head. "No, I need to know this. I deserve to know this." When he only glared at her, she turned to the other basniins. "Please. You chose me to be your queen. If something happened to my father, I would need to know this. It's imperative to keep our people safe!"

Only Nazan smiled slightly. The rest looked at their hands, the table, the ceiling, or the floor, none willing to meet her eyes. So she went on.

"I know something has happened that you're not telling me. Even foreigners visiting the market have noticed. The eighth spoke in the wheel. The uneven seal. The missing books at the library. The people with the blue bands." She pulled the paper from a hidden pocket in her dress, where she'd copied the picture from the sash the old man had given her. "What about this seal? It's blue. Because that's the missing stone, isn't it? Instead of the black stone in the crown. We should have blue as well."

It all made sense. The missing clan once had the eighth spoke of the city and the seal. And if they had been the original guardians of the kingdom, as their name implied, then the Justines must have taken the Sentinels' role upon themselves upon the Sentinels' exodus.

The knights from Sabra's story book were *real*.

"Daughter, not *now*." The king's eyes had grown dark and promised retribution. It was against the law to challenge the king publicly, and Sabra knew it. But she was done with the lies. Especially as those lies would determine her fate.

"No, Father. I'm not a child, and I'm not going to stay silent any longer. Not when a villain is demanding to lay beside me every night for the rest of my life." She looked at the others. "You cannot leave me out of this decision. Not anymore."

"Anyhow," her father said, still glaring at her as he turned back to the others, "what do we do? We have no defenses. We can't ask an ally for help, for we would be beholden to them for the rest of our kingdom's existence. There must be a way to stop them."

Yasin from the Sowens, sighed. "What if we have no choice but to give them what they want?" He briefly met Sabra's eyes and looked down. "I'm sorry, Princess. I don't wish it to be so, but I'm not sure how we would do otherwise…" His voice trailed off. "Just to save the kingdom, you know." His eyes darted to something behind her. "Demir would make an excellent king."

"One that's not about to give up that easily." Demir sneered from behind Sabra. "If you think I would sacrifice my cousin at the first sign of trouble, then perhaps I'm not as worthy of a crown as you think."

Annoying as he could be at times, Sabra had never adored her cousin more.

"Nazan is right," Sabra said, taking advantage of the brief silence. "If these guardians somehow broke their vow, they could return like she said and fulfill it!" It couldn't have been that long ago, if everyone here knew the truth but her. If the timing lined up with what she'd discovered at the library, the exodus of this mystery clan must have happened around the time she was born.

"I'm not comfortable with the idea of pawning off our crown princess to satisfy the demands of a rogue clan," Baran said, frowning down at his meaty hands. He dared to glance up at Sabra once before looking away. "It doesn't seem fair. Or good practice."

"Yes!" Sabra cried, still standing. "Let's do as Nazan suggested! Let's—"

"Demir." Sabra's father jerked his neck in the direction of the door. "Since my daughter refuses to recall that I'm still alive, and she's not queen yet, please escort her from the room until she can control her outbursts."

Sabra's mouth fell open, and for once, she had no words. She had just been chosen as the future queen, and her father was still keeping secrets. Even worse, he'd just humiliated her in front of the very people she would one day rule. Sabra's face heated with shame and anger as her cousin gently tugged on her arm. She turned to give him a warning glare, but he bent and whispered in her ear.

"I'll explain everything. I promise."

Still, Sabra hesitated. Giving up her position here was admitting defeat. As though she were admitting that her father was right. But unlike her father, it seemed, she knew her cousin kept his promises. And this one was too tantalizing to pass up.

Holding her chin high, despite the nausea churning in her stomach, Sabra stood and followed him out.

CHAPTER 11
TRUTH

Sabra waited to speak until they were safely in a storage room, where the palace linens were folded and kept until they were needed. The piles of folded cloth kept the room beautifully quiet, and Sabra doubted that the strongest of ears could have heard them. So once the door was locked, she folded her arms.

"All right. I'm waiting."

Demir grimaced and reached back to scratch his neck. "You're not going to like it."

"I don't think I have a choice now, do I?" None of the trepidation that had haunted her earlier was here now. Sabra was too angry. No matter what clan she was originally from, this was wrong. And her father's secrets only made it worse.

"You're right. You're involved now, so there's really no point in keeping it a secret any longer."

Sabra wanted to retort that she was also crown princess, but that would only delay his revelation.

"It happened when I was small." He went over to a stool in the corner and sat on it. "I was just old enough that I remember." His jaw tightened. "The Sentinels' abandonment is what led to my parents' death."

"I thought..." she frowned, "that your parents died when the Dune Pirates attacked."

"They did. But the Dune Pirates would have never sacked the city if the Sentinels had done their duty and protected it." His voice was harder now.

"What happened?" Sabra asked softly. "What made them leave?"

"To simplify a complicated story, the Sentinels claimed they were being treated unfairly, sabotaged even. I recall the basniins searching, but they found nothing to prove the Sentinels' claim true." His frown deepened.

"What kind of treatment did they say wasn't fair?" Sabra asked.

"I don't remember. I wasn't old enough, and after it was all over, your father made a decree that no one could discuss the incident. Simply put, they became angry and threatened to leave. So we investigated and found nothing." His voice darkened. "They left anyway."

"Where did they go?"

He shrugged. "That's just the strange part. No one knows. They were never heard from or seen again. The kingdom was left without guardians, and the Dune Pirates took full advantage of that. The kingdom was nearly ransacked, and would have been if the Justines hadn't figured out how to step in and stop them." His face hardened as he stared out the little window at the top of the linen room. "They deserved to disappear."

"How did the Justines stop the pirates?" Sabra asked. The dark look on her cousin's face wasn't a familiar one. Nor did she want it to be. "Don't the Dune Pirates use dark powers?"

"The Justines had an ancient trove of weapons from their forefathers that had been used before their tribe joined our clans. Some of them had passed the ancient fighting forms down as well. At least, that's what they tell me. I was only ten, so I wasn't present at any of the fighting." He frowned. "Based on what we know now, though, I wonder how much of their own dark power they're using."

"But why would Father keep all of this a secret?" Sabra shook her head. "I don't understand. It's not as though it was his fault." She paused. "And why would everyone else obey?"

"The Justines said they would henceforth take up the mantle the Sentinels left behind. It wasn't a difficult change for the clan of law to take up enforcement of that law. They told your father, and he agreed, that it would be more healing to simply move on and forget our betrayers forever."

"The sabotage," Sabra said slowly. "I wonder what they meant by that. Perhaps someone *was* sabotaging them."

Demir raised his eyebrows. "Are you defending the people who allowed my parents to be killed before my eyes? Because they knew what they were doing, Sabra. They'd been fending off the Dune Pirates for decades. They knew that the moment they left, a gaping hole would rip open, exposing the heart of our nation. And they left anyway."

"I'm not excusing them." Sabra made her voice soothing and low. Demir was difficult to rile. If he was this upset, she would need to take care if she wanted him to answer more of her questions. "I'm only wondering. Why would a clan abandon its home and people after four hundred years of faithful service? Assuming they were faithful."

Demir went to the window and ran his fingers through his beard. "I wouldn't know. Your father didn't share such with me at that age. He did the best he could to purge the kingdom of every record the Sentinels ever left behind. As requested by the Sentinels. They said it would be difficult to transition if everyone were still looking to those few of the Sentinels that remained."

"The Blue Bands," Sabra whispered. Demir just nodded. "Many of the elderly and the weak stayed behind. Your father extended them clemency on the condition they would integrate with the other clans."

Sabra wanted to note that they hadn't done a tremendous job, but she knew when to hold her tongue.

"It seems," she said instead, "rather convenient that the Justines happened to have a means with which to defend the kingdom." She joined her cousin at the window. "Four hundred year old weapons should crumble in battle. And it also strikes me as odd that they would know how to use such dark arts after so long as well. Generations would have passed by then."

"All I know is that if it weren't for the Justines, I wouldn't be alive today." Demir glowered at the afternoon sky.

"What do you mean?"

He paused for a moment, and when he spoke, his voice trembled. "The Dune Pirates were demanding access to our treasuries, our food stores, medical supplies, even our lumber supply. It would have drained the city of all we needed to trade and survive the next year. Your father refused to give them access as the stores were hidden. They threatened to kill his entire family one by one if he didn't give them what they wanted." Demir's voice grew tight. "They started with my mother, as she was the king's only sister. They killed my father at the same time to make sure he didn't marry again and produce more children. Still, your father refused. I was to be next in line."

Sabra put her arms around her cousin's waist and hugged him. "I'm sorry," she whispered. And she was. Demir had always seemed to fit in well with their family. She'd been surprised to learn as a small child that a cousin was not the same thing as a brother. But such memories, especially from such a young age, had to weigh heavy on his heart.

Demir put an arm around her shoulder and ruffled her hair. "It's not your fault. Nor is it mine." He took a deep shuddery breath and looked down at her. "But you understand now why I have little sympathy for the Sentinels. The pirates killed hundreds in their search for the stores and treasuries. All because one clan abandoned its post." His voice hardened. "My parents would be here if they had fulfilled their oath. There would have been no drowning. No beatings. No breaking into homes to kill whomever they pleased."

"I'm glad they saved you," Sabra said softly. "More than you'll ever know. But the Justines are the enemy now. They're not going to save anyone this time."

He turned away from the window and rubbed his left temple. "I know."

"Why are they doing this?" she asked. "Really?"

"I wish I knew. They say it's to prevent a curse, but I just…" He sighed. "I need to get back to make sure everyone is keeping order. If I bring you back in, will you stay quiet and hidden? I want you where I can see you." His eyes hardened. "I'm not about to sacrifice you to some monster to save my own skin."

Sabra bristled at the memory of that afternoon and the way her father had treated her. But Demir didn't need any more trouble right now, and she had much to think about.

She also, she realized, had a letter to write. More than ever, she needed George's help. Her father could purge their annals, but he couldn't purge the records of the surrounding nations. Perhaps his master would have information about what had happened all those years ago.

As she followed her cousin back to the throne room, however, she was jarred by the realization that the Justines would most likely also be overseeing the messages that flowed in and out of the city. And for some reason, being cut off from George shook her far more than anything else that had happened thus far.

CHAPTER 12
NO TIME FOR FEAR

It was decided in the end that the Sophians would do their best to find a legal loophole that explicitly stated that Sabra could take the throne, despite being adopted. Meanwhile, each basniin was to take a secret count of his or her clan's able-bodied men. The Woodsmen would stop their building and begin creating weapons in secret. Demir and those like him who knew something of self-defense would be put in charge of distributing those weapons as they were able. The Physics would begin preparing medical supplies for war, and the Sowens were to move their food supply stores to new locations underground and keep them known only to their tribe.

But, as Demir put it, such an effort was like throwing a pitcher of water at a house fire. The Justines knew every weakness, every plan, and every emergency plan following that. They were at every road that led into the city, every street corner and in every marketplace. From the layout of Sabra's room to the treasured stores of the Sowens' emergency seeds and the Physics' most costly ointments, the Justines had seen it all. And now, there was little chance of them missing anything with their many watchful eyes.

Sabra's mother prayed for a miracle. But Sabra prayed for answers.

Her father refused to discuss the kingdom's plans with her. Or rather, he couldn't find time to talk with her at all. For up through the evening following the attack, he was always busy, and when she insisted on following him around as the day drew to a close, she was inevitably sent off on some errand with Demir or her mother. And as much as Demir wished to have her within plain sight, it was impossible for him to be with Sabra all the time. This, of course, meant lots of sitting in the palace, waiting for the three days to pass without abduction.

Sabra didn't despair, though. Because the evening after the attack, she walked into her room to find a letter from George on her writing table. With it was a note.

Your Highness,
Yusuf apologizes for the delay in delivering this letter. There were delays in Kappadona, though he was fortunate to return before the Justines took control of the city. However, we could not find a way to bring you the letter unnoticed until now.

It was signed by the master stablekeeper, which made sense, as Yusuf couldn't read or write. And despite the delay, Sabra smiled smugly to herself. The Justines couldn't control everything. *Some* of her people knew what loyalty meant.

Dear Sabra,
I wasn't able to find much in our annals about these particular symbols. But I know I've seen them before, and my master will soon return from a journey of his own, so I'm going to ask him for assistance.
I have to say, I'm a bit concerned by the tone in your letter. Is all well? I know I'm far away, but please let me know if you need

anything else. I will continue searching for your symbols, but in the meantime, please let me know if there is anything else I can assist you with.

And Sabra? Please stay safe.

Your Friend,

George

Oh, just a short note, I apologize for the delay in sending this letter, and in doing so, keeping your messenger as well. I spent too many days searching for your symbols, hoping I could at least find the right language before replying. My master has still not arrived. Since I haven't yet found a satisfactory answer, it seems you'll just have to suffer through more of my letters.

Sabra had folded the letter and pressed it to her cheek, thanking the Maker for putting such a man in the world. Then, of course, she set about her reply.

But just as she had put pen to paper, someone knocked on Sabra's bedroom door. It had to be near midnight. Only then did Sabra realize she hadn't even changed out of her day clothes. She put her pen down and shoved the letter into the bodice of her dress. Then she grabbed the dagger her mother had given her the year before and held it behind her skirts.

"Who is it?" she called as she smoothed her bodice down.

"May I have a word, Princess?"

Saba froze at the smooth, familiar voice. Did he really have the audacity to speak with her at such an unholy hour? Fear, of course, had risen in her chest, but with it, annoyance.

"Do I have a choice?" she snapped.

His answer was to unlock her door from the outside and let himself in. Sabra stood and crossed her arms. "Apparently, not."

"I swear, Princess, this shall only take a moment." Mahzar bowed, his shaved head shining in the light of her candle.

Why did he even bother?

"Well, then. Get on with it."

"I simply wanted to make my intentions clear," he said softly. If Sabra hadn't known better, based on these words alone, she might have thought him a very gentle man. "I do not wish to take advantage of you, Princess. If there were another way to secure your withdrawal from the crown, I would have chosen that."

"So comforting." Sabra glared. "Is that all?"

"I promise, I will not be a tyrannical husband. I will provide you with everything you could wish for. You won't lack for anything, equal to your comfort here." He paused. "I will not even ask you to perform the wifely duties of bearing me children. If you wish to retain your own privacy for the rest of your life, I will grant that happily."

Sabra stared at him. She searched for any sign of falsehood or misgiving. But he held her gaze steadily. "You really mean that, don't you?" she whispered.

He bowed his head again.

Sabra walked over to her window, doing her best to keep her dagger hidden, and shook her head, as though that might make any of this less nonsensical. "You would give up your place as clan head in order to keep me from wearing the crown."

"I would."

She turned to face him. "But why?"

"I told you. To keep our clans' vows. To avoid having a curse fall upon our kingdom as it did when our predecessors left."

"You mean the Sentinels."

"I do," he said. "And our kingdom paid the price for their treachery. They paid as well, even more dearly."

She raised her eyebrows. "And you know that *how*?"

"They disappeared into the desert. No one has seen any sign of them for years. In the villages and cities nearby, their name is used as a curse."

"How do you know that was a curse?" Sabra asked. "And not just the consequences of poor decisions?"

He put his hand to his chin and tapped a few times, looking thoughtfully at her. "How much do you know of the Justines' origins?"

Sabra paused and thought back to her lessons. She knew her own clan's history best, but she had studied the others' as well. Unfortunately, the Justines had the least information available of all the clans.

"They were from the east. Their village had been destroyed in a flood, and they were searching for a new home."

He nodded. "And what did they do?"

"They were…" Sabra paused. This was the part that was always tricky. Even the Sophian scholars couldn't all agree on what the Justines had done before joining Segzein, and the Justines seemed perfectly content not to correct anyone. "Experts in language and law. They studied the connection between the two, specifically." From what she'd been able to glean, people from different nations would go to them for counsel and recommendations when building their own laws, or to use them as arbiters to solve conflict.

"In a way," he said, folding his hands behind his back. "But more importantly, and this is what few of our own people even know, we understood the power of words and why it was so important to use them precisely. And when we realized that it would be in our best interests to join the other clans, we realized that it was of the utmost importance to create a contract between the clans that would not only create a healthy bond but keep us and the others safe from despotism, mobs, and other forms of tyranny and chaos. So when we agreed to join, we requested that we be the ones to write the vows ourselves. Our ancestors built…locks into the vows, so to speak."

"What do you mean by locks?" Sabra asked.

"Words have power, Princess. The power to bring peace and prosperity." He said it gently, his head slightly tilted and his eyes warm, as though he were calming a confused child. "Or famine and chaos."

"So," Sabra paused, "when you *smithed* your words, so to speak, you created what you believed would bring the outcome you desired. How would this be possible?"

He smiled slightly. "There is a reason we prefer to keep our origins...vague."

"And what's the Maker's place in all this? Because what you're speaking of sounds a lot like the dark arts." Sabra narrowed her eyes. "And those are forbidden."

"We do not dabble, if that's what you're accusing us of attempting. It isn't dark if the power was yours to begin with. Our ancestors practiced such ways centuries before we became part of this kingdom. The dignitaries who created such bans never understood what gift we truly possess. Neither do they understand that we are using our gifts to protect others, not to harm them superfluously, as the intent of the agreement suggested."

"So you speak for the Maker, then? Cursing some and blessing others at your own caprice?"

"As I said, our people have been gifted. I know that's hard to understand from the outside, but it's true. With the kind of power we have comes unwelcome decisions we must make."

Sabra fingered the knife hidden in her skirts. "Why would you build a curse into the vows? What good would that even serve?" she asked.

"The organization that our ancestors came up with was a good one. It was in everyone's best interests to prevent that from changing."

Sabra paused for a moment to think this over. "I don't believe you," she finally said. "You speak of keeping the law. But it's against the Holy Writ to use the kind of darkness it takes to create such a beast as the one you conjured yesterday."

His eyes widened slightly. "Perhaps. But a little darkness is nothing if it accomplishes what is best for the kingdom."

"You don't use shadows to fight the night," Sabra said. "Only dawn can do that."

"Perhaps we're simply trying to keep our people from wandering in the night as we wait for morning to come." He gave her a sad smile. "A little healthy fear goes a long way to keep children in bed."

"This kingdom is not your child!" Sabra lifted her skirts and stepped around him and marched to the door. "I shall simply have to find my own light. One that doesn't give a flying hoot about your darkness." She opened the door and held out her hand. "Good night, sir. I believe we're done here."

He watched her for a long moment before slowly nodding. "Very well, Princess." At the door, though, he paused. "I do hope you'll reconsider tomorrow, though. If you do not, I'm afraid the consequences will be—"

"Out!" Sabra shouted.

"As you wish." He bowed slightly before leaving her room and walking down the hall.

Once she was sure he was gone, Sabra locked the door and leaned against it. Against her will, her chest heaved, and heavy sobs racked her body.

She had been so sure she was meant to be queen. In her moments of anger, she held to that conviction. But as much as she hated it, his threat filled her with cold, writhing fear.

Who would suffer next? Her people? Her family? There were a million ways Mahzar and his people could gut them all. Their society and cultures were vast and intricate but delicately balanced. All it would take would be one great gash to their animals or homes or families, and everything would tumble down with it.

Compromise. Demir was always talking about how she ought to compromise more, to play the games that politics required. Sabra had never been good at those games. Thus far, they had mostly worked out in her favor. In general, people liked her and thought her ideas were good. But with the walls falling down, she wondered if that favor might fall. And if it did, what did she do then? Did she marry the brute for the sake of her people? Did she placate the angry mob by giving up not only herself, but her ideals? And if she didn't give herself up, how many would fall in her stead?

For one brief, fleeting second, she allowed herself to admit that right now, perhaps she didn't want to be queen after all.

But that was the fear talking. So with shaking hands, Sabra returned to her desk, finished her letter, and dipped her seal into the wax. Now was the hour of need. There was no time for fear.

CHAPTER 13
MOTIVATION

Sabra knew what day it was as soon as she opened her eyes. She dressed methodically, her maidservant unusually quiet as she fussed over Sabra's clothes and hair. Today, she donned a deep purple tunic with gold threads woven into the cloth. She also wore a matching set of pantaloons beneath them. Her mother wouldn't be very pleased, but Sabra wasn't about to wear some ridiculous mountain of frills that might hamper her ability to run. Not today.

"You look lovely, Your Highness," Nisa said, her voice catching at the end.

"I'm not dying, Nisa." Sabra gave her handmaiden the best smile she knew how to give. But inside, she felt like she was halfway in the ground.

Nearly twenty-two years of training and duty. And it could all disappear in an instant. And yet...in that instant, would she be able to save her kingdom by sacrificing herself? Her hopes and plans for country and king?

Her hopes of a king whom she might have one day loved? Because never would she be able to love Mahzar. Especially not after this. The man must be mad to even think she could content herself with him even from across a house.

The blaring of horns from outside her window slashed the silence like daggers through silk. Sabra stood, and though she trembled, she squeezed Nisa's hand and went to the door.

Demir and her mother were waiting for her outside her room. Her mother's eyes were red and puffy.

"I wanted to see you more before this," she whispered as Sabra walked out, "but I was seeking more information about your birth."

Sabra kissed her mother on the cheek. "I know." Then she turned and joined what resembled a funeral march as everyone made their way through the palace halls to the throne room. Sabra avoided looking too closely at anyone's face directly. She was afraid of what she might see there. The basniins had considered her valuable enough not to give her up at the first sign of trouble. But she couldn't be sure about the laymen. The dragon had threatened their well-being too. Did they think she was worth sacrificing for?

When Sabra reached the throne room, it was nearly full to bursting. People were standing, three or four thick, against the walls. They parted to make a way for Sabra, her cousin, and her mother as they moved through to join her father at his throne on the dais. This time, however, there were no friendly smiles or greetings. Only fear.

"Princess."

Sabra turned at the sound of Mahzar's voice. He stood on the other side of the room from her father's throne, flanked by a dozen of his guards in their white uniforms. His beard was neatly trimmed, and his white clothes with gold thread were pristine. He lacked the haggard exhaustion of everyone around him. Sabra herself hadn't slept well since the attack, but she jutted her chin out and joined her father at his throne. Her mother and Demir went to stand on the other side.

Only then did she notice that Shakirat stood several men behind Mahzar.

Traitor.

"Sabra Kralicenina Capitan," Mahzar said with a bow. "Thank you for joining us today so that we may hear your choice."

Sabra's face heated at the insult. Her true title now was Erbasniin, not Kralicenina. But she smoothed her face of all emotion except cool boredom. This man didn't deserve her ire.

"I speak for my daughter." Her father stood. "I also speak for the other basniins." He gestured to their right, where the other basniins were standing. "And we will not allow you to dethrone our future queen to quell some strange notion in your head that an adopted child is not the same as blood."

"And you know this through your extensive knowledge of the law?" Mahzar tilted his head.

"No." Nazan of the Sophians stepped forward. "He is not an expert in the law. But I am. And there is nothing in our vows nor in our legal texts that forbids an adopted child from becoming queen."

"I appreciate your time and care in this matter," Mahzar said, dipping his head at her gently. "But with all due respect, you, madame, have studied our law from the outside. In our own halls, we are the true experts, for the law is why we live, move, and breathe."

He turned back to Sabra. "Have you given any more thought to what I said the other night?"

"What did you say the other night?" Demir growled from behind Sabra. "And when was this?"

"Why didn't you tell me about this, Sabra?" her father hissed from beside her. But Sabra didn't answer, and neither did Mahzar. They simply stared at one another from across the room.

"I have considered it," Sabra said, ignoring her father. "But I'm struggling to take your offer seriously."

Mahzar's brows drew closer together. "Why?"

"Because I don't take people seriously when they threaten violence against a peaceful party." In her head, she could imagine Demir cautioning her to take care with her words, but she was angry. Hang whatever game it was that he wanted her to play.

"That's not a very queenly position, considering what your people are about to lose, should you refuse me again."

"And what will they lose?"

"I ask you, Princess." Mahzar's jaw flexed. "*Please* reconsider. I promise, I will never take you by force. But I will give you as much... motivation as I believe you need."

"And I will answer for her." The king stood. "The answer is no."

Mahzar finally turned to acknowledge him. "You do? Do you not remember what you discussed with our previous clan head?"

"I have carried your dirty secret for far too long." Sabra's father snarled. He leaped to his feet and strode toward Mahzar. "But you push me too far! You are not within your rights, and you know it!"

Mahzar turned to the basniins, ignoring the king's outburst. "And as clan heads, you support your king?"

Yasin, Baran, and Esemeray looked at the ground. Ozge glowered at the wall behind Mahzar. Nazan alone glared daggers at the Justinian clan head. "We do," she snarled. "No villain shall steal our queen."

Mahzar sighed. "I had so hoped you would change your mind." Then he turned back to Sabra's father. "I thank you for keeping your silence. I only wish you could have kept it longer." He held his arm up.

Sabra gasped as it exploded with light, sparks flying around the throne room. People screamed and ran as Mahar's skin was replaced by scales, white with a green tint. His hand, now a claw, boasted talons at least a handspan in length. And without another word, he thrust those talons past Sabra and sank them into her father's chest.

Sabra screamed as blood began to pour. She was at his side to catch him just as Mahzar retracted his claws and let him fall. As Sabra held her father's shaking, bleeding body close, Mahzar looked over her head and faced the basniins where they stood huddled together. From behind her, Sabra could hear Demir's sword come out from its sheath, but she couldn't bear to look away from her father.

"Sabra!" Her father spoke through clenched teeth. Blood continued to pour out of his wound as her mother tried frantically to stop it. "Sabra, look at me!"

Sabra did look at him. He was shaking all over, and his eyes were too wide.

"Just wait," Sabra sobbed. "Hold on!"

"No time for that." He shook his head hard, which made him cough up blood. "Sabra, swear to me that you won't let him steal your crown. Swear to me that you will be queen!" He gripped her wrists. "Swear!"

Sabra's pain was choking her, so she nodded. "I swear," she whispered.

"The Maker gave you to us for *now*," he whispered as tears ran down his own face.

"You tend to work slowly," another voice said. "Let this be your incentive to make a decision on time for once."

Sabra looked up to see Mahzar looking down on them, having the audacity to give her a sorrowful look. As if he cared.

Demir had his sword out and looked very much as though he wanted to cut Mahzar's heart from his chest. But he had reined himself in enough to remain standing above Sabra and her mother.

Sabra watched in a horrified stupor as her mother took her father's body from her arms. Mahzar and his men went back out the way they had come, the crowd screaming and running even faster as the group in white descended the steps. As the last of their ranks exited, an explosion from somewhere outside rocked the palace.

"Princess! Princess!"

Sabra looked up stupidly as Nazan called her name. The Sophians' basniin grabbed Sabra by the arm and pulled her to her feet.

"You have to see this!" she shouted above the noise.

Sabra was too dazed to fight the older woman as she hauled Sabra to one of the gigantic windows on the south side of the room. With a narrow sliver of sense left in some corner of her mind, Sabra noticed that the crowd had begun running into the palace instead of away from it. She understood why, though, when she peered out the window.

Mahzar, in full dragon form, had risen above the city and was raining fire down upon it. The palace walls were too high for Sabra to see the aftermath in the streets below, but from the dragon's position, she knew it was hitting the Woodsmen's spoke. Her heart fell as a plume of black smoke billowed in the sky. So much costly lumber in their lumber yards. She could smell charred cedar in the air.

The smoke brought her back to her senses somewhat as she turned and looked back at the chaos surrounding her. People were screaming, crying, and fighting for the best places to hide. Her mother was still sobbing over her father's body as Demir tried to organize those who were streaming in.

"You are the next queen," Nazan said, her eyes bright. "Now act like it!"

Sabra didn't want to act like it. She wanted to storm outside and make Mahzar pay for what he had done. But Nazan was right. People were looking to her for answers, and she must give them. She nodded stiffly to Nazan and then ran back to Demir. She had trained all her life for this.

"There you are!" Demir looked relieved when he saw her approaching. "The Justines have closed all the gates, but they're allowing people inside the palace."

"Isn't it dangerous to have the whole city in one place?" Sabra asked, looking around. All they needed was one burst of Mahzar's flame, and they were all going to die.

"It is dangerous," Demir agreed. "But we can't stop them from coming, so we'll have to do our best with what we have. I've been separating them by spokes in different parts of the palace." He cleared his throat. "But you're queen. You'll have to choose what to do next."

Sabra glanced once more at her father's limp body in her mother's arms. She was queen. Which meant her father was really dead. She had to fight the need to gasp for air as she spoke.

"No, that's wise. Let's do that."

Demir nodded and shouted at the basniins to join their people. "Go find your people! The least you can do is calm them!"

"What about the ones in the city?" Sabra asked. "The ones who can't or won't come?"

"Unfortunately, they're on their own until the dragon stops flaming."

"Do you still have our extra supplies in the lower levels?" Esemeray asked, seeming to have awakened from her stupor. The Physic's lined face was pale, and she moved slowly, like a woman two decades older than she really was. But at least she was moving.

Sabra nodded. "They're in the left wing. But...wait." She ran to her father's body. "I'm sorry," she whispered as she removed the large key ring from his belt. "Here," she said, finding the correct key and handing it to Esemeray. "Your supplies are all there."

"Thank you. We'll begin preparing to treat the burns." Esemeray nodded nervously and set off, calling a few of her own people to her.

The smoke no longer smelled of cedar. Instead, sulfur filled the air, and people began to gag.

"You!" Sabra shouted to a servant nearby. "Grab several others and go to the kitchens. Get water and linens so people can cover their faces to keep out the smoke! Quick!"

Hours passed, but Sabra was so busy that she only noticed when it became dark enough that they needed lanterns and candles to see by. Her senses were too dulled to notice the hunger that should have been in her belly. All she could focus on was sorting the people who continued to stream into the palace. It was her duty, after all. It was what she owed them.

That, and if she stopped long enough to let herself feel, she might collapse from the weight of losing her father and having her kingdom decimated all in the same day.

"Here."

Sabra looked up when a flash of white moved into her peripheral vision. She straightened immediately when she realized that the woman in the white robe must belong to Mahzar. But the woman wasn't looking at Sabra. Instead, she was looking at Demir as she extended a sealed parchment to him.

Demir looked at Sabra before taking the parchment. Of course, Sabra realized. Technically, any messages should have been addressed to her, as she was in line to rule. Which meant the extension of the message to Demir rather than herself was a heavy insult.

But Sabra was too tired to quibble over semantics, so she nodded to Demir to take it. He opened it and read the document.

"What does it say?" Sabra asked, holding her hand out.

He put the parchment in it, but his brows stayed drawn together. "They're giving you ten days to change your mind."

Sabra froze, the paper still folded in her hand. "Or what?"

"He says for every day that you delay, he'll be forced to motivate you." Then Demir's frown deepened. "And he's just getting started."

CHAPTER 14

INTO THE DARK

ousin."

Sabra looked up from the map she was studying to see Demir standing at the corner. "Excuse me," she told the servant. Then she left his side and joined her cousin in the corner.

"What are you looking at?" he asked her, surveying the room. It was one of the palace's less impressive rooms, often used by her father to facilitate smaller, more secretive meetings. Now there were about a dozen Sophians in small bunches of two or three as they scoured the maps that had been smuggled out of the main library. Sabra felt as though she'd breathed, eaten, and slept in this room for the past three days since the dragon's attack.

"Several of the Sophians and Woodsmen were able to bring maps of the city and storehouse charts. We're trying to piece together which of the underground stores might not have been hit and how many resources we have left." She paused and studied her cousin's face again. "Why, did you have something you needed me for?"

He looked down at her, his brow slightly furrowed. "Actually, the basniins would like a meeting with us in a little while. I was hoping you might survey the damage with me first."

"Is that safe, my lord?" one of the older Sophians asked. "The dragon could return any moment."

"He gave us ten days, and we have seven left," Demir said unhappily. "As much as I despise them, I believe they will keep their word. They're too superstitious not to."

Sabra couldn't help being a little annoyed. She was the chosen future queen. If anything, the basniins should be asking her to join them for a meeting. Not to send her cousin to do their bidding. Still, it wasn't Demir's fault. If it hadn't been for him and his calm, steady presence, the palace might have shattered to pieces in the days prior. So for his sake, she said nothing, although she resolved silently to talk with them about respecting her first in the near future. She turned and smiled her thanks at the man.

"Thank you for your concern. I'll go with my cousin now, but I would appreciate it if you continue running your numbers. I'll bring you whatever information I can."

The man bowed, and Sabra turned to leave with Demir.

"Have they said anything about an emergency coronation?" Sabra asked softly as they walked.

"It's been brought up, but nothing official."

Sabra frowned. "I can't do anything binding until I'm crowned. I'm not sure what they're waiting for."

"I know." Demir's eyes darkened, but they didn't say anything else as they made their way through the palace. There were too many people crowded within the palace walls, some sitting or even lying on the floor. The air smelled of smoke and too many bodies pressed together. Sabra did her best to smile and nod at those she passed, but no longer was she met with smiles in return. Instead, she saw the haunted, ghostly expressions of those who had lost everything. And many that blamed her for their loss.

Eventually, they turned and made their way out onto the palace wall, where she'd walked with Abasi what seemed like a century ago. It was void of guards now. There were several able-bodied young men dotted along it, here and there. Not enough to fight, but enough to light their oil lamps for signaling in case the dragon appeared again.

"How is your mother doing?" Demir asked, his voice hollow.

Sabra drew in a measured breath. "Not well. She doesn't want to eat. She just sits and stares at his chair in their chambers." In truth, Sabra was more than a little worried. She'd heard of more than one person who had died of a broken heart. A familiar wave of guilt washed over her as she thought about how little time she'd been able to spend with her mother. How little she herself had been able to mourn at all. But there was too much to do to sit with her mother hourly, begging her to eat. An aunt had been given that task. Because as much as Sabra was hurting, she knew she couldn't collapse too. Not when the continuance of her kingdom was at stake. That's what happened when you were queen. And even though Sabra was not yet officially queen, the duties fell to her nonetheless.

But duties were good. As long as she was fulfilling her duties, she could push away the pain. She could fulfill her oath to her father. She could lead her people.

Anything to keep from thinking too deeply about losing him. Or whatever dirty secret he'd kept for his murderer.

"So," Sabra said with a little shake of her head. "Now that we're alone, I suppose you brought me up here for a reason."

"I wanted to see the city for myself, rather than relying on reports." He gave her a sideways glance. "I supposed you would like to do the same."

Sabra went to the edge and leaned against the waist-high wall. "You were right." Then she added in a lower voice, "It's worse than I thought. The clans report that they've started unearthing bodies in the rubble."

Rows and rows of homes and businesses were either charred beyond repair or burned completely to the ground. Mahzar might claim he was only trying to burn the buildings, but with such a large city, it was inevitable that people might be caught in the flames as well.

"The Capitans' spoke has been hit the hardest," she continued after clearing her throat. "Though, I guess that only makes sense, as *I'm* the one causing him trouble."

"He did the least damage to the Sophians' spoke," Demir pointed out. "The library was barely touched."

"I suppose that's something to be grateful for," Sabra said wryly. "If they value words as they say they do, it would be difficult for them to destroy our written sources of knowledge."

"What does Yasin think of our resources?" Demir asked, his eyes still on the damage.

"We should be able to make it through the winter, thanks to the underground stores." She hesitated. "As long as we don't lose anything else. Otherwise, we'll have to spend a fortune purchasing from other kingdoms. A fortune we no longer have. And that doesn't include the seed we'd need to buy to replant next spring." She studied him again. Lines that hadn't been there a week before seemed permanently etched into his young face. He wasn't even thirty-four years, and he looked as though he carried the weight of the world on his shoulders.

But that was her job.

"What are you going to do?" he asked quietly.

She ran her hands over her face. In front of others, she had to be composed and calm, but with Demir, she could be human. And she was glad of it. Being a marble queen was exhausting. Once again, as she often had lately, she wished George were in Segzein. He would make all of this easier, somehow. She knew it.

"I don't know," she admitted. "I suppose whatever is required of me."

"Except marry Mahzar."

She looked up at him and grimaced. "It sounds bad when you say it that way."

"I never said it was bad. I'm only clarifying your stance."

Sabra huffed and pushed a clump of hair out of her face. "You're right, but not for the reason everyone thinks."

He gave her a sad smile. "I'm not everyone. And for the record, if I ever get a chance, I'm stabbing him in the face before I let him even look your way."

"You're very sweet." She gave him a tired smile back then sighed. "I know everyone thinks I'm refusing him out of pride. Or because I'm obsessed with power. But that's not it."

"What is it then?"

She paused before answering. "It's hard to put into words. I guess...if I thought marrying him would really stop this, I would. Not that I would want to, of course."

"But?" he asked gently.

She drew in a deep breath. "But I don't think it would stop him. I think it would just be the beginning. It's like we're standing on a precipice, and the enemy is pushing to see how much pressure it will take to make us fall. And when we do, it's going to be nearly impossible to win back the high ground."

Demir leaned against the stone wall. "I just wish I understood their obsession with this superstition. It seems like such a risk for such a narrow interpretation of the law."

Sabra studied a group of brave citizens in the Woodsmen's spoke who were clearing away the charred rubble of their market. "I don't think it's superstition, exactly."

"What do you mean?"

"Mahzar came to my room the night before Father died."

Demir's dark eyes narrowed. "I've been meaning to ask you about that. Someone mentioned that they saw him lingering near your door. Why didn't you tell me? Or scream? I would have come!"

She leaned against his shoulder. "I know. But he seemed determined to give me information, so I decided I would take it. And like you, I knew he was too obsessed with his strange sense of morals to do anything untoward."

Demir growled. "Since you risked your life for it, what did you learn?"

"Apparently, the Justines believe they were blessed with an ancient gift. When they speak, their words have the power to change reality."

Her cousin blinked at her. "I have literally never heard anything like this in my life."

"Because he said they keep it quiet. They've been vague on purpose with what they've shared of their history before joining with the clans." She paused. "It seems that they insisted on crafting the original vows so that if they were broken, dark curses would be called down upon the clans. And they're so terrified about breaking those vows that they're willing to use the ancient dark arts to prevent it."

Demir stared at her like she had a third eye growing out of her head. "Why for the love of all that's good would they do any such thing? Even if they had a gift like that. Which I doubt immensely."

Sabra nodded. "I doubt it as well. Otherwise, they would have spoken me into capitulation by now." She gave him a dry smile. "But Mahzar said it was done to maintain the perfect society, which they believed they could achieve with the right wording of the vows."

"So power through manipulation." He shook his head. "That's insane."

"Agreed. But it still leaves us with the problem that they're convinced their words have power. And they're convinced that this power is theirs directly from the Maker. And that He won't stand in their way."

"So," he said with a gusty sigh, "they have no fear of Maker or man."

"I wish we had a way to put the fear of both in them," Sabra grumbled, thinking again of the way she'd begged her father to let her search for the Sentinels. She could have gone to George. He would have helped her find them, even if her own people weren't willing. Who knew what she might have unearthed with the help of him and his master?

Whatever they might have found, it would have been better than this sitting around and waiting for something to happen. Once again, Sabra was struck with a yearning in her heart to *do* something.

"We need to go." Demir squinted at the sun. "The basniins will be meeting soon."

Sabra nodded and turned to follow him. "Demir? What am I doing wrong?" she asked as they moved toward the stairs.

"You're reading at night when you should be sleeping."

Sabra rolled her eyes but couldn't help smiling. "I mean with the basniins."

This time, he neither turned nor laughed. "I don't know what you mean."

"I mean they don't respect me. Two weeks ago, I could do no wrong. And now they're calling meetings without me, they're ignoring half of what I say—"

Demir came to a halt and held his finger up to his lips. Sabra followed his glance over to one of the young men standing by the wall stairs with his lamp. He wore an old blade and looked terrified to be standing guard. Such a strange sight compared to the strong, white-robed guards of the Justines that usually took such posts.

Sabra nodded slightly and followed her cousin. It wouldn't do to have anyone knowing of her insecurities. She had enough insubordination in her ranks already.

Sabra and Demir were nearing the meeting room when Sabra heard a man's voice.

"Your Highness."

She looked down to find a man with a blue band tattooed on his arm, visible through his torn sleeve, holding his hand out toward her. She went to him and knelt beside him. After a moment of study, she realized that she was looking at the man who had sewn the blue sash for her in the eighth spoke.

"It's you!" she cried, unable to hide her surprise.

He gave her a wry smile. "I'm sorry I wasn't able to share more the last time we met."

"No. Please don't apologize. I was very grateful for what you did share." She scooted closer. "Could you tell me more? About your people, I mean? Where I might find them?"

"Princess."

Sabra looked up to see Demir gesturing toward the meeting room. "I apologize, but we have a schedule to keep."

"Of course." She looked back at the man. "I'm so sorry, but could we continue this conversation after this meeting? I should very much like to hear anything you can tell me."

His gaze drifted past her to rest on Demir. "Of course, Your Highness." But he narrowed his eyes at Demir as he leaned back against the wall. "If we are allowed such."

What did that mean?

Sabra joined her cousin, but she couldn't help noticing the light was gone from his eyes. He looked...miserable. There was no other word for it.

"What's going on?" Sabra whispered. "What's wrong?"

Demir just looked at the ground.

"Demir, so help me—"

"I never knew guilt before this," he whispered, still looking at the ground. "Not really."

Sabra's blood turned to ice in her veins as she stared at him. Without another word, he opened the door just as the bells pealed the fifth hour of the evening.

The basniins were all standing around the table in the center of the room. Everyone looked as though they'd aged ten years in just a few days. None of the drinks or food set out on the table had been touched. That alone was unusual, especially now that everyone struggled for time to eat a full meal at least once a day. Even more frightening, however, was the way none, not even Nazan, would meet Sabra's gaze as she entered the room.

"I don't recall requesting a meeting," Sabra said, doing her best to keep her voice from shaking. "What's this about?"

"You are our crown princess," Ozge said gruffly, still not meeting her eyes. "So we have a question to ask of you."

"Very well." Sabra came to stand behind the chair she should have been sitting in. Instead, she grasped it for support. "I will answer."

"Are you willing to do what you must to save our peoples?" Ozge asked.

"It's my duty to act in the best interests of our peoples," Sabra said slowly. "But you know this. So why do you ask?"

"We have all spoken with our clans," Esemeray said, her voice trembling. "And they say they cannot survive these continued attacks."

Nazan pursed her lips. So Sabra turned to her.

"This is true?"

Nazan looked down at her hands. "I'm afraid so," she said in a voice so low Sabra could barely hear it.

Sabra swallowed. "So what does that mean?

"We took a vote on whether or not to have you marry Mahzar." Ozge said, finally meeting Sabra's gaze with a rebellious look of his own. "And before you say it wasn't fair, we allowed Demir to vote, too."

Sabra swallowed hard. "And?"

"The vote was unanimous. You will accept his offer tonight. Demir will be king, and the dragon will stop."

She stared at him for a long minute before his words truly sank in, her breaths drawing shorter and faster as she turned slowly to look at her cousin.

Demir's eyes were wet and shiny, as though he was about to start crying. But that didn't make up for the fact that he had voted against her, too.

Sabra opened her mouth, but no words would come. There wasn't a name for the feeling that was settling inside. It was a deep sort of despair, one she hadn't known existed. Somewhere in her head, she was aware that her husband-to-be was the most evil man her kingdom had ever known, except possibly his ancestors. One who was steeped in ancient, forbidden evil. She'd been able to smell it when he was in her room, a metallic, smokey scent.

But even worse was the helplessness. She would not only marry an evil man, but she would watch her cousin rule a kingdom that was now subservient to that evil. Sabra had studied despots and tyrants, and she knew that they didn't merely exert their power one time. Once established, they grasped at that power until someone stronger yanked it away from them.

Segzein was about to be ruled by the dragon.

"No," Sabra said, shaking her head. "No, there has to be another way."

"There is no other way," Baran said as he tore his uneaten pastry to pieces.

"We despise this man as much as you," Yasin said, his long thin face seeming longer than ever. "But we have no succor."

"We have no army," Nazan said. Her voice grew louder with every word. "No weapons. No secrets. All because we were foolish enough to grant them what they asked for after the Sentinels were gone!" She grabbed the ink well she'd been toying with and threw it across the room. The air split with a crack as one of the window panes splintered upon its impact.

"But the Sentinels!" Sabra said, praying hard that someone would listen. "If we could only find them—"

"The Sentinels are gone, child." Ozge scoffed. "They died, lost and wandering in the desert for all we know." Then he sighed.

"For what it's worth," Esemeray said meekly, "I do believe he means it when he says he will treat you well. "The Justines may have a strange sense of honor, but when they make promises, they always keep them."

"I couldn't care less about how he treats *me*," Sabra snapped. Anger, hot and sticky, was rising quickly from her stomach. It heated every inch of skin as it spread throughout her body, chasing away the fear that had paralyzed her moments before. "This is a mistake. Not for my sake, but for the people. Because if you think that dragon will be appeased by this concession forever, you're deluding yourselves—"

"You're not queen yet!" Ozge growled. "You forget yourself."

"He set our kingdom on fire!" Sabra held her chin high, praying they wouldn't see how it shook. "He killed the *rightful* heir to the throne! He destroyed livelihoods. We're still getting in reports of people who died that are only being pulled out of the rubble now!"

"You wanted to lead!" Ogze's dark eyes burned into hers. "Sometimes, leaders must sacrifice."

Esemeray shook her head at the ground. "I just can't help thinking of all the victims my people will have to treat if this continues. We can't go on like this. Not without our supplies. And most of those have been burned."

"If you'd simply accepted his offer the first time," Ogze continued, "we wouldn't be in this mess now."

"That's enough." Demir held up his hand. "I'll talk with her." He opened the door and looked at Sabra. "Come with me?"

Sabra's anger had held her together throughout the meeting, the hot fury in her veins melding the pieces together like the orange metal in a smith's fire. But as she stared at her cousin, a new kind of rage threatened to break free. "You usurp me," she said, her voice trembling. "And then you ask me to walk with you? You couldn't have told me an hour ago when you had me alone?"

"Sabra, I—"

"I trusted you!" she spat through the tears that were moving down her face.

"If you come with me, I'll explain," Demir hissed between gritted teeth. Tears streamed down his cheeks as well, but they were meaningless to Sabra. His betrayal overshadowed it all.

As much as she had loved her father, she had never been anywhere near as close to him as she was to Demir. Demir had helped make her strong. He'd taught her staff and history and languages and numbers. He'd been the one to wipe her tears when she and her father butted heads, and he had been her support when the lessons got hard and her confidence failed her. No brother could have been closer. In him, she had found protection and solace. Even when trying to choose a stranger for a husband, Sabra had known that no matter who she picked, Demir would be there.

And now, he was not only allowing them to hand her to a monster. He was delivering her up himself.

The room seemed to sway, and Sabra's chest squeezed as she

struggled to draw air in. Her arms and legs were suddenly brittle, threatening to crack if she dared move.

But she wasn't given the chance. Demir grabbed her by the wrist and pulled her from the room. People parted, their eyes large as he dragged her into the hall. They must have been a sight, both cousins' faces streaked with tears and eyes rimmed red. But Demir didn't falter, and only Sabra's last ounce of pride kept her from shrieking what she really thought of her cousin at the top of her lungs. Whatever the basniins had done, the people didn't deserve to have their fears heightened. So she let him pull her down halls and around corners, moving lower and lower as they went.

Besides, this wasn't the end. Sabra would make sure of that. Her cousin might have succumbed to fear. But she wasn't beaten yet.

After several minutes of walking, they made it to Sabra's mother's rooms. As soon as the door was locked behind her, she yanked her hand away and folded her arms across her chest. "I don't care what the basniins voted. I'm not going to marry that man."

But Demir wasn't paying attention to her. Instead, he was pushing her parents' bed out of the way. Sabra's mother appeared and began to help him.

"Wait," Sabra said, stepping forward to see better. "What are you doing?"

When the bed was against the wall, Sabra's mother jumped up and grabbed a bag from beneath a cushion on the bed. "Quickly," she said, her voice catching in her throat. "Take this. It has food, waterskins, and money in it. And here." She wrapped a thick cloak around Sabra's shoulders. "This should serve as a blanket until you can get somewhere to purchase one. Now put your boots on."

"A blanket?" Sabra automatically lifted her foot up when her mother knelt down and touched Sabra's right slipper. "What do you mean?" She was only vaguely aware that her mother was putting her riding boots on her feet.

"You're not marrying that monster." Demir looked up at her, his eyes obsidian in their depths.

"But you said…" Sabra watched as he worked a floorboard loose. "What are you doing?"

"Do you think I taught you all the secrets of the palace?" He gave her a wry smile. Quickly, he had five more floorboards moved. "Now come. We need to get you as far from the palace as we can before someone realizes you're gone."

Sabra blinked at him. "You mean…you didn't vote for me to marry him?"

"Oh, I voted all right. I voted for it so I could buy you more time to escape."

Sabra's mother took Sabra's face in her hands. "You're going to run as far from here as you can. Find refuge with some kind soul until we can send for you again." Sabra froze as her mother pulled her into a shaking embrace. "I'm sorry," her mother sobbed into her ear. "You are everything I ever dreamed of in a daughter and more."

"We need to go," Demir said gently from where he stood in the hole in the floor. "You should have about three days, but the sooner you're gone, the better."

Sabra's mother stood back and nodded, sniffing and wiping the tears away from her face. "I know. I just needed to hold my baby one more time."

"I don't understand." Sabra took a step back. "What's going on here?"

"You're escaping." Demir gestured at the hole. "This leads to a set of underground passages. They were created when the palace was built in case the king needed a way to escape the city. When you get out, you're going to run until you find somewhere safe to stay. The farther away, the better."

"But Mahzar will know I'm gone. He'll be angry."

"He will." Sabra's mother stood taller and gave her a dry, tremulous smile. "But we're going to make him wait to find out."

"How?"

"I'll tell him that the basniins have ordered you to marry him, but you need a few days to prepare yourself," Demir said. "They won't be satisfied, of course, until they have you under their thumb, since they see you as a threat. But at least you'll get a head start this way."

"I may be your mother," Sabra's mother said. "But I'm not ancient. With the right veils and coverings. I should be able to pose as you sufficiently until the wedding itself. By then, you'll have traveled to the nearest town. Mahzar has no jurisdiction there, which means he'll be slowed in his search for you."

"When can I come back?" Sabra asked, her heart beginning to race so fast she felt dizzy.

"When all is safe, we'll find you." Sabra's mother pulled Sabra close again. As her mother's lips left her forehead, Sabra felt like her heart might shatter to pieces. This was real. She was leaving her family and her kingdom behind, possibly forever. Instead of being queen, she was escaping as a fugitive.

At least her cousin hadn't truly betrayed her. And yet, Sabra couldn't find much more joy in her new situation than her last. Either way, she was losing everything.

"Time to go." Demir disappeared into the hole. Sabra's mother pulled her in for one last kiss on the cheek, then, silent sobs racking her body, she let Sabra go.

Sabra wanted nothing more than to cling to her mother and never let go. She instantly regretted every moment she'd spent with anyone else over the last few days. Not only had her mother lost her husband, but she was now losing her daughter and putting her life on the line to help her escape.

Instead of clinging, Sabra whispered, "I love you."

Then she lowered herself into the hole.

Into the dark.

CHAPTER 15
ALLY

Sabra found herself in a dark tunnel. It was lined with stone on all sides, barely tall enough for Demir to walk through without having to bend. By the time she was inside, he'd already lit a torch.

"We'll go this way," he said, indicating straight ahead. Only then did Sabra turn to realize that the tunnel ran in the opposite direction as well.

"How did I never know about these?" Sabra asked as they made their way deeper into the tunnel.

"It's a secret known only to your father's line." He paused. "Well, them and the Sentinels. Supposedly, the Sentinels wanted a way to get the king out of the castle if something ever happened to put him in danger."

"Why didn't Father tell me?"

"Only the crown ruler and his spouse know. You would have been told if you were properly crowned, but there wasn't time."

"Why do you know then?" Sabra asked, shivering as Demir's flame threw light on a disturbingly large spider web that took up most of the right side of the wall.

"Your father showed me after you were adopted. He said if something were to ever happen to him and your mother, I was to take you and make my way out of the city."

They walked in silence as Sabra considered this. Even then, her father was protecting her to the point of breaking the rules. Sabra's chest squeezed tight.

In the darkness, it was hard to tell how far they walked. Sabra wanted to speak. These might very well be her last moments with Demir for years. And yet, she couldn't find a single thought that fully encompassed all that was on her heart.

Just as she was wondering if she should have grabbed some of the fruit off her mother's fruit stand, Demir stopped so quickly that she ran into him.

"I want you to know," he said softly, his eyes pleading. "I never wanted your crown. This was the only way I could think to get you away. I knew what they were planning to do, and I panicked." He paused, then added. "I know I'm always telling you to be diplomatic and compromise. But sometimes," he gave her a pained smile, "I wish I was more like you."

"Demir." Sabra wrapped her arms around him. "Thank you. For everything."

He put his arm around her shoulder and kissed the top of her head. And one of the knots in Sabra's heart unwound.

"The crown should be yours," he said, his voice quivering. "And I'll hate myself until I die for taking it."

"Don't." Sabra gave him one more squeeze before pulling back and letting go. "If it can't be me, there's no one else I'd rather lead our people than you." She gave a humorless laugh. "At least this way, you get to pick between Grandpa or Jitters instead of me."

He gave something that sounded halfway between a laugh and a sob then ruffled her hair. "Come on," he said, his voice gruff. "Let's go."

Sabra nodded, and they resumed their walk into the darkness.

For a long time, they were silent. Sabra spent the time doing her best to comprehend all that had happened. That she wasn't being forced to marry Mahzar was a relief, of course. But what of the cost?

Who would suffer for her absence? Would they know Demir had helped her? And who would the Justines crown in his stead if they found out? There hadn't yet been a decision reached as to who was in line behind him. Sabra hated to lose her place among her people, but at least she knew Demir would be a good king. But it was anyone's guess as to who they would pick if the Justines thought him unworthy as well.

"The tunnel will deposit you below one of the smaller cliff faces just north of the city. Head west to the coast. From there, you'll only be a day from Zeyteen. Their highway is usually safe and well-trafficked. Don't stay there, though. Only stop long enough to refill your water and purchase whatever you need. Then I want you to keep going until you find someplace to blend in."

"How far should I go?" Sabra asked

"We're here," he said, gesturing with the torch. Sabra leaned around him to see a wooden door. A large stone, nearly as tall as her knee, rested against it. With a slight grunt, Demir moved it out of the way with his foot. Then he opened the door. Sabra blinked as light from the sunset flooded the dark. "I know your mother told you that we'll send for you once everything is set to rights. But unless you see me searching for you in person, I want you to keep running until you're far away. Destin. Ashland. Staroz. Anywhere but here."

Sabra stared at him. "You really mean that?"

"I do." He paused. "And Sabra? Don't come back."

Sabra's heart stopped. "I won't see you again, will I?" she whispered.

He shook his head. "I don't think so."

Sabra launched herself at him for one more hug. Then, in a move that felt as though it broke every single bone in her body, she released him and turned to face the high desert. About a hundred paces away, she turned for one more look. But the door was already closed.

For the hundredth time that day, Sabra wanted to fall apart. But she'd already done enough of that to last the rest of her life. Her cousin and mother were risking their lives to set her free. And she had never felt more loved or more brokenhearted.

But she wasn't about to flee to Zeyteen or any other little farming town. Not when her family and people were in jeopardy. In spite of her tears, Sabra dared to smile. She'd been praying to the Maker for the opportunity to do something. Maybe now was her chance.

She turned and headed north instead of west.

Her mother had told her to find an ally, someone she could trust. Well, she already had one of those, even if she'd only seen him once in the last seven years. She'd never been able to send out any more letters, and the blockade would have prevented any more of his letters getting through. That was well and good, though. She would go and see him herself.

CHAPTER 16

SERKAN

Sabra's trek toward the northern road that led to Kappadona began in surprisingly high spirits. It was still only late afternoon by the time she got her bearings, which meant she had several more hours of travel time before she was forced to find somewhere to sleep.

She wasn't on her way to cower in the corner of some nameless little town, waiting for death to take her. She was going to find George. And together, they would search for a way to bring the Justines down. After all, the Justines weren't the only ones with access to power in this world. There were plenty of people who had been gifted by the Maker with special powers of their own, the kind that could destroy the ancient dark arts that Mahzar had admitted to practicing. She *would* see her mother and cousin again, and her kingdom *would* be restored to order and prosperity.

The rocky terrain had a calming effect, as well, after the smoking chaos of the city. Tufts of green trees stuck up here and there, though there would be fewer of them as she moved north. The natural stone cone-shaped chimneys to her right, formed by ancient water and wind, were her favorite part of the terrain. They stood taller than the palace, dotting the land in bunches, as though defying the sky by piercing its distant plane without ever leaving the ground.

As a child, Sabra had wanted to climb one. Many of the chimneys even had hollowed out caves at the bottom, according to Demir, even larger than the caves that dotted the hillsides beside the chimneys. It was the perfect place to camp, she'd reasoned. Demir, who had been sixteen years at the time, had thought this a splendid idea, and they had been packed and ready to head out until Sabra's mother had found out. That had put an end to their adventure, something Sabra had always regretted.

Perhaps not a wonderful place for a five-year-old to play, Sabra was now forced to admit. But one such cave might provide a good shelter to sleep in that night. Usually, the ride between the two cities could be made in one long day or two half days. Without a horse, though, Sabra could only guess that she would need at least two, maybe three days to get there. Staying off the road would make the walk more difficult as she navigated the rocky terrain.

Hope and a strange sense of peace she hadn't felt in a long time settled over her. She was going to *do* something, finally. After about an hour of walking, however, Sabra had the strangest sensation of being watched. But every time she turned around, there was nothing but the rocks, the high desert hills, and random scatterings of trees. She had been walking closer to the hills in order to stay away from the road in case someone came searching for her. But the many hollowed out cave openings in the hillside began to make her feel more exposed than she might have near the road.

An hour after the sensation began, a crack sounded behind her, and she knew she was being followed. Under normal circumstances, Sabra might have tried to outrun whoever was following her, or might have even moved toward the road to force whoever it was out of hiding. But her patience was short today. So instead, she slowed until she could hear footsteps behind her. They were surprisingly quick and often came to a pause followed by a thump as if the traveler were…jumping?

When the steps were almost upon her, she whirled around and grabbed the culprit by the shirt. Then she was so surprised she let go.

"Serkan!" She gaped at the little servant. "What are you doing here?"

"You were leaving." He grinned up at her and wriggled his eyebrows. "So I followed you."

"What... How?" Sabra shook her head. "How is that even possible?"

"I saw your mother packing a bag of your things. So I figured what with them wanting you to marry the dragon and all, you were leaving."

"Yes, but how did you find me? And how did you know that? That was secret information!"

He shrugged, his grin impish. "I have my ways."

Horse hooves thundering in the distance made Sabra look up. Two riders were galloping toward them, their white cloaks streaking back in the wind behind them. She grabbed Serkan by the wrist and dragged him toward the hills.

"What are you doing?" he cried.

"The caves!" She yanked him around a boulder.

They were too winded to talk much after that as they scrambled up the foothills, the Justine guards closing in fast behind them. Though the slope up to the caves was gentle, the gravel and smaller rocks were loose, and Sabra and Serkan slipped on them often. Sabra would have made her way up quickly enough on her own, but towing Serkan behind her took twice as long.

The guards were almost to the foot of the plateau by the time Sabra pulled Serkan into the mouth of one of the caves. Just as she'd expected, the cave was small, but it opened up to neighboring caves on both sides. Without pausing, she pulled him into the cave to her left, dragging him to the very back and dumping him against the wall.

"Stay here," she whispered. "Don't let them see you!"

Serkan nodded and huddled in the corner, his typical hubris gone.

Thankful that he was listening for once, Sabra looked up. Years after her mother had put an end to their plans to sleep in some of the stone chimneys outside, Demir had still somehow convinced some of the guards to take him out to the plateaus so he could have a look around. And when he'd gotten back, he'd told Sabra how many of the caves not only went sideways, but up.

Sure enough, there was a hole in the ceiling. It was too small for Sabra to squeeze through, but the cave to her left had one that was larger. Motioning for Serkan to stay down, she snatched up as many rocks as she could hold and dumped them into her bag. Then she gathered her skirts and began climbing the sandstone walls, using natural pocks in the wall as footholds and praying its rough texture would keep her from slipping.

She made it to the top, albeit a bit winded from all the extra weight. A few more openings allowed her to look down at the caves below her, and she was even able to see outside. Just as she'd hoped, the guards had dismounted from their horses and were running up to the entrance of the cave she and Serkan had entered first. She pulled the stones from her bag, wishing she'd chosen some that were slightly bigger. But these would have to do.

She readied herself and waited.

They were more hesitant than she'd hoped, staying to the edge of the first cave after entering. For a moment, she was afraid they might not go all the way in at all, but she was rewarded for her patience when one called to the other from across the cave to look at her and Serkan's footprints. As the guards did so, they came frighteningly close to the corner where Serkan was hidden. She could see him shivering on the other side of the stone divide that served as a wall.

Just when they were about to enter his cave, they moved close enough. She pulled her arm back, just as Demir had taught her, and beamed the rock at the closest guard's head. He let out a cry, but she hit him again before he could turn around. The other whirled around and was hit in the nose for his efforts, blood gushing down the front of his uniform.

"Serkan! The horses!" she shouted. The first guard was slumped on the ground by this time. The second immediately started looking for another entrance to the higher caves.

And within seconds, he'd found it. He ignored Serkan, as Serkan streaked out of the cave. Instead, he found Sabra's opening in the cave ceiling and began to pull himself up. Sabra's breath caught in her throat as she realized she was trapped. She looked around wildly. The darker caves that led deeper into the mountain would be a last resort, as one could get hopelessly lost in them. But no. There was another shaft of light farther down.

"Princess!"

Sabra turned to see the guard gaping at her. He must not have recognized her until now, she realized with a sinking heart. And now the three days Demir had bought her would be worthless.

She turned and sprinted toward the shaft of light. Sabra tried to think as she ran. If these guards didn't recognize her before this, that meant that she truly had gotten out of the city undetected. Unfortunately, now they would not only know that she was missing, but what road she was following.

They wouldn't be able to tell the others for a while, though, if she and Serkan got their horses first.

When she reached the next cave opening, she rejoiced to see that Serkan was already standing by the horses, and she praised the Maker silently for making him a clever boy. She stuck her legs out the cave entrance, preparing herself to jump, when fingers wrapped around her wrist, pain radiating up her arm.

The guard yanked her back inside. Sabra knew he was going to drag her back away from the hole, and if she didn't escape now, she wasn't going to. So she turned her feet so that they hooked onto the edges of the opening. Then she gritted her teeth, and with a painful yank, she threw her weight back toward the hole. Her landing was awkward, and she turned her left ankle when she hit the ground. But her escape was successful. The man let out a yell as he raced back to the larger hole to climb down again.

"Serkan! I'm throwing you on a horse!" she yelled as she limped toward the horses and the boy.

"I've never ridden before!" he cried as she half ran, half slid down the rocky slope. Her ankle screamed with pain, but she didn't dare stop. She could hear the *thump* of the guard's feet as he hit the inside of the cave.

"You'll learn today!" Sabra grabbed the boy by the waist, and with a strength she didn't know she possessed, tossed him into the saddle. The horse snorted in protest, but Sabra didn't have time for protests of any kind. With her good leg, she climbed up on a boulder then threw her leg over the other horse. "Hang on!" she shouted, grabbing the reins of both her horse and Serkan's. Then she clicked and squeezed her legs. The guard was nearly upon them when both horses shot off toward the road.

When Sabra dared a glance behind her, she let out a laugh of surprise. The second guard was still lying on the cave floor, and the first was just standing there, watching.

"Are we safe?" Serkan called, his voice breaking as he clung to the horse's reins. Only then did Sabra realize the danger of what she'd done. Throwing a boy who had never ridden on a horse and then dragging that horse across the desert in a full gallop could have ended badly. But there was nothing to be done about it, as being taken captive by the guards would have been an even less desirable outcome. So, when they were nearly out of sight of the guards, Sabra slowed the horses to a walk, thankful again that these horses were royal and well-trained.

"I'm sorry about that," Sabra said, trying to catch her breath as she watched Serkan's hands tremble. "We had to get away from them, or they would have dragged us back to the city." She paused. "Speaking of which, I'm very curious as to how you escaped."

His face, which had begun to regain its color, paled again.

"Especially," she continued, "as the guards found me only minutes after you showed up."

He looked down at the saddle he was sitting on. "I heard your cousin and your mom talking about where you would get out. So figured I'd just meet you there. I couldn't use your secret tunnel, though, so I slipped out using the main road and figured I'd find you if I looked long enough."

Sabra stared at him. "Child, you're insane." What were the

chances he'd not only gotten out but that he'd actually found her? That tunnel could have led anywhere.

Apparently, when this whole Mahzar nonsense was over, she would also have to better seal the palace doors and windows. Who knew what information could have been lost with eavesdroppers such as Serkan?

He shrugged. "A trader was leaving to go to his home country, so the Justines were letting him out. I snuck onto his cart and hid under a blanket." He twisted his lips. "I guess I didn't hide well enough."

"And they probably scared that poor trader out of his wits, accusing him of sneaking children out of the city." Sabra frowned at him. "I'm just not sure what I'm going to do with you. Why did you come anyway? What I'm doing is dangerous."

"I wanted to go with you," he mumbled, glaring at the back of the horse's head. "You always know what you're doing. And sitting around in the palace made me bored."

Sabra stared at the boy. She had come up with many theories by now, theories that usually had to do with foolish hopes for adventure and fun.

But then again, Serkan was an orphan. Sabra had felt the world on her shoulders these last few days. Her father was gone, and her kingdom was in peril. She, however, had had every adviser and resource possible at her beck and call up until this afternoon, not to mention her cousin and mother.

Serkan had none of that. Everything he'd owned was his at the mercy of those around him. Irritating as his rashness could be, Sabra supposed she couldn't blame the boy. As a servant, his treatment of her was nothing less than insubordinate. As a boy, though...

He just wanted an anchor of his own. And for some reason, he had decided she was his.

"Well, I can't send you home like this, can I?" she gave him a wry smile.

His brown eyes widened. "You mean I can come with you?"

Sabra closed her eyes and took a deep breath. "On one condition."

"Oh?" He frowned. "What's that?"

"You have to do exactly as I say. No more of your foolish antics. No pranks or jokes, or we'll both die. I'm going to keep us alive, and you're going to help me in any way I need. Do you understand?"

He scoffed. "Who made you queen of the road?"

She laughed. "My cousin said that if I was going to travel with him, he wasn't going to be towing around some useless girl who was scared of her own shadow."

"What does that mean?"

"It means I was taught how to survive. But only if you don't go pulling any more stunts like what you just did. Understand?"

He scowled, but with a glance back at the city, which was now growing distant, he nodded. "Very well."

"You sound incredibly convincing." She chuckled. "Well, if we're going to make this journey on horseback, it's going to be much faster. Unfortunately, you're not a horseman."

"What does that mean?" he asked suspiciously.

She grinned. "We might as well get you started now."

CHAPTER 17

HOPE

By the time they stopped for the night, Sabra was unexpectedly pleased. Not only had they escaped the guards, but now they had horses and the basic emergency supplies that came with them. The Justines would make their way back to the city, but walking rather than riding should slow them some. To be on the safe side, though, Sabra refused to approach the road. Instead, she kept them close to the plateaus, traveling parallel, weaving the horses in and out of clumps of trees and looking for a place to sleep.

The sun was nearly down, and they'd ridden at least an hour by the time she was satisfied. Not that she wanted to stop. Now that the guards knew she was missing, they would be all over the place in no time. But Serkan wasn't an experienced rider, and his legs hurt so badly that tears were streaming down his face as he begged to stop. They wouldn't be able to go on like this. Not tonight, at least. So Sabra found the smallest, darkest cave she could and let Serkan rest there on a blanket she found in one of the horse packs. Then she tended to the horses at a nearby stream.

"I wish I could give you something better," she said, rubbing the horses down, "but this will have to do for now."

As they were settling down to see what kind of food was in the packs they'd taken from the horses, a strange sound broke the shuffling quiet of the moment. Sabra's hand went to the knife she'd found in the pack, but the second time the sound occurred, she knew exactly what it was.

"Serkan!" she cried as his boy's pack began to move. "You didn't!"

"Did what?"

Before Sabra could answer, a clear *mreow* sounded from inside the bag, and Sabra stared at it as a pink, skinny body wriggled its way out.

"You brought Thing?" She turned to glare at Serkan.

Serkan, however, was unrepentant. He just shrugged. "He wanted to come. He would have missed you!"

"This cat hasn't missed a human a day in his life." Sabra grunted as she lifted the animal all the way out of the sack and into her lap.

This boy was going to be the death of her.

After feeding the cat scraps from their supper, Sabra put him back in one of the big sacks. For a cat, he was oddly content with being shoved in small places. Which was good, because over the next few days, he would have no choice.

She lit only the smallest of fires to warm some of the fist-sized river stones she'd gathered. Then she put out the fire and slipped the stones underneath Serkan's blanket at his feet. Tonight would be chilly. For though it was early summer, the temperature could fall sharply once the sun went down. Hopefully, it wouldn't be too cold for the horses, but the only sort of stable she could find was to put them in the cave next to the one she and Serkan were sleeping in, as the caves were rather small.

Serkan, exhausted for possibly the first time in his life, fell asleep without protest. A beam of moonlight slipped silently into the cave's opening, revealing his soft, sleeping features in a way Sabra had never seen them before. Probably because he was always up to such mischief, a sly smirk on his ornery little piqued face more often than not. But here, all huddled up under his blanket from the cold, he looked very young.

He looked alone.

She reached out and smoothed his dark, rebellious curls once before moving to set up her own bedding. Despite her father's assurances that she was meant to be queen, it was rather chilling to consider how close she had been to being just as alone in the world as this little boy.

"Where'd you learn to do that?"

Sabra froze before looking back down again. "I thought you were asleep."

"I am mostly." He yawned and turned slightly. "But where'd you learn to heat the stones and all that?"

"I told you, my cousin said if he was going to take me gallivanting all over the countryside, he wasn't about to have some silly, useless child on his hands. He taught me to make a fire, find water, and to treat basic wounds." She sighed. He'd taught her the staff, too. But what good was all of that when a dragon was about to destroy everything she loved? What good were etiquette lessons, geography, mathematics, and civics when none of these things would stop the enemy?

"Will you sing to me?" he mumbled.

Sabra turned to look at him. "What?"

"Sing to me. You've got a nice song voice."

She sat up on her elbows. "And how do you know that?"

He grinned sleepily. "I've heard you. In your room when you think no one's listening."

"Serkan, how often do you sneak into my room?"

"Not usually." He rolled over again. "Just the roof. You keep your window open a lot."

Sabra rolled her eyes.

"But will you?" he asked again, quietly. "Sing for me?"

"I probably shouldn't, since we're trying to hide." She sighed. "But very well. Just a little. And very quietly, mind you."

"Good." His words began to slur. "My mum used to sing to me. Before she died."

Sabra's heart squeezed a little, but she cleared her throat and very quietly began to sing a lullaby her mother used to sing to her.

As promised, Serkan drifted right to sleep, a contented smile on his face. Sabra wished for that kind of peace. She should feel grateful. She had shelter, provisions, horses, and at the moment, was far from her captors. And yet, there was an emptiness inside.

Never had she felt George's absence more sharply. Which was strange, as she'd only seen him a few days every year. Maybe, though, part of her longing was for steadfastness. If George was anything, he was steadfast. He'd been steady when they were children, and as they'd grown, more so every year. Of course, Sabra didn't have a lifetime witness of him to prove his behavior true all the time. But everything in his manner and language the last time they'd spoken had been exemplary. No one was perfect. Sabra knew better than to expect that. And yet...

At this point in time, George was the only hope she had.

CHAPTER 18
HIDE

Sabra awakened several times that night, expecting to hear the clink of armor or the beating of scaled wings. But each time she opened her eyes, the world was still, bathed in the gentle glow of white moonlight, the only sounds Serkan's steady breathing and insects singing softly through the night. The next morning, however, didn't start out with as much promise.

"Blasted, stupid—" Sabra began.

"What is it?" Serkan whined, rubbing his head with a scowl on his face.

Sabra mashed her lips shut and swallowed the colorful word she'd been about to utter.

"The horses are gone. They must have headed home while we were sleeping." Served her right for allowing herself to slip into a deep slumber in the dark, early hours before dawn. She looked at Serkan with a grimace. "We're going to have to walk."

"Oh!" He beamed. "My backside likes that."

She gave him a wry grin. "It might not when your feet are about to fall off, and Thing insists on riding your shoulders. Come on, let's get packed up and fill the waterskins. We've got a long day ahead of us."

"How long until we get there?" he asked, as they went down to the brook.

"Well, if we'd had the horses, we would have been there midday. But since we're walking, just pray we don't have to sleep outside again tonight."

His jaw dropped. "It'll take *that* long?"

Sabra laughed. "What did you expect when you chased me out into the desert?"

"I don't know," he grumbled. "Something different, I guess. I've never been to another city. How was I supposed to know how far away they were?"

Sabra rumpled his hair. "Well, you'll learn now, I suppose. Let's pack up and move out."

An hour later, Sabra had destroyed all evidence of them ever being at the cave, and they were making their way along the plateaus, darting between each copse of trees in an effort not to be seen easily from above. Sabra had no idea whether or not Mahzar would come this way looking for her in his dragon form, but she decided it was better not to take a chance if she could help it.

"So who is this man we're meeting?" Serkan asked.

"A friend of mine. We first met when I used to accompany my cousin to the trade meetings before they were moved to Segzein."

Serkan gave her an ornery grin. "It's not the one you were kissing in the square, is it?"

"I've never kissed anyone." Sabra slapped him playfully on the arm. "So don't go telling people I did. You truly are the worst gossip in the palace, you know that?"

"But is it him?" Serkan pressed.

She sighed. "He is the friend I *spoke* with that day, yes."

"And do you love him?"

Sabra stopped short, then scowled at the little boy. "No, I am *not* in love with him. But what the princess does and doesn't do with her emotions is none of your business."

"Well, the princess doesn't usually sing servants to sleep either." He raised his eyebrows and grinned. "Or kiss them goodnight on the forehead. But we've sailed right past that, haven't we?"

Sabra watched him in shock as he cackled and ran ahead.

Maybe the Maker was trying to teach her patience. Her mother *was* always going on about it not being her strongest point.

"So why are we going to find this guy?" he called over his shoulder.

Sabra squinted at the distant road in the early morning sun. Yes, they were still going parallel. "Because I think he can help us."

"Can he kill a dragon?" Serkan asked skeptically.

She rolled her eyes. "Not that kind of help. I'm looking for help finding out what we need to defeat the Justines. There are lots of other people in the world who have power from the Maker. Good power. Not dark power like the Justines."

Serkan scrunched up his face. "How do you know their power is dark?"

"I was curious. So I accused Mahzar of using the dark arts, and he all but admitted that that's exactly what he's doing."

"Why do you think this friend can help you find that?"

Sabra smiled. "You have a lot of questions for so early in the morning."

"Oh, I have questions all the time. Cook says if she had a piece of bread for every question I ask, she'd feed everyone in the kingdom." He beamed as though this were a great accomplishment. "So why do you think he can help?"

She took a deep breath. "Because he's apprenticed to a scholar. With us being neighboring kingdoms, I'm hoping they'll have information that will help us figure out what the Justines' weakness is."

Serkan frowned for a moment. "How do you know they have a weakness?"

"Everyone has a weakness."

"How do you know that?"

And so the morning continued. Serkan peppered Sabra with questions, which she just barely managed to answer before he hit her with more. Then, when she put an end to the questions, Serkan chattered on about everything and nothing as they made their way across the desert. Sabra, however, was lost in her thoughts and heard little of it.

Serkan's question rolled around in her head.

How *did* she feel about George?

It was a silly question, really. Did her feelings truly matter? Because if all went according to plan, she would be back on her throne and ready to choose a husband again when this was all over. Then she would be in the same place she started. And what did she really know of him? He was funny and thoughtful and a hard worker, to be sure. At least, he'd been so as an adolescent, and still more from what she'd seen of him during his one visit. But she didn't really know him. Not really.

There could be some pretty little maiden he saw every day in the town square who smiled at him whenever they passed. Maybe she brought him lunch or pastries from her family's shop. And why shouldn't she? He was kind and responsible and intelligent, and, well...probably better looking than was good for him, with a chest like armor and—

"When are we going to eat again? I'm hungry."

Sabra shook her head as she fished a biscuit out of the pack and handed it to Serkan. None of that really mattered. What counted was that she trusted George. For better or worse, she'd given her trust to a man she couldn't have. And in doing so, had inadvertently placed the fate of her people in his hands.

"I see it, Sabra! I see the city!" Serkan's excited whoops pulled Sabra from her reverie. She'd almost corrected him on his inappropriate address, more for his sake than hers, when she, too, saw the city. The sun would be setting in under an hour, and both their feet hurt, but Sabra's heart leaped into her throat and made it impossible to respond. This was it. She was going to save her people.

Also, an annoying voice in her head whispered, she was going to see George.

She distracted herself by lecturing Serkan on how they needed to conduct themselves inside the city.

"We want to draw as little attention to ourselves as possible," she said as she studied the distant gate. "Once we're within the city gates, Mahzar will no longer have unopposed jurisdiction. But we still don't want to share identities upon the chance he sends emissaries to ask about us. Better if no one knows who we are at all."

"Except your beau." Serkan snickered.

"And that's another thing. We're only friends. So you will be in trouble like you've never known if you make things awkward by mentioning anything about my *love life* while he's present. Or rather," she paused, "at all. Just don't speak about it from this moment on."

"You sure enjoy spoiling fun, don't you?"

"I'm more concerned with saving our kingdom from a dragon bordering on insanity than anything else at the moment." She looked around again. Still no pursuers. Yet.

"Do you think they're still looking for us?" he asked in a quieter voice.

"I'm sure they are. But the Maker has kept us safe thus far, so rather than question that, I'm just going to get inside those gates as soon as possible. We'll worry about the rest later."

"How are we going to find him?" Serkan asked.

"I'm not sure. I do have the location he told me to send messages to, but I'm not sure where that is. I suppose I'll have to ask someone."

He gave her a look. "You're not going to hide very well in *that* dress."

Sabra looked down at her dress and sighed. Unfortunately, he was right. The fine cloth was now wrinkled and covered in dirt from walking and sleeping in it, but the bright blue with its fine sheen was far above what any common woman would wear. And the material wasn't the only detail that would call attention to Sabra's station. The outfit itself was one of those specifically sewn so she could prac- tice the staff with her cousin, which meant that the skirt was split with two loose pantaloons sticking out from underneath. Nothing a proper woman would be wearing in public, particularly made of such ostentatious cloth.

But there was nothing to be done for it. The faster they could find George, the faster she would be out of the public eye.

An invisible burden slid from her shoulders as they passed through the city gates. They'd made it. For some reason, the Maker had seen fit to get them through. Even better, everyone was so busy that few took notice of them as they moved quickly past the city guard and into the throng. Men and women and children loaded up their goods from their market stalls onto their animals or carts, the time for trading finished for the day. Sabra searched for George's grandfather's stall, but in the cheerful chaos of the evening, she couldn't find it. Then she heard a shout.

Three riders with white cloaks were barreling through the crowd, the gate guards in fast pursuit. People screamed and leaped out of their way as they rode straight at Sabra.

Sabra shoved Serkan behind a stall, which hadn't yet been cleared, and ran in the other direction. Perhaps he would be able to escape as they chased her.

Unfortunately, it was only seconds before Sabra was surrounded on all sides by the three riders. She tried several times to dart out of the circle they made around her, but the horses were too well-trained to let her through. She nearly let out her own scream of anger. They hadn't given up their search after all. They'd simply waited for her to appear. And she'd walked right into their trap.

"Princess." One guard jumped off his horse and bowed his head. "The dragon bids you come home. It needn't be this way."

"Tell me that if he wants me, he can come get me himself," she snapped, still turning in search of a way out.

"Unfortunately, he was obligated to remain at home. But if you come with us now, you can join him." One of the guards took Sabra's arm. His grip was so strong it hurt.

"There she is!" Serkan's young voice pierced the air. "They're going to take my sister! Please save her! Save her from the marauders!" Tears ran down his face. Though when Sabra stared at him, he had the audacity to wink.

A man in fine clothes broke through the crowd. He had dark skin and a beard that reached all the way down his chest, and he looked utterly annoyed. "What's going on here?" His gaze narrowed at the Justines. "Are you from Segzein?"

"We are," answered the guard that Sabra guessed to be the group's leader. "And we've come for a prisoner that's escaped."

"She's not their prisoner!" Serkan sobbed. "She's my sister, and we live here!"

"Your law says," the guard continued, "that we're allowed to take our own prisoners from within your borders. And our law allows the same."

"Is there anyone here who can attest to their citizenship?" The man with the beard looked around as he asked.

"Please! Don't let them take me!" Sabra used their distraction to yank her arm free. She pulled it free, but her elbow screamed in protest. She cradled her arm, looking about her, begging the onlookers to show some sort of pity and claim her. Inside, her own pleas made her cringe. She hated looking weak, but this wasn't about her. To help her people, she could *not* let them drag her back to the palace. So she tried harder. "They killed my father!"

The tears this time were not so hard to muster.

The villagers looked at one another with wide eyes, but no one made a move toward her. The Justinian guards began to relax slightly as the man with the beard began to shake his head.

"Then I'm afraid I'll—"

"She's with me."

CHAPTER 19

GEORGE

Sabra's heart nearly stopped. And when it picked up again, it was going twice its usual rate. George had appeared at the edge of the crowd, like some sort of summoned sorcerer from ancient times. Somehow, even in the few weeks since their last meeting, she'd forgotten just how deep his voice was. And the breadth of his chest, as well as the way his jaw flexed when he was upset. He began to make his way toward them, the crowd parting for him as he went.

"George," the bearded man called. "You know this woman?"

"I do." When he reached the circle of guards, Sabra couldn't help noting with some pride that he towered over everyone else. "She's my intended."

Sabra tried not to let loose the little ripple of pleasure as he wrapped an arm around her waist and pulled her close to him.

It's not real. It's not real. It's not real, she chanted to herself silently. It was all for show, of course. It must be. But it sent her heart careening sideways.

The bearded man continued to frown. "But how come no one else knows her then?"

"She lives farther out," George gestured vaguely to the west. "I met her at a trade talk when we were much younger." His eyes

201

narrowed at the guards, who were still on their horses. "Which means *they* have no jurisdiction here."

Oh, he was good. Telling the truth...mostly, *and* making it sound completely believable without actually revealing anything.

The bearded man shrugged and turned back to the Justinian guards. "Well, you've heard the man. You have no right to be here."

"Sir," one of the guards said, "she is a wanted criminal—"

"You'll have to go through your emissaries." The bearded man held his hands up. "But I'm afraid we'll have to escort you out from here."

Sabra held her breath as the leader of the trio locked gazes with her once more. Out of the corner of her eye, she saw George's hand on the hilt of the sword she only now realized he was wearing.

After a long baleful glare, however, the guard finally broke eye contact and turned to his companions. "We'll notify him that she's here. At least he'll know where to look." The other guards seemed to assent to this, and they turned their horses and headed back out the gate.

"Come with me," George said in a near whisper as he let go of her waist. "Quickly."

Sabra looked around and was relieved to find Serkan at her other elbow. She mourned the loss of George's arm around her waist but was nearly as pleased when he intertwined his fingers with hers.

"Can you carry your bags a bit farther?" he asked softly. "I would take them for you, but I want quick access to my sword."

Sabra nodded, so he began their trek by leading them east.

Sabra had only ever been to the main market square and the streets in its immediate vicinity. She hadn't expected such a labyrinth of houses, stalls, businesses, and random patches of large gardens that seemed placed in no particular order. Every few streets, there was a larger building, houses of worship, a few mansions, and such. As they went farther out, Sabra began to realize just how hard it would have been to find George unaided. But with his hand in hers, she couldn't even bring herself to really stop and imagine what a difficulty that would have been.

They reached the edge of the city after about half an hour of walking. Several fields, some broken and others fallow, stretched before them. George led them through the fields, stepping on the flat stones that had been laid to separate the plots of land.

When they finally made their way into a little ravine, about ten minutes past the edges of the city, he stopped just beside a little bridge and turned to face her. Then he took her arms in his hands and looked her up and down.

"Are you truly well?" he asked. His gray eyes nearly glinted silver as he gently lifted her arms and examined them. He frowned when he discovered the bruises left by the Justinian guards back in the square.

"I'm fine," Sabra said as calmly as her thundering heart would allow. She did her best to smile without trembling. "Just a little tired."

George's eyes lingered on her a moment more before turning to Serkan. "And you?"

"I might die of hunger," Serkan huffed.

The corner of George's mouth quirked up. "That we can fix." Then any sign of humor disappeared as he glanced over her shoulder. "Come on. Let's keep going before they decide to come sniffing around."

Much to Sabra's disappointment, he didn't take her hand again. Not, of course, that she could expect him to. As far as he knew, she was already betrothed to someone else. Sabra motioned for Serkan to follow and then followed George over the little footbridge.

"I'm sorry for coming to you like this," she said, doing her best to direct her thoughts appropriately. "I didn't know where else to go."

"Tell me what happened when we get inside," he said. "Talking will be safer there."

Sabra nodded and followed in silence. They continued that way, darting in and out of trees along the stream as they followed some invisible path until they crested the last low rise. He led them up to the highest point just as the sun fell behind the nearest hill. Built into the side of the hill was a sprawling house, like an ornament chiseled directly into the rock.

"It's lovely!" Sabra exclaimed, then remembered with regret to lower her voice. "And much larger than I expected," she said more softly. Large stone bricks the length of her forearm and the color of sand were stacked expertly into smooth, flat walls. Sconces were lit outside with tiny flames that danced, throwing sparkles and shadows across the smooth walls. The square windows were surprisingly many in number, and they all looked as though they held real glass.

"Come," he said, holding his hand out once more, and she was all too glad to accept. "We'll go in the back way this time. Just so you can get settled first." He pulled her around the side of the house to a cave with a ceiling that was so low even Serkan had to hunch slightly. George moved several fist-sized stones and then took a larger rock, nearly the size of Thing, and moved it, revealing a dark hole that went down.

"Wait here," he said, turning and lowering himself into the hold. A moment later, a dim light shone from below. "Come on down," he called.

"You go first," Sabra whispered to Serkan, "And don't touch anything."

"I know that." He scowled. "I'm not a baby."

"Well, sometimes, you could fool me." Sabra gave him a light poke. "Now down you go."

He made a face at her but did as he was told.

Sabra followed. The opening looked dark at first. But once she lowered her legs inside, she found steps. Carefully, she turned around until she could continue the descent facing forward. At the bottom, she and Serkan found themselves in a large room with smooth clay walls and a surprisingly even stone floor. A small fire was lit in the hearth on their left, and to their right sat a small bed with several knitted blankets folded at its foot, a rectangular table, and a small cupboard on the wall. A waist-high pile of wood pieces was stacked beside the hearth with six corked jugs on its other side.

"What is this place?" Sabra asked.

George went back up the steps, and his head and shoulders disappeared. He grunted slightly before reappearing again. Sabra could only guess he was moving the stone back into place.

"When my grandparents moved here, they didn't have enough money to buy a home or the materials to make one. So they created a simple home for themselves in this cave. Once my grandfather went to work smithing in the city, they were able to build the larger home you saw out from the hillside, adding a little at a time." He dusted his hands off. "We do keep this entrance hidden, though. My grandparents call it a safeguard of some kind." He rolled his eyes.

"And how will they feel about two complete strangers coming into their sanctum?" Sabra asked.

George laughed. "Well, we'll find out, won't we?" Then his eyes rested on her once again, and she could feel the blush rising to her cheeks.

"I never got to thank you for helping us," she said quickly, turning to inspect the bed. Then she laughed a little. "You don't even know what we're running from. Your grandparents might not be thrilled to know they have two fugitives on their hands."

"There's food in here!" Serkan cried, having opened the cupboard.

"Help yourself," George said, keeping his eyes on Sabra. "What happened?" he asked more gently.

Sabra took a deep breath and ran her hand down her now messy braid. "It's a long story." Then she looked back at him. "I'm actually rather curious as to how you happened to wander up at the exact right time."

"I visit the market every evening to help my grandfather pack up his stall. But that's not what I want to talk about right now." His brow furrowed. "The tenor of your last letter concerned me. You sounded frightened."

Sabra groaned. "I didn't mean to. I was just so focused on getting the information I needed that I suppose it came out that way."

He pulled a stool out from under the table and motioned to the bed. "Sit and tell me."

And so Sabra told him about her research that she'd gathered over the years. "When you appeared that day and asked all the same questions I'd been pondering for years, I knew it wasn't just a problem with me." She took a deep breath. "So I kept looking."

George listened quietly as her story unfolded. And as the words spilled out, Sabra felt the tightness in her chest begin to loosen, the same way her muscles relaxed after climbing out of some oppressive formal gown and into her nightclothes. His eyes narrowed when she told him of Mahzar's demands, and his jaw tightened when she related the basniins' vote to force her into marriage, but to his credit, he didn't interrupt.

Of course, he had always been a good listener. It was one of the things Sabra had always loved about him. No matter how many things he wanted to tell her at their yearly meetings, he always let her go first.

"I'm sorry," she said, looking at her hands, "for thrusting problems into your life. My goal wasn't to get you caught up in international unrest."

He pinched the bridge of his nose and closed his eyes. "First of all, I don't care how long we've been apart. The fact that you feel the need to apologize for asking me for help is by far the most ridiculous thing you've ever said to me." He opened his eyes. "And you've said some doozies."

Sabra rolled her eyes, but she couldn't help the smile that touched the corners of her mouth without her permission.

But then his humor died, and to her surprise, he leaned toward her, his elbows on his knees. Even in the relative dimness of the room with only the fireplace to provide light, Sabra's breath caught. He was so familiar, and yet, such a stranger at the same time. How much of that contradiction was true inside as well?

After all, this was his grandparents' house. And though she had met his grandparents several times at the marketplace, there was a good chance they would want nothing to do with her once they knew who she was and what she was running from. She wouldn't if she were them. And if he did put his grandparents first, which he owed them to do, of course, where would she stay? How would she feed Serkan?

"Sabra."

And just like that, the way he said her name, like a warm breeze rustling the trees, she was brought back to *him*.

"When I said that I wanted to help you, I meant it. Every word."

She looked at the ground to avoid staring into the steel-gray depths of his eyes. If she looked too hard, he might see right through her. And not even she was ready for that. Not now, when everything else was falling apart.

"You might be ready to rescind that invitation in an hour or so." She nodded with a smile at Serkan's sleeping form on the floor. After eating most of the food in the cupboard, he'd managed to steal one of the blankets from the bed and had fallen asleep in the corner.

"I meant to ask you," he laughed, his tone lighter again, "when did you get a little brother?" His eyes widened and his smile disappeared as he jumped to his feet, nearly stumbling in his haste. "And what in the world is that monstrosity?"

Sabra turned to see what he was looking at and saw that Thing had crawled out of Serkan's sack and was now curled up on top of the boy.

"He's not a monstrosity!" She went to the cat and picked him up. Thing purred as she held him close and stroked his head. "This is my cat, Thing."

"That is not a cat. But it is aptly named." George stared at the cat, a look of mild horror on his face.

Sabra stuck her tongue out. "My father got Thing for me when a traveling animal caravan came through the city several years ago." She stroked Thing's bare, wrinkled skin affectionately.

"Let me guess." George rolled his eyes. "It was love at first sight."

Sabra gave him a wicked grin. "Actually, I wanted a tiger. Thing was our compromise."

George shook his head and held his held hands up. "While that's more disturbing than I can express, I'm still curious about the little brother."

It was Sabra's turn to roll her eyes. "I didn't inherit a little brother. He's actually a palace servant."

"And you *chose* him to accompany you on this assignment?"

"Not at all. This little reprobate overheard that my cousin was sending me away in secret, and he decided to follow. Unfortunately, he's the one who led the guards to me before they even knew I was missing."

"You don't think he's working for them, do you?" George looked back at Serkan with a new frown.

But Sabra just shook her head. "I've known Serkan for too long. Cook found him next to naked and fighting mad, trying to steal from a nearby market when he was very small. She took him in, and the palace as a whole has been trying to reform him since. He changes duties the way a servant changes bathwater. And while he might be a pain in the backside, he's loyal as they come. Besides," she said, leaning down and tucking the blanket better around the boy, "if it hadn't been for my parents finding and taking pity on me, I would have been just like him."

"It seems like he's not too alone."

Sabra looked up to see George looking at her again with an expression she couldn't quite decipher. So she looked back down at Serkan.

"What will you tell your grandparents?" She chuckled. "I'm supposing you're not planning on keeping us down here unbeknownst to them forever."

"If you're hungry, we'll go up, and you can meet them right now."

"Starving."

"Good." He stood and went to the far wall. Sabra watched in amazement as he pulled on one of the large bricks. With that brick came the whole section of bricks.

"A trap door!" Sabra exclaimed. It swung open, revealing tiled stairs on the other side of a now gaping hole. Then he gestured for

Sabra to walk through. "We'll leave this open for him so he can find us when he wakes up."

Sabra nodded and began to walk through. But before she started up the stairs, she felt his hand on her arm again.

"She'll be delighted to see that I've brought home a young woman," he said, his own face looking a bit red. "But let me start the conversation."

"You don't think they'll object, do you?"

He paused. "I'm not sure what they'll do. But there's a reason, unbeknownst to me, that we live all the way out here in a house with secret rooms." He shrugged. "We might as well be prepared for a little suspicion on their part."

Sabra nodded her assent and waited for him to walk up the stairs first. But as she trailed him into the main house, she was sincerely doubting she would ever be truly prepared ever again.

CHAPTER 20
BY BIRTH

The bedrooms are that way," George pointed left down the hall once they reached the top of the stairs. "And on the other side of the house, Grandfather keeps his workshop in one of the larger rooms that was built just for weapons making." They rounded a corner to the right.

"George? Is that you?"

"Are you in the kitchen?" he called back.

"Yes. Who are you talking to?"

Sabra turned another corner and found herself face-to-face with a handsome woman with graying golden hair and a bowl of dough in her hands. Despite being at least in her sixth decade, she looked strong with a straight back and lean, muscled shoulders. She went to the other side of the table now and pulled teacups down from the wall, where they hung on pegs.

"Grandmother," George called as he and Sabra came into a warm, spacious kitchen, "do you remember Sabra?"

"I'm so sorry! I wish I did," the woman said, giving a little laugh. She shoved her bowl of dough to the middle of the table and put the teacups down. "Forgive my old memory. Where did we meet last?"

"Hello," Sabra said softly, suddenly feeling shy. She also doubted, from looking at the woman's well-toned arms, that anything about this woman was old, much less her memory. "I used to come with my cousin to the trade talks. Until they moved to Segzein seven years ago, that is."

"Sabra," George said, "this is my grandmother, Maria."

"Now I remember you," Maria said with a laugh. "George never got his chores done so quickly as on those days he knew the trade talks were taking place."

"She's here with her little brother on some unexpected business," George said, seating himself on a stool at the table. "I thought they might stay with us." He nodded at the hall in the direction from which they'd come. "Her little brother is already sleeping because he was so tired when we got here. I let her get him settled first."

"Of course!" Then his grandmother paused her mixing to look up at Sabra again. "You're not here with your cousin?"

"Not exactly." Sabra sat on George's other side. "The journey was a bit of a surprise."

"Well, you can put them up in the room on the south end." Maria poured them each a cup of tea. Then she went back to the dough and began to knead it. "I just cleaned the blankets in that room this morning." She grinned at Sabra. "We have an extra room on the other side of the house that we sometimes use to house the men my husband hires to harvest the orchard on the other side of the property. But we won't have them again until next fall."

"Actually..." George paused, his brows furrowing slightly. "I put them down in one of the lower rooms."

Maria stopped kneading and looked directly at George. Her eyes were the same steel-gray as his, and Sabra got the feeling they could cut just as well as any sword. "Why did you do that?"

He grimaced. "They had a run-in with some foreign guards in the market today."

Maria smiled at Sabra a little again, but the easy flow of her movements was gone now. Instead, she moved like a cat ready to pounce.

"Where are you from again?" Maria asked lightly.

Sabra hesitated. And yet, she might as well tell her the truth.

These people were taking her in. She owed them an explanation.

"I'm from Segzein," she said, picking up the cup of tea Maria had pushed in front of her. Only as she finished uttering the words did she realize George was subtly shaking his head, his eyes wide.

But the damage, whatever it was, was done, it seemed. Because Maria had frozen in place. "What clan are you from?" she asked faintly.

Sabra glanced at George, but he was grimacing. "Um...The Capitans?" It came out like a question, rather than a statement.

Maria turned to George slowly. The sweet, cheerful woman she'd just met was gone. "You told me she was from one of the outer farms," she said, her voice smooth and hard, like a cold river stone.

"I said she was from farther out, and that her cousin brought her to the trade talks," he said, holding up his hands. "And that much is true."

Apparently, the bearded man wasn't the first person to have heard this story.

But Maria whirled around to face Sabra again, her gray eyes burning. "What is your position in your clan?"

Sabra blinked at her. How did this woman know so much about her people and their culture?

The woman's eyes somehow grew colder. "I asked—"

"I'm the crown princess."

George's grandmother dropped her cup.

The crash of clay against the stone floor brought a man running into the kitchen from the second hall.

"Are you all right?" he asked his wife. Then he stopped and looked around. "Well, hello," he said, turning to George. "Want to introduce your friend?"

"Tell your grandfather what you've done." Maria turned the full power of her steel eyes onto George.

Sabra glanced back and forth between them, not sure what to do or say. At this point, she hadn't even asked for anything. Well, she'd meant to ask for help, but she hadn't even been able to present her case. George had given all his help freely. But perhaps his grandparents weren't as generous as he was. Or as trusting.

If they turned her out, where would she go?

"Grandfather," George said, cautiously, "do you remember little Sabra? The one who would come in during the trade deals and spend time with me once a year?"

His grandfather, a man who had always reminded Sabra of a muscled, bearded wolf, opened his eyes wide in surprise. "It's been a long time, Miss."

"Miss is the wrong title, Alner," Maria said quietly. "You'd do better to call her *Your Highness*."

Sabra felt her face pale as the smile disappeared from Alner's face.

"Highness?" he repeated softly.

Sabra looked nervously at George, who took a step closer to her.

"She needs help, Grandfather," he said. "That's why she came to me." He brought his hands to rest lightly on her shoulders, and in spite of herself, Sabra had to fight for concentration as the tips of his fingers sent little tingles through her sleeves to her skin.

"I think," his grandfather said, giving Maria a long look, "that we'd better sit down for this."

A few minutes later, they were all seated on stools around the table. The shards of the broken teacup had been cleared and disposed of, but Sabra got the feeling that cleaning up the mess she'd made wouldn't be nearly so neat.

"So." Alner, nodded at George. "How about you start at the beginning?"

Sabra looked at George. "Maybe I should go first."

Alner frowned slightly but nodded. So Sabra took a deep breath. Obviously, George's family had secrets. But she wasn't going to unlock any without giving up some of her own first.

"Although I have been raised as princess, I was not born to the king and queen. Not by blood, at least. I was found abandoned in the Capitan District when I was not even two years old. My parents—the king and queen—had decided to adopt an heir when they couldn't have children. So they went to the nearest children's home and chose to adopt me."

Sabra took a deep breath. "This never caused any trouble until it was time for my Inquest." She paused and gauged her audience. "Does this all make sense?" She had no idea how much they knew of her people and customs or how they even knew what they did already.

"It does." Sabra's grandfather nodded impatiently. "Go on."

George gave them a strange look. "I'm not sure I follow everything, but keep going."

So Sabra told them of Mahzar's objection and his failed Challenge and the ensuing chaos that had unfolded as the Justines asserted their authority.

"He killed my father in front of me." Sabra swallowed hard, willing the tears not to fall. She hadn't yet allowed herself even a full day of mourning since he was killed. And now was not a good time to start. "And when I refused to marry him, he and the other Justines locked down the city and bullied the basniins into taking a vote to force me into marriage."

"Wait," George said. "I'm confused. Why would they want you to marry this...Mahzar? So he could be king?"

"In Segzein," Maria said, keeping her eyes on Sabra, "basniins cannot marry one another. It's a way to keep the power in balance. If one basniin marries another, the one with more seniority or power gives up his place and becomes merely the spouse of the one with lesser power." She nodded at Sabra. "So if the princess were to marry the Justine basniin, he could retain his position, but she would lose hers."

Sabra nodded, praying they could see her sincerity. "I'm sorry if I've put you all in danger. I didn't mean to cause any trouble. I just..." She drew in a shaky breath. All the pain and terror she'd been repressing until now was trying to rush out like a flood. And yet, she shoved it all back down once more. "I didn't know where else to go," she whispered.

George took her hand beneath the table and squeezed it. Sabra squeezed back.

"How much did you know of what was going on?" Maria asked George.

"I hadn't seen her in seven years until a few weeks ago. She sent a letter that raised my concern, but I couldn't put the pieces together."

"My tea." Maria sat upright. "You bought it there, didn't you? Instead of getting it from a trader?"

George winced, probably realizing his slip about his secret visit to Segzein, but then he nodded. "I did. Master Gregory sent me to speak with a certain master learner. I ran into Sabra in the market while I was there."

"I wish you would have told us," Maria said as she poured herself another cup of tea, spilling it twice as she did.

George leaned forward. "I know you don't like the city, so I didn't want to worry you." He paused. "But why is that?"

His grandparents exchanged a troubled glance. "What do you know?" his grandmother finally asked.

George frowned at the table. "Nothing about your dislike of the place. I only began to learn more myself when Sabra asked me to look into the symbols—"

"What symbols?" Alner interrupted.

"They're old. I found them in a book," Sabra said. "I wish I had them here to show you, but they came from a picture. They encircled a hand holding a sword." She frowned down at her tea, as though it held the answers. "I can't read them. They're all foreign to me, probably ancient from their shapes. That's why I sent it to George. I knew he was with a scholar, so I hoped he might..." Sabra let her words trail off as Maria got up and left the table. Sabra looked back at Alner, but the old man just glared at the table.

"Did it look like this?" Maria returned, and she was holding out a familiar blue sash. At the bottom of the sash was an embroidered design that by now was all too familiar.

"These are the symbols!" George jumped up and grabbed the sash. "I've been looking all over Master Gregory's library for this!"

"Where did you get this?" Sabra asked, leaning closer to George to see the sash better. Of course, that meant leaning close enough to smell his intoxicating mixture of ash, sage, and something she couldn't name. Not that she minded at all.

"I have it," Maria said with a pained look, "because it's mine."

Sabra and George both looked up from the sash.

"But this." Sabra ran her hand over the white stitching in the sash. "I've seen one of these before," she said softly. Then she looked up. "It was given to me by a Blue Band in Segzein."

"That's because those people are *our* people." Maria pulled up her sleeve and revealed a familiar blue tattoo, a band of swirled blue ink that stretched all the way around her arm. Sabra hadn't realized before how intricate the detailing was.

"It's beautiful," Sabra whispered.

George looked like he might fall over. "I always thought those were something you and Grandfather received on your wedding day!"

She gave them a grim smile. "Oh, they were. All our people... Well," she grimaced, letting her sleeve fall again, "they *were* our people. Before they were clanless." Maria paused and looked at Alner.

"Just tell them," Alner said in a rough voice. "They might as well know now."

George sat up. "Tell me what?"

"We are from a clan called the Sentinels," Maria said, standing tall. "Our people had a long, proud history. One that dates back to the Fortiers in Destin."

"Wait." George shook his head. "I'm confused. How are we a part of these...Sentinels? And why haven't you told me all this before?" His words had a hard edge. "You always said we were from a city out west."

But Sabra was enthralled. Everything was falling into place.

"When you went to Segzein," his grandfather asked, "did you notice the spokes?"

"Of course," George said. "There were eight. One for each clan. Except, if I remember right, there are only seven clans?" He frowned.

"Seven." Alner rolled his eyes and snorted. "As though you can simply wish a people out of existence."

"Exactly," Maria said. "Because once there *were* eight."

"When the clans were originally united," Ahlner growled, "they were given their responsibilities by what gifts they brought to the others. The Sentinel...a man who eventually joined his family with the other clans, was a younger prince from the Fortier family, third in line for the throne. After his eldest brother was crowned, he chose to explore the realms, getting married and having a family along the way. By the time he reached the valley Segzein now occupies, he was middle-aged, and his children, who were quite numerous, had large families of their own."

"In those days," Maria picked up, "there were marauders in the area. And not just one kind. Many. A great earthquake had taken place not long before, displacing thousands of families, even entire villages from the surrounding areas. They camped around the lake there, where they could get food and water from the streams in the nearby hills."

"The valley itself wasn't settled?" Sabra asked.

"No. Some had tried, but the land was said to be infertile, probably because the salt lake was so close," Maria added. "And there were too many underground rivers near the lake that would cave in if even a horse walked above them. The refugees had to take care."

"And because there were multiple camps in this particular valley," Alner said, "marauders would raid them again and again, until the people were so desperate that they joined together to make one large camp to protect themselves."

"There was one particularly dangerous group," Maria added, "that attacked the people with unusual cruelty."

"The Fortiers today are known throughout the world for their unearthly strength," Alner continued. "And they were back in that day as well. Unusual even for the Fortiers, though, was that the third son's sons and grandsons had retained that strength. Most of the Fortier children cannot pass on their particular power to their children if they marry and live outside the Fortress from which their strength is rumored to come. Only those directly from or attached to the Fortress can wield its strength."

Sabra felt that she should probably check Serkan to make sure he was still asleep. But she felt frozen in place. She knew about the Fortiers of Destin, of course. Everyone did. Segzein might be in the southern realm, and Destin in the west, but no king in recent history had wielded such a power as theirs or such influence. Their infamous thousand-year-old blue fire was said to be the most potent gift of the Maker in the world. In fact, it was in search of power similar to theirs that Sabra had gone in search for.

Alner nodded as though reading Sabra's thoughts. "The Fortier prince and his sons protected the other people in the valley as the marauders continued to attack. In return, the other clans began to prepare food and other services for the Fortiers in order to keep them strong as they stayed on constant guard."

"But when the marauders learned that it was unproductive to attack the Fortiers or their allies, they turned their attacks to the one group that hadn't chosen to join with the others under the Fortiers' protection."

"Which group?" Sabra asked, her heart beating fast. Apparently, her friend's grandparents, whom she'd greeted for years, had the answers she'd sought all along. And they weren't even under her father's edict of silence. Which meant they could have told her years ago if she'd only known to ask.

Mentally, Sabra kicked herself for never even thinking to ask foreigners while she was at the trade talks.

"You know them as the Justines." Alner gave her a grim smile.

"They refused the Fortiers' offer of protection," Maria added with a scoff.

"But why?" Sabra asked. Not that she doubted it. That was exactly the sort of thing the Justines would do.

Alner shook his head. "No one knows. But the night after they refused protection, the Fortiers felt the sunset give rise to something dark."

Maria shivered, and Sabra felt herself shiver in response. "There was fire from the sky," Alner said, "and in the morning, the marauders' camp had been burned to the ground. Not a single tent pole of the marauders stood in place. Not a single soul had survived."

"What was it?" George leaned forward. It seemed he'd never heard these stories either. He was just as ignorant of the truth as she was. But Sabra decided to think on that later.

"No one knows for sure," Alner said. "But the marauders gave them no trouble after that. And not long after, another displaced group arrived that *did* choose to live under the protection of the Fortiers." He nodded at Sabra. "You know them as the Sowens. They claimed they could properly farm the land in the valley. Sure enough, they were able to create irrigation systems that made the valley fertile, and not long after, the groups encamped together chose to form their own new kingdom. Each group took a new name to represent their willingness to start over. It was agreed that each group would, however, continue in its own specialty, adding to the symbiotic nature of the new kingdom. And this time, the Justines agreed to join as well, saying their understanding of knowledge and words would be their own contribution."

"The Fortier descendants took on the title of Sentinels," Maria said, staring down at the sash.

"And they lived that way until recently?" Sabra guessed.

Maria stood. "I'll get supper. Alner can continue to tell you." Her words were measured and calm, but Sabra sensed an enormous sorrow in the woman as she stood, her steps heavier than they had been since Sabra had arrived.

"George, how much do you know of the Fortiers' gift?" Alner asked, his long face even longer in the evening shadows now that the sun had set.

"They have an incredible personal strength," George said slowly. "And the kings and queens control some sort of blue fire."

Alner nodded. "More than that, many of them have a very personal connection with the Maker himself through their Fortress. And because they have such a high sense of connectedness through the Maker, they are often very sensitive to evil as well."

"You mean like Sorthileige?" George asked.

"What's Sorthileige?" Sabra asked.

"It's the most tangible source of evil in the world." Alner stared at the table. "It bubbles up from the depths of the earth. Like grime, the Holy Writ says, sloppy leftovers from the Maker's enemy attempting to steal the Maker's glory."

"Most people die upon its touch," George added in a flat tone, his eyes distant.

"Or go mad," Alner nodded. "But there are some whose greed is strong enough to sustain or even strengthen them when they come into contact with it. It's said to have the most power when people open themselves up to be used as an empty vessel. The Fortier monarchs are some of the few known individuals that can destroy such potent evil. And as I said, strangely for the Fortiers, or the Sentinels, as they were now called, their power that had come from the Fortress didn't seem to die away with the new generations. Instead, their power was concentrated, and they learned how to use it in a new way."

"Isn't that a good thing?" Sabra asked, noting the new sadness in Alner's voice.

He gave a gusty sigh. "Yes. Unfortunately, however, it also made them particularly sensitive to concentrated evil, such as Sorthileige." He glanced up at George. "About twenty years ago, they began to get sick."

"*We* began to get sick," Maria added in a harsh voice from the counter where she was slicing bread.

"We tried to tell the other clans," Alner said, leaning back on his stool. "But they couldn't find any sort of contaminants in our seed or water. There was nothing visible, at least. The Sowens and the Physics searched for any signs of poison or other causes for weeks before giving up."

Sabra sat up. "Before he died, my father said something about keeping a secret for Mahzar."

Maria and Alner exchanged a meaningful glance. "Do you know what the secret was?" Maria asked.

Sabra shook her head sadly. "He died just moments after. But," she paused, "I believe it was one that made him feel terribly guilty."

Maria snorted and turned back to preparing the food. "It ought to have."

Sabra's chest wanted to crack into two. Losing her father was bad enough. Learning that he was at least partly responsible for what had happened to George's family...

It only made losing him even worse.

But no. She would deal with that later.

Alner frowned at his wife. "Maria." Then he intertwined his fingers and shook his head. "Eventually, we grew so sick that we could no longer fulfill our duties. We went to the king...your father, who was still rather green. He'd been crowned only a few years before. And we demanded recourse. But because we were unable to produce proof of what was happening, the basniins said that there was nothing they could do."

"So we took our own vote," Maria said, placing a basket of steaming bread on the table. Next to it, she placed a small dish of oil. "Most chose to leave, though there were some who stayed. The other clans informed us that we were breaking our vow. Not that any of that mattered. By that time, the vast majority of the people were so sick they couldn't even pack all they owned." She closed her eyes. "Even so, we left too late. Our people were so sick that we died in the desert before we could find anywhere new to settle."

The table was silent for a long moment. Sabra had thought the smell of bread heavenly just a moment before. But now, she had the horrid desire to dry heave.

"How did you survive?" George finally asked, his voice shaking slightly. Sabra looked back and when she saw his face, her chest hurt. She couldn't read his expression. But she knew it was one of pain.

Maria glanced at her husband. He gave her a sad nod.

"Your father came to us when he realized what was happening. We weren't family, but we were old family friends. He begged us to take you to one of the surrounding villages. He told us to drink deeply of the clean water and to eat good food and to keep you safe."

"But why me?" George asked, his brow furrowed. "Why not everyone else as well?" Then his eyes opened wide. "And by my father, don't you mean your son?"

Alner took a deep breath. "The nearby villages had already told us not to seek shelter. There were too many of us, and they were afraid they would be overwhelmed. But he sent you alone with us because we were healthier than many in the group." He took another deep breath. "And no, we're not your true grandparents. But we were stronger than most, so your father placed you in our care because he didn't want the line to die out."

George stared at them. "His line—"

"By birth," Alner said slowly, "you are a direct descendant of the Fortier prince's eldest son."

"The prince of our people," Maria added. "Sometimes called a clan head. Or a basniin."

Sabra felt all the air rush out of her lungs. The disappointment was so thick she could hardly swallow.

That shouldn't be, though. She'd already known George wasn't someone she could consider as a future husband. She'd known that from the start.

Amid all the more important things, like discovering that her father had betrayed his own people, why did this knowledge make her wish to fall to her knees?

Sabra felt Maria's gaze, and looked up to find the other woman carefully studying her. And though she had no way to prove it, Sabra got the feeling that George's grandmother - or whatever relation she was to him - knew exactly what Sabra was thinking. Not that it mattered. Because even armed with knowledge as she was now, Sabra was no more powerful than she had been an hour ago.

"Why didn't you tell me this?" George asked, sounding somewhat strangled.

Maria looked at her hands. "We wanted you to grow up without the fate of your lost people on your shoulders."

"What would you have had us do?" Alner asked, raising his eyebrows. "Tell a child that his parents and entire people died because they were forced to break their four hundred-year-old vow?"

"I'm twenty-four years." George's hands were in fists at his side, squeezing so tightly that his knuckles turned white. "You could have told me when I was seventeen. Or nineteen. Or twenty-one years. But you wait until I'm—"

"It wouldn't have done much good if we had," his grandfather scoffed.

"And why is that?"

"Because you can't use the full extent of your powers." His grandfather gave him a sharp look. "Not yet.

George rolled his eyes and then turned to Sabra. "Did you know this?" His eyes were hard and his voice cutting.

Sabra stared at him. He'd never used that tone with her before. And after the last few days she'd had, she didn't much care for it. "I was ten when we met!" she snapped. "Do you think I *asked* you to come sit next to me at the fountain?"

He glared at her then at Alner, his eyes hardening again. "I don't know what you expect of me. What anyone expects of me now that I know. I don't see what difference any of this makes."

"It seems," Alner said, avoiding the sharp gaze of his wife, "that the Maker planned not to let you avoid it after all. If you met the princess by coincidence as a boy, there's little we can do now to sever such a connection."

"Alner—" Maria began in a tight voice.

"Maria." Alner turned to her, his voice gentle. "We prayed for a way to help him."

"By taking him to Destin!" Maria cried. "Isn't that what we've been preparing for all these years? Not by sending him back to the people that tried to kill him!"

"Sending me to Destin?" George looked at them like he was about to fall over. "Is that why you wanted me to be a scholar?"

"The Fortiers are legendary fighters," Maria said, keeping her eyes on her husband. "But they're also well-known to be incredibly intelligent and highly educated. You've already learned the art of war from your grandfather. We wanted you to stand out as much as possible before you approached them."

"Your grandmother thought it would be prudent to give you every edge in competition to attract their interest," Alner said with a scowl. Clearly, he wasn't in such agreement.

"To do what?" George walked in a circle and gave a half-choked laugh. "Waltz in and announce that I'm some long-lost relative, and would they please take me back?" He shook his head, his eyes hardening to a near silver. "I'm not going to Destin."

"How about," Alner said as Maria opened her mouth, "we eat our bread and retire to bed? In the morning, we can continue this discussion when we've had some time to think and pray and rest."

Though just an hour ago Sabra's hunger had been so sharp it was nearly painful, the suggestion of sleep made her nearly sway on the spot. But now her chest felt as though she might just burst. Anger and indignation formed in her eyes as angry tears, and she pushed her empty plate back and got off her stool so quickly she nearly fell off.

"Good night," she whispered as she hurried back to the room where Serkan slept.

If they didn't decide they were done with her, that was.

When she reached the secret entrance, Sabra stopped and leaned against the wall, closing her eyes and breathing in and out in slow, controlled breaths.

George's anger was understandable. She was still reeling with her own revelations about her father's past, though his role was perhaps less surprising to her than these truths would have been to George. But still, George had always been a safe soul to Sabra. Welcoming and warm and gentle. Even when they weren't seeing one another in that seven year absence, she had thought of him with a particular fondness she'd never felt for anyone else. To have him angry with her, especially for a history she'd never known about until now...

If George abandoned her, where would she go?

He was hurting. That much she could see. As little time as they'd spent together over the years, only one day at a time, she'd never seen such sadness as was now etched in his face. And, to an extent, she couldn't help feeling that it was all her fault.

Heavy steps interrupted her thoughts. She opened her eyes and gave a little jump when she found him standing only a few feet away.

His eyes were wary, and he held two folded blankets.

"Can I help you?" she asked in a petulant tone. Probably not needed, but she couldn't stifle the sting of his words at the table.

He looked down at the blankets. "Sabra, I'm...I'm sorry for what I said back there."

"It's all right," she said without thinking.

He shook his head. "I didn't...I mean..." He ran a hand through his hair. "I always knew there were things they hadn't told me. But I assumed it was that my father was some sort of highwayman or my mother had some sort of scandalous past." He swallowed. "I never thought it would be this."

"I didn't know, either," Sabra whispered.

"I know. And I'm sorry I took it out on you." He held out the blankets. "Peace offering?" The corner of his mouth turned up sheepishly.

She gave him a tired smile. "Of course." Then her smile died. "And I'm so sorry for all my father did. I know that doesn't really fix anything, but I am. And I'm also sorry for...all this." She gestured back at the stairs. "It was never my intent to dredge up old skeletons. When I ran, all I could think of was finding you."

"It seems the skeletons have been there a while." He took a slow, deep breath in through his nose before giving her a tight smile. "Still, I'm glad you're here. If it has to be this way..." He took another deep breath and turned toward the stairs. "Good night Sabra."

Sabra stared after him. "Good night, George," she whispered.

CHAPTER 21

THE SENTINEL'S SONG

Sabra should have slept well that night. The bed was comfortable enough, Thing was cuddled up against her, and the fire kept the little room cozy and warm. She and Serkan were the safest they had been in weeks, and there was food guaranteed for them when they got up the next morning.

And yet, Sabra struggled to fall into the arms of slumber. Instead, she was tossed around between whirlwinds of half-dreams that circled in her head.

A dragon with scales like moonstones.

A city on fire.

A clan in anguish.

A man in pain.

In her brief moments of lucidity that were scattered between dreams, Sabra could only imagine what kind of pain George must be in. She'd always known she was adopted. Of course, trouble had only arisen recently because of her past, but at least she had known. George, however, had just learned of his people's painful deaths. His grandparents weren't even his true family, and he was the prince of a clan that was dead.

Sabra tried not to think too much about that part. But her befuddled, exhausted brain didn't pay her much heed.

By the time morning arrived, Sabra was more than ready to escape sleep, or rather, her lack thereof. Judging by the light coming in around the edges of the large stone George had placed in the back cave entrance, it should be late enough to politely go to the kitchen.

The fire had gone down to embers during the night, so Sabra stumbled over to the hearth to rekindle the flames. As she stoked the fire, she tripped on something and heard a groan.

She grabbed the little table's edge and caught herself before falling flat on her face. "Serkan?"

The boy groaned again. "My stomach hurts."

Her eyes were adjusted enough to see him leaning against the wall with his legs, which she must have tripped on, splayed out in front of him.

"Probably because you ate like a little piggy last night without any self-restraint." She went to his side and put her hands on her hips. "Are you too sick to go to breakfast?"

He quit moaning. "There's breakfast?"

"Only if it doesn't make you sick." Sabra tried to hide her smile.

"I'm feeling much better now!" Serkan hopped up, grabbed the indignant Thing with one hand, and ran to the bricks in the wall. She laughed and shook her head as she removed the bricks, then they climbed out and made their way up to the kitchen.

The house smelled of bacon when they reached the top of the stairs, and Sabra felt just as hungry as Serkan acted. They followed their noses to the kitchen, where Maria was putting platters of food on the table.

"George is out feeding the animals," she said as she handed them each a mug of steaming milk. "Eat up quickly." Her mouth tightened a little. "His grandfather and I have something to show you when you're done."

"Is it more about the Sentinels' history?" Sabra asked as she bit into a piece of flatbread. It was even softer than it looked, and she could taste cheese. Whatever Maria's troubles, the woman could bake. Sabra broke off a piece of bacon and handed it to Thing, who sniffed it before deigning to take the offering and hopping down to hide with it under the table.

"Somewhat, yes." Maria paused, and frowned slightly at the back window. "It also might be the key to defeating your dragon."

Sabra needed no more encouragement to hurry after that. She inhaled what was on her plate and then dragged Serkan with her, pausing only when he pleaded that she let him grab some bacon to bring with him. On her way out, she bent and snatched up the cat, who protested loudly.

Sometimes, she could swear the cat was silently cursing at her.

"Fine then." She made a face. "But if you get lost or eaten by some desert animal, don't blame me."

Maria led them up a set of stairs to a higher level of the house and into its north wing. They exited the hallway and emerged on a balcony that went all the way around a square, indoor courtyard, not unlike the one Sabra would practice staff in at home with Demir. Unlike her practice room at home, natural light poured in from the windowed ceiling above. The ground was made of soft dirt, and there were a somewhat alarming number of weapons racks hung on the walls around the main floor. Alner was standing at one of the racks, examining a sword.

Footsteps sounded to her left, and Sabra turned to see George approaching them. He didn't look angry or frustrated the way he had the night before when they'd said goodnight. Instead, his face was a mask, closed off from any detectable emotion.

Sabra decided she preferred the anger. This George, devoid of feeling, was all wrong. As little time as she'd gotten to spend with him growing up, Sabra had always known George to be expressive and full of passion. It was one of the things she'd always loved about him. Unlike her subjects, he didn't dull his responses to life merely because he might risk offending her.

Until now, it seemed.

"You said you have something to show me?" He faced Maria, crossing his arms over his chest.

Sabra definitely disliked this calm, cold version of her old friend.

Of course, it only served as a reminder of how little she really knew him. So instead of studying the way the morning shadows fell on his face the way she wanted to, she turned back down to look at Alner.

"You need to see this." Maria glanced, unsmiling, up at Sabra. "Both of you."

"You said it could lead to helping my kingdom?" Sabra clutched her skirts to still her shaking hands.

"It could." Maria looked down at her husband. "But it will come at a cost." Then she looked behind them. "And you, boy, will help me gather eggs. Let me show you where to begin. George, go down with your grandfather. Pick a sword. You're going to face off today." Then she turned to guide a protesting Serkan back down the hall.

George stared after her for a long moment. Then he gave Sabra an unhappy half-smile and went downstairs.

Sabra watched George's face carefully as he joined Alner. She couldn't hear what they were saying, but whatever it was made George's mask flicker, and Sabra watched as true worry sharpened his gaze. And even though her nerves were battered, she couldn't help smiling a little. George might not be openly happy with the people who raised him, but he did *care*. There was that compassion she knew. He shook his head vehemently as Alner began to argue loudly enough for his voice to carry slightly. Before Sabra could make out any words, though, Maria returned.

"Are you ready?" she called down.

"Yes," Alner replied.

George glared at him, but after a moment, stalked over to the wall and chose his own sword.

"George has been training with the sword since he could hold a small wooden one," Maria said quietly.

"Is he good?" Sabra asked.

"Good is an understatement. The power is passed to all Sentinel sons, but the original blood of that Fortier prince still flows through *him* particularly."

"What kind of power?" Sabra asked, standing straighter. Her heart began to pound with unspoken hope.

"You'll see." Maria leaned over the edge of the balcony and nodded. In response, Alner and George began to circle.

Sabra had never trained with a sword, much to her chagrin. Her mother said it was bad enough having a daughter who was proficient with a staff. But she'd watched enough of Demir's lessons to have a rudimentary understanding of the basic forms. She recognized the crouch Alner fell into now.

George moved in for the attack. Despite Alner's age—which was probably in his sixth decade—they seemed evenly matched. George's attacks were forceful and bold, but Alner's grace and skill kept him dancing just out of George's reach. For several minutes, the only sounds were those of their feet on the soft dirt. Then the fight truly began.

While Sabra was amazed at Alner's swift, clever moves and his stamina, especially considering his age, once the men were in motion, she could hardly take her eyes off George.

She had always known he was exceptionally strong for his age. Several times, she'd watched him smith for his grandfather as a boy, and even then she'd been impressed. And every year when she'd come back to Kappadona, his shoulders had been wider and his arms thicker. But now, as he fought in only a simple shirt, leather jerkin, and trousers, she couldn't tear her focus away from his lithe, lethal form. His powerful shoulders moved with each strike, and his legs, which she hadn't given much notice to as a girl, reminded her of her father's pet jaguar at home, sturdy and agile, never missing a step. And it wasn't very long before he was able to drive the old man back into a corner.

Then Sabra jumped when Maria began to sing. Her voice was strong and clear.

> Grab your lance and nock your arrows.
> Hold your sword up high.

As she sang, Alner's steps and sword began to meet with the music, synchronizing in turn. The rhythm was deliberate and accentuated, and as Alner joined with its pattern, Sabra felt the immediate urge to move along with him.

For to war we have been called,
And now we're going nigh.

"It's a dance!" Sabra exclaimed as Alner continued to move to Maria's song.

As she spoke, a new sensation filled the air. The hairs on her arms tingled. Her skin wasn't wet. She knew that. And yet, her arms and face and other areas with exposed skin could *feel* the air. She could feel the drops of moisture separating from the dry air as the morning sun rose. The smells around her were accented. Time seemed to slow. Every sensation was heightened. But somehow, that wasn't even the most impressive part.

As the song progressed, Alner's sword moved faster until he was truly doing what looked like a dance of death, driving a very startled George back as he did. And as he did, blue fire swirled around his blade. Sabra heard George gasp at the same time she did. Some part of her wanted to look at him and see his response to such a display, but the flames were mesmerizing, and she couldn't look away.

And then, in one swift movement, he'd stripped George of his sword, and the fight was over. Maria stopped singing, and Sabra's senses returned to normal. Still, she felt frozen in time. Seeming oblivious to the change around them, or perhaps just used to it, Alner carefully placed the sword back on its wall hooks. George picked up his sword and slowly walked back up the stairs.

"The lullaby," George whispered as he came to stand next to Sabra. His eyes were distant as he stared at his weapon, his chest still heaving.

Sabra turned to look at him. "Lullaby?"

He nodded, looking up at Maria. "You sang me to sleep with that song for years," he whispered.

"Of course we did." Everyone turned to see Alner coming up the stairs. "You needed to know the Sentinel's Song."

"Sentinel's Song," George repeated slowly.

Alner wiped the sweat from his brow. "The Fortier prince wanted to pass the art of battle on to his sons. So he and his wife took one of the ancient songs of the Fortiers and moved it to a cadence that matched their forms. They realized not long after that the Maker had chosen to use it for them as well. The song serves to kindle the power within."

George said nothing. Once again, he was wearing the impassive mask on his face as he stared down at the sword he still held.

"There are several others," Maria added. She bent to pick up Thing, who had twined himself around her ankles. "But this is the one every Sentinel child learns from birth up."

"Do the girls have the gift as well?" Sabra asked, giving Thing a dirty look. The ungrateful cat never twined himself around *her* ankles.

Maria gave her a sad smile. "Unfortunately, we do not. We are, however, given the power to sing for the men. They cannot sing for one another." She held her head slightly higher. "Which means, they cannot go to battle without us. Not if they wish to fight their best."

Sabra thought as fast as she could. Maria had said this might be the Maker's way of saving her kingdom. That meant that George's family might be the way to save her kingdom. This was slightly disappointing, of course, as Sabra had hoped for a slightly larger contingent of warriors to beat back the dragon. But she had hoped and prayed for something or someone extraordinary.

And this latent power of the Fortiers certainly seemed that. Then something occurred to Sabra.

"Maria, can you sing for George?" she asked, interrupting whatever George's grandfather was saying.

Maria glanced at her husband. "Unfortunately, I cannot. I can only sing for Alner now."

Ideas and hope were swirling so fast in her head that Sabra could barely think straight enough to utter the next words. "Could I sing for him?"

This was perfect. They could all return to Segzein. George and

Alner could challenge the dragon. Surely, the legendary Fortress's power would be enough to defeat the Justines' stolen strength. She and Maria could sing, and George and Alner could fight.

Her heart fluttered when she imagined George fighting. The best man she'd ever known driving back the evil that had taken her kingdom and threatened to swallow her whole. She couldn't think of a more worthy opponent for Mahzar.

Only then did she realize that Alner and Maria were looking at the ground. Even George had lost his aloofness and was staring at them with a slight frown.

"What is it?" Sabra asked. "Is it because I'm a Capitan?"

"No," Maria said slowly. "A woman of any birth can technically sing for a Sentinel warrior."

"But?" George crossed his arms.

Maria pursed her lips. "George will first need to pass through the Sentinel's Cave."

"Sentinel's Cave?" George interrupted.

"I'll explain later," Maria went on. Her words were slow and measured. "If he passes the trial there, he'll be ready for battle."

"But who will sing for him?" Sabra asked.

"Anyone can sing for him." Maria turned and studied Sabra, her gray eyes sharp. "But not without making difficult choices first."

George rubbed his hands over his face. "Grandmother—"

"The song is a wedding vow," Alner said. "It's a sacred part of Sentinel tradition. The song will only work for a married couple. During Sentinel weddings, the bride would sing the song as the groom performed the forms for their guests. When his weapon flamed blue, the marriage was complete."

Sabra could only stare at him. She wanted to speak, but words wouldn't come. George, she could see out of the corner of her eye, seemed to be doing no better.

After several tries, Sabra finally managed to swallow the lump in her throat. "So...if I sang for George—"

"You would become his wife," Maria finished quietly.

Sabra took a long, shaky breath. Because while marriage to

George would be eternally preferable to a marriage to Mahzar, George was also a basniin.

She would still lose her crown. She would break her vow to her father. Her people would still be without a queen.

All of this. Her father's death. Her city burning. Running for her life.

It would all be for naught.

She was also growing increasingly aware of how close George was standing, and of the fact that he was watching her face closely. Taking a deep breath, she turned and did her best to face him with a calm she didn't have.

"You don't have to do this." She attempted a smile, though it probably was more of a wince. "I'm not going to ask you to sacrifice yourself needlessly." She sighed. "Especially for people who wronged your family such in the first place."

His eyes sparked. "You don't think I can do this."

Sabra blinked at him. "That's not what I meant."

"Then what did you mean?"

"Let's give them a moment," Alner whispered to Maria, taking her by the waist as he headed down the hall.

Sabra held up a finger, gesturing for him to wait while she gathered herself. She must use careful words, or this could all go very wrong. "What I mean," she said slowly, "is that it would be wrong of me to ask you to risk your life fighting for the people who practically exiled your family and sentenced them to death." She sighed. "We made our bed. Now we must lie in it."

She went to the nearest window and looked out at the high desert. She could feel his gaze, and shame covered her like a veil as she simultaneously wished that he would look longer.

"Come with me," he said.

She turned. "Where?"

"My master's home." He shook his head. "I know what I just saw. And looking back on my life...it makes sense. But I need to do some more research." He gave her a wan smile. "If for no other reason than to clear my head."

"All right." She paused. "Do you think the Justines will be there?"

"They might, but..." his face reddened slightly. "If we pretend to be a couple and keep our heads down, we should be harder to identify."

Sabra felt her own face redden as she realized what he was proposing. It was just for show, of course. That's why he had suggested it. But would such pretending be wise? The hope in his eyes was impossible to miss, as was the way he was leaning slightly toward her.

And yet, such a suggestion wasn't bad. After all, they might have more information in his master's books than was available in Segzein. That's why she'd come to Kappadona in the first place.

Also, it was perfectly normal for two old friends to spend a day reading books.

She nodded and let a tentative smile slip. "Let's do it then."

CHAPTER 22
BE GENTLE

George joined his grandparents in the kitchen where they were drinking tea, dragging Sabra along behind him. She had to smile to herself as she followed. He hadn't dragged her around like this since she was thirteen.

What she wouldn't give to be that girl again. Living in the moment without a care in the world. Well, that wasn't true. She'd had cares back then, too. But there weren't any dragons in those days, at least. And her father had been alive.

A sliver of anger leaped up like a tongue of flame in her head, but she stomped it back down. *Not yet.* Anger would distract her. And there was no place for distraction now.

After George had told his grandparents what they were going to do and asked them to watch Serkan for Sabra, he headed up to his room to change. Sabra excused herself quickly and headed down the hall to her room as well, but she was stopped by Maria on the stairs in front of her hidden room.

"Sabra...Your Highness."

"Please." Sabra did her best to smile. "Call me Sabra."

Maria nodded, but she didn't smile. "I know you're here for your people. You wouldn't be a good queen if you weren't."

Sabra nodded slowly. "I wouldn't have come if I'd known any other way."

"I understand that." Maria glanced up the stairs. "I just ask you one thing."

Sabra turned to face her. Agreeing to a request before knowing it was a bad practice for anyone in power. "I'll do my best," she said.

"Please," Maria said softly, "be gentle with his heart."

Sabra froze, a sudden heat and cold seeming to sear her face.

"You may or may not know this," Maria went on, "but he's been in love with you since the day you met." She paused. "And I can see it in your eyes, too. You want to be his nearly as much as he wants you for his own."

Sabra looked down at her hands. "I never meant—"

"I know." Maria's mouth tightened. "But if you're set on being queen, just remember. He's a basniin. And if you're determined to keep your place, so are you."

Sabra mulled over Maria's words as she put on the change of clothes her mother had put in her bag. Part of her was incensed. This woman had known her less than a day. And while it was possible that she might know George's feelings on the matter, she was quite possibly mistaken there as well. Sabra doubted George had loved her from that first day, young as they were. But even if George considered himself in love with her, how dare the woman assume she knew the depths or directions of Sabra's feelings or the direction of her intentions? Sabra had come to George as a friend she could trust. Her goal had never been manipulation, nor had she entertained even the slightest hopes for what would be an impossible relationship with him.

No, it was better she put all of that out of her mind here and now. Maria was wrong. George and Sabra weren't children, and they understood the boundaries that separated them. That was all there was to it.

When she hurried outside, George was ready. He had on a fresh leather jerkin, and he'd changed the shirt underneath and was now wearing a sword. As she came closer, he finished putting on a cloak and then held one out for Sabra as well.

"If we wear the hoods up, we should be a little less conspicuous," he explained.

She took it from him shyly and draped it over her shoulders. Her fingers fumbled the clasp several times as she tried to fasten it. What was wrong with her?

"Here, let me help." He took the cloak and pulled it more evenly around her shoulders. Sabra's heart hammered in her chest as Maria's words echoed in her head.

He's been in love with you since the day you met.

Could that be true? They'd only seen each other two days now in the last seven years. And before that, they were just children. Surely some other young woman had caught his eye, or at least made him wonder what life would be like, married in this little city with the simplicity his grandparents had raised him with.

And yet, she shivered as his thumb brushed against her collarbone while he fastened the clasp.

Thankfully, she didn't have time to dwell on this as he stepped back and offered his arm. Of course, Sabra didn't miss his grandmother's slight frown from the door as Sabra accepted. But, Sabra argued in her head, it wasn't as though they were sneaking out for a secret tryst. Going to the library was the responsible thing to do, after all, to seek out information about her kingdom's enemy. She couldn't very well show up on his master's step alone.

And yet, strolling toward town on his arm felt so...

"What will you tell your master?" she asked him, determined to distract herself from the thoughts swirling around in her head as the door closed after them.

But he stared straight ahead as he walked. His eyes distant as he glared at the road.

"George?"

He sucked a breath in and shook his head. "Sorry, what?"

She stopped walking and turned him to look at her. "Before we go any farther, just spit it out."

"Spit what out?"

She gave him a wry grin. "Whatever has you so broody."

She expected a laugh from him. George had always been anything but broody. Now, though, he only studied the hand she'd put on his arm to turn him, his brow furrowing slightly.

"If I help, I could bring down whatever darkness was unleashed on my people."

All of Sabra's desire to laugh was gone.

"I never meant to ask you—" she began, but he only shook his head.

"I can't abandon you, Sabra."

"Yes," she frowned up at him, "you can. You didn't make that vow to protect Segzein. Your ancestors did. Besides," she sighed, "it sounds like my people broke the contract first. You had nothing to do with all this."

"I'm not so sure we can pin this on all your people. But even if we could, what would we do about you?"

"I'm not your responsibility." Why did she suddenly sound so breathless? She wasn't even walking.

He took her hand in his and twined his fingers through hers. It was a simple gesture, one they'd done a dozen times as children, dragging each other around the square as they sought to enjoy everything as fast as they could before she had to leave again. But now she could feel the calluses on his hands and the strength of his fingers, which were now so much bigger than hers, and she very much did not want to let go. She should object, in light of his grandmother's warning. She couldn't find the right words, though, so instead, she turned and began walking again. He followed but kept her hand in his.

"I think I always liked being around you so much when we were little because you were like me," he said softly.

Sabra let out a surprised laugh. "Really? I was always embarrassed by the ridiculous number of guards we brought in compared to everyone else in the market."

"It wasn't that. Here, we'll be at the town's edge in a few

minutes, so let's stop and put our hoods up. It's windy enough no one should think it odd."

Sabra paused and did as he suggested, somewhat thankful when he had to let go of her hand to do so.

"How did your grandparents not know I was a princess?" she asked when they were walking again. "They met me several times over the years."

He held his finger up to his lips, and they were silent until they were on another less crowded street.

"I, um…I might have told them that you were part of your cousin's entourage and that you lived on a farm outside of the city." He gave Sabra a small, mischievous smile. "I knew they wouldn't want me spending time with anyone from Segzein."

"Why?"

He shrugged. "I never knew the reason for their suspicions. I always assumed that they were afraid to lose me since they lost my parents, and big cities made them nervous." He kicked a rock. "I never thought it was because they weren't actually my grandparents or that they were tasked by royalty with keeping me safe."

Sabra nodded slowly. "I suppose I can see that." Then she shrugged and snorted. "If it makes you feel better, apparently, my father and the rest of the kingdom have been hiding the death of an eighth of my people from me for my entire life. And then lied about it to my face repeatedly. Then I found out about my father's involvement seconds before he was killed in front of me." Sabra frowned at the ground. "I'm used to knowing what to do and say. But these last few weeks…" She kicked a rock. "I'm not even sure where I stand anymore, let alone where I'm supposed to be." Or who, she almost added. But that wouldn't do. She knew exactly who she was and who she was supposed to be. Mahzar couldn't take that from her too.

"Sabra."

She gave a humorless laugh. "I feel like a small child throwing sticks at a bear to take it down. And somehow, I've convinced you to help me."

"Sabra," he said again.

Sabra looked up to realize that they'd come to a stop outside an adobe house shaped like a beehive. Surprised, Sabra looked around to realize that the other houses surrounding this one were shaped like mud beehives as well. Apparently, she'd been so busy the day before that she hadn't noticed any of the local architecture. She'd never seen anything like this in Segzein.

"Where are we?" she asked.

"We're here," he said. But instead of knocking immediately, he gave her a sad smile. "But before we go in, I want you to know something."

"What?"

The fingers of his right hand twitched, but he kept them at his side. "One step at a time. We're going to go in and search for any information we can find on this dragon and his people. We're not going to worry about your cousin or your father or my grandparents." His gray eyes searched hers. "Just here and now. Understand?"

Sabra couldn't help smiling. "Not three steps down the road. Got it."

He grinned and ruffled her hair through her hood, despite her protests, before turning and knocking on the door.

Sabra was about to give him a playful shove when the door opened, and somehow, she managed to pull herself together and behave, ignoring the urge to elbow him back.

A small, thin man opened the door. His white hair stuck out in every direction, and he wore a simple black robe. He was just tall enough that his head reached George's elbow. "You're late," he said to George. Then his eyes moved to Sabra. "And this would be?"

"Master Gregory," he said in a low voice, a smile playing on his lips, "I have a story for you. But you have to let us in first."

The man's eyes only widened. "Oh? And why should I admit a stranger into my sanctuary?"

George glanced at Sabra and grinned. "This story involves a princess."

CHAPTER 23

YOU KNOW

The old man stared at Sabra for a long moment before seeming to remember himself. Then he gave a little cry of what sounded like dismay.

"Your Majesty!" he hissed. "Come inside, quick! Before someone sees you!" He gave a little start and gestured behind him before darting around behind them and closing and locking the door. Then he ran around the room, closing every window he could find and locking his back door as well.

"Are any of the authorities looking for her?" George asked, ushering Sabra over to a long, rectangular table in the corner by a small hearth. She sat on one of the wooden stools that surrounded it.

"Not officially." The man checked every lock and window once more. There weren't many windows, as bookshelves took up most of the wall space. And desks. Lots of desks. There were four that were scattered haphazardly around the room, besides the table, and most of them were covered in books. "But there have been strangers in the square, loitering and causing quite a stir. The merchants are displeased."

George looked down at Sabra and frowned. In spite of the locked doors and closed window, Sabra shivered and leaned toward him a little. Being near George was calming. It always had been. Even more so now that he was a gigantic, full-grown man.

"What possessed you to bring her with you?" Master Gregory finally came to a stop in front of them and put his hands on his hips. "Especially after that show you put on yesterday to drag her out!"

"You saw that?" Sabra asked.

"No, but word travels fast. It's all anyone can talk about this morning."

George stared at him. "Um, I thought she could help me search for answers."

"And I couldn't do that?" Master Gregory raised a bushy white brow.

"I was hoping to see for myself," Sabra said, hoping to placate the little man's anger. "I love books." She pulled the little blue book from her bag.

The old man's eyes widened as he took the book and reverently ran his hand over the cover. "Yes, I can see that," he said softly. He opened it and gasped as he flipped carefully through the pages. "This is a treasure, I hope you know. I've never seen its like."

Sabra took the book back and hugged it to her chest.

"While we're on the topic," George said, looking at the ground, "this will be my last day with you for a while. I'm not sure when I'll be coming back."

"Sit." The little man gestured at the table, looking surprisingly unsurprised. "I'll get some tea, then we'll discuss this properly."

A few minutes later, everyone had a cup of steaming tea, and Master Gregory had seated himself across from them. Sabra tried not to be so very aware of how close George's arm was to hers, resting so close on the table that she could feel its warmth.

She also tried not to think about how much she wanted to touch it.

"So I have come across some information since you asked me about that language," he said, looking pointedly at a pile of books at the end of the table. "But before I tell you what I found, I want to know exactly how the two of you came to know one another."

Sabra and George looked at one another.

"It's nothing spectacular," Sabra said. "As a child, I accompanied my cousin, Demir, on his trips to attend the trade talks that used to be held here. When I was ten, I met George in the square. We met every year after that until the talks were moved seven years ago."

"And I became reacquainted with her when you sent me to Segzein a few weeks ago," George added.

Sabra fingered her teacup. The handle was incredibly delicate, painted with gold luster. "We exchanged a few letters after that. Then when the trouble started in Segzein," she continued carefully, "my cousin helped me escape the city." She shrugged. "George was the only person I could think to turn to."

The old man worried his beard as he studied them. Then he leaned back and gave George a strange smile.

"When you asked me to search out information on the mystery of Segzein, I knew you had a reason. I didn't realize, though, how deeply the Maker, apparently, had entwined you in this destiny already." The smile he gave George was cynical and amused, similar to the expression Master Mirac wore often at home.

"What do you mean *this* destiny?" George asked.

Master Gregory tapped his fingers on the table three times before he got up and began to gather books from the desks. "Did you know that I spent a decade studying with the master Sophians in Segzein?"

George shook his head. "I didn't."

"Yes. And it was wonderful. So much knowledge and history in one place." His eyes grew distant, and it was several moments before he seemed to recall himself. "That's why I came to call myself a master when I took up my own place of study and consultation. Anyhow, I know Segzein well." He paused, and his brow furrowed slightly, drawing his eyebrows nearly together. "I knew your people well."

"My people?" George glanced at Sabra. She knew exactly what he was thinking because she was thinking it herself. How much did this man know? And how did he know? He must have hidden it well if George was pretending to be ignorant of it now.

"Your eyes are a dead giveaway, my boy. Your people mixed with the locals in many ways, but those eyes - gray, almost silver - have stayed strong and true for all these years." He shook his head and stood before he began to shelve a pile of books. "Anyhow, after word went out that the great Sentinels had been cursed, most people around here locked down and hid in fear that they would attack and demand supplies and shelter in desperation." He scowled. "They did no such thing. But not long after word had gone out that the warriors were dying, word around town had it that there were a few survivors who sought refuge. So knowing what I did of your people, I sought them out."

"You weren't worried about a curse?" Sabra asked.

Master Gregory snorted. "In all the time I'd spent with the Sentinels, the last thing *they* would knowingly bring upon themselves was some curse. Which I have doubts about, by the way. Either way, though, when I found your grandparents living in one of the caves east of the city, I did my best to help them."

"How was I kept ignorant of all of this?" George asked. His voice was tight, and against her better judgement, Sabra reached out and wrapped her hand around his arm, which he pulled closer to himself.

"Your guardians, or grandparents, rather, discussed this at length with me. They themselves were weak and had little money and almost no supplies. So I, along with several sympathizers, helped them create a home in the caves and supplied them until they were strong enough to work again." Master Gregory scratched the back of his head, getting his fingers knotted in his hair in the process. When he was done untangling them, he came and sat down again. "Your grandfather knew how to make weapons. It had been his primary occupation in Segzein. And he did sell some in the marketplace, but only just enough to keep you all alive."

"Some people were willing to buy from him then?" Sabra asked. She tried to make sense of how the master swordsmith barely sold enough weapons to provide for his little family. Ever since she had first laid eyes on him, she had assumed him to be wildly successful, judging by the beauty of his craft.

"Mostly travelers on their way in and out of the city. People who didn't know of the supposed curse the silver-eyed Sentinels had brought upon themselves. And the longer the family was here and didn't cause any trouble, the less people feared them."

George stood and paced back and forth once before returning to the table. "I still don't understand how I was kept ignorant of this my entire life."

Master Gregory let out a short laugh. "My boy, why do you think you had so few friends as a child?"

As he said the words, Sabra was reminded of that first day, how George had been the one to introduce himself and had offered to spend time with her. Her heart twisted as she realized just how lonely he must have been.

"I was the one who suggested your grandparents take you to Destin, you know." Master Gregory sipped his tea with a satisfied grin. "You might as well return to your roots and see what they could offer someone with your...talents."

"Why now?" George asked. "Why wait until I was nearly grown to apprentice me and then suggest my grandparents take me away?" His jaw worked back and forth, and Sabra hoped desperately that it was with anger. Not sorrow.

George didn't deserve any more sorrow.

"Well, we'd hoped to find a way to return you home to Segzein. For a long time, they hoped the king would realize how he needed his people and call you all to come back. But when word had it that the Justines were getting more aggressive in their pressure on the Capitans, we knew Segzein would no longer be safe. So I suggested I teach you all I could in the next few years. The Fortiers are building a library at their Fortress that just might grow to be larger than the one in Segzein. They're even employing people from around the world to write books about every place and subject imaginable so they might have knowledge of as much of the world as possible."

Sabra felt a stab of longing as she wondered if she would ever set foot in the library again. Would she never speak with Master Mirac?

"You're an excellent swordsman," Master Gregory continued,

"but as the Fortiers value intelligence as well, your grandparents and I decided we ought to make you as desirable as possible. Then, surely, they would have use for you somewhere." He paused, and his eyes softened slightly. "You could be somewhere you belonged."

George didn't answer. Instead, he stared off into space.

"I am curious," Sabra said slowly, as George seemed lost in his own thoughts. "What about whatever it was that made his people sick to begin with? Even if George and his family returned, couldn't it make them sick again?"

"Ah." Master Gregory's face darkened a shade. "That was another concern we had with a return. Because George is capable of wielding the Fortiers' power—"

"That hasn't been proven yet," George said in a flat voice.

"Something that can be easily remedied." Master Gregory waved his hand dismissively. "As I was saying, those who are capable of wielding power from the Maker are generally sensitive to Sortheleige as well." He frowned at George. "And from what I what understand, it's extremely unpleasant."

"What is?" Sabra asked.

"Sortheleige. Stolen power. Dark power. It's what your Justines used to create their dragon. At least, that's the only conclusion I've come to with Maria and Alner."

Sabra straightened. "What makes you think that?"

He gave her a sad smile. "Alas, it isn't sure. My knowledge and books aren't that ancient. But I do know a bit about Sortheleige itself." He turned to his right and picked up a large book with red leather covering. The pages were yellowed and rough as he opened it. After scanning a few lines, he nodded.

"Here it is. Sortheleige is power that was originally gifted to the world by the Maker, but it was stolen and misused for purposes other than what it was intended for." He skipped to the next page and continued. "It often bubbles up from the Deeps of the ocean, where the merpeople are, or from deep chasms in the earth. There are some, though," Master Gregory frowned, the lines in his face deepening, "that can steal the Maker's gifts directly from others and use them for their own purposes. That misuse taints the gifts. Curdles them like milk." He took a deep breath and rubbed his eyes with the palms of his hands. "All that to say, we decided as George got older that it would be better that they not move back, even in secret, until we knew whether or not they would become sick again."

"There are some who still live there," Sabra said, thinking of the old man who had embroidered the symbol for her. "They seem to be well..." But even as she spoke, her memory of their pale, pinched faces flashed in her memory.

He glanced at George. "That's actually why I sent him there when I did. I wanted to see how he fared."

"I was fine," George said in that same flat voice, not moving his eyes from the wall where he'd been staring for the last five minutes.

Master Gregory snorted. "You had a headache for three days." Then he turned back to Sabra. "So it doesn't seem as though whatever was there before is killing them now. But if you asked them how they feel, I would venture to say they're in a great deal of pain."

Sabra stared at him in horror. Had the Blue Bands been in pain her entire life?

Oh, Father, she thought with a grimace. *What have you done?* But there was nothing she could do about that right now. So instead, she swallowed hard and continued. "Did you ever learn what happened to them? That made them sick in the first place?"

He widened his eyes. "As you're the princess, I was hoping you could tell me."

She gave him a sad smile. "I only learned of the Sentinels' existence a few weeks ago."

"I had a hunch it was such as that."

"So what now?" George growled.

They turned and looked at George, who was glaring at his teacher. In the light of the hearth's fire, his eyes did nearly look silver. Not quite. But almost.

"Well," Master Gregory said with a shrug. "You have several options. The first is to hide here and hope the Justines don't choose to increase their borders or continue hunting the princess. Keep her safe and do your best to continue living as you have been. The other option is to go to Destin. Your grandparents are strong enough now, and I believe they have the money for the journey."

"And the third option?" George stared his teacher down.

Master Gregory sighed and looked down at his hands. "I'm afraid it's one you won't survive." He glanced at Sabra, though she didn't know why. "At least, not as things stand now."

"But?" George prodded.

"But," Master Gregory continued, "should you choose to return to fight the dragon, which I can only assume you would do for the sake of the princess, you would need a miracle from the Maker." His sharp eyes rested on Sabra again. "Honestly, though, with the depth at which the Maker has seemingly entwined your lives, I'm not sure you have any other choice at this point. For the crown princess and the lost prince of the missing clan to meet and grow as close friends, completely unaware of their connection, is not something I can write off as coincidence."

Soon after that, Sabra and George said their thank-yous and goodbyes to Master Gregory. Well, Sabra said them. George just stared blankly ahead. They made their way back home through one of the smaller markets. Master Gregory advised them against returning the way they'd come.

For a few minutes, they walked in silence. Sabra did her best to catch glimpses of his face beneath the hood, but they were few and far between, and whenever she did see him, his face was that of a statue, chiseled void of emotion.

Finally, she could stand it no longer.

"You don't have to come, you know."

George blinked a few times and looked at her. He didn't speak, but his eyes flared briefly before returning to that irritating aloofness.

"You're not beholden to me or my people," she continued. "Especially after what they did to your people." It felt traitorous to say. At home, people were scared and possibly dying. But they had made their choices. And it wasn't fair to hold George responsible for them.

She briefly closed her eyes. Anger at her father and the other basniins flashed inside of her. She wanted to scream at him. She wanted to shout. To demand he explain himself to her. But that wouldn't get her anywhere here and now. Now, she would just have to focus on finding another way.

He stopped walking, and as her arm was linked in his, she was forced to stop, too. He took her chin gently in his fingers and lifted her face so she was looking directly into his.

He really was the handsomest man she'd ever laid eyes on. But it wasn't just his chiseled jaw or the breadth of his shoulders or the way his hair was fairer where it was longest.

Oh, how Sabra wanted to touch that hair.

More than anything, she was captivated by the burning of his eyes as they looked into hers, seeming to see into her soul and beyond. It made her feel thrilled and mortified at the same time. As though he was wondering which part of her he might unlock first.

He lifted one hand up and brushed her cheek with the back of his finger. It was a simple movement. And yet, in that moment, Sabra's skin might as well have been ablaze.

Why couldn't he have been among her suitors on the platform? They might have changed everything together.

He opened his mouth, but before he spoke, his focus narrowed to something over her shoulder. In one motion, he swept her behind him and had his sword out of its sheath and pointed at the man who was running straight toward them with sword drawn.

CHAPTER 24
I WAS RIGHT

The two men clashed so hard that Sabra was knocked to the ground. But George absorbed the blow and struck back, advancing against the man before he had even gained his balance. But as he pushed their attacker back, Sabra found her arm gripped by another man whose face was hidden by his brown hood.

If only she could find something like a staff! But they were in the middle of a market, and there were no long poles to be found. So Sabra, remembering her cousin's basic instructions on how to flee an attacker, let her weight go dead against the ground. This seemed to take the man by surprise as he stumbled forward. Before he could regain his feet, she fisted her hand and punched just behind his left knee, and he went down.

"George!" Sabra screamed as she jumped to her feet. Before she could run after him, though, her attacker grabbed her cloak, and she was yanked backward, hitting the ground hard. Her head vibrated with pain. She tried to push herself to her feet, but the man rolled over and knelt on top of her, one knee on each side while pinning her arms to the ground.

"It's time to come home, Princess," he said while she writhed and fought him. "Your mother is worried. She wants you to come home."

Sabra nearly paused at the mention of her mother. But she had enough sense in the moment to know that her mother would never want her to return to the future Mahzar had planned for her in Segzein. So she screamed George's name again.

The man gathered her wrists in his hands as though he might bind them together, but a flash of silver appeared above him, and Sabra could hear the *thunk* as the butt of George's sword slammed into his temple. George grabbed him by the collar and threw him off of Sabra.

"Are there any more?" she asked breathlessly as he pulled her tightly against him. He held his sword in a ready stance as he scanned the crowd that was growing larger around them.

"We need to get out of here," he whispered. "I shouldn't have brought you."

"Are you all right, George?" a man called out from the crowd. Only then did Sabra realize that their first attacker had already been bound and gagged. A few men rushed to help with the unconscious one on the ground.

"I am, thank you." George relaxed his stance slightly.

"What do they want with you?" a woman called out. Sabra couldn't help but think her tone was slightly accusatory. "That's twice in two days that girl's been attacked."

Sabra's heart beat erratically as he held her so close she could feel the heat through his shirt and leather jerkin. And it wasn't because they'd just been attacked.

"I'm afraid I've frustrated a very rich man." George stood straighter, though Sabra could feel the coil of his muscles, still taut and very ready to strike. "He had his eye set on my betrothed." He gave the people a saucy grin. "But she said yes to me."

"Well, you'd better marry her soon then," the woman called back. "So the rest of us can buy eggs without avoiding henchmen on a daily basis."

"I'll keep that in mind." George nodded and gave them one more grin before turning and pulling Sabra down a back alley.

They hurried in silence until they were out of town. Only when they were over the brook, sheltered by a copse of trees, did he stop.

Without speaking, he motioned for her to climb up into one of the trees behind him. She wrapped her skirts around her wrist and followed. Climbing was slightly more difficult than it had been when she was younger and would follow him up trees on the edge of the main market, due to the fact that her skirts were longer and fuller than they had once been. But she did make it up into the branches and seated herself on a branch near his.

He held a finger to his lips and motioned with head down at the ground. They listened for several minutes, but all they could hear was the gentle rustle of wind on the early summer leaves and the sound of the water gurgling below. Eventually, he got up and motioned for her to stay put. Then, carefully, he picked his way around the trunk, across to the other side of the tree, where he lowered himself down to peer farther back up the road. After a moment, he nodded and went back to his original branch.

"I think we're safe. There were only the two that I saw, but it was impossible to be sure."

"You don't want to lead them back to your home," Sabra guessed, and he nodded. Then he took her hands in his.

"He didn't hurt you, did he?" His voice was low and gruff as he pulled her sleeves up to examine her arms.

Sabra let him examine her, but more for the sheer pleasure of his attention. "A few bruises and a slight headache. Nothing more." She had to focus on her words rather than the way his fingers brushed up and down her arms. It was only to check for injuries, she knew.

But oh, how good it felt.

"They hit you on the head?" He let her hands fall and took her cheek in his right hand and began to feel the back of her skull with his left. Such a gentle touch for such a large man.

"Um..." *Focus, Sabra. He asked you a question.* "I hit it when he yanked me back onto the ground."

"Well, there's a knot back there. But," he studied her eyes carefully, the gray in his irises growing and shrinking as he moved them from side to side, "your eyes seem fine, so I'll wager to say you'll do well enough."

His quick examination seemed to be finished. And yet, she couldn't seem to tear her eyes from his. He continued to stare into hers as well. There was an openness in his expression, one that reminded her of the boy she'd known years ago. How she missed that boy, back before lineage or history had intruded into their lives so violently. And yet...

"I'm not going to leave you to them."

She blinked. "I'm sorry. What?"

His jaw flexed, and his eyes looked more silvery than they had a moment before. And she could have sworn she'd seen a fleck of blue for just a moment in their depths.

"You said in the market that I didn't have to go with you. That I owe them nothing." His right hand, which was still cradling the left side of her face, loosened slightly as he ran his thumb down her cheek.

Sabra closed her eyes, his thumb leaving a tingling trail behind it on her skin.

"And you're right," he said, placing his left hand on her other cheek. "But that doesn't mean I don't want to."

She opened her eyes and stared into his once more. If she had doubted his grandmother's word about his feelings toward her before, she found herself hard pressed to do so now.

"Why?" she whispered. "What am I to you?"

"You were always my friend."

She snorted. "A friend that ordered you about once a year like the spoiled child she was. You've only seen me three days in seven years, and I've done nothing but make your life harder."

"Since the day I first met you, you've been a pillar of stalwartness in my life."

Sabra raised her eyebrows. "Stalwartness?"

"You follow what you believe is right, and nothing moves you from that place." He slid his hands down from her face to her fingers and stared at them as he lightly held them there. "You heard when we were in Master Gregory's house. I had few friends as a child." He paused. "Funny, I didn't know what they meant back then with all the ways they excluded me. I only knew it was an insult. But knowing now what I do, I think a few of my neighbors even tried to warn you off when they saw us together once. I didn't know *why* at the time. But I did understand that for some reason, they thought the young princess should have nothing to do with me."

Sabra frowned. "I don't remember that."

He gave her a small smile. "You probably don't. You laughed as though they'd said the funniest thing in the world and then carried on with whatever nonsense we were up to. But up until that moment, I had lived in dread every year that one day you might appear and have realized that I was just another commoner." He paused, and when he spoke again, his voice was quiet. "But you were faithful even when the world wasn't."

"Huh." Sabra gave a little laugh. "That sounds about right. I don't exactly like being told what to do." She looked at him. "Or who my friends are."

He leaned closer. "You stayed by me all that time when you had no reason to. You were popular and beloved and beautiful and everything I was not."

Sabra had the vague feeling that she should stop him before he went too far. But she couldn't remember why she should, nor did she really want to. Because the way he was looking at her now was the look she had longed to see in her suitors. Not like an acquisition or some sort of untouchable goddess. She'd had enough of those looks. They were meant for creatures of her suitors' imaginations, creations of their own mind.

This look was for *her.*

"You might die," she whispered. "Not just from the dragon, but the land itself."

He gave her a sad smile. "That's just a risk I'm going to have to take."

"But—"

"Sabra, my life has, apparently, been planned in every way possible."

Sabra opened her mouth, but he cut her off.

"With all the best intentions, I know. And before you ask, yes, I've forgiven my grandparents already. Not that I'm going to tell them that immediately."

She gave him a wry grin as he continued.

"But you heard Master Gregory. What kind of coincidence is it for the daughter of the king to befriend the one boy in the world she shouldn't, according to her people?" He shook his head, a piece of hair falling over his forehead. "The Maker put you in my life, and I'm not about to abandon you now."

Sabra wanted to laugh and cry at the same time. So this was what love felt like.

While she was the last person in the world to rein in her natural enthusiasm, Sabra had always been more than careful with her heart. Playful aloofness was the safest way for a princess with a duty to marry. And even when that carefully constructed aloofness failed her, Sabra had imposed her iron will upon herself.

But never had she felt so completely helpless. There was no wall she could erect against the feelings and emotions that were bouncing around in her head and chest now. She wanted to pull him against her and to kiss him until they had drunk their fill of the joy. She wanted to take his hands and promise him forever, and then plunge into that promise with a running start. Their minds and hearts and bodies never looking back.

And yet...

Grief hit her like a rockslide. The weight of her crown had never been heavier. And if she wasn't careful now, it might crush her completely.

But how did she tell him? He was looking at her now with the same intensity she felt raging in her chest.

"You always thought you were a commoner." She put a hand on his face as he had done to her and gave him a smile that felt like it might break into a thousand pieces. "But I never thought that." She drew in a shaky breath. "And, it seems, I was right."

He stared at her for a long moment before understanding dawned in his eyes. And Sabra hated herself as he slowly nodded.

"You are correct." He gave her a poor smile. "But then, you always were." He sat back and studied the plateau. "We should probably be getting back. Supper will be ready soon."

Sabra let him help her out of the tree so she didn't trip on her skirts. Then she forced herself to withdraw her hand from his.

"I want you to know," he said softly, "that when I said I would protect you, I'll do that, no matter what choices you make." Then he turned and led her back to his home.

But her heart hurt every step of the way.

CHAPTER 25
SHE WAS IN LOVE

When George and Sabra reached the house, they said quiet goodbyes and Sabra excused herself to change clothes. Thankfully, Maria had offered some of her old dresses for Sabra to wear while she washed the clothes she had traveled in. The dress laid out on her bed tonight was simple but pretty, a blue-green gown with a white lining that reached just below her knees. Thin white trousers lay beside it. Sabra ran some water from the ceramic bowl through her hair and then brushed it before changing.

And the whole time, she was ignoring the emotions that were trying to burst from her chest.

She was in love.

What a strange thing to imagine. After so many years of keeping her heart safe for the sake of whomever she married, and after a lifetime of hearing how free she was to be allowed to choose her own spouse from her people...she was in love with one of the few men in the world she couldn't have.

And to make it all worse, it was the same man who was risking his own life in countless ways to save hers.

"You're not making this easy," she whispered to the Maker. But the empty room didn't answer her. Instead, she heard Maria calling everyone to supper.

Supper with George was the last place she wanted to be right now, but ignoring her host's meal would be rude. So Sabra picked herself up and joined everyone else in the kitchen. And to her great horror, found Serkan in the middle of what, judging by the grin on his dirty little face, was a delightful tale.

"And there was another one she called Grandpa," he cackled to George and Alner, who were sitting with him at the table. Maria was bustling around the kitchen with the food, but there was no way she was deaf to Serkan's words. "He was so old his beard was whiter than the rocks outside. And he had a round belly." Serkan stuck his stomach out so hard he nearly fell off his stool. George and Alner shared an amused glance.

"Sabra would always suggest they take walks when he called. He was huffing and puffing after just a few minutes."

"Serkan, how on earth did you know that?" Sabra glared at him. "I never told you such a thing."

"No." Serkan stuck a huge slice of grapefruit in his mouth and grinned at her, juice running down his chin. "But you told Nisa. And I heard that."

Sabra wished she had some sort of power that would shut the naughty boy's mouth for the remainder of the night. Instead, she glared at him. "I'm sure our hosts have no desire to hear about my suitors."

George leaned back in his chair and put his hands behind his head. "On the contrary," he said, his eyes dancing. "I'd love to hear more."

Sabra wondered if it were possible to die of mortification. Or dread. The last thing she wanted was for the man she loved to hear about the fools who had sought her hand. Perhaps worse, though, was the realization that if all went well and he succeeded, she would still have to marry one.

"Sabra liked to play jokes on another one," Serkan added, seeming very pleased with himself. "She called him The Scholar."

"And why that particular name?" Alner asked.

"Sabra said he was—"

"Not overly thoughtful." Sabra sat down in a stool and scooted herself far enough beneath the table to kick Serkan gently in the leg. "What's for supper, Maria?"

"Did she hate all of her suitors?" George asked.

Sabra glared at Serkan, but he just lifted one eyebrow and grinned back.

"There was one she didn't seem to mind," Serkan said, obviously not taking Sabra's hint. He grinned at her. "Actually, I believe she said he was quite nice to look at."

"Serkan!" Sabra cried. "If you utter one more—"

"Supper's ready," Maria announced in a firm voice. "That means you need to wash up." She took Serkan by the shoulder and turned him to face the door. "I don't know why I even let you sit at the table like this. One would think you'd wrestled with the chickens."

"With the goose, actually!" He beamed.

"Was I that bad at that age?" George asked as they watched him wash himself in the basin outside, grumbling all the way.

"Heavens, no. I don't think I've seen any child who's such a heathen as this one." And yet, Maria's eyes softened as she watched the boy, still grumbling, scrub his face. Apparently, she'd trained him well in the little time he'd been in her care. Better than any of the palace staff had managed.

"So," George said, turning his gaze back to Sabra, "who was this one who was quite nice to look at?"

Sabra felt her face heat, but it was Maria who answered with a snap of her dish towel.

"You mind your manners, too. She may be eating in our kitchen, but she's still Crown Princess."

At the reprimand, George's smile faded. He pulled back to sit straighter in his chair, and Sabra watched with growing chagrin as he nodded once. "Of course. My apologies."

Well, this was all just fantastic.

"Speaking of the princess," Alner said, glancing back and forth between his wife and George, "you were saying something about an attack this afternoon?"

"Justines," George said. "They weren't wearing white, but I'm pretty sure I recognized both attackers from yesterday."

"You said there were three the first time." Alner stroked his beard. "But only two this time? That's a bit disconcerting."

"I know." George looked at his plate as Maria set it before him. "That's why I want to leave tomorrow."

Alner's eyes went wide. "Tomorrow?" he asked as Serkan came back inside. Maria took one look at his hands and promptly sent him back out again. "George, we're not ready to travel. And you're not ready to fight a monster of the darkness."

"The longer we wait, the stronger he'll get. And the more soldiers he'll send after the princess," George said.

Sabra flinched internally when he used her title instead of her name.

"That may be true. But if you're not able to fight using all your natural abilities," he said after his gaze had flickered briefly to Sabra, "you at least need to ensure you're better than every other average human." He paused. "You need to at least go through the cave."

"You keep talking about this Sentinel's Cave," George said. "What is it?"

"Let's say thanks and then we'll tell you," Maria said as she finally allowed a sullen Serkan to take his seat.

After the prayer, Alner took the honey and dripped it on his flatbread as he spoke. "The Sentinel's Cave is where every man must go before he's allowed to join the Sentinels' ranks. He must pass its trials in order to be deemed ready to fight."

"When the Fortier prince came, he had retained a gift from his father," Maria said as she passed around the dishes. "A part of the crystal from the Fortress's foundation. Such items, however, are coveted by many as talismans. So he placed it in the cave for safekeeping. When he came back, he was shocked to find that the crystal had grown into the cave walls itself and multiplied there. Then while he was in there," Maria added, "he was attacked by a monster."

"Did it eat him?" Serkan asked, his eyes lighting up.

Alner gave him a look. "*No*, it did not eat him. But he did fight it. When he defeated it, however, it dissolved into a mist. He didn't have time to examine it, though, because another creature came at him as well."

"Did that one eat him?"

"No, but I might be tempted to see if it will eat you if you don't eat your own food," Alner told the boy. Then he looked back up at George and Sabra. "He realized that the creatures were monsters the Fortress and its monarchs had encountered over the years. They weren't real, just shadows of their real selves."

"The Fortress had absorbed its monarchs' memories of their enemies," Maria said, refilling everyone's mug with chilled milk. "And the Fortier prince realized that the Maker must have chosen that cave for a special purpose, just as He had once chosen the location of the Fortress."

"It became a sacred place of testing." Alner sat up straighter. "The young men were sent through it when they were of age. If they emerged on their own on the other side of the mountain, they were deemed ready to fight."

"The cave goes from one side of the mountain to the other," Maria added.

"What if they didn't come out?" Sabra asked, her appetite suddenly gone.

"They never died, if that's what you're wondering. But they could be injured. And if the one being tested didn't emerge by nightfall, the elders had to go in and get him. It was a sign from the Maker that he was not yet ready."

"So why do I need to go through this mountain?" George asked, staring hard at his plate. "It's not as though we have any other choice."

"Because," his grandfather said gravely, "if you can't defeat the shadow monsters within the cave, you won't stand a chance against a dragon in real life." His frown deepened the lines on his weathered face. "And I'd much rather pull you from a sacred cave, injured but alive, than watch as a dragon picks you apart."

George nodded slowly. "Then I'll go tomorrow."

"No, tomorrow you will train."

"Why?" George crossed his arms and leaned back. "I've been training my whole life. It's not as though a few more practice rounds are going to drastically alter my skills."

"You're going to train with me, and that's final." Alner's voice was quiet and terrible. "And if you don't, I'll not show you where the cave is at all."

George ground his teeth, but Maria lay her hand on his arm. "I know," she said softly, "that we aren't your real grandparents. Not by blood. But you are everything to us. And you're all your people have left, scattered and poor as they are."

Sabra thought back to the Blue Bands at home and shivered.

"Please let us help you one more time. Train with Alner. While you do, I'll prepare for the journey. We'll all go together then."

George still looked like he wanted to argue, so Sabra spoke quickly.

"I think that sounds wise." She met George's eyes, pleading silently for him to agree. As much as she wanted to save her kingdom, she didn't want to do it at the cost of George's life. Not when a few more days of training might possibly save him as Alner seemed to be convinced they could.

He stared at her for what felt like eternity. Then he slowly stood. "Very well."

CHAPTER 26

IF YOU DON'T KNOW

Sabra would have spent the next day in fits of anxiety, but Maria didn't give her time.

"If they're going to be fighting that beast," Maria said, gathering a pestle and mortar, bowls, and several flasks of unmarked liquids, "we'll need to have as much elixir on hand as possible. I doubt they'll have any left in Segzein."

"Elixir?" Sabra asked.

"A salve that can speed healing faster than any traditional poultices." Maria picked up a small burlap drawstring bag. Sabra gaped as she opened the bag and pulled out a blue crystal the size of Sabra's thumb.

"How so?" She watched as Maria put the crystal in the mortar and began to crush it. Her pulverization of the stone was impressive. Sabra doubted she'd have been able to do it so easily.

"This crystal is from the Sentinel's Cave. If we crush it into a fine powder," she scraped the sides and began again, "we can then mix it into a drink for the organs or a salve for the skin."

"I've never seen this in Segzein," Sabra said, leaning closer. The powder, though a light dust, still sparkled in the sunlight coming through the window.

"That's because you have none. Before we were exiled, we would make annual treks to the Sentinel's Cave to harvest the crystal where it grows." Maria's voice strained as she pressed the pestle even harder. "At the end, when the Sentinels grew too weak to travel and most of us were gone, there was no one to get the crystals or make the elixir." She paused and pushed some hair out of her face and added smugly, "I'll bet the Physics had a good time telling their customers they couldn't make any more."

Sabra stared at the powder. In chasing out the Sentinels, her people had lost not only their greatest defense, but also this miracle healing elixir. What else had they lost?

Once again, Sabra had to shove down the rage and frustration she wished she could take out on her father. But since he wasn't here, she allowed herself to be distracted when Maria began to name the ingredients as she mixed them in. Olive oil. A hint of peppermint oil. Aloe. Soon Sabra lost count and had to settle for simply watching the process. Her anger still simmered below, but it was easier to ignore as she watched the older woman work. Maria seemed as though she could have made the elixir in her sleep. Without spilling a drop, she poured the viscous liquid into a small blue glass jar the size of Sabra's fist and stopped it up with a wax seal.

"This," Maria said with satisfaction, "will come with us to Segzein. And I'll be making more tomorrow."

But they didn't go the next day. Or the next. Or the next. Instead, the next three days seemed merely designed to torture Sabra. George practiced endlessly with his grandfather, his grandmother singing until she went hoarse, and all Sabra could do was watch, pray, and mull. Not even Thing wanted to sit with her. Instead, he was off getting fat and happy eating mice in the animal stalls as Serkan played happily in the yard.

All that would have been bearable, though, if George hadn't been so focused. Not that she didn't want him to be focused. She wanted him to be as prepared as possible. But the long hours spent practicing made her feel restless and unnecessary. Even worse was the wall George seemed to have erected.

It wasn't a cruel wall. He still smiled and teased, but it was there, nonetheless. He no longer opened up to tell her what he was really thinking about unless it was something trivial.

Not that she blamed him. He'd opened up to her, and she'd practically announced to his face that she was marrying another man. Not now, perhaps. But one day, if all went well. So it only made sense for him to close himself off to her.

That didn't mean she had to like it.

And, of course, there were the whispers in Sabra's own head, the doubts that would never quite rest. *You could do it*, they always hissed with glee. *You could marry him and increase his power tenfold.* Sabra knew exactly what Alner hadn't said when he'd said that George was going to fight without access to all his abilities. He'd meant that Sabra *could* marry George and sing. His power would be increased greatly. He'd stand more of a chance of defeating the dragon.

But it wasn't so simple, Sabra argued with herself. She *could* marry George *and* probably increase his chance of victory against the dragon. But then the crown would be gone, and she'd be back to where she'd started. She'd promised her people so much, and if she did this now, she would have no chance to keep those promises.

Even more important was that because of this adventure, she now knew more than the vast majority of her advisers, at least about more recent history. This journey had taught her what her father had feared her learning and more. Many at home would be unwilling to believe what she had learned about the Sentinels and their mystery illness. If they had been unwilling to believe back when the Sentinels had been there, wasting away in front of them, how could she expect them to believe the truth now? And while Demir would be in every way qualified for kingship in his own right, his blind prejudices against the Sentinels frightened her. The way he'd spoken of them before she'd left...she couldn't guarantee that George and the Blue Bands would be treated as they ought, even if he defeated the dragon. She could still recall the fire in her cousin's eyes as he blamed the Sentinels for his parents' deaths.

Of course, there was also her vow to her dying father.

No. It was better this way. Besides, George was holding his own against his grandfather, even without the blue fire. If anyone could fight the dragon and win, it would be him. Then she, as queen, could put her resources, limited as they were, into helping his people either truly clear their land and resettle or move on. As queen, she could even call on King Everard Fortier for help with whatever darkness had settled in their land. Such a call wouldn't be possible for the wife of a basniin. Basniin spouses didn't have authority of their own accord. But with the crown, she could call in every resource available until they found a way to rid Segzein of the... What had Master Gregory called it? Oh, yes. Sortheliege.

Then George could finally choose to have a life in his own right, no longer running and hiding from the Justines or living under the lie that he was cursed. He could have a home of his own, move his grandparents in with him, get married, have a family...

Sabra groaned. The thought of this triumphant ending was not cheering her as it should. She did her best to focus again on the practice fight going on below the balcony where she sat.

Eventually, George and Alner stopped to get something to eat, and Serkan scampered along after them, peppering them with questions about their weapons. Sabra stood to follow. She hadn't eaten anything since the early breakfast they had all shared, but once she was on her feet, she realized she had no desire to eat. Her stomach soured at the thought of it. She was restless and needed some way to channel the frustrating thoughts in her head instead.

And then her eyes rested on the staffs pegged on the wall below.

Surely they wouldn't mind if she borrowed one. She just needed a chance to work her frustrations out with some movement.

She hurried down the steps and went over to the wall with the staffs. She had realized the day before that each wall had weapons on it, and there were more than just swords. Lances, pikes, bows, crossbows, daggers, spears, maces, halberds, and, of course, staffs. The draw to examine and handle every single one was present, of course, but Sabra ignored that desire and instead went straight to the staff section. She lovingly ran her hand along several of them. They were finer than anything she had ever trained with. Some were smooth, with patterns and mysterious symbols carved and painted beneath some sort of shiny finish. Others were rough and simple. Some had hooks and spikes, and one had holes that Sabra could see no purpose in at all.

Remembering that the men would soon return to resume their training, Sabra picked the simplest of the staffs and tested its weight. Handling it was like touching balance itself. She took it reverently to the center of the training square and closed her eyes. Then she began to move in the most recent form Demir had taught her.

She had been right. Movement was exactly what she needed. The more she moved, the more her mind cleared. Her troubles didn't fade, but they were shuffled into a neater box, rather than rolling all about her mind like the glass marbles her father had gotten her for her tenth birthday.

Breathe in.

Breathe out.

Spin.

Strike.

Block.

Strike.

Spin.

Sabra nearly fell over when the smooth arc of her strike struck something hard. Her body jarred as she opened her eyes to see George. He had blocked her strike with the fancy painted staff.

"Your posture is good," he said, taking a step back and pulling his staff with him.

"But?" Sabra gave him a knowing smile. "I can hear the 'but' coming."

He gave her the smallest of smiles. "If you fight like that, you'll be knocked over in the first three steps."

She frowned. "I haven't missed any."

"No." He put his staff on the ground to the side. Then he put his right hand over hers and wrapped his left hand around her left. She was now pressed against his chest, and the warmth against her back made her breath hitch.

What were they talking about again?

"Ready stance," he said.

Oh, yes. She fell into a ready stance. Or what she thought was one. She couldn't remember for sure at the moment.

"You move through the form with grace, but it has no purpose. Show me what comes next."

When Sabra remembered, though she wasn't sure how, his arms willingly followed hers.

"Here, try again. But like this." The muscles of his massive arms tensed against hers, and with a power like she'd never felt before, she was in the second position.

"Do you see what I mean?" he asked, his lips against her hair.

Unable to speak, Sabra nodded.

"Good. Now the next one."

Step by step, move by move, George guided her through the form. She lost track of time, and if he had asked her what part of the form they were in, she wouldn't have been able to tell him. She could only think about how she wanted to stay here, safe in his strong arms where she knew no one would harm her.

They must have finished because George finally stepped back. The lack of his chest at her back cleared Sabra's mind enough for her to realize that they must have finished. There were slight sweat marks on his shirt, and she could smell a little of his scent on her own clothes. Not that she minded.

"You can fight until you drop," George said, wiping his forehead on his sleeve. "But if you don't know why you're fighting, you're going to lose."

Sabra stared after him as he swigged from a waterskin. She was thirsty, too, but for some reason, she couldn't get her feet to cross the floor.

Hurried steps sounded on the balcony above, and George and Sabra looked up. Maria's eyes were wide and fierce.

"We just received word from Master Gregory. Justines are all over the town. The local authorities are trying to get rid of them, but there are too many."

"Are they coming here now?" Sabra asked.

"Not that I'm aware of. They're searching houses within the town." She frowned. "But they will be."

"Well," George turned to Sabra, "it looks like I will be taking that trial sooner than later after all."

CHAPTER 27
TRY

Sabra was instructed to remain in the house when George and his grandparents left early the next morning.

Sabra didn't listen.

This was her kingdom at stake, and George was her friend. She needed to see what happened, even if only from a distance. It wasn't as though she would interfere. Trailing them unnoticed was difficult, though, and she had to work not to make any sounds as she stumbled along behind, following Alner's dim lamp. This was especially hard when she stepped on a rock the wrong way and twisted her ankle. She bit her lip hard so she wouldn't let out a cry.

They were making their way down the range of hills, past the plateau in which their home was built. Sabra had left Serkan with instructions not to leave the house or cause trouble. Her severity must have been convincing because for once, he just looked at her with wide eyes and nodded. Finally, moments before the sunrise, Alner stopped the group at the foothill of a small mountain, one that rose up higher than the hills around it. Judging by the change in the rock formations around her, Sabra guessed it had at one time been a small volcano.

She hid behind a large boulder and squinted up at them. It was still dark enough that she had difficulty making out the large cave entrance above. When Alner spoke, his voice was nearly inaudible.

"When you get inside, use your sword to draw blood from your hand. Put your palm on the standing crystal at the opening. When you do, you'll see the crystal flash. This signals that the crystal recognizes you as an heir of the Fortier fire. You'll begin your test from there."

"What will I do?" George asked.

"Simple," Maria said. "Survive."

"You need to push through the cave to the other side. That's the only way out. If you can make it through to the other side..." Alner drew in a breath that rattled so loudly Sabra could hear it. "You might survive the dragon."

Sabra peeked around the boulder once more to see Maria pull George's head down to place a kiss on it. Alner looked up at the young man who towered above him and squeezed his shoulder once before turning and going down the mountain.

Sabra watched him hesitate a moment as he watched them go, and a mad impulse took hold of her.

What if she followed him inside the mountain?

Surely the shadow monsters or whatever they were wouldn't attack her. She wasn't a Sentinel, and she wasn't going to use her blood. She would just follow from a distance and watch. Demir would most definitely forbid it if he were here, and her mother would be horrified, but they weren't here. She was. And she was their queen, after all.

She waited until George's grandparents had gone far enough that they were unlikely to turn again. Then she darted up the foothill, slipping twice, and into the mouth of the cave.

The entrance was impressive, at least twice Sabra's height, which made its interior even more surprisingly unimpressive. The cave itself was just a small room, no bigger than the room she was staying in beneath George's home. She didn't have time to examine it too far, though, because George was standing before the largest crystal Sabra had ever seen. It had sprouted up from the ground and would have been up to her chest had she been standing just beside it. Even in the dull gray of the early morning, its straight blue arms seemed to flicker in the darkness. The hair on Sabra's arms stood on end, and she wrapped her cloak more tightly around her. The early morning breeze was stronger at the mouth of the cave, but she knew that if she went any deeper, he would see her. So she shivered and watched from her corner.

He slowly drew his sword from its scabbard and looked at his left hand before raising the blade to it. The cut was small but made Sabra flinch as he pulled it across his palm. Then, as the blood dripped down his arm, he pressed it against the crystal.

For a moment, nothing happened, and Sabra wondered if the cave had died along with its people. But then the cave began to groan slightly, a strange warm breeze playing with her hair as it exited the cave. She looked back down at the crystal to see a blue spark at the crystal's base. Swirling blue danced up within the rock, moving like smoke as it filled every arm and crevice.

Then the cave exploded with light.

Floating points of brilliant blue hovered at the ceiling, lighting a path that moved deeper into the mountain through a tunnel that Sabra could have sworn wasn't there before. Similar blue clung to the cave walls, just bright enough that Sabra could see the crystal covering nearly every inch of the cave, floor to ceiling.

As if in a daze, George walked slowly deeper into the cave. Sabra followed as closely as she thought safe. Never in her life had she seen anything so beautiful.

The only warning was the whisper to their left. Sabra turned her head just in time to see a cloud of bright blue smoke materialize into a glowing creature.

Although it wasn't just one glowing creature staring up at them. It was hundreds. Hundreds of rats…the biggest rats Sabra had ever seen, larger than Thing, stared up at George. George stared back at them, seeming unsure of what to do.

One crawled up to him, holding its paws up in the air, sniffing curiously. Scooting a bit closer, it sniffed his boot.

And then bit it.

George cried out as the rat's teeth went straight through the leather. His sword, which was already drawn, cut the rat neatly in two, but as it died, the horde facing George began to chatter. Then, as though with a single mind, they began to climb George.

George shouted, raking his sword dangerously close to his own body in an effort to sweep them off. But each time he did so, they simply climbed him again. Sabra felt sick to her stomach as they bit and scratched him. Their squeaks formed a malicious cacophony that echoed through the chamber. Sabra squeezed the rock wall inside the tunnel until her fingers hurt as she watched him try to slash and squish them against the wall.

Just when he seemed ready to topple over, he freed one of his hands. This allowed him to grab one of the large torches, alight with blue flame. The rats screamed loudly and darted down his body away from the flame. This time, he was able to scrape them off. He kept the torch in his hands as he turned and ran deeper into the cave. The rats tried to chase him, but whenever they did, he slashed his sword in their direction, and they fell back again until he'd reached another tunnel. Sabra hesitated a moment before running after them. Thankfully, the rats didn't seem to notice her, or if they did, they didn't care.

George and the rats went through a narrow tunnel, but as Sabra came closer, the creatures squealed and darted in all different directions. By the time Sabra reached the tunnel and followed him through, there wasn't a rat to be seen. Still, instead of following him out, she hid just inside its mouth and peeked out.

George had stopped again on the other side. This time, however, there was a very large creature in front of him. A wolf, Sabra realized in horror. A wolf nearly as tall as he was with teeth jutting out of its jaws at crooked angles, teeth so long its lips couldn't cover them. It had a dead rat in its jaws, bleeding bright blue drops on the ground. But as George and the wolf eyed each other suspiciously, the wolf dropped the rat carcass on the ground.

This time, George didn't wait to be bitten. Instead, he sprinted to the side and climbed up to a rock ledge higher than Sabra was tall. He ran along the length of the wall this way, pausing every few yards to slash down at the wolf below. The wolf gave chase, its teeth missing George by a hand width each time George had to pause or prepare to jump over breaks in the ledge. The farther they got, the louder the creature's snarls as its blood became matted with fur.

Sabra continued to trail behind, still unsure about whether or not the other creatures could see her, but also too nervous to lose sight of George. The last thing she needed was to be sealed inside some magic mountain when he was finished with his trial or she got too far behind.

Unfortunately, George found himself at the wrong side of the room, the tunnel opening all the way down the length of the blue-lit wall. Sabra watched in horror as the wolf gnashed its teeth at him again and again. He was cornered.

Clinging to the edge of the wall, he nearly stumbled but caught himself. Just as it looked as though he might swing himself over the wolf's head, using parts of the rough wall for a grip, he turned midair and came down on the animal blade-first, the wolf letting out a gurgled cry as it slumped to the ground.

There was no time to celebrate, however, because as he jumped to the ground and yanked his sword out of the wolf's body, something large and fast swooped down, letting out a shriek that echoed through the cave before knocking his head with its sharp beak.

Sabra could see where a trickle of blood ran down the side of his head and nearly gave herself away as her instincts screamed at her to go check his injury. But his quick movements and stance of alertness were enough to assure her that he hadn't been too badly hurt. The creature, some sort of bird of prey, swooped back up to the ceiling as it let out another shriek. As it swooped down, Sabra could see, however, that it was no ordinary bird. Its body alone was nearly the size of the wolf.

George used the time that it spent gliding to sprint back toward the tunnel he'd come from, but he wasn't able to make it fast enough before the bird struck again.

Sabra blanched and was momentarily frozen as, in her head, she could see Mahzar sweeping down from the sky, fire in his jaws the way this bird's beak was full of blue flame. The bird wasn't anywhere nearly as large as the dragon. But the sensation of danger from above was too familiar for comfort.

Again and again, the bird hit his head with its beak, until in the dim light, she could see at least three trickles of blood rolling down his face and neck. Sabra had made it to the far tunnel now and had hidden herself in a shallow opening beside the tunnel.

George did his best to fight the bird as it dove at him from above, but he could do little. The bird pivoted in the air, dancing just out of reach every time he tried to slice at it from below. The only progress he could make was short sprints each time the bird flew back up in preparation to dive again.

Just as he was nearly to the tunnel, though, the bird made a sharp turn and hit him harder and faster than before, slamming into George so hard that he fell to the ground. And he didn't get up.

Sabra's heart was in her throat, making it impossible to breathe. Had he been defeated so soon? Forget the dragon, would he even make it out of this test alive?

Sabra had nearly gone to his side to examine him when the bird swooped down once more. This time, however, it perched on his still arm. Just as Sabra was about to begin throwing rocks at the cursed thing, George flipped over and ran it through with his sword.

Sabra nearly fainted with relief.

He got to his feet with only one or two wobbles before straightening his shoulders and passing carefully through the tunnel into the next chamber. Sabra carefully followed.

To her surprise, though, there were no animals in this chamber. No birds of prey or even sparrows. After walking for a few moments, however, they did discover people.

There was a small group of what looked like confused peasants bunched in a corner on the other side of the room. They looked distressed. George paused and frowned. The path to the next tunnel was clear, but Sabra could only guess he was wondering if he ought to see what had them so upset. Of course, they weren't real. They were made of the same bright blue the way the animals in the last cave had been. But at the moment, they didn't seem intent on killing George.

An old woman on the fringe of the group hobbled away from them. She appeared lost and confused. George ran to her side and put a hand on her shoulder.

"Madame, are you lost?"

The woman turned, and Sabra could see now that she was weeping.

"Madame?" he repeated.

"No," she sobbed, her hands over her eyes. "I'm in mourning."

"For whom?" he asked, more softly this time.

She pulled her hands away from her face and looked at him with large, luminous blue eyes. "For you." Then she pointed to the other side of the cavern, and Sabra gasped when she saw an army of blindingly blue soldiers approaching them. When George turned back and looked over his shoulder, there were soldiers coming from the next tunnel entrance as well. They were banging their swords on their shields and chanting in a language Sabra didn't recognize as they marched toward George.

Sabra pushed herself against the cavern wall, her breath coming in and out too fast as she prayed these soldiers wouldn't see her either. But she needn't have worried. They went straight for George.

This time, he didn't hesitate as he did with the rats. He grimly held up his sword, and by the time the first enemy had raised his own weapon, George was charging forward.

Sabra could only catch glimpses of the fight. There were at least three dozen, and they were all coming closer and closer to George. His sword was strong and fast, though, and they couldn't seem to pierce the circle he created around himself with it. One after one, they began to fall. Instead of falling back, though, they merely transformed into clouds of swirling vapors before rematerializing again. Then they darted back to attack him again.

Unfortunately, after a while, George began to tire. His steps became sloppy, and she could see that the tips of their weapons were beginning to nick his skin here and there.

He needed to remember the song. Sabra opened her mouth to call out to him, to remind him to do the dance of war, when one of the soldiers turned and looked at her. He turned away from his brothers and reached out for her.

Sabra didn't mean to scream, but she must have, for George's head snapped up.

"Sabra?" he shouted. When they made eye contact, even in the dim light, she could see his strength renew. His steps became sure again as he began to strike the enemy down, two or three at a time, until he reached her. By then, the soldier had taken her wrist in his hand, but he did no more, as George's sword ran through his chest.

"Run, Sabra!" George shouted as he struck the soldiers who came at them again.

Sabra was out of her hiding place in a second. Now that he had joined her at the wall, they had a clear path to the next tunnel. He took off first, cutting down the soldiers that got in their way. She bolted after him, sure that they would make it in time. But just as they neared the end, the soldiers and the villagers faded away.

Only one man stood in their way. The general who had commanded the horde stood before the tunnel, staring at George. Heat emanating from his body made the air hazy. In fact, it quickly began to scorch Sabra's face. Turning away briefly, she realized quickly that she could indeed be hurt in these tunnels just as easily as George.

This complicated things.

"What do you want?" George called out, grabbing Sabra's hand and pulling her behind him.

Without answering, the man's face began to contort, and as it did he smiled. His nose melted into his face, and his eyes widened until they were impossibly far apart, shrinking to slits no wider than several stacked pieces of parchment. Then he burst from the form he'd just taken into a cloud of blue vapor that floated through the air.

It moved closer, thickening again into its strange form an arm's length away from them.

George and Sabra stumbled back as it leered at them.

"What?" it asked in a raspy voice. "Never seen a fae before?"

George didn't answer, only held his sword up higher and tightened his grip on Sabra's hand. "I don't want to kill you. I simply want to pass through."

"Oh, but I so want to kill you!" It raised a long knife at George and brought it down hard above George's head. George met its attack and even drove a few of his own before the creature dissolved again. Seeming unencumbered by gravity, it floated up above their heads before beginning to materialize again. George shoved Sabra back against the wall as the creature fell on him.

Somehow, he blocked the creature's blade and shoved it off. But the creature...fae, it seemed, wasn't daunted. Again and again it came at him from every angle. And after an eternity of hand-to-hand combat with this unearthly creature, George began to tire. He stumbled once. Twice. A third time, and the creature managed to hit him hard with its fist, which was air one moment and solid the next.

Time seemed to freeze as Sabra realized two things. One, that if this strange, human-sized creature of magic defeated George now, there was no way he'd be ready to fight the dragon. Provided they made it out of this cave alive. She also, however, realized that they had forgotten something.

"The song!" Sabra screamed from her place at the wall. "Move to the song!"

"What?" George's voice was hoarse and desperate.

"George, fight to the song!"

Sabra peeked out again from her hiding place to see George take a few more steps. But they were clumsy and not at all to the rhythm of the Sentinel's Song. Then he cried out as the fae slashed at his shoulder.

He was fading. He needed help.

Just a hint. She would give him a hint of the song. Surely that would be enough for him to remember. Not the whole song, of course. She wouldn't need to do that. Just a few words.

"Grab your lance and knock your arrows..." she sang. Fear shook her so hard her voice cracked. But she sang nonetheless.

Both George and the fae froze and looked in her direction.

"The song, George!" she called. "Fight to the song!" When he stayed still, she sang again. *"Hold your sword up high."*

Then everything changed.

George's eyes began burning blue, lit by what looked like the same light as that which came from the crystals surrounding them. His sword glowed as well. And not only his sword. The entire cave lit up, and the room, which had been dimmer than if lit by a mere candle, flared nearly as bright as day.

"Now, George!" Sabra screamed.

This time, George listened. His footsteps fell into the familiar rhythm. Sabra had heard Maria sing the song so many times she could have chanted it in her sleep.

The fae seemed to have the opposite reaction. It dropped its weapon, and it materialized fully in front of George. Its eyes were wide and distant as it stared at George's blazing sword. Which George ran right through its chest.

"Come on!" he yelled, not waiting to see if more creatures appeared behind them. Sabra grabbed his hand, and they ran through the tunnel into the largest cavern yet.

It was at least as high as her throne room at home. The blue lights on the walls became lost in the distance, seen only as a sort of blue haze that made the path inside just visible enough to see. Standing beside the path was a man dressed in long robes and a jeweled diadem. He held his sword, point down, his hands resting upon its pommel. His body was also lined by the mystical blue light. A long beard reached down to his finely swathed chest, and rings of blue fire blazed in his eyes.

"Come," he said to them, indicating that they stand before him.

George lifted his sword a little. "You don't want to kill us, too, do you?"

The man…he looked like a king, gave them a patient, gentle smile, the kind Sabra's mother used to give her when she was full of childish nonsense. "No," he said in a deep, rich voice. "Now, come here, and I shall tell you of your final test."

George and Sabra came slowly. When they were finally before him, Sabra realized that this man was even taller than George.

"Your next test," he said in that same rich voice, "will be one in which you must make a choice." His eyes settled on Sabra. "There will be a rockslide."

George stood straighter. "A rockslide?" He looked at Sabra, his brow furrowed. "I don't know how to fight a rockslide."

The man gave George a sad smile. "You can't."

Sabra's chest tightened. "You mean…"

"We all have our limits," the king continued gently. "Sometimes, though, when we are faced with insurmountable circumstances, we still must make a choice." His eyes flicked back to Sabra. "No one can make our choices for us."

"But George—" Sabra began.

"Sometimes," he said again, "we still must try."

The floor began to quiver. The cave thundered, and before their eyes, the king began to disappear. And behind where he had been standing was a beam of light.

"The cave entrance!" George cried. "Come on!"

They began to run toward the entrance until it felt like they were flying. But the rocks that had begun rolling along when the cave shook were now making their way to the path. The ceiling also gave a tremendous crack before chunks of it began to fall, pounding the earth below as it smashed down all around them.

George held up his sword above their heads, Sabra guessed in an attempt to break any large rocks that fell their way. But they were still too far from the entrance. They wouldn't make it in time.

Sabra could hear George singing as they ran. It was more like a recitation, as he was out of breath, and the words came in gasping groups.

"Grab your lance…nock your arrow…hold…sword up high…"

Sabra joined him.

"For to war we...have been called. Now we're...going nigh."

She hadn't meant to sing the song on her own. She'd merely meant to aid George, to help him as they ran the rest of the way. But as soon as the words were out of her mouth, the blue fire seemed to explode from within him again. And as the stone ceiling collapsed in, George yelled,

"Jump!"

They landed hard in the gravel. But Sabra hardly noticed. She scrambled up onto her elbow to look behind them, sure the mountain would fall in on itself. But the cave mouth was black and silent, just as it had been on the other side before George had used his blood to awaken it. There was no shaking from within nor any strange, wispy, glowing blue.

And somehow, it was already late afternoon. How had they been in that cave for most of the day?

George and Sabra looked at one another, their eyes wide and their breaths coming in gasps.

"You didn't..." He swallowed and tried again, still struggling for breath. "You didn't sing the whole song, did you? Just the beginning?"

"No." Sabra let her head fall back on the dirt, not caring how dirty it got. "I just wanted to remind you. You were forgetting..." She let the words die on her lips as he nodded.

"Thank you." Then he frowned and looked at the ground. After another moment, he spoke again. "You don't think this would disqualify me, do you?"

Sabra thought for a moment. She hadn't considered that. Only keeping George alive. "What would you do if it did?"

He shrugged. "I'd fight the dragon anyway."

She nodded. "Well, then. Maybe it is what it is."

It wasn't cheating, she assured herself, as they made their way back to the edge of the small mountain where he was to meet his grandparents. She'd briefly powered his eyes and sword. But they had only glowed for a minute. It wasn't as though she'd held the fire there.

"Sabra," he said, stopping before they moved into the shade of the mountain, out of the late afternoon sunlight. "Why did you follow me?"

Because she needed to know he would survive so her people would survive.

Because she needed to know he was well.

Because she couldn't bear to let him go alone. Not when it was her fault he was being tested so soon.

But her lips wouldn't utter those words. Instead, they told the truth, "I just knew I needed to go."

He stared at her for an eternity. She could feel his nearness just as she had felt the nearness of the crystal cave. As though he were radiating its power. Every hair on her body was standing on end. Gone was the wall he'd carefully created over the last few days.

He finally blinked, breaking the spell that had held them both there, and nodded. "It would probably be best if you stayed out of sight, though, and followed us home. I'm not sure my grandparents would understand."

She nodded.

"And Sabra?"

She met his eyes. They were gray once again, no hint of the brilliant blue remaining. But sharper than ever.

"Thank you."

As Sabra washed and brushed her hair that night, determined to remove any trace of her adventure, she couldn't help but wonder.

She had sung for George. And though the song wasn't complete. Far from it, the power within him had leaped to life. Not just his power, but the dark itself had become like a brilliant light. But she wasn't his wife after all.

So what did it all mean?

CHAPTER 28
I'M READY

Supper that night was strained. George and his grandparents talked quietly of their preparations while Sabra and Serkan ate. Every few bites, Serkan glared at Sabra over his bowl of soup, but to his credit, he didn't say anything to give her little adventure away. He was jealous, though, that she'd gone with George while Serkan had been forced to stay behind and feed the chickens, and she knew he was waiting for their first moment alone to let her know just how much he had disliked it.

"I'll call on Gregory tomorrow," Alner was saying as he dipped his bread in oil. "He'll stay with the animals if I ask him to." His words were easy, but Sabra didn't miss his heavy sigh.

"I'll pack what we need tonight," Maria said. "Whatever we don't need, I'll take to market tomorrow to sell." She glanced up. "We might get some money for the curtains and sheets, too. And the blankets. I'll pack some, of course, but..." Her eyes slowly swept across the house, and Sabra's food lost its taste.

"Wait." Serkan looked around. "You're not coming back?" He turned to Sabra, his brown eyes large. "They can come back, can't they?"

"If they wish," Sabra said, doing her best to force a smile. But inside, she was breaking. "And I'll make sure they get back everything they gave up and more."

Serkan nodded glumly and went back to his food, but Sabra just wanted to vomit hers. They were giving up everything for her. Their adopted grandson. Their house and animals and everything they had worked for. Possibly even their own lives.

Alner nodded and started eating again. "I can sell most of the weapons, too. We'd get a better price for them if I waited, but it'll be better than nothing."

"I'll see what we have in storage," George said.

"What we get should be enough for a cow and a few chickens when we get settled again," Alner said. Of course, he left unsaid the possibility that they would never get settled again in the case they didn't survive.

Sabra closed her eyes. Her rash decision to run to George might end up in his entire family's deaths.

"I'm sorry!"

Everyone looked at Sabra, and she felt mortifyingly large tears well up in her eyes.

"For what?" Maria asked, looking genuinely confused.

Sabra dropped her spoon in her bowl with a clink and put her hands on her face. "When I came here, I never meant to ask this of you. All I knew was that I was being chased, and George was the only person I knew, and—"

"Child."

A warm, rough hand touched her face, and Sabra looked up to see Alner looking at her, his eyes, soft and warm.

"Of all the people you met on that day in the market, George should not have been one of them. The likelihood of the princess and the lost basniin befriending one another was too small to have happened by chance."

Sabra tried wiping the tears off with her hands, but just succeeded in smearing them all over her face, which was probably red and splotchy. "But you're risking everything." She caught George's eye, and he stared back at her, his face unreadable.

"Yes, there is much risk," Maria said slowly. "But seeing as the Maker has orchestrated everything thus far, worrying about risk seems a bit foolish now, doesn't it?" She gave Alner a strange smile. It seemed as though they'd discussed this at great length. Maria hardly seemed the same woman as she had that first day, when she'd realized who Sabra really was.

He returned the smile with a sad one of his own. "There's an older saying among the Sentinels. *Run the path laid before you. Do not veer for the broken sapling.*"

"That doesn't make any sense." Serkan made a face at his food.

"It means that if we were each put on the path created specifically for *us*, the Maker doesn't expect us to repair what lies in someone else's path or garden. That is his work. He created everything with its own purpose, after all, just as we were created for ours."

"You ask about risk in battle," Maria said. "Our people were born for battle after all." Her eyes flashed. "Is action truly foolish when it's what you were created to do?"

A crash sounded in the front of the house, and Sabra turned to see men in white climbing through the broken windows. In one movement, Alner had yanked Sabra out of her chair and swung her to the side. With the other hand, he grabbed the little table and threw it at the men closest to them.

Maria had Serkan and yanked him into the kitchen, where she grabbed a hot tong from the fire and held it with the same familiar expertise George and Alner handled swords with.

George took Sabra from Alner and half-pulled, half-dragged her toward the weapons room. "Grab a staff and stay behind me," he said tersely as they ran. "Whatever you do, don't let them take you."

Three men followed close on their heels. George and Sabra had barely made it down the stairs into the training square when their pursuers reached the balcony above. Sabra dashed over to the wall and grabbed the painted staff because it was the longest. George darted around the training area, loading his person with weapons. Then he turned to face their attackers as Sabra pressed herself against the wall, and George squared off with them at the foot of the stairs.

They were definitely Justines. Their white cloaks and black undergarments meant they weren't even hiding their origins now. They had come with the intent of making sure no one but Sabra would live to testify against them. And if they got her now, Sabra had little doubt they would make sure she couldn't speak publicly again, aside from her involuntary wedding vows.

Two of them went straight for George while the third came at her. Sabra met him with her staff, bringing it down as hard as she could. The blow pushed him back a few steps, but he blocked it easily.

A distance. She only needed to keep him at a distance. Sabra had no doubt George would beat his rivals. Then he would come to help her if she could only last that long. At first, her nerves made her clumsy and slow, and the man drew so close that she was forced to pull back. He followed, of course, using her mistake to push closer until she was very near to being backed into a corner.

"One down!" George called to Sabra. She and her opponent glanced over to see one of the men in white fall at George's feet. The shout broke through the fog of frustration filling Sabra's mind, and she recalled Demir's training. She took advantage of her opponent's distraction to sweep his leg. He rolled and was on his feet quickly, but he wasn't quite as close as he had been before. Her moves weren't nearly as smooth or practiced as George's, but she was able to keep her attacker at bay, just far enough away that he couldn't grab her.

That changed, however, when he yanked a whip from his belt and unfurled it. Then he snapped it in the air and wrapped it around Sabra's staff. With a flick of his wrist, he yanked it out of her hands and flung it to the side. Sabra turned to run back to the wall of staffs to grab another, but with a painful snap, he had the whip around her waist. Try as she might, she couldn't unwrap it in time, and he began pulling her closer to him. She threw herself on the floor and managed to grab a second staff as he pulled her back. But by the time she was able to turn around again, all as she was still being dragged through the sand, she was too close to use it.

"Basniin Mahzar has no wish to hurt you or your friends," the guard said as he wrapped one large arm around her and yanked her to her feet. "If you'll agree to honor the clan vows, we'll cease fighting immediately."

Sabra managed to wiggle one arm free and elbow him in the jaw. "Mahzar can worry about honoring his own vows before he worries about mine."

The man spit out blood and began to advance toward her again, this time, his eyes narrow and bright. But he froze and then cried out before falling to the ground. George stood over his body, his blade red as he pulled it from the man's back. Sabra looked around to see not two but three other bodies lying on the ground. Apparently, they'd been joined by a fourth guard at some point.

"Are you well?" George asked in a flat voice.

Sabra nodded. "And you?"

"George!" Maria screamed from above. "Come quick!"

George and Sabra sprinted toward the stairs and climbed them as fast as they could. They arrived in the kitchen, which was covered in broken pottery, blood, and more bodies. Maria was on her knees, holding Alner on her lap. Serkan was sitting beside her, clinging to her arm.

Alner's face was ghostly white, and his long hair, which was always pulled back neatly, was strewn everywhere, matted with blood and dirt. He coughed several times and moaned as Maria tried to wipe the sweat from around his eyes.

"Get me the elixir!" Maria cried when she saw George. George darted back down the hall, and Sabra, knowing best to stay out of the way, gently pulled Serkan into her own lap so Maria would have space to move. He clung to her, his whole body trembling as she hugged him close.

"They kept me safe," he whimpered as she stroked his hair. "The Justines kept coming, but he kept pushing them all back!"

"What happened?" Sabra asked Maria. She could hear George's clomping footsteps as he ran back up the stairs.

"He was doing well until he slipped on some spilled oil and fell on a piece of pottery." She nodded down at where her left hand was pressed down on his stomach with a swatch of torn skirt.

George sank to his knees beside Maria, and Maria slid her hand over a little to peer at the wound again. After a moment of quiet discussion, they determined that the bleeding was stopped, and George began to clean it.

"I'll add the elixir and stitch it up," Maria said. "But he won't be able to travel for weeks."

George paused in his work. "But the elixir—"

She gave him a sad smile. "The elixir will help. But your grandfather isn't a young man anymore. He'll still need time." She put her hand on his shoulder. "It appears your path is alone. And that saddens me greatly." Her smile faded.

George's hand shook slightly before he began cleaning the wound again. "I understand."

Alone. George would be fighting the dragon alone. His grandfather wouldn't be by his side, fighting with the legendary blue fire while his grandmother sang the Sentinel's Song.

"Sabra!"

Sabra realized that Maria had been calling her name. "Yes?" She blinked and looked around. Serkan was gone. Maria must have sent him on some errand while she was daydreaming.

"Go pack for yourself now. You and George must leave before light comes, or they'll find you."

Sabra looked back down at Alner. "What about you—"

"We'll be fine. Go!"

Sabra turned to go, but Maria called to her once more.

"Yes?" Sabra answered breathlessly.

"Leave the boy with us. He'll only slow you down."

Sabra stared at her for a long minute before nodding and turning to leave again. Her head was a muddled mess, turning uselessly in circles. But at least her body seemed capable of obeying. Two minutes later, she was downstairs, throwing her belongings back into the satchel her mother had given her. Her mind was numb as she tried to remember what else they might need.

"Where are we going?"

Sabra turned to see Serkan standing behind her. He was trembling. Sabra took a deep breath and forced herself to smile. "Where's your new cloak?"

He went to his little bed on the floor and picked it out of the pile of blankets. Sabra took it and fastened it snugly on his shoulders.

"It was kind of Maria to give this to you," she said. "Make sure to sleep with it on tonight. There's a good chance Maria won't be able to tend to your fire."

He looked down at it and fingered the hem. "She said mine was too small. This used to be George's."

"You've grown this year."

He nodded. "Do you think we'll ever see them again?"

"You are going to see them a lot."

He took a step back. "What do you mean?"

Sabra followed and shook her head. "We're going to be traveling fast and hard. It will be easier for you if you stay here with them."

"No! No, no, no." He shook his head vehemently. "I'm going with you."

"Serkan—"

"Won't I see you again?" he whispered tearfully.

Probably not. But Sabra wasn't about to frighten him further. It was funny how things had changed between them in the past few days. "If things go as planned at home, I will make sure you and I are together again so much of the time."

The look the boy gave her told her that he wasn't fooled.

"Go see if Maria needs help with anything while I finish here." Sabra ruffled his hair and gave him a gentle shove.

Five minutes later, there was nothing else to do. Sabra had made up the bed and folded the blankets, reset the furniture, and holed up the wall of bricks. She went to the kitchen to find all the pottery swept up and the table and stools set to rights again. Alner was in bed, according to Maria, who had piles of supplies on the table.

"I've got little bags of almonds and dried apricots for you," she said as she filled Sabra's waterskin. "George is also getting the dried mutton strips. I think I can fit several rounds of bread as well, but they'll mold fast if they get wet. And this." She held up a blue bottle of elixir. "Do *not* spill this. You can't get any more where you're going, and I had to use the rest of what we made on Alner today."

"This is quite a bit," Sabra said as she began tucking the little drawstring pouches in her bag. "Are you sure it's not too much?"

"We'd been planning for a long time to make our way north to Destin." Maria paused and sighed. "If we choose to go one day, we can always prepare more." Then she caught Sabra by surprise and pulled her into a fierce hug. "I know you think you're honor-bound to this way of life," she said softly as she held Sabra close. "But honor comes in more than one color."

Sabra pulled back and studied her. "You seem so confident."

Maria arched one eyebrow. "To a point, yes. But paths bend."

George came in carrying a sack of flour on his shoulder. He set it down on the kitchen floor. "I wish you would let us stay one more day to help you," he said, surveying the room with a frown.

"You act as though I haven't cleaned up your messes all your life."

"And if they come again?"

She scowled. "Surely, you don't think I'd be so foolish as to sit out in the open and leave your grandfather exposed like that." She shook her head dismissively. "If you help him downstairs into the second lower room, I'll have this place looking as though we've been gone twenty years. If they come, we'll be living like kings, and they'll be none the wiser. It will be worse for us if they find you here again than if you're gone." She rubbed Serkan's head. "Besides, Serkan will be here to help, won't you?"

Serkan glared up at Sabra. "I still want to come with you."

She knelt down and hugged him tightly. As far as servants went, she had probably ruined him for life on this trip. He would never be just a servant to her family ever again. That was all right, though. He would be better loved here than he ever had been before. And he would be safe.

"You'll take care of Thing for me, won't you?" She did her best not to sniffle as she shoved the naked cat into the boy's arms. "He's not partial to dragon fire, and I'd like him not to scratch me up when we find the dragon."

"You're leaving both of us," Serkan pouted.

Sabra stared at him. When had he become so fond of her? Had he always been that way? "I will come get you as soon as I can. If you still want me to, that is." She bit back the urge to cry. Crying was the last thing the boy needed. So instead, she forced a laugh. "Who knows? Perhaps you and Thing will decide you like chasing rodents and sheep out here."

He threw his arms around her neck and clung to her. "I love you, Sabra," he whispered.

"I love you too," she whispered back.

On the other side of the kitchen, another goodbye was taking place. Maria went to George and pulled him close the way she had Sabra. But there was a special fondness in the way she turned her head and kissed his hair. Tears ran down her cheeks, and her voice trembled as she spoke. "We may not be yours by blood, but I've never been prouder than I am of you now."

Sabra, having gone to stand by the door, felt her own tears brim over as Maria put a hand on George's cheek and wiped it dry. "Face your enemy with courage. Fight to the song. And when you're finished, you'll find us waiting for you." She sniffled. "Always."

"Come here, boy." Alner, who was now laying on the couch and wrapped in blankets, motioned to George. George went and knelt at his side.

"Go." Alner had to stop and breathe between words. "Go down to the weapons room. Take down the old shield."

George's eyes widened. "The old one?"

Alner nodded and closed his eyes. "And get the matching sword."

George disappeared down the hall and reappeared a few

moments later with a silver shield and sword. The silver was scratched and nicked all over, as though it had seen many battles. They were large, the sword nearly as long as Serkan was tall, and they both looked heavy. George held them out to Alner as he returned to his side.

"These…" Alner panted, "…belonged to your ancestor. They were gifts from his father, the King of Destin, when he left the Fortress to make his way in the world."

"That's why you wouldn't let me touch them as a boy," George whispered.

"Your father sent them with us so we could give them to you when you were of age." Alner swallowed. "Look closely. The sword's edges and the inside of the shield are both lined with blue crystal."

"The crystal from the cave!" George exclaimed.

Alner nodded. "The shield should protect you from the dragon's fire, and the sword should be sharp enough to cut through his scales."

"Thank you," George ran his hand along the smooth inner surface of the shield. Sabra edged closer so she could touch it as well. It was cool and smoother than glass, perfect despite the rough appearance of the other side.

"It was an honor to keep them for you." Alner ran a shaking hand along George's face. "Just as it was an honor to keep you."

One more round of tearful hugs and kisses and blessings were given after that. Then George carried Alner downstairs to the second hidden bedroom beside Serkan's, and Maria shooed them out the door for fear they would lose precious travel time.

The night was chilly when they set out, and there was a sharp breeze that blew erratically. They headed southwest to slip around the town. Then they would follow the road from a distance, just as Sabra had done on her way to Kappadona. Sabra was sure she could find the way back into the palace through the underground tunnels. They had discussed taking horses, but George had decided it was too dangerous. They were too hard to hide if they were spotted. Sabra understood this, of course, but now that they were actually leaving, their walking speed made her somewhat anxious. Anything to keep her from her own thoughts.

"Are you all right?" she asked quietly as they trod over the soft soil.

A beam of moonlight appeared before them, and when she looked at his face again, all signs of tears were gone. His jaw was hard, and his gray eyes nearly glowed.

"More than that," he whispered back in a voice so sharp it made her shiver. "I'm ready."

CHAPTER 29

BETTER THIS WAY

They spoke little as they traveled. George kept his eyes on the horizon, barely visible in the moonlight, and Sabra was too busy worrying to even bother finding words.

Since Demir had sent her on this journey, she'd done her best not to think about him or her mother. They had sent her out to stay safe. Worrying about them would only lessen her readiness. And she had done everything in her power not to think of her father and the chaotic mess he'd left behind. Instead, she'd filled her time with watching George, helping Maria, and managing Serkan, tiring herself so that at night she could fall into bed, too tired to do anything but sleep.

Now, though, in the dark with only the sounds of the night surrounding them, anxieties crept in like a chill in the night. Had Mahzar realized that they'd helped her escape? Had he punished them for it? She doubted anyone would punish Demir too harshly, as the Justines believed him to be the next rightful heir. But her mother was of little use to them. Would they condemn and dispose of her quietly, or would the Justines' odd sense of self-righteousness keep her alive a little longer?

There was also, of course, the question of the people's future. Even if George pulled off a miracle and slayed the dragon, how would they survive? She shuddered to think of how much food Mahzar had burned by now in his desire to contain her. Hopefully, he'd stopped punishing the people as soon as he knew she'd escaped. The Justines were severe, but they weren't known to be cruel for cruelty's sake. Still, even with the damage that had been done before she left, what was left of their winter stores had been unpredictable at best.

Of course, then there was George. She had endangered his family by running to him, and now she was endangering him further by bringing him back to the monster from which she'd escaped.

Without the legendary blue fire which should be his by right.

Sabra felt dirty inside.

This is all your fault! She wished she could scream at her father. No wonder he'd spent his life worrying about her or worrying that she would discover his dirty secrets. Her mouth tasted sour as she thought of all the times they'd shared where she'd convinced herself that he was acting as he did out of a motivation to protect.

Had he been protecting her? Or had he been protecting himself?

"We'll stop here for the day," George said, interrupting Sabra's internal turmoil. "I don't want to be traveling in the direct sunlight if we can help it."

Sabra looked up to realize that they'd come to one of the desert hills that was riddled with caves. But George wasn't looking at the hill. He was looking at the biggest stone chimney Sabra had ever seen. She'd been so deep in thought as they'd approached that she'd somehow missed it.

The stone chimney had the general shape of a round triangle, as wide at the base as Sabra's bedroom and growing thinner until it reached its point at the top, which was at least fifty feet higher than Sabra's head. Several cave entrances opened up on the ground and above.

"My grandfather took me here to practice when I was a boy," he continued, walking up to the opening at the chimney's base. "We should be safe here during the day."

"They nearly caught us in a cave on our way to Kappadona,"

Sabra said as she drew nearer. "It was purely by the Maker's mercy that they failed."

"This cave is a little more than it seems." He gave her a dry smile, barely visible in the reflection of the moon. "Follow me."

Sabra followed him into the cave. But instead of stopping in the first open room at the base, he continued to lead her deeper and higher into the chimney up a set of stairs so smooth they looked as though a human had carved them by hand. The only light came from small holes in the walls that let in tiny moonbeams. "Are you sure we won't get stuck if the floor gives out or something else happens?" she asked, feeling foolish even as she asked. Of course, he wouldn't lead her somewhere dangerous.

Why didn't they bring a light?

"Are you afraid I'm going to strand you in some cave until you agree to marry me?" She could hear the smile in his voice. "Am I some villain now?"

Her heart pounded even faster at these words. But not because she was afraid. And honestly, she didn't even want to know why. So instead, she reached out and whacked him on the back of the arm. "You know what I mean. What if they trap us in here?"

"My grandfather used to take me into these caves to train, so I've prepared for that very scenario. We ran and fought in these caves so much that I could walk them blindfolded. He searched for any terrain within walking distance and was always going on about how I needed to be ready for anything. He also told me that years ago, people used these stone chimneys to hide from pursuers." He paused, and Sabra ran into his back. He reached back and steadied her with his hand. But when he started moving again, he didn't let go. "I wonder sometimes," he said, the humor all gone now, "if he somehow knew deep down that a day like this would come." At the top of the stairs, her eyes took a moment to adjust. But then she was able to make out a round room with a high, conical ceiling and a floor made of stone. It was wide enough that Sabra could have lain down head to toe three times over. There was no hint of a former human presence, other than that the floor was so perfectly smooth and flat, but it immediately felt like they were standing in someone's home.

"You do seem to collect trouble," she said when she was done assessing the room.

"Oh, do I now?" He pulled her gently to the left, away from the edge.

"You befriended me, didn't you?"

He laughed. A real laugh, not the kind he'd often pretended at his grandparents' table during these last few days. It made Sabra's chest warm.

"I suppose I did, didn't I?"

Ten minutes later, George had lit a small fire. "There are small holes in the wall that will let out the smoke," he said as he added a bit of kindling from his pack. "We won't need to keep this lit for very long. The sun should be up in an hour, and it will warm the room nicely. Let's get our bedding rolled out quickly. I don't want anyone seeing the smoke."

Only then did it occur to Sabra that they would be sleeping, unaccompanied, in the same room. Not that she feared that George would do anything...ungentlemanly. Still, it was somewhat of a scandal for Sabra to even sit in a room with one of her suitors unaccompanied or without someone nearby for propriety's sake. Here, they were miles from any living soul, let alone a chaperone.

George seemed to realize the same thing. "I, uh, I'll just sleep on this side near the door." He unrolled his mat on the opposite side of the fire. "You can have that side."

She gave him an awkward smile. "Thank you." Thankfully, they were spared the need to talk again, as Sabra was exhausted from their walk, and all too willing to do as he said. But just when she had her blanket spread on the ground and her bag set on it as a pillow, George jumped to his feet. A second later, his knife was in his hand, and he was gesturing wildly for Sabra to join him against the cave wall.

She obeyed quickly, alarmed at the fierceness in his face.

We've been followed, he mouthed. Then Sabra could hear it, too.

Footsteps. She listened harder. Strange, though. These footsteps were small and quick. Not the large stomping kind the Justines usually took.

Just as she wondered at this, George leaped out from his place against the wall and grabbed their stalker in his left hand while holding his knife with his right. A familiar shriek sounded, and Sabra jumped out from her hiding place, fearing what she would find.

Sure enough, the shriek belonged to Serkan. George had the boy by the collar, and though the knife was nowhere near him, Serkan was screaming as though he were already being gored.

"Sabra, help me! He's going to kill me! I'm going to die!"

"See what happens when you sneak around like a thief?" George put away his knife, but he held onto Serkan's collar. "You're going to get killed with that kind of stunt."

"Serkan, what have you done?" Sabra cried. "You were supposed to stay at the house where it was safe!"

"I wanted to be with you!" Serkan protested, briefly meeting Sabra's eyes before turning to glare at George. "You said you may not get to come back. So I decided it would be better to not come back with you than to wait on you and have you not come back!"

"Oh, Serkan." Sabra rubbed her eyes. "I thought we were past this."

"He needs a good spanking." George released the boy and glowered down at him. "But since we can't well spank you and have you further alerting every Justine in the region to our position, we might as well put you to bed." He folded his arms across his chest. "I suppose you'll be needing a blanket?"

"Of course not." Serkan scowled. "I brought my own pack. I'm not a baby." He beamed at Sabra. "I brought Thing, too." As he spoke, the bag he had strapped over his shoulder *meowed*.

George rolled his eyes. "Of all the ridiculous—"

"Let's get this all sorted out in the morning." Sabra shook her head. "Lay your blanket out between mine and George's. On this side of the fire. There you go. And...give me the cat, I suppose."

Soon, everyone was either lying or sitting on their blankets. And though Sabra knew she should feel as afraid as she had earlier - even more so, as Serkan had just complicated everything exponentially - she felt oddly at peace. If for only one moment, she was surrounded by people who cared for her. Even Thing curled up against her chest. They were safe. They were warm. And they were going home.

Sabra awoke with a jolt to find a hand covering her mouth. She struggled and nearly screamed until she realized that it was George's hand. He had her tucked against his chest under one arm. Serkan, whose mouth was covered as well, was under the other.

Shhh, George mouthed as he looked pointedly up. Sabra followed his gaze to realize that it must be broad daylight. The little holes George had spoken of the night before were now letting in streams of sunlight.

Sunlight that flickered across Sabra's face as Thing twitched his tail back and forth, seeming just as agitated as George and offended at whatever had interrupted his nap. Sabra peered out slightly through one of the small holes in the walls to see boots below.

"The dogs keep leading us here," one of them called out. "But I can't see what they're going on about."

"They must have been here," another answered, this one's voice gruffer. "Take them closer to the river. They might have headed there to throw off the scent."

Dogs. They were being hunted with dogs. Sabra shut her eyes and prayed for them to go away. And yet, for some reason, when she opened her eyes, George was smirking.

"Here!" the first called. "Down by the river!"

George's smirk grew to a full-fledged grin.

When the dogs' barking had faded into silence, and the men no longer called to one another, George slowly let go of Serkan and Sabra. But he put his finger to his lips for quiet and then motioned for them to stay by the fire. Then he vanished back down the tunnel through which they'd come.

Sabra looked at Serkan, who was also awake now, but he shrugged. Trying to shake off the fear that made her muscles seize up, she shook her head and pulled a little bread out of her bag and handed it to the boy. Hopefully, he'd brought food as well. Otherwise, their rations would be rather meager. Back at the house, Serkan had eaten almost as much as George.

George returned ten minutes later. He plopped down on his blanket on the other side of the fire and dug into his sack. "I knew that would get them."

"What did you do?" Sabra asked.

"After you went to sleep this morning, I got up and made sure to touch a lot of the rocks and shrubbery on the path we were on. Then I extended it down to the water and a little on the other side. I figured they might use dogs if they got desperate enough." His mouth twitched as he looked down at the naked cat, who was glaring at him as it licked its paws. "I might also have borrowed your cat."

So in the last twenty-four hours, Thing had not only been shoved in Serkan's backpack, but he'd been abducted to be used as a ruse for the enemy's dogs. No wonder the cat was so indignant.

Sabra shivered again at the thought of her own guards using dogs to sniff her out, but Serkan sat up, his eyes bright.

"Did you leave *your* scent like a dog?"

"Serkan!" Sabra stared at him. "We're eating!"

But George just winked as he chewed. "I couldn't say. Whatever got the job done."

"Oh, ugh," Sabra groaned. But inwardly, it made her feel happy to see George and Serkan getting along.

That was still so strange to contemplate. Not long ago, she'd been surrounded by advisers, servants, and subjects. She uttered a word, and it was done. Today, her closest companions were a childhood friend and a servant boy, and they were joking about urinating on bushes.

And yet, she was happy. Happier, possibly, than she'd been in a long time.

"We'll continue tonight at nightfall," George said. "They can't search all day. And we'll be better able to hide if we move in the dark."

The day was actually rather relaxing. They took turns sleeping, and between their naps, they nibbled on food and listened for footsteps outside. When the afternoon shadows began to fall, though, Sabra found that she couldn't sleep any more.

"Can't sleep?"

She sat up and looked at George. He was carving foreign symbols into her staff.

"I'm afraid not." She sat up and looked at Serkan. "At least he's getting some rest. Hopefully, you won't have to carry him tonight."

George kept his eyes on his work, but the corner of his mouth twitched. "While he's asleep, I have a question."

"That tone frightens me a little," Sabra laughed softly. "You seem far too pleased with yourself."

"Oh, it's not about me." He turned his clear gray eyes on her. "We never finished our conversation before. And now I want to know about the one that was... Oh, what was it? 'Quite nice to look at,' if I remember correctly."

Sabra stared at him for a long moment before groaning. "You can't be serious. You want to hear about my *suitors*?"

He shrugged. "You might as well tell me. I could use some entertainment."

His laugh was light, and his body relaxed, but there was a light in his eyes that Sabra couldn't quite read. It was sharp. Like Thing when he wanted her cantaloupe. His obsession with cantaloupe bordered on unholy.

She took a deep breath and blew it out in a puff. "Well, there's not much to tell. The one I referred to as Grandpa was three times my age. Jitters was so nervous he made himself nervous. There was a set of identical twins for a while, but they couldn't agree on who would get me, as though I would choose one, so they called it off after two weeks and left." She shrugged. "None I could actually stomach the idea of marrying. I suppose I could thank Mahzar for sparing me at least that pain."

"What about the one who was nice to look at?"

"You're not going to let that go, are you?"

He just raised his eyebrows.

"Fine. Abasi was quite handsome." She gave him a challenging look, "but he wasn't an option after all. When he came, he didn't realize that I had to marry a citizen of Segzein." She wrinkled her nose. "Besides, he was a little too enthusiastic about his work. I'm not sure how many nights I could have stomached listening to him discuss all the gory details of disposing of vermin before going stark raving mad."

That light in his eyes brightened, and his smug smile widened slightly. "Yes, but did he bring you home to be interrogated by his grandparents?"

Sabra laughed. "Your grandparents didn't interrogate me!"

"My grandmother did."

"Well, fine. If you want to call it that. But they had good reason."

Serkan, who was stretched out between them, began to whimper. Sabra shifted to go to him, but George was closer. He reached over and put his hand on the boy's head. Then he began to sing. It wasn't the Sentinel's Song, but its melody was sweet and haunting. Sabra watched George's face, mesmerized as the music floated around them, almost an entity of its own. After a moment, Serkan relaxed, and his breathing deepened once again.

"That was beautiful," Sabra whispered. "I didn't know you could sing so well."

George shrugged. "My grandparents sang to me my entire life. I have dozens of songs memorized."

"It's interesting that the power for fighting is activated by a song." She paused. "Is it that way for the Fortiers?"

"I don't think so. Not that I'm an expert in their gifts. But when we were training, I asked my grandfather about it." George paused and frowned thoughtfully. "He said that because the power originates from the Maker, the Maker can choose to distribute it any way he wishes. For one reason or another, he chose to hand it down to my people through song."

"Do all your people's songs have power?" Sabra glanced around the cave, wondering if she would see any of the blue flames floating in the air.

"No. Just the Sentinel's Song. But, apparently, my people were a musical one." He looked down at Serkan, his smile gone. "I wish I could have known them more."

Sabra sighed. But before she could join him in mourning, that sharp light was in his eyes once more.

"Tell me," he said, "did this handsome foreign suitor dance?"

Sabra chuckled. "Oddly enough, that question never crossed my mind as he described the best way to bash out a rat's brains."

In one graceful movement, George stood and extended his hand. Surprised, Sabra took it and allowed him to pull her to her feet. When she was standing, he put one hand around her waist, making her breath hitch at his sudden nearness. He caught her hand in his other and began to slowly spin. And as they moved, he began to sing a song, so low she could barely make out the words. But the melody sent shivers up her spine.

Or maybe it was the fact that he was here, holding her in his arms, spinning her with the same grace that he fought with.

What would happen if she closed the gap between them? As the scent of his clothes and the roughness of his hands saturated her senses, she closed her eyes. What would she taste if she kissed him? She let her head fall back so the sensation of circling could envelop her completely. It was hypnotizing, this giving up control. For once, she wasn't the queen or even the crown princess. She was a woman who was in the arms of the man she adored, and he was spinning her around as if there were no dragon at all.

He pulled her closer until her head was resting against his chest. Their turning slowed, and he wrapped his arms gently around her shoulders. "Tell me about Segzein," he whispered. "Why do you love it so much?"

"Hmm," Sabra kept her eyes closed. "I think I love it because it's like a well-oiled wheel. Every part has a purpose. Everyone has a reason for existing, and for the most part, they love it." She thought for a moment. "I guess I like being a part of that. I like knowing my purpose."

He was quiet for a moment as they turned in slow circles. "It's strange to think that I only recently visited the place that should have been my home. I can't help wondering what life would have been like if everything had gone as it should, and we had never left." She could feel him take a deep breath as his chest rose and fell. "Do you think we would have met?"

She lifted her head from his chest to look at him. "Oh, undoubtedly. Our fathers were both basniins, so we would have been dragged to their meetings together. And considering the nearness of our age, we probably would have grown up very good friends."

He searched her face, looking suddenly very young and vulnerable. And as he did, she felt her happiness fade. As wonderful as this was, spinning in his arms in what felt like exquisite comfort, it couldn't last. He was a basniin. So was she. And if she wanted to keep her promise to her father and make sure that her people were taken care of—George's remnant included, she would have to make sure it stayed that way.

"I...um, I think I'll try to rest one more time. Before we have to go, I mean." She gently pulled back and watched his arms fall to his sides. And she was suddenly forcing a smile even though she was closer to bursting into tears. It took all of her mother's lessons on diplomatic detachment to keep a neutral smile on her face. "Thank you, though. You're a gifted dancer."

She went to her pack and laid down, refusing to meet his eyes again. It was better this way.

It was better.

CHAPTER 30
BECAUSE YOU CHOSE

They set out again that night after dark. And as they began, the urgency Sabra had felt before was still there. At least, she still felt the pull to give her people what they needed.

There was, however, also a new desire to stay. To remain like this without the complications of dragons or politics or history that had been thrust, uninvited, into both their lives. Her zealous determination to become the queen that Segzein needed was now riddled with doubts as to whether she had the fortitude to stay the course. Doubts that only grew worse every time she glanced up to see the tall, foreboding figure leading the way through the moonlit desert.

No one spoke for a long time. Every once in a while, Thing would let out an offended hiss when she jolted her backpack too hard. But other than that and the quiet hum of a few early cicadas, the night was quiet.

At least the way George was leading them provided some measure of distraction. Sabra had believed they were traveling close to her first path, but George knew all sorts of hidden paths that he said would be safer than the way she'd come. It was also beautiful. Slowly, the dark dirt beneath their feet was turning white, and after a while, there was a nearly blueish tint to it. Then, without warning, they were at the edge of a cliff.

Staring down, Sabra realized where they were.

"The thermal pools!" she exclaimed. Jutting out below them, scaling the low grade of the cliff, were the world-renowned thermal pools of the region. The cave-dotted hills still stood behind them, but before them the half-circle pools stuck out, each forming another layer that moved in a slope down to the bottom. Some were large and others were small, but even in the dark, they made quite a sight as they sparkled, limestone and water, in the moonlight. The edges and sides of each pool were encrusted in limestone that looked like ice, which Sabra had seen only in pictures. Clear, blue water filled the half-circles, their steam making Sabra's tired joints ache with just a glance. Many came here for healing. Others believed the warm waters to have mystical powers. Sabra's own people, especially the Woodsmen, often came out to collect the limestone.

"How far are we from Segzein?" Sabra asked George.

"Not as far as you think. I decided to take the route a little less frequented after our attack last night. But it shouldn't add more than a few hours to our walk."

Sabra nodded, silently a bit envious that he knew all of this, and it was only a little ways from her home.

They walked a little way along the ridge, Sabra wondering if she dared ask whether they might risk soaking their feet just for a few moments, when George came to a stop and held up his hand. "Wait."

"Do we get to rest now?" Serkan grumbled, walking over to the edge of one of the pools. Sabra grabbed him by the shoulder and yanked him back before he stuck his feet in, shoes and all.

"No," George said, his eyes scanning the dark horizon as he drew his sword from its sheath. "Something's wrong."

Sabra gripped her staff harder with one hand as she pulled Serkan closer to her. George stood poised like a leopard, every muscle tense.

"Let's start down," George said quietly, edging closer to the nearest ledge. "Sabra, I want you and Serkan to go down first—"

A man jumped out from behind one of the larger boulders behind them and grabbed Serkan by the arm. Sabra managed to land a good whack on the assailant's head with her staff, but a second man jumped out as well and ran at Sabra, forcing her to pull back, Serkan's other arm still in her hand.

George was already a blur. He disarmed the man who had taken hold of Serkan, freeing the boy. Then, using the first cliff, he quickly disposed of the one who was attacking Sabra. But as he did, four more guards in white streaked down from the nearest cave-pocked hill. Then two more. They kept coming until Sabra could no longer count. Yanking at her arms, hitting her legs, they pushed her toward the edge of the nearest thermal pool. George, leaping from boulder to boulder, never keeping still, killed them just as fast as they came, but their numbers seemed endless.

"Hide in that chimney!" Sabra hissed to Serkan as more guards streamed down from the cave. She yanked the protesting cat from her backpack and shoved it into his arms. "Go!"

For once, Serkan did as he was told, clutching the cat and sprinting toward the nearest stone chimney. Once he was gone, Sabra did her best to distract the guards who were going after George, attacking them from behind with the staff. They paid little attention to her, though, unless she directly engaged them. Their tactic seemed to have changed. They'd stopped trying to take her and focused solely on George. Soon, they were so thick around him that she could barely see him.

"Sabra!" George cried from inside the melee. "I need you to sing!"

Sabra looked up from the man she'd just knocked unconscious. George couldn't be asking her this. Not here. Not now. She wasn't ready! In her mind flashed her people. Mahzar and his demands. Her years of training. Those who wore the blue sashes. The hatred in Demir's voice as he recounted his parents' deaths. Her vow to her father.

There had to be another way.

"Sabra!" George sounded desperate.

Sabra yanked her pack off and dumped everything out, thankful that the guards, for once, were ignoring her. They must have known they wouldn't be able to take her without getting rid of George.

Please let him hold, she prayed as she tore through the pile to find what she needed. There. Flint and a knife. Sabra cut two long strips of fabric from her cloak and tied one around each end of her staff. Then she grabbed hold of the flint and struck it. Her hands were shaking so hard, though, that she didn't even get a spark. She tried again. And again. Angry tears filled her eyes as she tried again and again to light the fire.

"Sabra!" George screamed. "Sing the song!"

Sabra tried again, but just as she was about to give up, two small hands took the flint and the knife from her hands. Sabra looked up to see Serkan smash the knife and the stone together. She began to laugh through her tears when the cloth caught fire. Quickly, they lit the second cloth. Then, with both ends of her staff blazing, Sabra ran straight into the heart of the fight.

She knew better than to try to fight the guards this time. Instead, she set the ends of their cloaks ablaze.

And she succeeded. When each one turned to see what she had done, he immediately dropped to the ground to put out the blaze. This gave George time to finish them off quickly.

By the time everybody on the ground was still, Sabra had counted eight. Eight men had ambushed them. And there could be more on the way.

"Why didn't you sing?"

Sabra looked up to see George lean on his sword. She ran forward to help support him, but he stepped away from her. Sabra stared at him, feeling as though she'd been slapped. Those gray eyes were no longer a soft silver in the moonlight. They were dark and hard like storm clouds.

"I'm sorry," she whispered. "But I thought—"

"You thought what?" he exploded. "That you could still defeat the dragon yourself if I died here? Good luck getting your crown that way!"

Sabra stared at him. Her thoughts were a jumble in her head. Not that it mattered. There weren't words deep enough to express the pain and shame that battled inside.

"You were willing to sing in the cave," he continued. "But not now. Now that we're close to your beloved throne, you couldn't bear giving it up. Even if it meant keeping us alive!"

"That's not true!" she managed to shout back. Her ferocity was ruined, however, by the tears that were streaming down her face. "You act like you know what you're doing, but the truth is that you won't last five minutes without me as queen!"

"I always wondered what you thought of me," he said, gesturing in the air with his sword. "It's good to know the truth at least."

"Which is?" she glared at him through stinging eyes.

"That dying a queen is preferable to marrying me as a nobody."

Serkan had watched this exchange through wide eyes. Sabra turned to him and grabbed his hand. "Come," she said, her voice wavering dangerously. "We're going to finish the night in the caves." She marched back to where she'd dumped her bag. Once everything was in the bag again, she marched them up to the nearest set of caves in the hillside. Ironically, they were the ones the guards had hidden in to attack them from.

Serkan let her lead him away, but he watched George over his shoulder as she pulled him behind her.

George dropped down over the edge of the closest thermal pool and disappeared. And though she glared, Sabra secretly wondered if he just might be angry enough to leave them. Unsure of what else to do, she went to the hillside and chose one of the caves above the ground. The only entrance was a hole in the ceiling of the lower floors. Somehow, she managed to get herself and Serkan up into the cave before falling apart. Then she let it all go and sobbed profusely as she set up and lit the little fire inside the cave. Serkan just continued to watch with large eyes as she unrolled their blankets and made the beds, crying the entire time.

Because he was right. She had asked everything of him. And she was stubbornly holding onto life the way she wanted it to be. But, no, that wasn't fair. There were good reasons, honest reasons for her to retain the crown. She was too upset to put them into words at the moment, but they were there. Still, George was doing what few men in the world would do, Sabra was sure. He was risking his life for a woman he loved and couldn't have, in order to save a people who had been somewhat responsible for the deaths of his family and clansmen.

What was he getting from this? Even if he was successful, what would he receive that could repay all he'd given? The heart and hand she knew he longed for the most weren't even hers to give.

"Is he coming back?"

Sabra looked up from her dark musings to see Serkan curled up on his blanket, pale-faced and small. She gave him a sad smile.

"I don't know."

Serkan nodded a little and frowned. After a moment, Sabra went back to getting the supper ready when the boy spoke again.

"Do you know why I followed you? The first time, I mean?" He paused. "Well, and the second time."

In spite of herself, Sabra gave a little laugh. "I've wondered that often."

But he didn't smile. "You're my clan."

Sabra paused what she was doing and looked at him. "What?"

"Cook found me in the market, stealing, when I was little. She took me in and gave me a place, but..." He shrugged his skinny shoulders. "I never knew my clan or my people. Then, when I was little, I found out that you were like me. Without your real parents." He looked down at Thing, who was lounging in his lap. "I didn't want to be alone."

Sabra put down the food she'd taken from her pack and went over to sit beside him. In a motion that never would have been acceptable for the crown princess to a servant, she swept him up into her arms.

"You're not alone." She hugged him close and laid her cheek on his head. "Meddlesome, maybe. Troublesome, always." She pulled back and looked at him until he met her eyes, then she gave him an ornery grin and ruffled his hair. "But not alone."

He leaned into her, and she closed her eyes. Though she was insane to even think it, she realized in that moment that she was more than thankful the Maker had let the little troublemaker slip into her life.

"Why didn't you sing for George?"

Sabra sighed and reluctantly let go of the boy before tending their dinner. It seemed silly to continue on as if nothing had happened, and their guide and guardian hadn't abandoned them. But Sabra didn't know what else to do. "It's complicated."

"It's not, actually."

Sabra and Serkan turned and looked at George, who was pulling himself up through the hole in the ground. Sabra stayed silent as he pulled a large stone over the opening in the floor before turning and meeting their gazes. "It's not complicated," he said, looking at Sabra, "because I never should have asked it of you." He nodded down at the entrance. "I created a stronger scent that led to another set of caverns. Hopefully, if they're still tracking with dogs, it will take them there instead of here, long enough to slip away."

Sabra nodded and simply watched as he got himself some of the food she had prepared before retreating to the empty side of the room. Minutes passed before she could stand it no longer.

"George, I'm sorry—"

"I mean it, Sabra. I was wrong to demand that of you. And *I'm* sorry for doing so." He ran a hand through his hair, making it stand on end. His chin was covered in stubble that she, in spite of her angst, wanted to run her hand over.

"I was afraid," he said in a softer voice. "But being afraid doesn't mean I had the right to take from you what's only yours to give."

She shook her head as a lump rose from deep inside her throat. "You had every right to ask." She looked down at the food in her lap. "You're giving me everything. And if I didn't have Mahzar to deal with, and if my cousin didn't hate your people..." She closed her eyes. "I promise. This choice isn't about you."

"Your cousin is next in line for the throne, correct?"

She nodded and opened her eyes. "And while he's dearer to me than a brother could have been, he's always blamed your people for the death of his parents. And for that reason, I'm not sure I can trust him with the fate of your people."

George's frown deepened. "You think he'd hurt them?"

"No, not that. It's more…I'm not sure he would seek their best. I think he's ready to force them into assimilation with the other tribes. In his eyes, it's the best way for everyone to start over, including them." She sighed. "If we're going to be successful, I must have the authority of the crown. As it stands, when we get there, we'll have to issue an official Challenge against Mahzar, or he'll have his men kill you on the spot. You'll never even reach him."

"Why would a Challenge stop him?"

"A Challenge is one of the final stages in disagreement between clans. It's somewhat barbaric." She shuddered. "But because it was in the original contracts and vows between the clans as a way to mediate, the Justines never let us remove it." How ironic, Sabra thought, that it would now be used against them. "Basically, when all other avenues of mediation have been tried and have failed, one clan can challenge the other to a contest of physical combat by representative. And whoever wins the combat, based on the stakes agreed upon, wins the argument."

"So why do you need to be queen for this?"

"To keep the Challenge from being used often, all of the other basniins must be in agreement that it's the last way to solve the problem." She traced the swirls in the rock she was sitting on. "And while the others might be convinced, I am absolutely certain that my cousin will not."

Why did she sound like she was trying to convince herself?

"Of course, that's not all," she hurried on to say. "If, or rather, *when* we defeat Mahzar, your people will need help. There are many in the city who were too sick or weak to make the journey. They chose to remain behind. And as queen, I can send a formal request to King Everard to come down and help us clear the land of whatever is making them sick." She gave him a sad smile and shrugged helplessly. "As the…" she paused and felt herself blush, "*wife* of a basniin,

I wouldn't have the power to send such a request. Not diplomatically, anyway. And as much as I love my cousin, I'm afraid his pain has blinded him to the needs of his people." She sat taller and swallowed. "*Our* people. People who are homeless in their own home. They're hurting, and they need someone to remind them of their own name." She shook her head. "And that's assuming Demir could even take the throne. He helped me escape, so who knows who Mahzar might have found to take his place."

A snore erupted, and they looked over to see Serkan sleeping on his blanket. When George looked back at her, his eyes were soft and gentle again, and Sabra felt her skin tingle. She had a sudden desire to get closer, to trace his face with her fingertips and to let him pull her into his arms.

"I understand," he said in a deep voice that only made her yearning grow. "And I'm glad of that. Truly. But for the sake of knowing..."

This was a bad idea. Whatever he was about to ask could only hurt them more. She was sure of it. And yet, she heard herself speak. "Yes?"

He spoke slowly. "If I had been eligible to take the platform when you had to choose a husband, would you have considered me?"

This, Sabra could answer. "In a heartbeat." She gave a rough laugh. "But I'm not sure that makes this any easier."

He nodded and laid down on his blanket.

"We'll sleep here tonight. Day will come in just a few hours, and I would prefer to make our stand against the dragon well-rested. There won't be any more hills by the time we reach the bottom of the ledge. From there, it'll be straight through the desert until we reach the mountain that you said you escaped through. Even if we take the rest of the night and tomorrow to rest, we'll be there tomorrow night."

Sabra nodded, suddenly too tired to form complete sentences. Slowly, the fire began to dim, and the room grew dark with the exception of the small beams of moonlight filtering in through the holes in the side of the cave from above.

"Sabra?"

"Mmm?" she murmured, half asleep.

"If you ever do sing for me, I want it to be because you chose to sing. Not because someone forced you to. Understand?"

Sabra was wide awake again. "I understand," she whispered. And she did. Which only made her want him more.

CHAPTER 31
LET ME

When will we get there?" Serkan asked as they set out the next night. They had spent the day before sleeping as much as possible. George even gave Sabra and Serkan some herbal tea that made them tired that afternoon, when sleep had become difficult. They would need all their strength in the coming days.

"Before the sun rises," George said. Then he looked at Sabra. "Are you ready?"

Sabra drew in a deep breath and let it out slowly. "No. And yes. As ready as can be, I suppose."

He nodded and turned to face the low mountain that was barely visible in the distance. A dozen times, Sabra wanted to break the silence. But every time she was about to open her mouth, she couldn't think of the exact words she wanted to say. Hours later, after they'd painstakingly descended past the limestone pools and moved into the valley, he broke the silence for her.

"You said we're going through a secret entrance to the palace?"

Sabra glanced back at the thermal pools in the distance, which they'd left behind several hours ago. How had she been so ignorant that her city was so close to the pools? They could have done so much with the pools had she known this before.

"Sabra?"

She shook her head to clear it. "Yes. The Justines control the roads into the city, so if we want a chance at this, we have to reach the basniins first."

He frowned. "They tried to force you to marry him. Why do you think they'll entertain me with the idea of a Challenge?"

"I'm not sure they will," Sabra admitted. She'd spent the better part of the day thinking through all the possibilities. "But our ultimate goal is for the other basniins to bless our Challenge."

"What makes you sure Mahzar would agree?"

She twisted her lips thoughtfully. "The Justines may be evil to the core, but they have a strange adherence to the law. If you challenge Mahzar to his face with witnesses present, Mahzar will want to honor a rightful Challenge. It will stop him from sending out the guard." She gave him a dry smile. "You're a good fighter, but I think challenging the entire Justine guard at once might be something we want to avoid."

"But how would this Challenge change that?" George asked.

"You're from the lost clan. Your people took an oath to defend Segzein. This gesture would be interpreted as you fulfilling the oath of your people. Besides," she tossed her hair. "He's vain. He'll answer the Challenge as though dealing with an imaginative child, rather than a real threat."

George gave her a wry smile. "Should I turn back now?"

But Sabra couldn't bring herself to smile back.

"Sabra, look at me."

Sabra kept her eyes on the ground until he gently took her hand and pulled her to a stop.

"Sabra."

Unwillingly, she met his eyes.

"I know what I'm doing," he said softly. "You haven't tricked me into anything. I'm going into this of my own volition."

"That's what makes it all the worse," she whispered. Then she turned and began walking again. "We need to hurry. The tunnel is long, and I want to get to my mother's quarters before the servants wake her."

When they neared the low mountain, Sabra had a brief time of panic as she wondered if she would be able to find the tunnel entrance again. But George, who was taller, spotted a metal piece sticking out of the stone. It reflected the moonlight at just the right angle, and Sabra sent up multiple prayers of thanks as they hurried toward it. She panicked again when she wondered if they would be able to get the door open. But George quickly figured out the mechanism there as well.

"The Sentinels must have helped design this," he said, frowning thoughtfully at the little circle that had been cut into stone. "My grandparents have a trunk with this exact mechanism as a lock."

Once they were inside, George locked it, correctly this time, as Sabra must have left it partially open upon her escape. Then they paused for him to light the small oil lamp he'd carried with them and made their way back up the tunnel.

Serkan eventually tired, and Sabra took the lamp so George could carry him. Nothing seemed to have changed since the last time she had followed her cousin through this passageway. At least, she prayed it hadn't. She prayed that the Justines hadn't discovered this apparently heavily guarded secret.

"What are you thinking about?" he asked softly.

Sabra paused to pull Thing from her pack, where he'd been peeking out from beneath the cover. "Let's sit for a moment. You can rest your arm, and I can get out the rest of the food. I'm not sure when we'll be fed again after this." She expected George to argue that he was fine, but to her surprise, he simply lowered himself to the floor before carefully laying Serkan on the blanket she pulled from her pack.

"That doesn't answer my question, though," he said when they were eating. "What were you thinking about?" She gave him a guilty look, and his smile grew. "Contemplating my incredible good looks then. It's all very well. You don't have to be embarrassed."

Sabra laughed. "And your humility." She knew he was trying to make her feel better, and though she was determined to punish herself for her selfishness in wanting him all to herself, it was working. Then she sighed. "I was thinking about how I could be walking us into another trap, like the one from last night. But only worse. I've been gone a week now. Everything could have changed since I was gone."

He stared at the stone wall. "I think—"

"That's not all." She willed her eyes to meet his. "I need to say this before I lose my nerve."

He stared at her with wide eyes, reminding her of the boy she'd loved as a child. To give herself something to do, she began to rub Thing's belly. The ridiculous cat stretched out across her lap and began to purr, as though they weren't possibly hours from their doom.

"I keep thinking about how if we're successful and we defeat Mahzar, I'm still going to have to stand on that platform one day and choose a king." Her voice cracked. "And then I'll spend the rest of my life staring at you from across the table at Assembly meetings. Official ceremonies. Everything in-between. And we'll both belong to someone else." Her voice cracked. "Until the day we die."

George stared at his hands for a moment. She saw his fingers twitch several times before he sighed deeply and moved to sit beside her against the wall. She could feel him, even though they were a handspan apart, and she had to fold her hands in her lap to resist the urge to reach out and touch him. As she was fighting this desire, though, calloused fingers worked their way into hers. She was terrified of what it might do to her heart when they were done and this could only be a memory.

But for now, she squeezed his hand tight, wishing with all her heart that it could be more.

There were more thoughts on her mind, but the kind she couldn't even share with George. How the thought of marriage to another man was nauseating. The kind of intimacy one must share in such a union was still vague and nebulous to Sabra. But watching her parents' marriage alone had provided her with enough to know that what was shared after vows were said wasn't the kind of knowledge one could take back. Her mother had assured her when she'd asked once that she would learn to love her husband, whoever he ended up being. If he was a man of integrity, she would learn to love his heart, and the rest would follow.

But that was back before Sabra had given her heart to someone else. Before she had found the man with whom she longed to share her hopes and dreams and deepest desires.

"I have a question."

Sabra looked up to see George playing with a loose thread in his cloak. "What's that?"

"Why are you so desperate to be queen?"

Sabra laughed softly. "I can't tell you how many times I've asked myself that question."

"Have you come up with an answer?"

"I have." Sabra drew in a shaky breath. "It sounds arrogant, but I swear, I don't mean it to be."

"Sabra," he poked her gently in the ribs. "Just tell me."

"Fine. I've been raised being told that it's my duty to guard these people. That when my father died, I would be the one looking out for them. My whole life has been shaped around leading my people. My education, relationships, everything has been for the sole purpose of becoming queen. And while I don't for a moment believe myself to be the greatest leader of all time, I do believe that I've been put in the position to know what they need."

"A position your cousin isn't in."

"A position he never wanted to be in. After his parents were killed, he blamed the Sentinels, and I think he developed a blind spot where he should have been asking questions. And now that I know what truly happened between the Sentinels and the Justines, something I know for certain he isn't aware of, I think I can maneuver the politics of the basniins in our favor." She huffed. "Also, I swore to my father as he died that I would lead these people as queen. And I know that seems a poor line of loyalty—"

"Sabra."

"What?" she forced herself to look up at him. When she did, his features were surprisingly soft.

"I understand."

She blinked. "You do?"

He gave her a sad smile. "I can't imagine my attempt being viewed by an outsider as anything but hubris. Who am I to think I can challenge a dragon? Especially without..." He cleared his throat, and guilt stabbed at Sabra's chest. "I'm most likely sacrificing myself for something that seems to have little to do with me. But this is the cup I've been given." He touched her nose. "Whether it's what I want or not."

Responsibility kept poking at the edges of Sabra's mind, reminding her that they needed to reach her mother's quarters before light. But she felt as though she were standing on the edge of a precipice. And if she didn't pause now, she might never pause again.

"We need to be going," George finally said, seeming to read her mind. "My arm is sufficiently rested, enough to at least throw a rock or two at the dragon. And I think our little mischief-maker is beginning to wake."

Sure enough, Serkan was beginning to stir, so Sabra and George gathered their belongings up once again, gave Serkan something to eat, and continued up the tunnel. An eternity later - or was it just an hour or so? - they found themselves at the end of the tunnel, the familiar ladder leading up to the trapdoor through which she and Demir had come.

"Sabra," George said, taking her hand once more before she could start up the stairs.

She looked up at him, drinking in one last view of his face, half-hidden in the flickering of the lamp.

"If this is your calling...to be queen, then I don't want you to apologize. I want you to hold your head high and fight for it with every last breath in your lungs." He took his own deep breath. "But I ask this of you as well."

"What?" A strange dark foreboding dripped in her stomach at the determination in his voice.

"I know you're angry with your people. But...please don't be."

She blinked at him. "But they..."

"I've been thinking about that. And no, they didn't. Those were the decisions of a select few. Most of Segzein clearly has no idea what truly happened." He shrugged. "You and I didn't know any better until we learned the truth. And it would be nothing short of further injustice to blame them for what they had no control over."

She swallowed. "And second?"

He studied her fingers entwined with his. "If this end is really my destiny... If I'm to fight the dragon, live or die, please don't try to stop it." He met her eyes. "Let me be me."

CHAPTER 32
BUT FIRST

Sabra made her way up to her mother's chambers while George and Serkan remained below until it was time to call them up. At first, she was afraid she wouldn't be able to get the trapdoor up. Thankfully, her mother's bed was high enough off the ground that she was able to get the trapdoor open wide enough to crawl through it, and she was able to push aside the loosened floorboards without making too much noise. Then she lay beneath the bed until she was sure no one else was in the room.

"Thing!" she hissed as the cat darted out from beneath the bed. He darted up to his favorite perch on one of the wardrobes. But the room remained dark and still, despite the cat's disobedience. So when she was satisfied, and her eyes were adjusted enough to see the familiar outlines of furniture, she rolled out from under the bed, her heart thumping with the anticipation of being held in her mother's arms again. Really, what she wanted to do most was curl up in her mother's bed and rest against her chest, the way she had when she was a small girl.

But the bed was empty.

This was not good. Sabra's mother was many things, but an early riser was not one of them.

There might be an explanation for this. There had to be. Perhaps she was getting up to help feed the citizens that were living in the palace halls. Or to assist with the sick or expectant women. Her mother had a servant's heart, so it wouldn't be uncharacteristic for her to rise before sunrise in a time like this if there was a true need.

All those comforting possibilities, however, seemed weak when she realized that the bed was still made. And the fireplace was cold. Her mother hadn't slept here all night.

Sabra closed her eyes and sucked in a deep breath through her nose. There wasn't any more time for second-guessing herself. She couldn't hesitate or let the fear hanging over her head bury her. She had been trained to alter plans in cases of emergencies. And she would do that now.

A moment later, a plan had come to her, and she crawled back down to the trapdoor and whispered for George and Serkan to come up, George holding the lamp. As soon as they were all standing, she explained in hushed, quick whispers that there would be a change of plans.

"George, you and I will make our way to the secret room where the basniins meet. We'll take the servants' hallways so we aren't seen by those who are living in the main palace halls. And you," she bent down to Serkan so they were eye-to-eye. "Remember when I would despair of your sneaking in and out of the private quarters?"

Serkan nodded, eyes wide.

She gave him a little smile. "I'm going to need you to do it again."

When everyone knew his role, Sabra exchanged her torn cloak for a new one in her mother's wardrobe. Then she and George watched Serkan slip out of the room before taking off through one of the more hidden servant doors. She would leave the cat here. Hopefully, Shakirat wouldn't see him, as he was probably the only person who would know the cat's presence would indicate Sabra's.

They blew out the lamp and made their way silently through the back halls, Sabra sending up prayers of thanks the whole time for all of her curiosity as a child. The walk was quiet and quick, and they only ran into two servants. Each time, they bowed their heads and let the servants pass, and neither of the servants seemed to even take notice of them in their dirtied travel clothes.

Still, despite the success of the trek, Sabra was not as hopeful as she might have been. Even in the depths of the palace walls, the air smelled of sulfur and smoke. How much more of the city had Mahzar burned?

Why had Mahzar destroyed the city? Demir had been willing to take the crown as Mahzar had demanded. So why wasn't the dragon yet satisfied? The alarm this raised in Sabra's chest spurred her feet even faster.

The servants' halls didn't take them all the way to the secret room, which Sabra desperately hoped was still being used for that purpose, so they were forced to walk the regular halls together in plain sight for several turns. But to her relief, most of the people on the floor were still sleeping or barely paid them heed. The smell of human odor and refuse filled her nose and made her nearly gag, and Sabra's heart clenched as she realized just how far they'd fallen.

George was right. This wasn't their fault. They had been lied to and forced into silence the way her father had attempted to silence her. Even the basniins had been hushed. Red hot anger flickered in her vision and threatened to distract her, making her close a door behind her a little too loudly, with George giving her a questioning glance. She quickly fought to control her focus once again, allowing it to steel her resolve to see this plot through.

They arrived unaccosted at the meeting room but didn't breathe a sigh of relief until the door was shut. Dawn was just close enough that thin gray light made its way in through the window, and they could see the furniture that had been squished into the room.

"We'll hide behind the sofa in the far corner," Sabra whispered and pointed. "We'll need to wait until they all arrive so the word doesn't get out. Then I'll show myself and address them. Don't get up until I tell you."

He nodded, and they made their way over to the corner behind the sofa. It was diagonally placed against the wall, and they had to take care not to bump the tall candelabra behind it. One they were there, they had to squeeze in so their sides and shoulders were pressed up against each other.

And all that was left was to wait and pray.

She had just begun to despair of Serkan's success when a familiar voice broke the silence in a shouted whisper as the door swung open.

"I don't see why we had to be roused from our beds before dawn. Not even a reason! I would have thought Mahzar's torment of the poor man would have tired him out by now."

Sabra stiffened. It was Basniin Ozge, from the Woodsmen. And there was only one person he could be speaking about. She must have made some sort of sound or movement in her fear because George, with what little space he had, squeezed her arm gently.

"If Demir is calling us to meet, there must be a reason," came Esemeray's nervous response. "I told him to stay in bed unless Mahzar had called him. As it is, it will take him weeks to heal."

Sabra winced. What had Mahzar done to her cousin on her account?

"How much longer do you think he'll be able to hold out?" This calm and collected voice could only belong to Nazan of the Sophians.

"Where are Yasin and Baran?" Ozge snapped. A chair scraped against the floor then a thud sounded, as though someone had collapsed into it. "The sooner we can get this useless meeting over, the better." In a lower voice, he added, "I detest sitting in the dark. It's like we're bats, and we've been chased out of our own caves."

"Do you have somewhere better to be?" Nazan asked, her voice laced with dark humor.

"Each time we hold one of these, we put ourselves in danger! Mahzar is going to find out if he hasn't already. Honestly, I don't know why we even bother with the charade."

"Sorry, we're late." Baran was breathing hard. "One of the busybodies from Yasin's clan spotted us on our way here and demanded he hear her complaints on our way here."

"She was rather long-winded," Yasin mumbled.

"You speak as though your people are the leaders and you are not," Ozge chuckled.

"Where is Demir?" Esemeray asked. "Perhaps I should go—"

"I'm here."

Sabra nearly leaped out from behind the sofa to throw herself at her cousin. But she knew better than to show herself before the door was closed and locked. They had to keep this from Mahzar for as long as possible. At least...as long as it took to convince her people to stand behind her.

"Now that you've chosen to grace us with your presence, what did you drag us out of our beds for?" Ozge asked.

Sabra was really, really starting to dislike that man.

The lock on the door clicked, and Sabra felt her heart take off like a bird.

"He didn't," she said, standing. "I did."

The basniins gaped at her, but Sabra stared at her cousin.

Thin scars, several inches long each, covered his face and arms. His eyes had dark bags beneath them, and he looked as though he'd aged ten years since she'd left. He was leaning on a cane, and he held his other arm close to his ribs.

"Demir," she whispered, taking three steps before she ran into the corner of the couch.

"What are you doing here?" His voice shook. "Sabra, if you knew what we've suffered here since you left, you would have never returned."

"Is Mother still alive?" She held her breath. Until now, she'd denied the possibility that her mother could have been killed for her actions. Because admitting the possibility would have brought her to her knees. But now that they were in the heart of the enemy's grasp, she needed to know the truth.

Demir glared at her. "She's injured. But alive. In the hands of some Justine for safe-keeping. They—"

Before he could finish, someone knocked violently at the door.

Everyone turned to look, and Sabra couldn't breathe. Had they been discovered?

"Let me in! I know the princess is here! I have vital information I need to share with her!"

"It's Master Mirac!" Sabra nearly laughed with relief as she hurried toward the door. She unlocked it and ushered the master learner inside before locking it behind him again, thanking the Maker that her mother and Master Mirac were both still breathing, if nothing else.

"I'm sorry, Your Highness," he said, glancing first at Sabra and then at Demir. "But rumor had it that you had returned, and I had to see for myself."

"If he's learned about it, it's only a matter of time before Mahzar knows, too," Nazan said, leaning back in her seat. "You'd better make this fast, Master Mirac."

Master Mirac scowled and pushed his spectacles farther up his nose. "Hence, my insistence!" He gave Sabra an exasperated look. "Your Highness, I really do need to show you this. It will answer the questions you've been asking for years."

"I do want to see those answers. And I'm so very glad you've come." Sabra took a few steps back toward the corner sofa. "Because I have something I need to show you as well." She turned her head to look over her shoulder. "George?"

George stood, and Sabra wondered for a moment if Yasin might collapse from a heart attack. So she took the opportunity to speak.

"This is George Basniin Sentinel." The words were bittersweet as they rolled off her tongue. "The Maker seems to have intertwined our destinies, for we met, ignorant of his position, when we were young while I accompanied my cousin to the trade talks in Kappadona."

"How did his parents not recognize you?" Ozge sneered. "The Sentinel basniin would have recognized a trading party from his own kingdom."

"His parents are dead." Sabra stared at the Woodsman. "He was raised by one of the few Sentinel couples that survived when the rest of the clan died of their mystery sickness in the valley."

Esemeray put her hand on her chest. "We sent searchers out. They never found any bodies."

"My grandfather...the man who raised me said that several weeks after they left, a massive dust storm covered the city and the nearby valleys." George paused, and his voice softened. "My grandparents believe it was the Maker's way of burying those who had none to do it for them."

The room was quiet for a moment, and to Sabra's satisfaction, most of the basniins had the decency to look somewhat ashamed. Except for Ozge, of course.

"Even if that is true, how do we know you're Hakan's son?"

"He could be Hakan's twin," Nazan scowled. "Are you really that blind?"

"It really is incredible," Esemeray murmured. "He looks just like him."

Sabra glanced at George, hope springing within her chest.

Yasin simply stared at George as though he'd seen a ghost.

"While family resemblances are all very interesting," Demir said, sinking into a chair, wincing on the way down, "I would like to know exactly why you came back." His eyes flashed at Sabra. "Sentinel or no Sentinel, I told you never to return."

Guilt tried to slash at Sabra's confidence, but she batted it away. "Because with George, we have a chance to save Segzein."

"He's one Sentinel, yes." Demir's voice hardened. "But if I recall, the Sentinels never fought alone."

"Actually," Master Mirac laid a large, dusty book on the table, "I think she may be right." He met Sabra's eyes. "In fact, I think he might be our only chance."

Demir glared at him but waved his hand.

"There are a good number of the Justines who disagree with what Mahzar has done. But they're too frightened to speak out. One of their scholars, however, gave me this several days ago." He gestured to the book.

"What is it?" Baran asked.

"It's a history of their people. From the beginning."

Nazan gaped. "This can't be real!"

"Why can't it be real?" George whispered to Sabra.

Sabra whispered back. "The Justines have guarded their history jealously. They have refused to elaborate when any of the other master learners have asked for information about their clan from before they joined Segzein. There are some general stories known by all the clans, but nothing specific about their origins."

George shot her an incredulous look. "And no one thought this was important when the clans were joining forces?"

Nazan gave him a wry smile from across the room. "They were masters of language. They wrote the vows. Unfortunately, no one was knowledgeable enough to examine the vows well enough to ask questions until years later. Only then did the others realize that the Justines had legally given themselves a wide berth to harbor whatever secrets they wished."

"They were masters of language indeed," Master Mirac said. "People would come for miles to their original country to have them write contracts and give legal advice. Kings would hire them to create trade agreements. They were also considered to be masters of literature and other ancient texts." He paused and glanced at Sabra. "But secretly, they had mastered the language of the Dark Arts as well."

Sabra's blood ran cold. "So they didn't just dabble in Sortheleige—"

"It was their medium."

The room was so silent that it was possible to hear Baran's still slightly labored breathing.

"Now, if you'll listen, I'll tell you what I've found." Master Mirac cleared his throat.

"When the earthquake decimated their city, they changed their name and were vague about their origins. There were many groups in the region that had lost their home, so few were concerned with the intent and origins of others. Most were concerned only with competing for available food and resources. And the marauders were so thick in this region that the groups camping near the lake were desperate for more numbers because more people meant fewer attacks."

"What about the Sortheleige?" Esemeray asked, glancing

nervously at Nazan. "Surely, we would have known if they were using it among us." Her hands shook slightly. "Especially if the Sentinels were present. They would have..." Her voice trailed off, and she paled as she looked at George.

"Felt it?" George asked, his deep voice reverberating in Sabra's chest as he fixed Esemeray with a cold stare. "I think they did."

"It is thought by some of their own master learners," Master Mirac said quietly, "that they had accumulated so much Sortheleige in one place, that the earth very possibly opened up to swallow it, unable to tolerate so much on its surface. It might just have been the reason the earthquake happened in the first place."

"They could have brought some with them," Yasin said slowly, twirling his beard. "It can be stored and carried in clay jars."

Nazan nodded. "Something like that would have been easy to hide. They could have hidden it for centuries, and no one would have known. If it were properly sealed at least."

Sabra had never seen Sortheleige for herself. But Maria had told her once that it was slimy and black, like squid ink. One very small drop could do immeasurable damage.

"So the creature my grandfather spoke of," George addressed Master Mirac, "the one that burned the marauders before the Justines joined the other clans—"

"I'm afraid it is." Master Mirac shut the book. "The Justines have kept their history tightly guarded. It wouldn't be unreasonable to think they might have saved this knowledge and passed it down from generation to generation, each basniin teaching his successor his secrets when he was ready to pass on the position."

"Apparently, more than just the basniin," Nazan snorted.

"I don't think many have the use of Sortheleige itself," Master Mirac said. "It would have to be too heavily guarded, and a people of this size wouldn't be able to keep that kind of knowledge hidden." He paused and opened the book once more before tracing a few lines with his fingers. "The core of the clan most likely knew of it, though. That would explain why so many guards followed blindly."

Sabra folded her arms. "It makes sense that they were the ones to so quickly fill in the vacuum left by the Sentinels."

"Rather convenient," Baran said, nodding his head profusely.

Demir cleared his throat. "As interesting as all this is, I don't see how one warrior is going to defeat the dragon that's taken down the entire kingdom."

"Think about it, Your Highness," Master Mirac said. "The dragon was created using stolen power. Because that's what Sortheleige is... power that was stolen and twisted for selfish purposes. The only way to fight darkness is with light. And whether or not you like it, that light, in this case, the blue fire of the Fortier line, flows through the veins of this young man here." He looked at George. "In my humble opinion, Sire, this young man isn't just a possible hope. He's our only hope."

"Mahzar won't like it." Baran shivered. "He hasn't liked anything we've offered so far." He glanced at Demir then back at his own lap. "Let alone a Challenger."

"Young man," Nazan said, looking straight at George. "Do you really think you can best him?"

But Demir held his hand up. When everyone was quiet, he pointed at the window. "Sabra. Go peek out of that window. Don't open it. Just look through the curtains. Tell me what you see."

Sabra did as her cousin said. And she lost her breath. The entire city was blackened. Even the grand library was scorched.

"When you left, Mahzar refused to make me king in your place until I gave you up, or you were recovered. And since then, he's not only been pleased with torturing me in body and soul," Demir's voice hardened, "but for every day that he has been unable to recover you, he's destroyed more of the city." He sat up straighter, wincing again as he did. "If you truly think your friend will destroy the dragon's hold on this city, then I will bless this venture and stand behind you. But if you have any doubts..." He fixed his eyes on her with a weight that threatened to crush her soul, "then leave with him now and never come back. Because if he does find that we've been hiding you from him, I'm not sure he won't burn the entire city completely to the ground."

Sabra couldn't breathe. She stood there, trapped in her cousin's icy gaze. Was he right? Would it be better if she left now and never came back? Because she did have doubts. Lots of them.

But then she felt George move to stand behind her, and she could feel her own strength and assurance returning as she drew from his.

"The Maker led me to George before we were old enough to know anything of our pasts or destinies." Sabra lifted her chin and even dared to smile. "George was meant to challenge this villain. And so are we."

Demir watched them for a long time, long enough for the sun to break over the horizon and accentuate the puckering scars on his face. Then he shook his head.

"I'm sorry, Sabra." His jaw flexed as he looked from her to George and back again. "I can't agree to this."

"Demir—"

He stood and used the table to make his way to her. Leaning against it, he grabbed her by the arms. "Sabra, if you go through with this, Mahzar will charge you with treason." He glanced once more at George. "And he won't be happy to take George alone. He'll demand you both."

Sabra had to struggle for a long moment to find her voice. Because he was right. And worse, she could see that it was eating him from the inside.

"I was chosen to be queen," she finally whispered. "And now I'm back to take what is mine by right." She turned to the basniins, a new fire burning in her chest. "I know you chose differently the last time I stood before you. But I ask you now. Will you accept my sacrifice and that of the Sentinels?" She leaned forward and willed them to meet her eyes. "Will you make me your queen? And after that, will you support George in his official Challenge to Mahzar?"

The basniins were quiet, and for a long moment, Sabra was afraid they would say no. This was it. She had no more plans. If this didn't work, she had no idea where she would go.

Most likely, out to meet Mahzar as his bride.

But just when she was ready to despair, Nazan stood. "Well then, let's issue the Challenge." She stood stiffly, but Sabra detected the slightest hint of a smile on the woman's lips. "But first, let's make you queen."

CHAPTER 33

THIS ODDLY BEQUEATHED SENSE OF HONOR

Sabra held her held high as she made her way toward the palace entrance, flanked by George, the other basniins, and a very unhappy Demir. She was wearing her mother's finest court gown, sewn with real gold threads and trimmed in ruffles embroidered with vines and flowers. The late morning light made it nearly glow as she passed by the large hall windows. Her mother, she learned from Esemeray, had been removed from the palace and placed under constant supervision. Mahzar had been demanding her cooperation to find Sabra, but she'd refused to help. So he'd locked her in one of the smaller houses in the Justines' spoke of the city. She was also being treated by a personal Physic because of lung damage created by all the smoke. Apparently, Mahzar seemed to think this was incredibly compassionate.

Never mind that he'd been the one to create the smoke in the first place.

Sabra desperately wanted to free her mother first, but she knew that wasn't possible. Not now, when it was difficult enough to find one of her court outfits appropriate for the Challenge. Thankfully, Serkan had come through once again, somehow locating the queen's wardrobe - even though it had been moved - and snatching one of the gowns for Sabra to wear. So now, arrayed in gold that glinted in the setting sun as the evening shadows began to lengthen, Sabra walked through the halls lined with the people who loathed her almost palpably. Their hate was painful, but the fine golden robes made her feel once again like she was where she belonged. More noticeably, her mother's crown weighed heavily on her head.

I'm keeping my vow, Father.

A vow she wouldn't have had to make if he'd only done what was honorable.

The walk wasn't without great effort. She could feel the eyes of her people on her, whispers, scoffing. A few even spat. They stopped, of course, when Demir followed in her wake, but she could feel their hostility nonetheless.

Not that she could blame them. To them, she was the princess who had fled and left them to the dragon determined to destroy them until she gave herself up. To them, she was a coward. Meanwhile, Demir had remained, doing his best to protect them while surviving the enemy's torture. No wonder they despised her.

She could accept that, though. She wasn't doing this for herself. She was doing it to save them. She might go down in history as one of the most cowardly royals ever to inhabit the palace. But at least her people might live on to tell of her supposed cowardice. Her father had said that she had been placed here and now for a purpose, even if it meant they hated her for doing so.

By the time they made it to the palace steps, word must have gotten out that their wayward princess was back. And not only that, but that she had been named queen by the other basniins.

When they were all out on the large front entrance at the top of the main steps, Sabra thumped the bottom of her large ceremonial scepter. The sound echoed throughout the palace walls and into the city.

"Citizens of Segzein!" she called when the talking quieted. "I am aware that there were certain names and subjects of which you were not allowed to speak under my father's rule." She looked around at those who were close enough to meet her gaze. "As your queen, I hereby revoke those commands. I will do so in writing at another date. But in light of recent events," she glanced back at George, "and recent discoveries, it has become necessary to make great alterations for the preservation of our lives and ways of life." She took a deep breath. Now for the hard part.

"Who made you queen?" someone shouted. "You abandoned us, and now you waltz back in to claim your throne?"

"Contrary to what the Justines may claim," Nazan said in a dry voice, "the basniins have not lost our ability to crown the queen. Whether we're in the throne room or a little hovel."

"But Demir was supposed to be king!" someone else called. "Now the dragon will punish us!"

Demir stepped forward. His face was cold and unmoving. But to his credit, he bowed his head. "The dragon would not recognize my kingship until I helped him locate the princess." He looked at Sabra, his eyes accusing. "And that was something I couldn't in good conscience do."

This was getting out of hand. Sabra needed to take back the situation now.

"I know some of you have heard rumors that I escaped when the dragon required my hand in marriage," she said loudly. "The rumors are true."

Murmurs so loud they hardly counted as whispers sprang up from the crowd, resulting in a dull roar that Sabra had to bang her scepter on the ground once again to quiet.

"I was not, however, abandoning you." Her heart was beating erratically, as though it might tire and stop at any moment. But her voice stayed calm and strong. She had trained for this. Her entire life had been spent preparing for this moment. If she couldn't use her knowledge and training now, she might as well pack up and leave. "I searched to see what I could learn about the dragon. How we might defeat him."

Another rumble broke out in the crowd, but Sabra spoke over it.

"I found knowledge, but even more importantly, the Maker led me to find the basniin of the lost eighth clan. He is the last of his line.

And as a Sentinel, though he hasn't been here since he was an infant, he has promised to fight the dragon."

At this point in her speech, Sabra expected shouting and protests to break out. But instead, those who had gathered near scattered like bugs from light as a large shadow was cast from the west.

The dragon, reeking of smoke and sulfur, landed on the tiled platform before her.

"You've returned, Princess," he said in his low, rumbling voice. It reminded her of rocks banging against one another.

"I have." She stood straighter. "But I am no princess. And I have joined with the other basniins to issue an official Challenge."

"So you have," he said, already looking at George. "And tell me, young basniin. Have you come to fulfill the oath your ancestors made to protect the people of Segzein?"

George met the dragon's stare. "I've come to fulfill the oath I made to the queen."

The dragon chuckled, an unpleasant sound. "I could argue that you're free from such an oath, as she is not rightfully queen. And yet..." He tilted his head. "I'm intrigued by your sense of honor." The dragon turned back to Sabra. "You do know that an official Challenge must have an agreed upon point at which one party forfeits."

"I do."

"And you also know that a Challenge of this magnitude can only end in death. And if, for some reason, the battle is not finished by the end of the first day, it must resume again the day after."

Sabra took a deep breath. "I expect no less."

The dragon paced a few times, his white serpentine body nearly blinding as it reflected the sharp light of the late morning sun. "You also know," he finally said, pausing, "that if he dies, so shall you. That is, if you are issuing the Challenge with him."

Sabra opened her mouth, but in two long strides, George was between her and the dragon. "I issue the Challenge alone."

The dragon looked back and forth between them. "You have no singer."

His words felt like a knife to Sabra's heart, and from the way the dragon was still watching them closely, it seemed he knew it.

"What I have is my business," George growled.

The dragon shrugged. "Very well. I was simply curious. I wasn't sure how well you knew the ways of your people. Not that it matters to me." And yet, Sabra was sure that she saw something very akin to relief in the dragon's expression as he looked to the others standing behind her. "And the other basniins recognize this Challenge?"

"We do," Nazan said.

"And you will bow to the demands of the victor?"

This time, Nazan's voice was slightly tremulous. "We will."

The dragon looked around. "Very well. While this queen is a pretender to the throne, I accept this Challenge and recognize it as valid." He eyed George. "Largely because this oddly bequeathed sense of honor intrigues me. Meet me at the lake this evening at sunset. We will begin then." And with a flap of his wings that nearly knocked Sabra over, he took off into the sky.

CHAPTER 34
WHAT HAVE YOU DONE?

The day was torture. Sabra reviewed the contract Mahzar had written and sent to the palace. It was tightly worded, as Nazan confirmed. He made it clear that no other warriors would be allowed to come to George's aid. Not that Sabra expected any. She'd seen little to none of the Blue Bands since arriving back at the palace. Demir might have offered to help, had he not been so badly injured from Mahzar's torture.

The basniins muttered amongst themselves as the day progressed and they waited for evening. George paced, and Demir spent the whole time glaring. The one time Sabra asked if he had any advice, he growled and retorted that she should have disappeared with George while she had the chance.

But that was not what she'd sworn to her father. She also wouldn't have gotten this far without the crown that she'd used to leverage this contract. Still, all the while, though, Sabra couldn't help thinking...

She should be with him. She should be his singer. She should be there beside him now, holding him close as he prepared for what might be his final battle. She shivered as she imagined what it might be like to be that close. What would it feel like to know he was hers?

She thanked the Maker when the sun finally began to fall and there was no more time for what-ifs. Excusing herself, she made her way down to the armory where George was preparing for the battle, not sure what she would do when she arrived. George would be preparing there. Nazan said it was where the Sentinels had once refreshed themselves between guard shifts and where they had kept many of their weapons. Now it was largely a storage room, but there were still a few cots and barrels of weapons in the corner.

She peeked inside to see George. He was wearing a long tunic that went down to just above his knees. He also wore leather sandals that were wrapped and tied snugly around his feet. And in his hands, he was holding up and examining what looked like armor.

"George?" she called out softly.

He turned, and the relief in his eyes was so warm it made her want to weep. "Sabra. I didn't hear you at first." He gestured to the armor. "Nazan gave me this. She says it was worn by some very famous Sentinel years ago that I don't know the name of."

Sabra smiled in spite of herself. "How do you get it on?"

"First I need help tying this scarf. It's supposed to keep the metal edges from rubbing my neck." He held up a scarf. "And then help me tighten these leather ties on the chest armor, if you would. I'm not sure they're secure."

Sabra went to him and began to tie the scarf loosely around his neck. Then she helped him adjust the leather straps. The top part of the armor looked and fitted like a jacket. But instead of being made of a single sheet of metal, hammered into body-shaped armor as worn by the Justines, this armor was made of dozens of long strips of metal that were attached together so the armor could move with the body. It was made of four parts that could all move separately. Two parts covered the shoulders, and the other parts were halves of the torso pieces.

Sabra moved closer and took the front straps in her hands. "You tied them tight enough, but I don't know how long this leather will last under stress. It looks rather old."

He grimaced. "I was afraid of that. But it's better than nothing."

"Your grandfather couldn't give you his?"

"He was making me some when you arrived. But there wasn't time to finish it when the Justines attacked. Only the shield and sword were ready."

Sabra tied the straps carefully. She could feel the heat radiating out from beneath the metal, and it took all of her self-control not to lean in closer. Instead, she went as slowly as she could, relishing every accidental brush and the feeling of his breath against her neck as he watched her.

The irony wasn't lost on her that she was doing what a wife should have done before sending him to fight the dragon, only she was doing sending him without the help he needed most. As it had since she'd uttered the words, her oath to her father weighed heavily on her heart.

What if she sang now? What if she pretended she'd never taken the oath at all?

"Don't."

Sabra blinked a few times to clear her head. "Don't what?"

He gave her a sad smile and put his fingers under her chin. "Regret your choices. You're serving your people in the best way you know how. That's all anyone can ask of you."

"I could serve in another capacity," she mumbled.

"It's possible." He paused. "But who knows what else I'll need from the basniins. I know nothing about this world and all the politics involved. You're queen now. If I need something, you're my best chance at getting help."

She tried to smile but couldn't. "Or I could sing and help you defeat him once and for all."

He wrapped his large hand around the back of her neck and pulled her toward him gently, resting his forehead against hers and closing his eyes. "I told you, Sabra. Fulfill your destiny. And let me fulfill mine. If the Maker wishes me to live, then he'll somehow provide a way."

Sabra nearly argued then and there. She nearly sang the song. But the binding ropes of her oath kept her tongue still.

"Where do you think we should put this?" George asked, holding up Maria's old blue silk sash.

Sabra did her best to smile. "Your grandmother actually did show me this." She helped him loop it over one shoulder and across his chest, tying it down at the waist. When they were finished, she stepped back to look, and it took her breath away.

He could have walked right out of the pages of her little blue book.

But no, as much as she wanted George, he wasn't hers to have. She had chosen her path. The path of responsibility to her people.

And it might just kill her.

They exited the palace just as the sun set over the edge of the distant western mountains. Mahzar was waiting in his human form outside the city grounds at the edge of the lake. Sabra and George made their way to him through the Sowens' spoke, Demir and several makeshift citizen guards following. It took all of Sabra's control not to reach out and take George's hand. But they had to be strong now. They had to show the dragon that they were dangerous as well.

George certainly looked the part. The gold discs on his leather belt glinted in the sunlight, as did the discs on the leather straps that hung down from the belt in the front. He carried his metal helm under his left arm, and though his sword was sheathed, he left his right arm free. On his back he wore a long, thin lance and a crossbow with arrows.

They came to a stop about ten paces from Mahzar. Close enough they could talk without shouting, but far enough to stay out of the dragon's reach, should he act dishonorably.

"Strange as it might sound, I am glad to see you both here," Mahzar said with a small bow. "Though I disagree with your methods, I am glad to know that the Sentinels didn't all fall prey to cowardice."

George's jaw clicked audibly, but Mahzar simply turned to Sabra. "You know, Princess, that if you lose this Challenge, you agree to marry me."

"I signed the contract," Sabra said in a monotone voice. "I'm aware of what was inside."

As if hearing her thoughts, Sabra felt George's hand on the small of her back, and she lifted her chin a little higher. Even if few others believed in her, George did. And that was what made this all the more painful.

"And just a reminder," Mahzar turned to George,"this is to the death. If you injure me and throw down your sword, I have every right to fry you like a piece of pork."

"A chance I'll make sure not to provide." George looked at Sabra. But this time, his voice was too quiet for the dragon to hear. "I can see you wavering."

"It would be simpler to give up this whole thing and just sing."

"We wouldn't be here if you'd agreed to sing for me. You've gotten us this far. Walk your path." George's gray eyes burned into hers. "I'll walk mine. And when it's all over, our consciences will be clear before the Maker."

Sabra held his gaze, unsure whether her conscience could be clear either way. But when his lips turned up at the corner, she was unable to fight the feeling of peace that seemed to emanate from him.

"Is there a problem?" Mahzar called out.

"No." George broke the trance he'd trapped her in and turned to Mahzar. "I accept your terms."

Mahzar bowed his head. "Very well. As soon as the princess's entourage has returned to safety, we will begin."

Sabra had never been one for titles and great shows of decorum, but Mahzar's constant attempts to usurp her authority made her bristle now. She turned to go, but before leaving, she put her hand on George's arm. "Hand his tail to him on a platter," she snapped.

George's eyes glinted that near silver as he smiled, a new smile that was feral and very unlike the gentle man she knew. "With pleasure."

Demir hurried Sabra much deeper into the city than she would have liked.

"I want to see!" she protested as he moved her and their guards through a field of saplings.

"I promise, you won't be able to miss it." He pursed his lips. "Though I would have given anything for you to do just that."

They were interrupted by the sound of the gong, signaling the start of the battle. Sabra ran up the steps of the closest guard tower that overlooked the lake and the valley. When she was at the top, she had to admit that Demir had been right. From that high, she could see everything.

Mahzar still stood as a human, but something was different about him. Sabra squinted and realized that he was being surrounded by a thick, black mist. It swirled around him like a whirlwind of ash and smoke. Faster and larger it swelled until it abruptly broke apart to reveal the white dragon.

Sabra had seen more than enough of the dragon for one lifetime. And yet, it still made her blood freeze in her veins. Even from the distance she stood at, the dragon was enormous. On its hind legs, it towered over George at three times his height. Its tail was at least the same length as the rest of its body, possibly longer. The beast shook its body out, revealing a wingspan that would have spanned the width of the throne room alone. Sharp-hooked talons were on the end of each wing, though they were invisible when the dragon folded its wings back onto itself. It looked up to the sky and roared, shaking its head as it let forth a burst of fire.

"Sabra," Demir whispered. "What have you done?"

Sabra gaped as the beast let out a roar. Even if George had the legendary blue fire, would he have stood a chance?

The dragon's roar was cut short when George charged him. It lifted into the air and immediately came down behind him.

"Come on!" George shouted, banging his sword and shield

together. "Aren't man enough to fight me? Or are you going to spend the whole time flying away?"

"He's either the bravest or most foolhardy man to have ever walked the planet," Demir said.

Sabra didn't bother to reply. She was too busy praying.

The dragon drew in a deep breath, during which George slammed the pointed bottom of his shield into the ground. Just as the dragon let forth a stream of fire, he ducked behind it.

The stream was so thick that George was lost within it. Sabra let out a little shriek. Would this be the end? Would all their struggles and journey end in a few short minutes?

George, however, did not collapse under the flames. Behind the shield, he had held his ground.

"How in the sands...?" Demir muttered.

"The shield!" she said, her voice wavering uncontrollably. But she was so happy she didn't care. "His grandfather gave him the original Sentinel's sword and shield. They're lined with crystal from the Fortress!"

Demir looked at Sabra but seemed unable to utter a word.

The dragon let out another shriek before blanketing George with flame again. Once again, George withstood the flame.

"But he has to do more than survive." Demir gripped the end of his cane until his knuckles were white. "He has to win."

Sabra's joy began to disintegrate. As much as she hated to admit it, Demir was right. George couldn't win by hiding from the dragon's flames. He had to go on the offensive somehow. But how could he do that when the dragon wouldn't give him the chance?

The dragon and George were circling again. The dragon opened up his mouth a third time, as if to flame him, but just as George raised his shield, the dragon's tail snapped around like a whip.

George was knocked several feet away and landed hard on his side. He had just enough time to roll beneath his shield when the dragon sent yet another river of fire at him. Then, just as he got to his feet, the dragon hit him with its tail. Again and again, it smacked him down. Its fire never seemed to touch him, but he wasn't able to get his bearings.

"He's getting tired," Demir said, frowning as George once again pulled himself to his knees. Sure enough, he wasn't fast enough, and the dragon leaned forward. Instead of hitting him with its tail, though, the dragon smacked his shield with its head. George went flying backward. This time, though, when he stopped moving, he didn't get up.

Demir held Sabra's hand so tightly it hurt, but she squeezed right back.

The dragon moved its head close to him to sniff. Just when it was inches from his body, though, George smashed the dragon's face with his shield.

The dragon reeled back, its ear-piercing scream making Sabra's ears pound. George didn't waste any time watching. Instead, he jumped up and began sprinting toward the nearest hill.

"He's hurting," Demir said. "Watch him hug his left arm to his side. He's limping slightly, too."

He was indeed limping. But he scrambled up the side of the hill anyway.

The dragon didn't immediately give chase. Its nose was dripping with blood, and it looked to be in a good deal of pain. When it turned, though, Sabra knew the second it spotted George. Its eyes narrowed, and like an arrow, it shot into the sky.

By the time the dragon neared him, George had made it to the top of a cliff that jutted out over the lake. It wasn't terribly high, probably only three stories in her palace. But then Sabra realized what he was going to do.

Like them, George seemed to have realized that he couldn't simply win by surviving.

"He wouldn't," Demir whispered.

But as the dragon neared him, its wings flapping in the air, George took a running start and propelled himself off the edge of the cliff.

Sabra was so horrified she couldn't speak. She could only watch as George's blade sliced through a large portion of the dragon's left wing. And then George and the dragon tumbled toward the water.

They both landed in the lake's shallow end. And neither of them moved. The crowd that had gathered at the edge of the valley seemed to be holding its breath. Before Sabra knew what she was doing, she was down the steps and sprinting back out to the battlefield.

"Sabra!" Demir called from behind her, but Sabra didn't slow. Instead, she pushed faster. And by the time she reached the lake, her run was hardly faster than a walk, and her side had a piercing pain beneath her rib cage. She continued to push, though, until she was in the water and at George's side.

I don't know what I'll do if I roll him over and he's not breathing, she told the Maker as she knelt in the water.

This fear was nonsensical, a distant part of her mind whispered. That was the goal of the fight: to the death. And yet, Sabra didn't know if she could handle turning him over to find that the man she loved was lying dead in her arms.

He was on his side, his head barely out of the shallow water. She did her best to roll him over, but the armor he wore made him heavy, and she couldn't quite turn him all the way.

Sabra hadn't realized she was crying until Demir reached her side. Gently, her cousin pried her hands off of George and turned him slightly until he no longer had the side of his face in the pink, salty water.

"He's breathing!" Demir exclaimed.

Sabra felt more than ready in that moment to faint, and for the first time in her life, she might have allowed herself to do so if she hadn't seen Mahzar's men running over and examining their master as well. Sabra stood and walked a little closer.

"Is he dead?" she asked. Oh, how she prayed he was.

But Mahzar's captain, a mustached man who never left Mahzar's side, just shook his head. "No." He looked back down at the dragon, whom his men were now attending. "But he is in a great deal of pain."

"We agreed to a truce, should the original match not be finished today," Sabra said, willing herself to speak calmly and clearly. "Perhaps you would be in agreement to wait until tomorrow to end this."

"The offer...still stands...Princess."

Before their eyes, the dragon shifted back to his human form, and then sat up, panting heavily.

Sabra jumped back slightly, but Mahzar waved her off. "I have no plans to break our treaty." He winced as one of his men rolled him onto a crude leather stretcher, carried by four poles on his men's backs. "Tomorrow will be as today should have been." He paused, breathing hard. "Unless you choose to marry me now and forfeit all the discipline I must exercise against our people when I take my victory by right."

"No!"

Everyone jumped. George, who had been unconscious just half a minute before, had raised his head. He glared at Mahzar. "I'm not finished."

Mahzar's face remained impassive, but Sabra thought she detected the tiniest glimpse of disappointment in his eyes. Then it was gone so soon she might have imagined it.

"Very well," he said. Coward. He had been hoping she would concede so he wouldn't have to fight again. She was certain.

Sabra felt her face harden into a mask of fury. "We will meet here tomorrow at sunset. As planned." She turned to Demir. "Let's get him back and let Esemeray look at him."

Demir nodded unhappily, and Sabra made her way back to the palace, leading the way as servants carried George behind her. On the outside, she was all confidence and cold grace. But on the inside, she was dying already. The only thing that held her together on that long walk back to the palace was the anger that was boiling hotter by the second.

CHAPTER 35
SEE

I'm going with Esemeray to see George," Sabra told one of her servants quietly as they neared the palace. "My cousin paused to speak with someone else, but please find him and tell him, so he won't worry."

The servant bowed and ran to do as she said, and Sabra followed Esemeray into the palace. They had cleared different rooms in different wings to try to accommodate the different spokes. Several rooms had also been cleared for each spoke's use for whatever they needed. The rooms Esemeray had received for healing were small, but more numerous than anywhere else in the palace, simply because so many people had needed treatment after the dragon had appeared. Lung damage and burns were frightfully common. And now, as they cleared a small room for George, she was thankful to have made that decision.

The men who carried George gently laid him on the raised pallet that had been set in the middle of the room. Esemeray thanked them and sent them away. Once the door was locked, she lit a candelabra. Then she went to a small drawer and rummaged through the bottles and jars until she found a small brown bottle.

"What is that?" Sabra asked. She'd watched a number of healings by the Physics, but she couldn't remember having seen this particular bottle before. She tried to recall from her brief training what remedy would be used for such injuries, but none sprang to mind.

"It's an ancient concoction," Esemeray's feathery voice whispered in the silence. "One created by the Sentinels to heal their own people. I was gifted several bottles for those who stayed behind as the others were leaving."

For one brief moment, Sabra felt unbridled joy. "Wait! I have more!"

"You have *what?*" Esemeray cried. But Sabra was already gone. She tore through the palace, practically shoving people out of her way until she reached her room. There, she went inside and thrust her hand into her bag. For a moment, she feared it was gone. Someone must have stolen it. But then, just as she was about to panic, she realized it had gotten wrapped up in one of her shawls. Grabbing the bottle, Sabra raced back down to the room, and she thrust the bottle out at Esemeray.

"Use this!"

Esemeray took the bottle reverently. "How did you—"

"George's grandmother sent it." She held her breath. "Will it work?"

Esemeray removed the wax and sniffed carefully at the substance inside. Usually, the woman was nearly as nervous as Sabra's old suitor, Jitters, but whenever she was in a healing room, those nerves melted away, and Sabra could see that she truly did deserve the title of basniin. Sure enough, she nodded confidently and went back to examining George.

During which Sabra nearly died of impatience.

"He has multiple broken ribs, from what I can tell," Esemeray finally said. "And he'll be bruised all over tomorrow at the very least. There might be several other broken bones, but I can't tell for sure." She pursed her lips. "I wish I had more, to be honest. But if I use this on his ribs and on his head for the concussion, it should be enough to keep him alive at least."

Before Sabra could respond, there was a knock on the door. She answered it and found the same servant outside.

"Your Majesty," he said. "I have a message I am to deliver to you from Basniin Ozge." He handed her a sealed note.

Sabra sighed as she broke the seal and read the note.

The basniins must meet tonight in the palace to discuss the situation at hand.

Her first inclination was to tell Ozge exactly where he could meet himself if he had a desire to leave his quarters. But she was queen now, and pettiness was not an option. More than anything, she wanted to tend to George and watch Esemeray treat him. She wanted it so badly it hurt. But showing her hand would be very foolish right now. Skipping that meeting could breed dire consequences. They needed all the support they could get, and a last-minute meeting with the basniins wasn't promising in and of itself.

"Very well," she said. "Tell all the other basniins who are not Esemeray to meet me in the throne room immediately."

"Of course." The servant frowned, his eyebrows drawing together. "Although...are you sure that's wise?"

"Which part?"

He bowed his head again. "I don't mean to be impertinent, Your Majesty. But since the day the king..." He paused and swallowed, and Sabra's own throat grew tight. "In recent days, the basniins have desired to meet in a more discreet location."

"I understand that. But I wish to meet them in the throne room nevertheless." She gave him a dry smile. "If we're going to fall, let's do it standing, not from our knees."

His eyes grew wide, but to his credit, he bobbed a nod anyway. "Of course, Your Majesty." Then he hurried to obey.

The throne room, though dirty, had been kept largely clear of sleeping citizens. There were, however, dozens who gathered in clumps about the room during the day, Sabra had noticed, probably because it was so large and they had a bit more space to breathe and move. Most of them glared at her whenever she walked by or watched her with suspicious, resentful eyes. Well, that was fine for them. They would simply have to trust her. She knew what she was doing.

At least, she prayed she did.

"That's everyone," Demir said gruffly twenty minutes later. For now, the throne room had been cleared of everyone but the basniins. When she arrived, it dawned on her that for such a meeting, she would be expected to sit on the throne. This nearly made her vomit. The last person to sit there had been her father on the day he was killed. But as there was no other choice, she marched up the dais and, as gracefully as she was able, seated herself in the large stone chair as if it had been hers all her life.

"Thank you, everyone, for coming at this late hour," Sabra addressed them. It was strange speaking to them from so high up. In her mind, this chair still belonged to her father. "Esemeray is tending to George. In the meantime, Ozge has something he wishes to discuss." She looked expectantly at the man and tried not to grimace.

Ozge was known as one of the least amiable men in all of Segzein. He was also known for despising every kind of work except his own. She had a feeling that his particular interest in this fight, whatever it was, would not be good.

"The dragon has promised to make our lives more difficult with each day that you refuse to give up your crown," he began.

Sabra nodded in what she hoped was a patient way. "Yes. I do recall that."

Ozge glared at her. "Another day of fighting means more punishment if he wins."

"You didn't object this morning." Sabra glared right back. "What makes tomorrow so different?" She leaned back. "Would you rather we surrender now? After we've stirred the hornet's nest?"

Ozge huffed and rubbed his left arm. "Yesterday, they hadn't yet burned down my people's last lumberyard."

"Today?" Baran paled. "He did that today?"

"Not him. His people. They set it ablaze the moment he injured his wing, I'm told."

And the Justines claimed to be upset because the Sentinels supposedly hadn't kept their word.

Hypocrites.

Sabra briefly closed her eyes. No wonder he was worried. Lumber was difficult enough to buy in the region when there wasn't a shortage. And now his people had lost it all.

"I'm sorry," she said quietly. "Truly, I am. And after all this is done, we'll see what we can do to replace it." She turned to the others. "If it makes any sense, though, this is all the more reason why we need to defeat him. If he's hurting you now to make a point, don't you believe he'll do it again?"

"I believe what you're saying," Baran said, his voice shaking. "But we can't keep holding much longer either."

Sabra frowned at him. "What happened?"

He let out a long sigh. "Before the battle tonight, he burned our seed reserves."

"I am very sorry." Sabra sat back in her chair. And she was. This was a loss for not just the Sowens, but the entire kingdom. "But our goal here is to eliminate his threat. It always was." She spread her hands. "I'm not sure what you want me to do."

"We need to set a limit." Ozge scowled. "Even if the Sentinel survives the night, and even if he's ready to fight again tomorrow, it must be the last time. Dragon or no dragon, we can't survive any more destruction."

"We can rebuild the city. And we can trade for new seeds," Yasin said, looking from one person to the next. "And surely it would be worth the destruction if we're free of Mahzar at last?"

"We don't have anything to trade with," Baran whispered. "The city won't survive the winter."

His words were followed by silence.

Sabra sighed. Yasin's support was a pleasant surprise, considering how he'd capitulated when she was first dethroned. Unfortunately, considering that quick capitulation, she had little confidence in his allegiance. Even worse was the loss of Baran's confidence. Young as he was, his loyalty to her had never come into question before the dragon came. If he was losing hope...was there any to be had?

Sabra looked to Nazan for support, but the woman was strangely quiet.

"You all know that if Mahzar gets his way now, he's not going to stop simply because his demands have been met." Sabra looked from face to face, incredulous. "He'll just do it again the next time he doesn't approve of something. And again. And again. And again. Why can't you see this?" As she spoke, she glanced back at Demir, who stood by the doors. He hadn't so much as moved the entire time. What did he think of this conversation? If he hadn't been inhibited by the torture's effects...if he were still the old Demir Sabra had grown up with, what would he have said about this conversation?

Today, he was as stone-faced as ever.

Ozge shook his head. "The more I think about it, the less I want to take the chance with tomorrow, either." He glared at her. "You have good intentions, Your Majesty, but you are young. Pardon me for pointing out that you've never seen your people starving." His frown deepened. "You've not been here to hear the cries of their babes as they hunger."

Fury and guilt crashed in Sabra's chest. "You speak as if I were gallivanting around the countryside for a picnic."

"Let's focus on the discussion at hand." Nazan folded her arms across her chest. "We agreed to a Challenge, and a stipulation of that Challenge was that a truce could be temporarily called. I think one more day is a reasonable thing to ask, considering it was part of the terms."

So Nazan also seemed to think that waiting two days was impossible. This was not going well. Sabra cleared her throat. "George has already declared that he's not giving up. And as Esemeray is using an ancient healing—"

"No offense, Sabra," Ozge said with a sneer, "but we're very familiar with the Sentinels and their elixir. You might be new to their ways, but *we* have lived and worked beside them for most of our lives."

"*Your Majesty*," Sabra said through a clenched jaw. "My title is *Your Majesty*. You will address me using the same respect you showed my father. "

"We might not be in this mess if we had shown him less honor as well," Ozge snapped.

"Ozge," Yasin warned, "you forget yourself!"

Even a month ago, making such a fuss over her title would have sickened Sabra. But this was important. Clearly, the basniins didn't have faith in her leadership abilities. And such slips were dangerous during war. Clear lines of authority were necessary to keep the structure of the kingdom sturdy. Without rules and regulations, questions would be raised that could break a kingdom in half. It had already nearly happened when the basniins had voted to offer Sabra up to the dragon. Now that there was some semblance of order once again, this was her one chance to restore the kingdom. If she failed, there would be no more Segzein. At least, not the one she knew and loved.

The law was on her side, whether Mahzar wanted to admit it or not. And strangely, even he was keeping to it more closely than the other basniins at this point, accepting the Challenge and keeping to its terms. Sabra needed something more than spineless advisers that changed allegiance with power.

Sabra had been staring at the door behind a still silent Demir as Nazan and Ozge argued. Then it came to her, like lightning before thunder.

She needed the Sentinels.

Sabra stood and pulled on her cloak.

"Where are you going?" Baran stared at her with wide eyes.

"To get help," she snapped. "And this time, if you would all be so considerate as not to scheme behind my back, it would be greatly appreciated."

The words probably weren't the wisest to say to the same people who had just made her queen. But Sabra wasn't in the mood for games. As she had told Demir on countless occasions, she wasn't good at them.

"Sabra," Demir said in a quiet voice when she reached the door.

She glared at him. "Are you speaking to me now?"

Hurt flashed in his eyes, and Sabra had to bite back guilt as she noticed again how many scars were healing on his face. Angry as she was, this wasn't his fault. She might not agree with his methods, but at least he had tried.

"I don't want to see you hurt," he said softly, staring at the floor.

She closed her eyes briefly and pulled him into a hug. "I know," she whispered. "But at this point, pain is inevitable." She pulled away and held his gaze. "I know this is risky—"

He snorted. "Risk is an understatement."

"Do you want to be a puppet king?

"No." His gaze hardened slightly. "Nor do I want you to be the submissive wife of a monster."

"Which is why I'm fighting with everything in me not to be." Sabra pushed the door open.

"Sabra, wait."

Sabra took a deep breath and turned slowly. "What is it?"

"It doesn't have to be one way or the other."

She turned to face him fully this time. "What?"

"I talked with Mirac last night. The Challenge can be amended if both parties are willing."

"What part would we amend?" The part where he burned everyone's food supplies or the part where he wanted to marry her? Because Sabra rather doubted Mahzar would be interested in either.

"If you loved...George." Demir looked as though it pained him to even utter George's name. "And you were willing to step down, we could marry you here, before Mahzar. He could be satisfied that your union would prevent you from returning for the crown." Demir took a deep breath, his eyes on the floor. "And you could marry the one you love."

Sabra wrinkled her nose. "Am I that obvious?"

"Your romantic whims are not something I particularly enjoy discussing. I would personally prefer to think of you as a child of five years for the rest of my life." He sighed. "But yes. I'm afraid you've been in love with that boy since before you knew what love is." He smiled, but it didn't reach his eyes. "Few people can ever boast such a childhood sweetheart such as yours. Why throw it away for a people who have abandoned you both?"

For a moment, Sabra hesitated. In a way, it sounded too good to be true. But that meant it most likely was. After all, George had sworn an oath, and she knew him well enough to know he wouldn't break it. Especially if breaking it meant leaving thousands of innocents in the hands of a man like Mahzar. And she, too, must heed the call and keep her promise.

"It's not their fault that the Justines committed an atrocity." She swallowed. "And my father with them. To shift the blame to them would only further the injustice." She took a deep breath and met Demir's eyes, which were growing more fiery by the second. "George would not break his oath. And neither will I."

"But he's going to fail, Sabra! Can't you see that?"

"We may fail. But that failure will be far more painful if we know we didn't try." And with that, she left the throne room and stepped out into the night.

CHAPTER 36
GONE

The streets were silent and deserted when Sabra forged into the darkness. The moon shed just enough light for her to pick her way around the rubble and debris from the repeated dragon attacks. And she was glad for it. The roads were barely recognizable, and more than once, she had to stop to get her bearings. So many buildings had been destroyed.

Hopefully, she would find them.

They weren't among the survivors living in the palace. Sabra had spent several hours searching before she was told that they had chosen to remain in the eighth spoke. As she got closer, she could see why. Mahzar had left the eighth spoke primarily untouched. There wasn't really a reason to attack it. It was mostly undeveloped land covered in shoddy shacks. Mahzar, horrible person he was, really believed he was doing the right thing by punishing Segzein into obedience. He could use the destruction of food and lumber and other supplies well for this task. Killing people in their homes didn't accomplish his purpose. Hopefully, it would stay that way.

Ten minutes later, Sabra was rewarded by a small batch of flickering lights. She ran toward them and was even more relieved when she saw their blue sashes reflecting in the moonlight. Were they wearing them for George? Had they perhaps changed their minds? But when she reached them, her excitement turned into panic.

"Are you leaving?" she cried.

The men and women in the clump nearest her turned, looking surprised. At their feet were bags. Some had carts with donkeys or a rare horse attached to them. Sleeping children were in the carts, and many adults had bags strapped to their backs. Sabra realized in that moment that she had never truly known the real numbers of the Blue Bands. They'd simply been staples, scattered about the city at random. But now that she studied the group before her, she realized that there had to be no less than three hundred.

"Your Majesty," a familiar voice called.

Sabra looked around until she recognized the man who had given her the sash the last time she'd visited the eighth spoke. He was also the one who had tried to stop her in the palace just before the basniins had agreed to give her to Mahzar, and Demir had spirited her away.

"What's going on?" she asked as he approached.

"We are leaving," he said in a kind but firm voice.

Sabra gaped at him. "But why?"

He gave her a sad smile. "It's time. The poison has receded enough that we have enough strength to go. And with the dragon distracted tonight, and unlikely to notice us, there's no better time."

"But George..." She sucked in a quick breath, remembering why she'd come. "George is going to fight him tomorrow! He can defeat—"

"No, my dear," the man said kindly. "He can't."

Sabra stared at him, open-mouthed. "What do you—"

"Not without the Sentinel's Song." He looked back at the others and sighed. "Though most likely not even then."

Sabra glared at him to keep tears of frustration at bay. This was not at all going the way she'd expected. "And how do you know that?"

"Where do you think the power came from that brought our entire clan to its knees?"

Sabra swallowed. "You know what happened?" Funny, how when everything was about to come crashing down, she might just get the answers she'd been seeking. Even if they were too late.

"Walk with me." He motioned to the others with his hand then drew Sabra to the side. There was a little walkway that wasn't as strewn with rubble as the road she had taken to get there. He led them down this path until they found a bench that miraculously hadn't been burned or broken.

"What did you learn while you were gone?" the man asked when they were seated. "Tell me of this long-lost warrior you found."

Sabra frowned up at the cloudless sky. "I know that there was some sort of poisoning that affected only the Sentinels. So the ones that could go left. George is the late basniin's son, and he was among those who left. He only survived because his father sent George away with a childless couple. They were able to hide in the nearest city and drink the clean water. So they survived."

The man no longer wore the patient look of a condescending parent. He leaned forward and gripped the edge of the bench.

"That man…" he paused to draw in a breath, his voice shaking. "You're telling me that young man is the *rightful* basniin?"

Sabra nodded. "That's the only way we could bring a legal Challenge."

The man scrunched his eyes shut and clenched his jaw. Then he pressed a fist against his mouth. After a moment, Sabra realized he was crying.

"So the boy lived," he whispered.

Sabra watched, unsure what to do. Obviously, the survival of his basniin meant the world to this man. But would it mean enough for him to stay?

"And the others?" he finally asked in a hoarse voice after clearing his throat.

"They died in the desert when the surrounding villages refused to share their resources with such a large group." She looked up at the man's weathered face again, its shadows sharp in the moonlight. "What is it?"

He drew in a long, slow breath through his nose and gazed out at the night. When he spoke, his voice was tight.

"We thought it was something like that. But we never knew for sure." His voice broke, and it was a moment before he could compose himself again. Sabra wanted to lean over and embrace him, to share in his pain, but she sensed he needed to carry this burden alone.

Finally, he drew in another shaky breath. "Prior to the poisoning, several of our people had begun feeling poorly. But they were perfectly healthy when the Physics examined them. So after much exploration, we did a secret investigation and learned that the Justines were experimenting with small bits of Sortheleige."

"Which is illegal."

"Yes, by an international standard, one agreed to by the kingdoms in this region. But international agreements technically aren't binding in our own law." He snorted. "The Justines must have seen to that when they wrote the vows for everyone else to sign, and the others were too incompetent to realize it until it was too late." He shook his head. "Once the discovery of Sorthileige was confirmed, our people made the mistake of taking it privately to the king." He glanced at Sabra. "Your father was young, then, and had only taken the throne five or six years prior." He paused. "To keep it from sounding as though I'm speaking evil of the dead, he wasn't a bad king. But he did choose sides."

Sabra's chest felt like it was being twisted in on itself. Would there be no end to these discoveries?

"Did most Sentinels know this?" she forced herself to ask. George's grandparents hadn't seemed to know.

"No. We feared it would cause outright panic, so we chose to discuss the charge privately with the king first. We believed he would take it to the basniins, which was custom. Instead, he made the mistake of sharing the charges with the Justines privately. And they made their revenge swift and painful." He glanced up at the others who were watching him from afar.

"Wait." Sabra sat up. "What about all their talk of curses and superstition and—"

He snorted. "Utter blather."

"How so?"

"They've never been superstitious a day in their lives. And there's no curse written into our vows. They can twist all the words they wish. It doesn't change what's actually there on paper." He scowled. "They were caught in the mud and didn't want everyone else to see the dirt on their faces."

Sabra frowned. That made sense. Much more than their strange claim of curses. Unfortunately, they'd done a wonderful job of convincing everyone else they were right.

"After their revenge had devastated our people," he continued, "the Justines somehow convinced your father to forbid anyone from speaking of the event, or even our people, ever again. They convinced him that censorship would be the best method of healing. We realized too late that the poison was in the water, but by then, we'd had our livelihoods and homes stripped from us and were told that we would need to live unaffiliated with our clan if we were going to continue in Segzein."

"That was their revenge, wasn't it?" Sabra whispered.

He nodded. "Brilliant, really, when you think about it. In small amounts, Sortheleige is impossible to trace in water unless you have a gift of your own, as the Sentinels do. So no one was able to see or sense it." He gave her a sad smile. "Save us. And there was nothing we could do to prove it to the rest of the kingdom except—"

"Except sicken and die."

"Except sicken and die." He nodded slowly.

"But that exposure didn't hurt anyone else?"

He huffed. "The Justines are skilled. Sortheleige is all around us in this world. In the ocean. The soil. All over the place. But most of it is so mixed with other things that our bodies filter it out. The Justines knew that pouring a nearly negligible amount in the water would leave the rest of the people safe, but it would injure us."

"So...why did the Sentinels who traveled die, and you didn't?"

"For all we can figure, they stopped poisoning the water supply as soon as most of the clan was gone. So the water they took in their waterskins and barrels went with them." He held up his hands. "My hands never fully recovered their skill. And most of us have been affected in some way." He tilted his head and gave her a strange look.

"You do know why the Justines chose your Inquest as the time to remove you, don't you?"

Sabra blinked at him. "I haven't the slightest idea. But wait. How do you know that?"

He chuckled. "We've been sick, Your Highness. Not deaf. And even the tight-lipped Justines can't keep all their talk at bay. Especially when poor, worthless merchants are sitting at their feet in the corners of squares."

"Oh." It made sense. The Blue Bands were known by their blue banded tattoos, but if they wore sleeves, no one would have known them from anyone else, especially if their pale eyes were cast down in the presence of someone more important.

He went on. "Apparently, your questions were more than they were comfortable with." He shrugged and twined his fingers. "They didn't want a queen who would somehow unearth the past they'd tried so hard to bury."

"So they decided to bury me too."

He gave her a grim smile. "You're a little harder to bury than we were." Then he sighed and briefly closed his eyes. "Those were dark days at first. So dark. But we've recovered enough over the last two decades that we're finally strong enough to leave. And we're not going to repeat the mistake of waiting to see how it turns out."

"So you think there is no hope?" Sabra slumped back against the bench. "That we're only digging ourselves deeper by challenging him?"

The old man took her hands in his. Their warmth was a painful reminder of what it had felt like when her father took her hands.

"Your father was frightened." He gave her a sad smile. "So he let them have their way. If he had fought with the tenacity of his daughter, things probably would have been very different."

"Why didn't you tell people before he brought the edict down? Spread the word? Surely the citizens would have believed you."

"Your father could be extremely effective where he wanted to be. And, unfortunately, once the Justines had him where they wanted, he excelled at silencing people."

"But—"

"Come with us," he said, leaning forward, his voice suddenly urgent and his eyes bright. "You have done more than enough for these people. You and George. Come with us and find happiness and peace!"

For one brief moment, Sabra indulged herself with her imagination. "Where will you go?"

"We're going to Destin. King Everard is said to be a good man. Perhaps he'll allow us some land there to settle and continue healing." He took a deep breath. "We've done all we can for these people. And they've turned their backs on us and embraced death by doing so. It's time to let go."

Something rebellious in Sabra itched to say yes. And this time, it was even stronger than when Demir had made the suggestion. Because this time, it was right in front of her. These people were leaving. It would be unfathomably easy to follow. How freeing it would be to take George and run. In just an hour or so, they could be rid of this mess forever. The farther they got from Segzein, the stronger they would be. She could marry George and never think about managing Ozge or Baran or Mahzar ever again. Her people could hate her all they wanted, and she would be too far away to even care. Demir would be king, and all would be right.

And yet, George had made the promise, as had she. And she had told Demir only an hour earlier that her people weren't to blame. Abandoning them would only further the pain.

Sabra's crown had never been so heavy. It pressed down on her temples with the weight of a tombstone. The weight of a promise to her father and her people.

"I can't," she whispered, unable to look up from her hands. "I made a promise."

The man's face softened. "One that you did your best to keep. But truly, how much more can you do?"

Sabra swallowed. Part of her wanted desperately to agree that there was nothing left. But Ozge's grumblings were too recent to forget. And while this man seemed certain George wouldn't—that he *couldn't* win, just giving up the Challenge would mean an immediate and lasting age of the dragon. Mahzar would put Demir on the throne and abuse him there until he found someone better. The guards stationed at the city entrances and in the streets would be permanent. Gone would be the free, creative people Sabra knew and loved. Segzein would enter a dark, gray existence governed by a king who ruled with the iron thumb of what he believed he knew better than everyone else.

Or she and George could stay and challenge him one more time. They could run and hide, or they could go down in flames.

"What did you come here for?" called a woman's voice.

Sabra looked up to see dozens of Sentinels standing around her. They'd come so silently she hadn't even noticed. The woman who had asked her the question stood about four feet behind the man she'd been speaking with.

"I..." Sabra paused. What had she come for? It wasn't to have her world turned upside-down, even though that's what had happened. "I was hoping you might have more of that healing elixir. For George, I mean," she said, knowing now that they would say no to the other question she had longed to ask.

The woman barked out a harsh laugh. "You think after twenty years of near death, we would still have a great store?"

But as she spoke, the man Sabra had been speaking with got up. He went back across the way to the cart he'd been standing by when Sabra found him. The woman was still shaking her head when he returned. This time, he was holding a familiar blue glass bottle. Sabra gasped when he handed it to her, as did the woman behind him.

"Vale! That's your last bottle!" she hissed.

But Vale, as it seemed the man's name was, paid her no heed. "Take it," he said gently. "Use every last drop."

"Thank you," Sabra whispered, her hands closing over the bottle as though in a dream. "But why?"

Vale put a hand on her shoulder and gave her a gentle smile. "Hakan was my older brother. George is my nephew. If I thought I could do anything by staying, I would." He looked toward the north, his smile fading. "But the dragon is asleep now for the first time in a long time. I'm going to lead what's left of our people somewhere new."

"You could..." Sabra paused. What could they do? She was going to say they could help George fight, but then she remembered the stipulations of the Challenge. Only George and the dragon. Of course, they could also stay and support him, but... Well, if they were determined to leave, they had every right. "The Maker bless you and keep you in your travels," she whispered. Then she turned and began to jog back to the palace, hoping that the darkness would keep her tears unseen.

After tonight, the Sentinels would truly be gone.

Segzein, as she knew and loved it, would be forever changed.

And now, she and George were truly all that stood between Mahzar and absolute power. And it was all she could do to pray that the elixir would be enough to prepare him to fight again.

We need a miracle, she prayed silently into the cold night sky. *Because we can't do this alone.*

CHAPTER 37

GET UP

If he were my patient in any other situation, I'd have him in bed another three weeks. None of this next afternoon business." Esemeray pursed her lips as she and Sabra watched George tie his leather sandals. As if to prove her right, he let out a pained hiss when the right side of his ribs touched his leg.

"I'll be fine," George grunted as he stood. He gave a long, hard stretch. "I'm feeling better by the minute. I just need to get moving."

Esemeray shook her head and closed her eyes.

"Did the extra elixir help?" Sabra asked.

Esemeray's eyes shot open. "Goodness, yes. If I hadn't had that, I'm not sure he'd be walking today."

"Is there any left?" Sabra leaned over to see Esemeray's makeshift work table.

"A little. But not enough to fix the kind of damage he suffered last night." She frowned again. "I'm afraid if he gets injured like that again, it's going to be permanent."

"Well, it's a good thing this fight is to the death then, isn't it?" George called with a saucy grin.

Esemeray glared at him before gathering up her tools and herbs.

"You're sure you're well?" Sabra asked quietly.

He gave her a wry smile. "Well enough, considering what I'm about to do."

Sabra looked down and opened her mouth, but George put his fingers to her mouth. They were warm and calloused, and Sabra fought the urge to grab his hand and kiss it.

"No apologizing. We discussed this." He chucked her chin gently. "We're all going to meet our Maker sooner or later, and when we do, you and I will have no regrets."

Sabra had loads of regrets. Regrets that piled higher with each word he spoke. But she just nodded. "Right."

His smile disappeared, and his eyes darkened. "Esemeray told me what the basniins discussed last night."

"They're terrified." She gave a humorless laugh. "As if I'm not."

"Your Majesty?"

Sabra unwillingly tore her gaze from George's face to look at the servant at the door. "Yes?"

The servant bobbed a curtsey. "Apologies, Your Majesty. But the basniins say it's time."

George took Sabra's hand in his. Gently, he pressed his lips to her fingers. "For my kingdom." Then his voice dropped. "And for my queen."

Sabra had cried enough in recent days to have run out of tears three times over. And yet, it was a moment before she could open her eyes and whisper back, "Let's go."

There was none of the ceremony from yesterday. Sabra and George simply walked from the palace down to the empty valley beside the lake. This time, Demir didn't appear. So Sabra and George walked alone, her makeshift guards trailing a distance behind. When they reached the edge of the lake, Mahzar was waiting for them. His arm was wrapped in a bandage, but aside from a few other bumps and bruises, he seemed nearly untouched.

"Princess." He gave a small bow. "I see no one accompanied you today?"

"They are their own people." She lifted her chin. "I have not told them what they can and cannot do."

"Of course not. I only mentioned it because I wonder if perhaps some are no longer able to support this Challenge?" He lifted one eyebrow. "Of course, my offer still stands. I will happily accept your forfeiture."

George snorted, and Mahzar turned to him. This time, suspicion filled his face as he looked George up and down. "You're looking exceptionally well for being nearly dead."

"I am, thank you." George's eyes glinted silver. "And how is that arm? Did you rest it last night?"

All traces of humor fled Mahzar's dark eyes. "I understand then that you're ready?" he nearly growled.

George gave him a feral smile that chilled Sabra with its ferocity. "I'm looking forward to it."

Sabra met George's eyes for a long minute, trying to memorize them, before turning and heading back toward the watchtower.

Demir was there when she arrived, but he didn't look at her or greet her. His beard was wilder and more unkempt than she had ever seen it, and from the bags under his eyes, she wondered if he had slept at all the night before.

Still, she went up to stand beside him.

"He's looking well," she said in a low voice.

Demir stared out at the valley below.

Sabra took a breath and tried again. "And at least Mahzar can't use his left wing today. George says that means he needs to go after his tail next, so he can't use it to—"

"I'm sorry, Sabra." Demir turned to face her, his eyes shining with unshed tears. "I have done everything I can to protect you. I've lied for you. I've been beaten for you. I have searched the law to get you out of this in a way that would assuage your conscience. But this is one time too many."

Sabra blinked. "What are you saying?"

"I'm saying I can't watch you purposely throw your life into the hands of that monster." He whirled around and stalked away.

Slowly, with shaking hands, Sabra turned back toward the valley. The battle would begin any second. But suddenly, her perfect perch was no longer perfect. She was having a hard time seeing through the stinging blur in her eyes.

The horn sounded again, just as it had the day before, so Sabra did her best to focus and pray.

The dragon began to circle again, as it had the day before. Instead of mirroring him, however, George darted forward and slid toward the dragon's belly, shield up and sword out. His shield protected him from the dragon's first explosion of fire, but just as he reached the dragon's underside, the dragon batted him away with its right foreleg.

He hit the ground so hard it made Sabra wince, and even from the distance she stood at, she could tell he was in pain. His shoulders curled in slightly as he pushed himself up, and Sabra prayed the bandages Esemeray had put around his ribs would hold.

Because the dragon couldn't fly well, it was forced to run toward George, giving George just enough time to stand and dodge the dragon's stream of fire. As soon as the stream was done, he would dart forward again.

This happened again and again, until Sabra began to notice a pattern that George must have been following. After the dragon flamed, he was unable to flame again for at least ten seconds. This gave George time to dart forward and attempt another slice at the dragon's scaly hide. Half the time, the dragon's tail kept him away, but on the occasions that George actually reached the dragon, he was able to deliver a short, quick slice, not deep enough to reach the heart or any other vital organs, but severe enough to draw blood. It wasn't long before the dragon's white scales were soon covered in sticky red.

After this back and forth had gone on for some time, whether five minutes or five hours Sabra couldn't actually tell, the dragon stumbled as it turned to keep up with George's quick, lithe movements. George sprang forward to seize the opportunity, but he missed the tail as it whipped around then wrapped itself around him, pinning his arms to his sides and lifting him into the air.

Sabra grasped the stone ledge in front of her until her hands hurt.

He had dropped his shield when the dragon began to lift him into the air, and as the dragon opened his mouth, she could see an orange glow emanating from within.

This was it. George was going to die by fire in front of her eyes. Sabra wanted to close her eyes and run, and yet, she remained fixed to the spot. It was for her that he was doing this. The least she could do was remain with him, in spirit at least, till the very end.

But the dragon, apparently, wasn't holding him tightly enough. George wiggled free just in time to slash at the dragon's face. Screaming in rage, the dragon dropped George. Sabra simultaneously rejoiced and also winced as she wondered how many bones he had broken in that fall.

George didn't seem to notice, though. Because he rolled over and up onto his knees and grabbed his sword and shield from where they had fallen. Then, in uneven steps, he limped behind the dragon, which was still clawing at its snout, and began to hack away at the underside of the dragon's tail.

Blood began to spurt from the wound, and the dragon let out an ear-piercing shriek that ripped through the sky. It unfurled its wings for the first time in the fight and began to move them up and down in uneven, short flaps. Its left wing, which was jagged and torn, was no match for its strong, whole twin, but the dragon somehow managed to lift into the sky anyway.

As he began to fly, however, he used his bleeding tail one last time to smack at George. George stumbled forward, unable to catch himself as he landed on a pile of large, sharp rocks. The dragon flew northwest toward the Justines' spoke, dripping blood from the sky as he went, dipping and rising unevenly in the sky.

George didn't get up.

CHAPTER 38

THE POINT

Sabra was out of the tower and running toward George when the sound of hoofbeats approached. For one terror-stricken moment, she was sure it was one of Mahzar's white guards coming to claim her. But it was only Esemeray, racing out on a stallion with her healing pack at her side. She stopped so Sabra could join her, then they raced on. As soon as they reached George, Sabra knew it was bad.

After leaping off Esemeray's horse, she knelt by his side and put her hands out but paused before touching him, unsure of what might or might not be broken. Blood covered his face, and it was impossible to tell where it all came from. His skin, already mottled from yesterday's battle, was a strange mix of blue and purple all over, colors that would definitely grow brighter.

Then Sabra thought to look at his chest.

"Esemeray," she whispered as the woman knelt at her side. "He's not breathing!"

Esemeray, who seemed so timid and quiet in the throne room, however, was in complete control, already listening to his chest, her hands sure and steady as she gently felt his arms and ribs.

"No, he's breathing. Barely, but he is still alive for now."

Sabra nearly fainted with relief.

"His ribs are broken again," Esemeray murmured. "His shoulder is dislocated. I can't tell about his femur. Here. We need to get him onto the stretcher. I'll know more back in the palace."

Sabra looked up to see that Esemeray's people had arrived once more with a stretcher. Their presence helped her snap out of her frozen state of confusion, and she backed up to give them room.

Minutes later, she was on Esemeray's horse again, speeding back toward the palace. But for all their speed, they might as well have been crawling.

She was the reason he might be dying. If this death was going to be long and painful, she wasn't about to let him die alone.

The wind helped clear Sabra's chaotic thoughts, and once they were back in the healing room, she was clear-minded enough to help tend to him.

When she was young, her father had required that she spend a month with each clan, learning their trades so she wouldn't be ignorant of their needs. During her time with the Physics, Sabra had spent time training under Esemeray herself, and for the first time in a long time, she fully appreciated her father's stubborn insistence on something. It was probably the only reason Esemeray didn't chase her out with all the others.

"Do you have any left?" she asked as Esemeray grabbed her bag of tools, including the elixir.

Esemeray shook her head. "Not enough."

That's what Sabra had feared. But there wasn't time to fear. So instead, Sabra helped. Time slowed down as she did whatever Esemeray asked. Clean cloths. The knife. The needle. Anything to avoid pondering about what came next. Sabra focused everything she had on obeying Esemeray. Obedience meant movement. Movement meant hope.

There had to be hope.

"Your Majesty?"

Sabra turned to see Nazan standing at the door, motioning for her to come out.

"Go ahead," Esemeray said. "I can manage from here on my own."

Sabra cast one more long look at George. He lay unchanged, eyes shut, perfectly still.

"He won't wake up, even if he can," Esemeray said softly. "I've got a sleeping compress over his mouth and nose so he doesn't pull at my stitches."

Sabra nodded reluctantly and exited the room behind Nazan. Yasin, Baran, and Ozge were waiting for her in the hall. True to his word, Demir was nowhere to be seen.

"So." Sabra drew in a shuddering breath. "What do you need?"

Nazan glared at the ground, and Yasin, looking pained, stared at the ceiling. Baran fiddled with his belt. Only Ozge met her eyes.

"Well?" Sabra swallowed and pulled up herself to her full height.

"We gave you the day—" Ozge began, but Nazan cut him off.

"It's time, Sabra." Her voice cracked.

"He's not dead yet," Sabra meant to sound commanding and strong. But instead, it came out as a whisper. "The fight was to the death." She looked around, her voice growing in volume. "He's not dead yet! And we don't even know if Mahzar survived! He was losing a lot of blood!"

"And if he did?" Baran kept his eyes down, glancing up only once. Her glare sent his focus skittering back down. "I know you don't want to hear it. But what kind of punishment is he going to give us for defying him?"

"It's only a matter of time," Nazan gave her a sad smile.

"But the law—"

"This isn't a matter of what's right by the law's standards." Ozge interrupted her. "At some point, we just have to survive."

Sabra opened her mouth but found no words. Instead, she stood there like a simpleton until the door opened behind her again. Esemeray stepped out.

"How is he?" Sabra asked, nearly tripping in her haste to reach Esemeray.

But Esemeray had no timid smile this time. "He's bleeding internally, Your Highness." She let out a long sigh. "It won't be very long now."

"You did your best," Nazan said gently. "Go spend what little time you have left together."

"I removed the sleeping rag," Esemeray nodded. "He should wake up anytime if he's able."

Every instinct told Sabra to fight. To push them to wait, even just a few more hours. After all, Mahzar might not have survived either. In which case, the Justines and the other clans would have to start from the beginning. But somehow, the energy to even utter the words was gone. The tongue of flame that had burned inside and carried her through every fight before this had always been strong. It had pushed her to the next hardship, sure she would find hope there as well.

But that flame was gone. It had been snuffed out by the winds of pain that tore at Sabra's heart and threatened to undo her. She'd tried. So many times, she'd tried.

And there was nowhere left to turn.

Sabra took a few steps then paused, hand on the door. She was too tired to argue. Bitterness, however, was present in full.

"I wanted to be just like you," she said before whirling around to face Nazan. "There was a reason I followed you around as a child. After my parents, you were a giant, strong and skilled. You used knowledge like a sword and wisdom like a shield." She held Nazan's red-faced gaze until the older woman looked at the floor. "But I suppose the Sentinels aren't the only ones who have fallen."

Nazan remained silent, and Esemeray looked back and forth between them nervously before finally skittering down the hall to talk with one of her waiting aides. Sabra sent Nazan one final glower, as though sending it might make it more felt, then went inside.

The door seemed to bang shut as it closed behind her. She walked slowly toward the center of the room, where George was laid out on the thin bed. There was a stool beside it, the one Esemeray had sat upon as she worked. Several candles flickered in every corner. Esemeray was adamant that she have good light whenever she was working. Now the candles cast shadows across George's face, making the angles of his cheeks, nose, and chin even more prominent, until he looked more like a painting than a man. The shadows danced, but even their dance seemed subdued now, as though they were just going through the motions.

Esemeray had removed George's armor and his tunic, but hardly any of his skin showed, so wrapped were his ribs in long, brown strips of cloth. His arms were bandaged in multiple places, as were his legs. His face was cleaner now, but Sabra could still see traces of fresh blood at the corners of his nose and mouth. She could only guess that this was how Esemeray knew about the internal bleeding.

Something inside of Sabra cracked, and she fell into the stool and put her arms and head on the table beside him. More than anything, she wanted to pull him close, but she was afraid she would injure him even more.

"It seems silly, doesn't it?" she whispered, putting her chin on her arms, where she could stare at the side of his face. "We worked so hard. I maneuvered so much, and you trained so hard..." She swallowed the lump in her throat. "And we still lost."

The silence was deafening. Not a movement from him, not even the flutter of an eyelid.

"I mean, I could have sung. Any time, I could have opened my mouth and sung the song. It would have taken so little time. And I keep wondering if I should have done that from the moment I heard your grandmother sing." She shook her head, as though he might see. "But then there would have been no way to convince the others to let us issue the Challenge. Not without my hand in it, anyway. Demir never would have assented. I mean, you could have taken the dragon on without a Challenge, I suppose, but that would have allowed the Justine guards to fight as well..." She let the thought trail off as an image of bloody carnage in the streets filled her mind. Mahzar had no desire to kill citizens needlessly, but taking control, in his mind, was necessary. The Challenge had allowed them to take him on without his hordes of guards at his flanks.

Not that it mattered now.

"What I don't understand is this." She sniffed. "My father always said the Maker had given me this path for a reason. He was convinced of it. He said he knew I was destined for great things from the first moment he laid eyes on me." She frowned. "I was on the path to be queen. And you were born prince of your people. All those years we spent training and studying. We took vows. And we *kept* them." Her voice broke as she laid her forehead on her arms and closed her eyes. "But for *what*?" Raising her head, she looked up at the ceiling, as though she might look into the Land of Bliss itself.

"Why?" she cried. "What was the point?"

With every step forward, she had felt as though they were poised on the cusp of history. They had nearly broken the forces of evil. Just as the Maker had put them there to do. The journey had been painful, but there was a reward in sight. Peace. Hope. A future.

And now, they were left, lying in the ashes.

"Why did you even bother?" she whispered to the Maker as she let the tears fall.

CHAPTER 39

ONE MORE DAY

Sabra couldn't remember falling asleep. One minute, she was watching George's chest, trying each time to discern its nearly immeasurable rise and fall. The next, Nazan was shaking her shoulder gently.

"I'm sorry," she said, not meeting Sabra's eyes. "It's time."

Sabra gave George one last glance. Regret coiled in her stomach, making her want to gag as she thought about just how close she'd been to kissing him in the tree. If only she'd had a smidge of rebellion in her body back then and pressed her lips against George's. She had never been kissed, and now she never would be. Because she would die before she let Mahzar's lips touch her own.

Nazan led her down several hallways and up a flight of stairs until they somehow ended up back in Sabra's chamber. Sabra was vaguely aware that Nazan was speaking to her, but she heard none of it.

Instead, she let herself indulge in all the what-ifs she'd been keeping at bay, terrified they might break her heart. Now, she might as well have them. Because they were the closest to real love she would ever get.

What would it have felt like to kiss him? A first kiss? A wedding kiss? The first kiss of forever. He could have touched her, not caring who knew or saw. At some point, she would have felt the flutter of his baby in her belly. She would have stood beside him, watching their children grow as lines of age and laughter formed on their own faces. Her hair would slowly gray, as would his, and they would play with their grandchildren together.

Of course, she couldn't necessarily imagine where this would have taken place. But that wouldn't have really mattered. Only that it would have taken place.

"Sabra?"

Sabra blinked a few times to see Nazan standing before her.

"Did you hear me?" she asked.

Sabra shook her head.

Nazan sighed and smiled sadly. "I said that you're beautiful."

Sabra glanced in the mirror. The delicate silk lace covered her long, dark hair. Her mother had worked on this dress with the local dressmaker for months so it would be ready when Sabra chose her husband. Now her husband was choosing her, and once they were joined, there would be no one to tell him what he could or couldn't do otherwise. The white purity of the silk mocked her, seeming to say in its pretty, gentle shine that in this dress, she would lose all hope of ever being treasured with a pure tenderness of true husband's genuine affection.

Compliments on this dress were the last thing Sabra wanted.

Instead, she cleared her throat. "My mother should be here. Not you."

Nazan flinched and looked down. As she should have. "Mahzar says you may see her once the ceremony has been completed."

The fire inside, the one that had been extinguished the night before, nearly sparked back to life. "My mother can't even be at my own wedding?"

Nazan raised an eyebrow. "Do you really want her there?"

No, Sabra realized. Not to see this.

All too soon, Sabra's hair, carefully pulled up on her head, was finished. She was decked out in the traditional charms and jewelry of the Segzeinian wedding ceremony. Her skin had been scrubbed, moisturized, and painted to perfection. Even her shoes were soft and new. Nazan pronounced her ready and led her back out into the hall.

Where Demir was waiting.

Sabra wanted to throw herself at him and wrap her arms around his waist, begging him to keep her safe the way he had when she was little and she'd seen a rabid dog. Instead, she kept her posture straight and merely stood beside him to look out the window as well.

"I thought you said you were done with me."

"I couldn't leave you to this alone," he whispered before meeting her eyes. "You know that."

She glared at him for a long moment, then couldn't help the small smile that threatened to curve her lips. "You were always lots of bark with less bite."

"Consider it an apology gift."

"For what?" she asked. "You did everything you could do—"

"For ever taking you with me to Kappadona in the first place."

Sabra studied him for a moment before taking a deep breath and turning away. The pain in her chest squeezed too tightly for her to breathe, much less speak. Not that she could respond to that anyway.

Two guards in white appeared from the shadows. Sabra swallowed when she recognized Shakirat.

He bowed his head and held out a hand toward the end of the hall. "Princess."

She regarded him for a long moment. One more soul she had trusted implicitly. That she had loved.

"I suppose you're here to escort me to my captor."

Shakirat flinched just as Nazan had. "Your intended," he whispered, keeping his eyes on the floor.

"We've known each other too long to tell such tales." She stared at him until he unwillingly met her eye. "Let's call it as it is, shall we?"

He closed his eyes and scrunched them tight. More emotion than she'd ever seen on his stoic face. "Princess, please—"

Sabra marched past him, unwilling to let him see the tears that were forming once again in her eyes. Was this penance for pushing away tears so often in recent weeks? Having them all spill at once?

The walk to the throne room seemed eternal. Images of her father, her mother, and George revolved in her mind with each step. And above all, the question of why.

Why had the Maker built everything up just to burn it all down?

"Princess."

She looked up to see Mahzar beside a holy man at the front of the throne room. Somehow, she'd walked to join them without even realizing it. The holy man kept glancing at the nearest doors, but Mahzar looked completely at ease.

Well, as at ease as one could look with an injured arm and a bandage wrapped around his rear end, its cloth so thick it made his rear twice its usual size.

If Sabra had been any less heartbroken, she would have found this quite funny.

Actually, he looked like he was in a great deal of pain. Good. Hopefully, it would haunt him until he died.

And yet, the pain didn't keep him from smiling as she joined him at the front of the room. Citizens filled all the extra spaces against the walls and in the balcony above, but from what Sabra could see, Mahzar was the only one who looked pleased.

He reached out and brushed his right hand along her jawbone. The light in his eyes was alarmingly warm and familiar, as though this were a day for contentedness and pleasure. Sabra wanted to make sure it wasn't, but her voice seemed stuck in her throat, and all she could do was turn her head away.

"I know this isn't what you hoped for," he said softly, "but in time—"

Sabra's voice returned miraculously at these words. "You should know right now that I loathe you. I despise everything you've ever done, and I hope for the sake of the people you rule and who surround you that the Maker brings you to an early grave."

His eyebrows went all the way up. Oddly enough, he looked truly confused. "Really?"

"I'm not finished. You said once that you would allow me to choose the depth of our affections if I wedded you. Well, I can assure you now that those affections will be non-existent."

Mahzar took her hands and looked down at them for a long moment. "I know you can't see it now, but I *will* be a good husband." He looked up into her eyes and gave her a small smile. "Believe it or not, I have never respected another soul as much as I do you. I may not agree with your interpretation of the law, but that doesn't mean I have come to regard you meanly in any way." He pulled her forward and pressed his forehead against hers.

George had done this very thing. And yet Sabra now found herself wishing she could scratch Mahzar's face off.

"You are a rare soul," he breathed. "And I intend to treat you as a queen as much in my home as you were ever treated here."

In his home. Sabra nearly passed out. Before this moment, she had never allowed herself to even consider the dragon's home as her own. But in just a few moments, it would be hers until the day one of them died.

Maker, she prayed, *if this is the way it's going to be, please don't leave me here for long.*

"Dragon."

Sabra's head shot up and she whirled around the best she was able to, as her hands were still in Mahzar's.

And there, in full battle armor, was George.

His eyes were red and glassy, and his left shoulder was slightly lower than his right. Black, blue, and red patches covered his visible skin. But he was standing.

He was alive.

Sabra had to restrain herself from running and throwing her arms around him. First, because she was terrified that if she touched him, he might go up in smoke. Perhaps her overtaxed mind had finally failed her. Maybe she'd lost her sense of reality and was now truly mad.

Madness was fine with her if it meant living in a world where George was alive.

Second, because shame kept her feet soldered to the ground. He might be alive, but she didn't deserve him.

Breathing was suddenly difficult, and Sabra hoped that even if only for a moment, he would look at her. She needed to see the forgiveness in his eyes, that he didn't completely hate her after all the pain he'd survived for her sake. But George kept his glower on Mahzar.

Mahzar gaped, and Sabra took advantage of his distraction to free her hands and take a half-step back.

"This is…unexpected," Mahzar said, his words clipped and stilted.

Guards garbed in white stepped forward from the shadows while a roar of whispers erupted from the walls and balcony.

Mahzar took two steps forward. Sabra expected him to grimace or gnash his teeth. But to her shock, he looked fascinated.

"Incredible," he whispered, walking a slow circle around George. "But how?"

George turned slightly with him, not allowing him out of sight. "I suppose the Maker decided to leave me down here one more day."

In spite of her shame and worry, Sabra wondered the same thing. She'd seen the extent of his injuries only hours before. How had such a miracle occurred? By Esemeray's judgment, he shouldn't have been able to stand after his fight yesterday, even without the mortal internal injuries.

Something extraordinary must have happened.

"So," Mahzar said, tilting his head to study George again. "You've survived. And not only that, but you're here again." He straightened and gave George a sad smile. "If only your people had possessed your courage twenty years ago."

George's jaw tightened. "If only your people had possessed a heart."

"A charge unproven." He stopped and took a deep breath. "What is it you want, Sentinel?"

"Our agreement was to the death." George held his arms out.

"And it looks as though neither one of us is dead, and you're trying to steal a bride."

The good humor evaporated from Mahzar's eyes. "Be frank, Sentinel."

"Fulfill your word. Fight me to the death." For the first time, he met Sabra's gaze. "Then you can have your bride." He looked back at Mahzar. "But only when I stop breathing."

Mahzar looked up at the people who were watching them. There were at least two hundred gathered in the room, not including the guards. He studied George for a long time, and Sabra could only imagine what was going through his head.

She had no doubt that whoever became king after George's death would be a puppet king. Mahzar could claim that he wanted to follow the letter of the law. But knowing what she knew now, that the Justines had really attacked the Sentinels to protect the secret of their Sortheleige, she knew that Mahzar's intentions were all selfish, rather than out of superstition. If Mahzar caved to George now, it would be out of a desire to make himself look fair before the people. Not because he actually had any intention of keeping his word.

"If I remember right," George added, "you're the one that flew off bleeding yesterday like an injured dog."

Mahzar paled, but to his credit, he nodded slowly. "Very well. We did have a deal." He looked up and smiled to everyone surrounding them. "It seems the Sentinel and I have unfinished business." He looked at George. "Shall we finish this outside?"

Ten minutes later, Sabra had a dreadful sense of déjà vu as George and the dragon faced off for the last time. Unlike the former battles, the entire kingdom seemed to have come out for this one. Every guard tower was full to bursting, and many watched from the ground bordering the valley and its lake. Once again, Demir stood beside Sabra, his hand on hers.

"This time," the dragon called out in its horrible, grating voice, "there will be no assistance. If we fall faint, we fall faint. Leave us there until one of us is finished." Even from a distance, Sabra could see his eyes burn a bright orange.

"This is torture," Demir groaned.

"If you think this is torture," Sabra gave him a wry grin, "you should try having to watch it in a dress."

Demir shook his head. "You're a better person than I, Sabra."

Sabra didn't answer. All she could do was pray. And pull her shawl tighter. It was unseasonably cool today, thanks to the wind.

The horn blasted, and for a third time, George and the dragon faced off. Watching George was painful. He walked with a slight limp, and his left arm didn't raise as well as his right. So when the dragon let out its first stream of fire and George stumbled, Sabra closed her eyes, sure George was done.

"Sabra, look!"

Demir was staring, open-mouthed. For when the flame dissipated George was already almost beneath the dragon, delivering a slice to its foreleg. Instead of dodging the flame, he'd rolled forward on his good shoulder *toward* the dragon.

He wasn't close enough to deliver a killing blow to the heart, but he did get close enough to make the dragon roar in pain. The sound was ear-splitting and made Sabra throw her hands over her ears.

By the time he flamed at George, George had retreated to safety behind a cluster of nearby rocks at the base of the nearest hill. The dragon stretched his wings, but Sabra could tell immediately that he regretted it. His bad wing hung limp at his side as he tried to raise himself into the air with his other. It didn't work, though, so he was forced to follow George on foot, flaming the whole way.

George must have slipped through the rocks to the other side, because by the time the dragon reached the place he had been, George darted out from a different cluster of boulders and slashed at the dragon's side before darting back in.

They played this game for what felt like hours. George's movements began to slow slightly, but every time Sabra was sure the dragon would catch him, George would somehow squeeze back behind the rocks. He was taking advantage of the fact that the dragon couldn't fly, and that its tail was unable to lash out.

"Coward!" the dragon roared.

No, Sabra thought smugly. *Just smart.*

Rocks began to roll down the hill toward the dragon. The dragon easily maneuvered away from them, even with his injured wing. But just as he settled out of the way of the rockslide, George ran out from the other side of the hill and raised his sword at the dragon's side.

This time, however, the dragon seemed to be expecting it. Rather than stumbling around, as he had before, the dragon swiveled sharply and swiped at him with its good foreleg.

George had raised his sword again, but not his shield. Not enough, at least. This time, the dragon caught him off guard. With his good foreleg, he swiped at George a second time and caught his claw on the shield. Sabra watched in horror as the claw pierced it all the way through. Then the dragon yanked its claw out, leaving a gaping hole that would fail George the first time it was flamed.

And the dragon knew this. It smiled as it crawled toward him then, its serpentine neck stretched toward him, already beginning to inhale deeply as it crawled closer.

"It tricked him," Demir whispered. "It drew him out."

CHAPTER 40

SING

Sabra frowned back down at the scene. Mahzar couldn't have done that. George had been the one outsmarting the dragon. But she could see now that Demir was right. Because the dragon was playing with him now. It had moved him just far enough from the hill to prevent him from running back to the boulders at its foot, forcing him backward until he was at the edge of the lake. It could flame and kill him anytime it wanted to.

Just as the dragon began to draw a deep breath in, George sheathed his sword and grasped his broken shield in his hands. With one powerful thrust, he threw the shield at the dragon's exposed neck. The dragon stumbled a few feet back, choking as George ran to retrieve his shield. Three more times, he hit the dragon in the neck as it struggled to breathe.

He might just win.

And I could make sure that he does.

Time seemed to stand still. It was as though a wave of spring air had washed over her. All the angst and shame and confusion melted away, and understanding was left in its place.

She had asked the Maker why He had let it come to this. And now the Maker had answered.

"Demir." Sabra turned to her cousin. "If you were to become king without the dragon, would you restore the Sentinels?"

Demir stared at her. "What?"

"If I made you king here and now, would you restore the Sentinels? Would you treat them as equals and seek to redeem their standing in Segzein?"

"Sabra, I—"

"King Everard can confirm their claims of poisoning. Ask him to come, and I'm sure he'll help." She grabbed his hand. "Now swear to me!" she cried. "Swear you'll do it!"

He still stared at her, shaking his head slightly. "But you promised your father—"

"I know." This time, she allowed herself a smile. "I said I would lead them as queen." She removed her crown and fingered it carefully. "And I have. But I think I've done all I can in that capacity. I've fulfilled that oath."

It was true. Sabra had become the queen her father had envisioned. She'd fought for her people. Journeyed for them. She'd led them, even though they hadn't wanted her to. She'd played the political games she so despised and given up the man she loved for them.

"I've asked the Maker a thousand times why He brought us to this." She smiled up at her cousin, feeling so much peace it was nearly absurd. "And then I realized that if it hadn't been for all of that, we couldn't be here now. I couldn't have fulfilled my duty and found my purpose here as well."

Demir's eyes narrowed. "Sabra, your purpose is to lead your people."

"Yes." She nodded and smiled. "But not as queen." She placed the crown in his hands and looked out at George, who was facing off against the dragon again. "Now I will lead them down another path."

Demir gripped her shoulders, his fingers digging into her skin as he bent down to see her face-to-face. "But you don't need to do this! He might actually win this time!"

Apparently, Demir knew how the Sentinel's Song worked as well.

Perhaps it was better this way. At least he wouldn't be surprised when she walked out to the fight in a moment.

"And my duty is to make sure he does."

Sabra pulled her cousin into a strong embrace. She could feel his arms shake as he wrapped them around her, his body racking with silent sobs.

"I swear," he whispered in her ear.

That was all Sabra needed to hear. She let go, and with a final smile, turned and climbed down the tower steps. Then she crossed into the battlefield.

In her free time at George's grandparents' house, when George wasn't practicing, Sabra had learned the Sentinel's Song. Not that she'd ever expected to use it. But for some reason, she had felt as though she would lose something if she didn't learn it as well. Now, she drew in one deep breath. Then another. And after her third, lifted her voice up to sing.

Sabra had been told that she had a very pretty voice. Nothing like the professional singers in the traveling shows that would come through Segzein from time to time. But respectable. When she uttered the first notes, however, a powerful sensation snaked its way through her. It was so strong she nearly stumbled. It twined with her voice and amplified it louder than should have been possible, echoing through the valley.

> Grab your lance and nock your arrows.
> Hold your sword up high.

Both George and the dragon froze. Sabra took another breath and went on.

> For to war we have been called,
> And now we're going nigh.

The dragon's scaly face was a mixture of horror and rage. But George...

George looked lost in wonder.

> For to our death it might take us,
> But we won't falter at night.

Something bright and blue glowed briefly on George's sword before disappearing. Sabra's heart briefly lost its rhythm, but somehow, she managed to sing on.

> We march on and hold the line
> So evil falls tonight.

It wasn't working. Why wasn't it working? She was singing, just as the brides did...

Then she remembered Maria and Alner.

"You have to fight, George!" she screamed, still only halfway to the lake.

She was close enough now to see the understanding dawn on George's face. As Sabra began to sing again, George turned and raised his sword.

Blue flame nearly engulfed him. It wrapped itself around his sword and down his thighs and across his fingertips. And this time, when the sword made contact with the dragon's shoulder, the dragon was knocked flat on its side, a black scorch mark marring its white, pearly hide.

The dragon flamed again, and Sabra's heart dropped for a long moment as George brought the broken shield up to cover his face. The crystal-coated inside of the shield and the edges of the sword lit up to match the brilliant blue that now covered George like a pillar of flame. And instead of letting the fire in through the hole, the crystal seemed to extend over it, protecting George once again from the flame.

George delivered strike after strike against the dragon, driving it back toward the water. Soon, they were in the lake, its pink edges getting higher and higher around their legs. Sabra wondered what George planning, but she was too busy singing to really concentrate.

Then the dragon raised its head and let out a roar.

The dragon had roared many times before, but this one was different. Sabra couldn't say why, but she knew as soon as white garbed guards began to pour into the valley.

The roar was an order.

Sabra did her best to keep singing as the guards came closer and closer, but fear made her mouth dry and her throat suddenly thick.

How would George fight them? He was beating the dragon, but there was no way to defend himself or her from the dozens of men running toward them with weapons drawn. Barely breathing her song, Sabra turned and sprinted toward George.

Unfortunately, silken wedding slippers were not good for running. And before Sabra had run ten feet, she slide and brushed against a particularly large rock that cut a gash in the side of her leg. She hit the ground so hard that the air was knocked from her chest. When she tried to get up, the pain in her leg throbbed. Even worse, she couldn't find her voice.

"Sabra!" George shouted. He was running toward her now, the dragon in hot pursuit. But the dragon forced him to stop and hold up his shield when it sent another stream of flame after him.

Sabra licked her lips. She had to sing. He couldn't fight them off if she didn't sing, and then neither of them would survive. But as the dragon and the guards charged forward, her chest still seemed to vibrate from slamming into the ground. Her breath was stuck, and she couldn't find the power to get it out.

But just as she began to despair, a familiar melody floated in on the breeze. Sabra looked up to see a group of women standing on the east side of the valley. They were singing, and across their chests were silken blue sashes.

And racing toward Sabra at an alarming speed were the warriors they sang to. Their sashes were worn to threads, and they moved more like Alner than George. But the songs pressed them forward, and faster than should have been humanly possible, they reached Sabra and ran beyond, meeting the white guards head-on.

The clash was audible as the Sentinels met the guards at full speed. All the while, the women sang from their side of the valley. And once again finding her breath, Sabra raised her voice to join theirs.

But when she looked around, she couldn't see George. He wasn't near her, nor was he near the dragon. Then she realized that the dragon was smiling. And he was pressing his large right hind leg down into the water.

Then he looked up from the pink water straight at Sabra.

"You cheated," she spat out, hoping her voice wasn't as warbly as it felt. "You called in your guards."

"You sang for him," the dragon snapped back.

"The rules never said I couldn't."

"I tried to be kind to you." The dragon scowled. "I promised you I would treat you well. I had every luxury prepared in my home to make you happy."

"You thought dethroning me, killing my father, burning my city, and dabbling in dark magic would make me happy?"

"You obviously don't see my gift for what it is." The dragon sneered. "And you obviously never will. I was gifting your beloved city order! You would have torn it apart!"

"And you're finally understanding." Sabra balled her fists, walking closer to the dragon despite the screams coming from somewhere inside her brain to run away as fast as she could. "I could never be happy with you."

"Then my patience has come to an end." The dragon stepped back and stood at full height. The water below him remained undisturbed, and Sabra's anger burned hotter.

He opened his mouth, and for the first time, Sabra could see the orange as it began to light the back of his throat.

Well, if she was going down, she would do it fighting. Sabra opened her own mouth and began to sing again. Even if George couldn't hear. Even if he was already in Eternal Bliss and could no longer gain, Sabra refused to be taken standing still.

> *For to war we have been called,*
> *And now we're going nigh.*

The flame began to roil and roll within the dragon's jaws. She could see it growing in power and frenzy as he kept it behind his needled teeth.

> *We march on and hold the line*
> *So evil falls tonight.*

The dragon leaned back, and Sabra whispered one final prayer in her mind. She was at peace with leaving the earth that George had already left. She only hoped it wouldn't hurt too much along the way.

But before she could finish her prayer, a man engulfed in blue flame shot out of the water. His outstretched sword bit the dragon's underbelly, sinking in up to its hilt.

The fire in the dragon's mouth fizzled out as George yanked his sword out and struck again. And again and again. Until the dragon's flame had been extinguished by the water he now lay in, pink steam hissing as it rose into the air around them, the serpentine body finally still.

Sabra ran to George's side, and he hugged her so tightly she could feel both of them trembling.

"Is he really dead?" she asked, staring at the still scaled form floating in the water before them.

George closed his eyes and pressed a kiss to her temple. "He is." Then he pulled back, his eyes widening. "But you...you sang!"

Sabra smiled and wiped a smudge from his cheek. "I did."

"But that means—"

"I kept my oath to my father. I was queen for three days. I led my people where I believed they needed to go, even if it wasn't where they wanted to go." She stared into his eyes, willing him to understand. "I did my best. Then I took up the next most pressing need." She put her hands on each side of his face. "Which was keeping you alive."

"You lost the crown, though." He frowned down at her.

She reached up on her toes and brushed her lips against his. Not a kiss. Not quite. He would need to kiss her back to complete it. But the feel of him was enough to send shivers down her spine. She let her lips linger against his as she whispered,

"Maybe. But I gained the man I love."

Whatever walls George had been clinging to seemed to crumble as he wove his fingers through her hair at the back of her head and pulled her to him.

Sabra had always wondered what it would feel like to kiss a man. At times, the thought had terrified her, particularly as she imagined having to kiss a man she didn't love or who didn't love her. But there had also been moments where she had imagined being kissed by *the* man, the one who wanted her as much as she wanted him. These thoughts had been brought to the forefront of her mind more than ever in recent days. And if she was honest, many of these musings had involved George.

But her wild imaginings were nothing compared to this.

His kiss was full of contradictions. Tentative desperation. Careful need. Hesitant hunger.

And she was all too ready to answer. She leaned into his chest, feeling his warmth even through his armor. His fingers tightened against her scalp as he deepened his kiss. And where he went, Sabra followed.

Finally, to her disappointment, he pulled back. They were both breathing heavily, though from the kiss or the battle, Sabra couldn't tell.

"Your cousin is glaring at me as though he wishes the dragon had finished the job," he murmured, keeping his mouth next to hers.

"It's not as though he can complain too much." Sabra gave him an ornery grin and pressed herself closer. "You did marry me. Which is more than he can say for any of the girls he's kissed."

George had lowered his lips to hers again when he froze, looking startled.

Sabra didn't like this and gave him a slightly absurd pout to show. But he didn't seem to notice. Instead, he let go of her and backed up. Burying his hands in his hair, he walked in a circle.

"Sabra...we're married." He ran back to her and grabbed her by the arms. "Sabra, why did you marry me?" He ran a hand through her hair, his eyes sad. "I might have won without you."

Sabra crossed her arms. "You mean the part where you nearly drowned?"

He gave her the hint of a smile. "Only because that's what happened after you helped me. Who knows what would have happened if you'd just waited?" All traces of his smile disappeared again as he ran the back of his fingers down the side of her face.

Sabra swallowed. "Aren't you glad?" She searched his gray eyes, fear rising in her chest. He'd been clear about his desires.

Hadn't he?

She faltered, struggling for words like she never had before. They came out too fast, like a pitcher filled with too much water. "I know you wanted to live out your path to its fullest, but..." Her breath caught in her throat as she got lost in his silver eyes. "I wanted to be a part of that path, too." She drew in a shaking breath. "You're not upset, are—"

He cut her off with a kiss so passionate that she briefly saw stars. Those stars began to disappear, however, when someone cleared his throat.

Reluctantly, George pulled away enough that Sabra found Demir standing across from them, looking more than a little uncomfortable. She tried to smother the smile that was threatening to make his discomfort far worse than it was already.

"The basniins want to talk with us later tonight after things are less chaotic," he said. His eyes darted unwillingly to George. "All of us."

Sabra nodded. "All right. We'll come."

Demir began to turn but then stopped and turned to George. "I know words can't...convey what I owe you." He swallowed. "What our people owe you. In more ways than one. But I hope you know that I'll do everything in my power to help your people."

George dipped his head. "I thank you."

Demir gave a nod of his own then whirled around and walked toward the palace with a sense of urgency.

"I killed the dragon," George whispered in Sabra's ear as they followed at a more leisurely pace. "Isn't he supposed to like me now?"

Sabra quirked an eyebrow. "Yes. But that was before he saw you kissing the face off of his baby cousin."

"Mmm," George growled in her ear. "Point taken. Tonight, though..." His fingers trailed down the side of her lacy gown.

Sabra's stomach nearly flipped inside-out at the rumble of his chest, and she had to keep herself from letting out a very stupid, very childish giggle. She did laugh outright, though, when Demir turned and gave them another glare.

"I think that's our hint to start walking." George pulled her more tightly against him, and Sabra just laughed again.

CHAPTER 41

MY LOVER AND MY FRIEND

Sabra and George trailed Demir back to the palace, George's arm wrapped tightly around Sabra's shoulder. She leaned her head against him and slowly drew in one long, deep cleansing breath. Then another.

They had made it.

"George."

George and Sabra turned to see Vale approaching them, the Blue Bands trailing him. They were dirty, and some were splattered with blood. Sabra was surprised to see how many there really were. She'd been so focused on George during the battle that her recollections of the battle that had ensued around them were fuzzy at best. But now the weight of their actions bore down on her as she remembered how they'd stopped the Justines from killing both her and George.

Vale opened his mouth, but Sabra spoke first.

"Why?" she asked. George gave her a funny look, but she kept her eyes on Vale.

"I suppose I can see how that would be confusing." He sheathed his sword, and Sabra wondered how she'd ever thought him a frail old man. He moved with nearly as much ease as George. His long, dark gray hair was gathered expertly at the nape of his neck the same way Alner had done, rather than hanging limply the way it had when he was selling bandages in the market. He wore armor like George's beneath his blue sash, which was tied so that it held weapons on his back.

"I'm sorry." George shifted and extended his right hand. "Apparently, I'm the only one who—"

The man grabbed his arm and pulled him into an embrace. George allowed the man to hold him tightly, but he looked slightly startled. Vale, however, trembled slightly and squeezed his eyes shut as he held the younger man.

"George," Sabra said softly, "Vale is your uncle."

George pulled back to stare at the man. "As in…" His voice shook.

Vale gently took George's face in his hands the way Sabra's father had once done to her. "I was your father's younger brother. When he left, I was too sick to follow." He glanced at Sabra before returning his gaze to George. "And when you returned, I was foolish enough to think we could use the chance for our escape." He turned and looked at the men and women who were now surrounding them. Each wore a tattered blue sash, and their arms bore the infamous band of blue ink. A few children had appeared at their legs as well.

"We tried to go," a woman said, sidling up to Vale. He put his arm around her and gave her an affectionate smile. "But the old fool didn't feel right leaving his nephew to fight the dragon alone."

"Speak for yourself, woman." Vale grinned. "You were the one who told me to turn around."

"None of us felt right leaving you behind," said a younger woman, stepping forward shyly. Sabra felt a stab of jealousy before realizing that this woman could very well be George's cousin.

George's cousin. George had a family. For some reason, this thrilled her.

"You take well to the elixir," Vale said to George with a smile. "It healed you better the second time than the first!"

Sabra gasped. "You're the reason he healed so fast!"

The woman at Hakan's side nodded. "We pooled all we had left. Then Vale snuck into George's sick room and treated him once that woman left."

Without thinking about what she was doing, Sabra threw her arms around the woman in a tight embrace. "Thank you," she whispered as tears threatened to fall. "Thank you!"

"Sabra!" Demir called out from behind the crowd.

"We'll continue this later," Vale said with a slight bow. For some reason his smile was amused. "Can't keep the newlyweds too long."

Sabra thanked them once again before continuing toward the palace, but George looked as though he were in a trance.

"Think you'll survive all the congratulations and well wishes?" Sabra laughed as they made it into the city. When he looked down at her, though, there was a curious look in his eye, one that seemed to grow more intense by the second.

"There's just...so much," he breathed, running a hand down the side of her face, his eyes still full of wonder.

"Sabra!" Demir called. "Come see your mother!"

In that moment, Sabra forgot that Vale existed. She forgot nearly everything when she saw her mother's tired face round the nearest corner of the palace gate up ahead.

"Mother!" She sprinted over the rubble and debris until she had flung herself into her mother's arms. She breathed her mother's familiar scent in deeply, and if she hadn't felt George's presence a little ways behind her, she might not have ever let go.

Her mother was in a wheeled chair which was being pushed by a Physic, but she held Sabra just as tightly as she ever had. They wept in each other's arms, and it was a long time before they were able to stop. Finally, her mother took a deep, shuddering breath and pulled back to smooth Sabra's messy hair out of her face.

"You're alive," Melisa said, letting out a sob of a laugh. "And you're back."

"I'm sorry I didn't listen to you," Sabra said, kneeling at her mother's side. "But I just couldn't sit back and—"

"I never thought you would." She wiped the tears from Sabra's face. "Your father knew you could be great. And you were."

"Mother?"

"Yes?"

Sabra took a deep breath and glanced back at George. "I got married."

Her mother glanced over her shoulder, too. Her eyes widened. "Is that—"

"The former basniin's son? Yes, but—"

Her mother put her hands on Sabra's shoulders and faced her directly. "Does he turn into a dragon?"

"Well...no."

Her mother grinned. "Then I think we're off to a wonderful start."

Sabra grinned as well. Then she turned back to George. "Do you mind if I talk to my mother alone for a few moments?"

He came forward and knelt before her mother, bowing his head. "Of course." Then he stood and smiled gently down at Sabra. "I think I'll go find my uncle again."

She nodded and watched him go until he disappeared in the crowd.

"You really do love him, don't you?" her mother said softly.

This time, Sabra was able to smile without reserve. "I have for a long time." Her smile faded, though, as she looked at the ring on her mother's hand. "What about you? Are you well?" She swallowed. "Especially considering that Father..." she couldn't bring herself to finish the rest of the sentence. But her mother merely nodded and took Sabra's hand before motioning for her escort to leave them.

"Push me into the gardens," she told Sabra. "It's not so bad there. I think the dragon was afraid burning them would jeopardize the palace's structure."

Sabra took her mother's wheeled chair and did as she was asked. They walked quietly until they'd reached the center of the garden, where crimson flowers lined the path and trellises stretched overhead, vines crawling in and through them.

"Here," her mother said. "We should have a little more privacy this way."

Sabra turned her mother's chair so that she would face the rock Sabra had found to sit upon.

"There are things you need to know," her mother said, folding her hands in her lap. "Things we wanted to tell you, but..." She shook her head. "Your father believed you'd be better off without knowing them, and nothing I said could change his mind. She paused, and her shoulders drooped. "I feel like whether we meant to or not, your father and I betrayed you. But he was afraid that if you found out what had happened, you'd hate him."

Sabra's jaw trembled, and when she spoke, it would only come out in a whisper. "I wouldn't have hated him if he'd told me the truth."

"He hated himself." Sabra's mother gave her a sad smile. "The guilt of what he'd done to the Sentinels, ignoring their calls for help, ate at him until the moment he died. He'd hoped that if he couldn't fix the situation, he could simply take his sins to the grave and have them die with him. You were worth more than a treacherous father, he would rant."

"Why did he ignore the Sentinels' reports?" Sabra asked. "I never imagined he'd ignored them like that before." The old, familiar ache of anger flared up in her chest, but she did her best to keep it hidden. Getting angry at her mother wouldn't do any good.

"It wasn't that he didn't believe them." Her mother stared down at her hands. "In truth, he was frightened."

Sabra frowned. That's what Vale had said.

Her mother went on. "He hadn't been king for long yet. And until then, his reign had been uneventful for the most part. But when the Sentinels came to him and told him what they'd discovered, he made the mistake of confronting the Justines directly, rather than making the issue public."

Sabra nodded. "Go on."

"The Justines didn't like the challenge. They became aggressive. They went to your father and showed him...terrifying things." Her mother shuddered. "Then they told him that if he didn't make up a story about their superstitions, they'd do far worse to the kingdom than he could imagine." Her mother looked at the ground, and her mouth tightened. When she spoke again, her voice was husky. "They said they would kill you."

Sabra froze. "But I wasn't adopted until after the Sentinels left...was I?"

Her mother sighed. "You were. We actually didn't have any children when they made the threat. We had been looking at adoption for a while, but after the threat was made, your father refused to adopt any until the situation with the Sentinels was over." She paused. "After they left, he thought it would be safe. But as you grew older and started asking questions, the Justines were quick to remind him of their threat."

"That's why he wouldn't tell me!" Sabra breathed. "All these years, it was to protect me!"

Her mother squeezed her hands and gave her a sad smile. "I know all of this has put his memory in a light that history will not look kindly upon. But I wanted you to know that there was a reason. He wasn't trying to be an evil man. Just a desperate one." She turned and plucked a flower from a nearby bush and twirled it in her hands, but Sabra wasn't able to stand just yet. She was still considering all the implications of this revelation. The dark cloud that had hung over her beloved father's memory, all those fights and arguments. He'd done it because he loved her. She briefly closed her eyes and drew in a slow breath.

Thank you, she thought to the Maker. *For letting me know.* It didn't fix things. But...at least it made sense. And for the first time in many days, she felt as though the vise the world had clamped on her heart was beginning to loosen.

"I know you need to go to your husband." Her mother took her hand. "And I'm rather sure my Physic will want to fuss over me again soon, so I'd better be quick." Her mother gave her a tight smile. "If your father could see you now, he would be the happiest he's ever been in his life. It was his greatest terror that he would leave you to shoulder the burden he created."

Sabra nodded slowly. Knowing didn't fix the heartache. But at least she felt some sort of resolution in her heart, and with that, the knowledge that this wound would one day heal. Because deep down, she would always love him. Just as she would always love her people.

"Speaking of happy," she took a deep breath, "how do I draw them together? Our people, I mean. The Justines, from what I understand, are a mess of their own. The Sentinels resent the Justines. And everyone else—"

"Nothing will reveal the true nature of the soul like pain and fear," her mother said firmly. "But the Maker gave you a heart of gentleness." Her grip on Sabra's hand tightened. "Don't give way to bitterness. Love them all as you always have and show them what it looks like to love their neighbors." Her smile grew slightly. "And even their enemies."

"I'll do my best," Sabra said softly.

Her mother pulled her into an embrace. "I know," she whispered in Sabra's ear. "And I couldn't be prouder."

"Sabra?"

Sabra turned to see Demir coming up the path, flanked by George.

"Sorry," Demir said to her mother. "The basniins have requested a meeting, so I need both of them."

"Take them and do your best to speed through that meeting." She gave Sabra a saucy grin. "These two have earned their rest."

"We sure have," George grumbled as they followed Demir into the palace. He sounded more aggravated than Sabra had ever heard him.

"Tonight," she promised. "If you can wait until tonight, I'm yours."

He arched one dark eyebrow while running a hand down her back and pressing her closer with his palm. "I'll hold you to that."

The meeting between George, Sabra, Demir, and the other basniins was more than slightly awkward. Sabra knew they'd done what they could to save their people, but she still felt more than a little smug that the very man they'd doubted and abandoned was the one to save them. And from the darting eyes and constantly shifting bodies, they knew it. Even Nazan seemed at a loss for words.

It was decided that while Demir would truly take the crown, Sabra would continue to help him reclaim the kingdom. Demir demanded the basniins assign her some measure of authority so that she could be more effective in her work. And though Ozge balked at first, probably for fear of retribution, George surmised afterward, the basniins eventually agreed. The Justines would need to be dealt with as a people, and the Sentinels would need to have their land purged of its evil. The damage to the city as a whole was unprecedented, and everyone had a different idea as to how repairs should be begun. In a strange way, though, facing the basniins together like this was a good place for George and Demir to find their own place of trust. Sabra watched in amusement as they began sending one another exasperated looks across the table. Demir looked like he wanted to be there about as much as George. Finally, after her husband had sent one too many longing looks at the door, Sabra stood.

"I believe my husband and I have earned a good night's rest," she said with a smile that dared anyone to object. "We will continue these talks tomorrow."

"You know you're no longer—" Ozge began, but George silenced him with a deadly glare.

"No longer *what*?" he growled.

Ozge looked at the window. "Nothing."

Sabra couldn't hide her smile as George indignantly stood and held his arm out, and she took it.

"Authority looks good on you," she whispered as they moved into the hall.

Before he could respond, Demir ran after them. He stopped and looked back and forth between Sabra and George. Then he closed his eyes and sighed.

"I know this isn't my place to meddle. What's done is done." He opened his eyes. "But Sabra, I have to ask." He glanced once more at

George. "Is this what you want? More than the crown? Because if you want the crown, say the word, and we'll set everything right."

Sabra felt George's eyes on her as well, studying her reaction, she knew. He had no reason to fear, though, because Sabra's smile felt like it lit her entire face. "I love him. I always have. And I know you might not believe it, but I am happy."

Demir nodded then looked at George. "As much as it kills me to say this…if anyone deserves her hand, it's you."

George opened his mouth to speak, but Demir continued.

"But if you ever hurt her, I don't care how many dragons you've slain. I will end you myself."

Sabra groaned, but to her surprise, George only nodded. "As it should be."

Finally…finally, they were allowed to leave the rest of the chaos and retire to Sabra's old room. They were allowing her to keep it for the time being, as the Sentinels had no true home. One day, a mansion would be built for them, as all basniins had mansions in their own districts. But for now, Sabra was just glad to be somewhere familiar and warm and not on the ground. Tomorrow, she would be able to spend time with her mother and all her other friends, and they would begin the real work to heal her beloved kingdom. But for now, they were alone.

Once the door was shut, however, Sabra and George seemed as though they'd both grown roots and were stuck where they happened to be standing when the door closed. The room was cleaner than it had been that morning when she'd gotten dressed for the wedding. Probably a gift from Nisa, even amidst the madness.

And George was staring at her as though he'd never seen her before in his life.

"What is it?" she asked breathlessly. Had her room always felt this small? Or this warm?

"I just keep expecting you to come to your senses and realize that you've given up the crown." He shook his head and ran a hand through his hair. "What with you trying to reclaim what should have been yours... Married to me, it's as if you've started all over again." He shrugged. "You could have been queen."

Sabra reached out and took his hand. She lightly ran her fingertips across the red, angry welts that had sprung up all over his palm.

"I won't lie. Not being queen or having that expectation will be a...an adjustment." She gave him a small smile. "But, as you can tell, I'm not terribly torn up about it."

"So why did you do it? You could easily have had the marriage annulled. I'm sure of it."

"Because I want you." She held his palm to her face and kissed it softly, then watched him tremble with pleasure. She leaned her cheek into his hand and smiled. "Don't forget, George, you're a prince in your own right. Not crown prince. But prince of your clan all the same." She laughed. "Besides, it seems you and I are bound and determined to do this all backward anyhow."

"But you've left the Capitans. And you were so determined to claim them as your own."

Sabra sighed and pulled his hand down where she could just hold it. "I did want the Capitans to be my people. Being crown princess then queen...I thought it would make me feel like I belonged. Like I knew where I was meant to be and whom I belonged to. And less like it was mere chance that my parents had somehow accidentally chosen me." It was true. As much as Sabra's fight had been for her people, there had been a part of her that was always fighting for her place in life. The part that had wondered for weeks, *if not a queen, then what?*

"And now?" he asked.

She smiled. "I'm right where I need to be. No matter which clan I belong to." She leaned forward and brushed a gentle kiss across his lips. "I'm yours."

In two seconds, George had swept her up in his arms and was carrying her to the bed. His mouth was on hers before her head hit the pillow, and Sabra allowed herself to get lost in the kiss as he hovered above her, his arms on each side of her shoulders. When he pulled away, they were both breathless. Instead of kissing her again, however, he put his forehead against hers and rested it there. His fingers twined with hers and pressed into the bed.

"I still can't believe we did it," he breathed.

She pulled her hands free and placed them on the sides of his face, memorizing the angles and contours she'd so longed to touch. "The Maker had a plan for us. And no amount of meddling on our parts or anyone else's was going to change that." She kissed his forehead. "I love you. I have since the moment I recognized you in the marketplace." Her smile widened as she thought back to her girlhood moments of gawking at him when he wasn't paying attention. "Maybe even before. And now we're going to help build our people up once again. We're going to find a way to rid the land of its sickness once and for all, and we're going to be happy because we choose to be."

He moved his lips to rest against hers. "And you," he said against them, "will be the kingdom's most beloved queen and princess for generations to come." He put one hand on her cheek. "You'll help me find my way when I feel lost." Then he slid his hand down to rest on her belly. "You'll be the mother of my children." His voice grew gruff. "You are the gift I'll never tire of receiving."

Sabra wondered briefly if it were possible to pass out from sheer pleasure.

For so many years, she'd feared living life with a man she could never love by her side. But now, she had the one person she couldn't imagine life without.

"And you," she whispered, "will be my protector. My lover. And my friend."

There were other words she meant to say, but his kiss silenced her. Not that Sabra minded. She'd forgotten what she wanted to say anyhow.

EPILOGUE

TWO MONTHS LATER...

Sabra snuggled deeper under the covers as the rays of the sun touched her face. Usually, she was up much earlier, as was George. But for the first time in two months, since the dragon had been killed, no one had come running and knocking on their door to ask them about this or consult them about that.

Instead, she was able to snuggle closer to George, basking in the warmth of his bare chest against her back. Even through her nightgown, he felt like a sunbeam against her skin.

As if reading her thoughts, he stroked her cheek with his knuckles, and Sabra closed her eyes, drinking in the peace like a dying woman finding an oasis in a desert.

His hand moved from her face down to her waist, where he wrapped his arm around her and gently squeezed.

"Are they sick?" he mumbled.

"Why?" she laughed.

"We haven't gotten to stay in bed a single morning since we got married," he growled in her ear. "They must all be ill."

She wiggled in closer. "Your grandparents are getting their own home soon. Maybe they're worried that when she finally has time to pay attention, your grandmother will chase them around with her broom for overworking you." Sabra had seen his grandmother do this once to Serkan. It was more entertaining than it should have been.

"Well, don't make any loud noises," he grumbled into her hair. "I don't want them to start now."

Sabra sighed with happiness as he placed a gentle kiss on the back of her shoulder. "You've worked just as hard as your cousin, if not more," he said, moving his lips down her arm and kissing her again. "You deserve a morning without them and all their problems."

"Mmm." She rolled over to look at him. Wrapped in sunlight that splayed across his chest, he was magnificent. "And what would I do with such a morning?"

He leaned down and pressed his lips against hers. Sabra's stomach erupted in fireworks as he slowly deepened the kiss. "I can think of a few things," he murmured.

A knock sounded at the door.

"Basniin George?" someone called out. "I'm so sorry, but we have a situation with a few Justine guards we found hiding near—"

George rolled onto his back and groaned loudly. Sabra was tempted to do the same, but George looked so put out that she had to laugh.

"It's not funny." He glared at her. "At this rate, they'll give us enough privacy to have children in a decade or so."

Sabra leaned over and kissed his forehead once more. "*That* will not be the case."

"And how do you know that?" George asked as the knocking started again.

Sabra went to her wardrobe, pulled a dress out and began to get dressed. "Easy. We'll threaten to stop fixing their problems."

As she spoke, Thing hopped down from one of the shelves on the wall and tried to walk across George's face. George picked up the cat and dropped him unceremoniously off the bed. "I'm pretty sure your cat is in league with the others as well."

Sabra just laughed and put Thing back on his soft bed in the window.

It seemed like such a simple solution, threatening a sabbatical from the demands on every side. One that Sabra had considered at least three times a day every day for the past month. But such, she considered, must be the fate of those who marry on the day their kingdom barely survives an attack from within.

"Get dressed," she said, kissing him once more. "I'll see you soon."

"Not yet, my love." He pulled her back to the bed. She sat beside him, curious.

"What is it?"

He rolled over to where his cloak was slung on the bedpost and pulled something from the hidden pocket on the inside. Sabra leaned forward to see.

"One of the Justines gave me this after the dragon was killed." He held it up in the light, and Sabra gasped.

"Is that a scale?"

It wasn't just a scale. It was white, the same white that had covered Mahzar, slightly colored when you turned it just the right way in the sun. It had been edged in silver and set in a silver band.

George turned the ring over in his hand. "He said he hoped it would be a reminder."

"A reminder of what?" Sabra asked.

"That not all Justines are men of Mahzar's heart." His smile faded. "I think, too, it serves as a reminder that any of us might fall prey to the darkness of arrogance. None are above it. And yet the Maker is powerful enough to bring light even from the dark schemes of men." His smile returned. "And I can think of none better to wear it than the queen who gave her crown to save her people." He took her hands in his and slid it on her finger. "It shines. Just as you do."

Sabra held her hand up to examine the ring in the light. Yes, this would be a lesson she would not soon forget.

She kissed her husband one more time. Or perhaps three or four more times. Then after pulling Thing from George's face, where the cat was once again trying to sleep, Sabra dumped her pet out in the hall where he could wander at will, and she made her way to the room where she knew the basniins and everyone else who needed help would soon be waiting for her.

The halls seemed strangely empty now that most of the citizens were no longer living in the palace. The houses were being rebuilt faster than Sabra had anticipated, as a number of the surrounding city-states had volunteered to send wood in exchange for future trade deals. While that meant Segzein would be bringing in less money than it spent for several years, it was better than having a third of the population homeless for the winter.

Things were looking up for their family as well. As soon as his grandfather was able to travel, George had sent a party to bring his grandparents back to Segzein. He'd even located the spot where their original house had been, and he was set on building their new home there once more. They were living with relatives for the moment, refusing to live off the charity of the palace.

Serkan, spoiled rotten by all Sabra's attention, was no longer fit to be a servant. The moment George's grandmother had returned, Serkan had demanded to be allowed to move in with them again, and when George's grandmother suggested she wanted him as well, Sabra had no qualms with handing him off. He made a terrific little brother, though, and thanks to George's grandmother, he was now cleaner and more obedient than he'd ever been. Of course, that didn't mean he didn't sneak back into the palace whenever he had the incli-nation. Sabra had been surprised more than once to find Serkan in a variety of odd places, the oddest of which was her wardrobe, where he was scarfing down some of Cook's best pastries, which Sabra was sure hadn't been a gift.

Still, he was proving quite proficient at smithing, according to Maria's letters, and Alner swore he'd make an honest man out of the rascal one day.

"Your...Princess..." The servant coughed nervously and bowed, returning Sabra's attention to the present. "Your first meeting will be in here today."

Sabra smiled and stretched her shoulders. She was technically still a princess, though merely one by birth now, rather than the crown princess. She was also princess of her clan. And, of course, she also had the new authority Demir had granted her as well. But no one seemed to know how to address her upon sight. That was all very well, though. Because Sabra wasn't doing this anyone else's way.

She and George were trailblazing their own.

I can't believe you got this much seed!" Yasin gaped at the numbers written on the parchment he was holding, and Sabra couldn't help smiling a little smugly. "It's far too late in the year for this!"

"When they heard about our situation, their ambassador contacted me. He says they grow an abundance of wild strawberries in their region and harvest those as well to save. They also have more fruits and several grains, if we're interested."

Yasin opened his mouth, but no sounds came out. Finally, when he looked up again, his eyes were wet. "I can't tell you how much this means to us." He looked up at Nazan, who had been listening to their conversation as she gazed out the window. She was supposed to be overseeing Sabra's meetings with the basniins as a consultant, as she was the senior basniin, having held her position longer than any of the others on the Assembly. She'd also studied Segzein's recent history enough to have a good understanding of what was and was not enough of this product or that product to see them through. But throughout most of the meetings, she simply stared out the window and listened, volunteering an opinion only when asked directly.

A far cry from the confident, authoritative woman Sabra had known all her life. Now the lines on her face were more pronounced, and she always looked tired, even though the dragon no longer reigned over the skies, and Segzein was free again.

Sabra gave Yasin a dry smile. "Well, considering that I do like to eat, and you provide the vast majority of the food for the kingdom, I can say that there was considerable incentive."

"Don't you think it's enough?" Yasin looked hopefully at Nazan.

Nazan blinked a few times before she seemed to remember what they'd been discussing. "It should suffice."

"We will, of course, need to continue purchasing food for this winter," Yasin said as he gathered into a pile the papers scattered around them. "But I do think we just might make it through. And we should have enough seed to start over again next year."

"Good." Sabra walked with him to the door. "Let me know if you need anything else."

Yasin bobbed a bow once. Twice. Three times. "Of course! Thank you, Your…" He blushed slightly. "Thank you, madame." Then he turned and was gone, already spouting orders to his apprentice. Nazan followed him silently. Sabra's heart twisted slightly as she watched them go. How she missed speaking with Nazan as she once had.

At one time, Nazan had been her hero. But, as with everything else, that had changed. And even though Sabra loved her new life, there were times where she felt it was moving too fast for her to get her bearings. As happy as she was, she often felt as though the waters she was treading were still too murky. Now she wondered if she would ever reconcile with the older woman. She hoped so. But Nazan would have to wish to reconcile too for that to happen. And at the moment, there seemed to be no desire for that.

Sighing, Sabra turned and began to gather her own papers. It was time for the noonday meal.

"Princess!" cried a familiar voice.

Sabra turned to find Mirac at their side. He looked a bit the worse for wear, his library robe more worn and more rumpled than ever and his beard untrimmed. But his eyes sparkled as he stood nearly bouncing in the hall.

"Do you remember, Princess, when you wanted answers?"

Sabra snorted. "I have more answers now than I ever had questions for."

"You and I both know that isn't true. You always have questions."

Sabra leaned forward. "Do you have something to tell me then?"

"How about you follow me down to the Sentinels' spoke, and you shall see."

"I'll come now." Sabra followed him out the door. He just grinned and marched on, seeming terribly pleased with himself.

"You're being more cryptic than usual," Sabra said as they made their way out of the palace.

"Because I don't think you would believe me if I told you."

"Should I call my husband then?"

"Let me guess, you haven't seen him in an entire hour."

Sabra rolled her eyes as Master Mirac chortled to himself.

"Actually," he said, "I believe you'll see him sooner rather than later. This involves him too."

Sabra sped up her steps, but she faltered when they rounded the palace wall and she saw an imposing figure in the distance.

The man, whoever he was, wasn't abnormally tall, but he wasn't short either. His shoulders stretched even wider than George's. He stood straight and alert, though he also seemed to be watching the rebuilding of a structure with great interest. And there was something incredibly familiar about him, though she couldn't say why.

"Who is that?" she whispered to Mirac as he tugged her toward the man.

"Why, Princess," he raised his thick eyebrows, "don't you recognize the heir of your husband's ancestors?"

Sabra stopped short. "It can't be."

As she uttered the words, the man turned and met her gaze. They were twenty paces apart now, but the moment her eyes locked onto his, she knew that this man could be no other than the great King Everard Fortier.

His short hair was fairer than George's, and his skin lighter as well. He looked to be thirty-five years, but could easily have been older or younger, depending on how the shadows darkened his face. The jawline was the same, though, and he had the same muscular build, though his muscles were perhaps somehow impossibly even *more* defined than George's. More telling than anything else, though, were the eyes.

King Everard's eyes were that same distinctive gray as George's. Even more than gray, though, as from a distance they seemed to glow.

As if in a trance, Sabra walked toward him, unable to tear her gaze from his. Sure enough, as she grew closer, she began to make out the legendary rings of blue fire that danced in the gray. They pulsed and moved to the rhythm of an unsung song.

"You're here," she whispered when she was six paces away.

His stern mouth turned up at the corner. "I am." His voice was rich and deep, just as velvet might sound if it could speak.

"But how?"

"Your cousin wrote to me after your..." his eyes darted up and glanced over the scene of charred destruction that surrounded them, "dragon incident."

Sabra looked at the Sentinels' spoke, where they now stood. "Do you think you can help them?"

He studied her for a moment. Finally, he nodded slowly. "I can." His eyes darkened. "But it won't be easy. No wonder they sickened. This land isn't fit to look at, much less live on."

Sabra nodded quickly. "I'll do whatever I can to assist. My husband as well." Then she sucked in a lungful of air. "Master Mirac, can you get my—" She whirled around to call Master Mirac, but when she found him, he was already on his way back to her, George at his side.

The fire in the king's eyes leaped when he saw George as well. His arms, which had been crossed over his chest, came down, and he took a step forward. "Incredible," he whispered.

"What is?" Sabra asked, looking back and forth between the king and her husband.

"The Fortress's power. It really does flow in his blood."

"How...how do you know that?"

He lifted an eyebrow slightly. "I can feel it."

Sabra gaped at him. George was still a good ten paces away. And yet, somehow, the king knew. She looked the king up and down again, the hairs on the back of her neck standing slightly. What kind of creature was this man? Stories of him filled the world. He was powerful, of course, filled with inhuman strengths of all sorts, supplied by his legendary Fortress, a gift of the Maker to one of his ancestors. But never in her wildest dreams had Sabra imagined such power to be so...

Potent.

Master Mirac deposited George at Sabra's side, though George seemed too caught up in his awe to really be aware of what the master Sophian was doing. As if in a dream, he bowed before slowly putting his arm around Sabra's waist, looking back up at the king with just as much awe as before.

"I wish we'd known about your people sooner," the king said kindly. "We would have helped before it came to this."

George glanced at Sabra. "To do what, Your Majesty?"

The king gave him a small smile as he drew his sword. "This." And with one hand, he swept Sabra out of the way as he lunged toward George.

Sabra screamed as George fumbled for his own sword, barely drawing it in time to deflect the king's first attack.

Sabra's felt her heart fall into her stomach, where it lay dead and cold, refusing to beat as she held her breath. The king advanced on George again and again. His attacks grew faster and more complicated, and George, the greatest swordsman in the kingdom, barely managed to stay alive.

"Please!" Sabra shouted, running after them. "Please don't hurt him!"

What was happening? Why would the king, known throughout the world for his good judgment and compassion, travel all the way down to Segzein to kill her husband, a distant relation of little consequence, as far as he was concerned? Was it because he was worried about a threat to his own throne? A question of inheritance? Such a trivial matter of obvious legality seemed beneath the great king.

But why else was he attacking George?

A crowd had gathered around them as they fought. People shouted, begging for mercy. Blue Bands came running, drawing their swords and shedding their cloaks as they raced toward the king. Before they could even come within striking distance, though, a ring of blue fire shot up, surrounding George and the king, keeping them inside and everyone else out.

"Sabra!" George shouted. "Sing!"

Of course. Sing. Sabra would have to get better at this. She took a deep breath. What were the words? She searched her memory, but no song sprang to mind.

George was going to die, thanks to her.

Grab your lance and nock your arrows.

One of the women behind her began. Sabra threw her a look of thanks and joined her.

Hold your sword up high.

Like a torch, George's sword blazed blue, and within seconds, he moved from defense to an attack.

If Sabra hadn't seen it herself, she would never have believed it. But as soon as George's power began to glow, she could have sworn the king smiled.

The king fought George for another minute or so. He was no longer on the attack, but his defenses seemed strangely lax for all the effort George was pouring into the fight. Then the crowd gasped as the king's own sword lit up. But it wasn't with the faint wisps of blue smoke or little tongues of flame that danced on George's blade. The whole sword was set ablaze, its blue fire leaping out around it. His eyes glowed brighter, and he was a blur in motion. One. Two. Three moves, and he had George pinned against the ground.

When George and Sabra had fought the dragon, she had been able to sing even after he'd fallen. Not so this time. Her voice cracked and broke as the king stood above George, like a wolf crouching over its prey.

Everyone was still and silent. George lay panting on the ground, his eyes desperate as he looked at Sabra. The horror in his gaze threatened to bring her to her knees. But like the crowd, Sabra felt frozen to her spot.

Then the king nodded once to himself and straightened. Sheathing his sword, he reached down and offered George his hand. George cautiously took it, seeming to decide he had no other choice. When they were both standing, the king turned to Sabra and smiled. Except, this smile wasn't the predatory leer that he'd worn while fighting. This smile was brilliant.

"The Fortier children generally cannot pass their powers to their children unless they're direct heirs." He turned to George. "I am more than a little interested to hear the full story of your people."

"What did you do that for?" Sabra blurted out, unable to fully recover from the shock of the fight.

The king chuckled. "I needed to see what he could do." He nodded to George. Then he looked back at Sabra. "And what you could do as well."

A test. The whole thing had been a test. One that George had obviously passed, judging by the pleasure on the king's face. Sabra wasn't sure whether she wanted to thank the king or slap him.

"The women of our clan must awaken the power," George said, pulling Sabra firmly against his side. His hand shook slightly, but Sabra didn't blame him in the slightest. "Only through the bonds of marriage, however."

"Perhaps." King Everard frowned slightly at Sabra. Then he held his hand. "But...may I?"

Sabra blinked. "I'm sorry?"

He held out his hand further.

Sabra glanced at George, who gave her the slightest of nods. So Sabra took a deep breath and put her hand in the king's outstretched palm. He'd better not pull his sword on her. She would be less understanding than her husband.

The king's eyes widened. After a few seconds, he let go of her hand and stepped back. "Thank you. I know this isn't probably what you were expecting." That hint of a smile returned. "I shall be happy to help your people with your land, just as you asked. After that, though, I have a request of my own."

Sabra and George shared a mystified glance. "Oh?" George asked.

"When your life here is slightly less hectic, I would love for you to join me and my family at our Fortress in the near future."

"You would?" George looked as though he might fall over, though from joy or trepidation, Sabra couldn't tell.

"I would. You are both capable of more than I ever imagined when I first read your cousin's letter. I would be honored if you would allow me to help you hone your abilities to better serve your people. And anyone else who has need of your services." His smile grew slightly. "It would be a relief if my family was not the only one the world called upon for help."

"Wait," George said. "What do you mean both of us?"

Sabra's heart beat so loudly she could barely hear through the pounding in her ears. *Both* capable?

"Didn't you know?" The king looked at Sabra. "She has Sentinel blood as well."

Sentinel.

Sabra wanted to laugh and cry at the same time. After all these years of wondering, she was a Sentinel. She had a clan.

In a strange, twisted way, Mahzar's greatest fears had been justified.

"But..." she searched for words, "I was found in the Capitans' spoke. I'm a Capitan."

"By adoption, perhaps," the king said with a smile. "But you have power in your blood as well. Not as strong as it is in his, probably because he's a direct descendant. But it's there." He looked out at the people surrounding them. "Actually, I would venture to guess that every Sentinel has it."

Sabra looked back and forth between the king and her husband. "But there's no history of the women holding their own power. The power comes from the vow..." She let her words die as her thoughts continued to spin. But if there were, how would anyone know? Until the king had arrived, the Sentinels had known little about their own power, only its source. King Everard was changing everything.

"Who says the gift can't manifest itself in multiple ways?" The king raised his eyebrows. "What you just did for your husband proves that the Maker created the women of this clan with a special purpose of their own." He rubbed his chin thoughtfully. "I'm curious to see if your gift is limited to these two abilities, or whether you can do more."

"But what does it mean?" Sabra whispered, her heart fluttering fast within her chest. Every time she thought she'd figured out her place in the world, the Maker threw her something new.

But as the king smiled at her, and her own husband glowed, the pride bright in his eyes, Sabra couldn't help but wonder if maybe... just maybe, that wasn't a bad thing.

Maybe she was exactly who she needed to be now. And would continue to become that person as the Maker saw fit. Maybe she would continue to become the person she was destined to be.

"What does it mean?" the king echoed with a grin. "We'll just have to find out for ourselves, won't we?"

The Seven Years Princess

A Clean Fantasy Fairy Tale Retelling of Maid Maleen

Dear Book,

Writing on such crisp, clean pages in such a beautiful leather binding seems nearly criminal, but no one has touched you for a long time, as I can tell by the fine coat of dust I blew off your cover, so I suppose you're not sorely missed elsewhere.

I'm writing here because I need to speak to someone. Anyone.

Even if it's only empty pages. I haven't spoken to a single soul (who will respond to me) in two weeks, and I'm beginning to feel the need to slam things just to hear some sound.

My companion, Jalyna, isn't speaking to me. Or perhaps she's simply not speaking at all. I understand that she's angry. It's my fault that she's locked in here, away from her family and friends for the next seven years. I'd be angry, too. But my uncle is truly the one to blame, and I'm not sure how helpful it is for her to take out her anger on me. All she does is mend and sew and wash all day long with the supplies they've sent up the pulleys, glaring at her work and occasionally, me. She doesn't hum or sing or even whisper to herself when I'm not looking.

I'm frustrated, too. I've been through the entire first two levels of books, and I haven't found a way to escape, a book that might tell me how to do so, or even a mouse hole. It's as if this were the stoutest, safest tower in all of the western realm, protected even from little whiskered creatures. Honestly, if one were to pop out and speak to me, I'd probably be tempted to talk back.

I thought for sure we'd only be here a few days, or maybe a week at most. My servants cannot be in agreement with this. Then again, they have no power to stop him, especially if he's been replacing the military with his loyal soldiers in the stead of mine. Surely political pressure then, I thought. But no. It seems my uncle is too afraid of betrayal to even keep his trading treaties with the most powerful kingdoms in the realm. I worry that if someone doesn't change something soon, not only will I be stuck here, but our kingdom will crumble. He's destroying our military and our economy, and I can't do a thing about it.

My greatest hope is Rob, who is the most resourceful person I know. He's skilled in military strategy, and he has a will of steel when he's put his mind to something. Surely he will save me. He said he loved me, and I believe him. For Rob will do many things on a whim, but offering his heart would not be one of them.

I wish I could have heard what happened the night we were thrown in, after the door was locked. But I've found with much regret that our building seems to be doubly reinforced. There's wool between the inner and outer walls. I know because while I was searching the writing desk, I found an old drawing of the plans for the tower's construction. Apparently, according to the small handwritten note in the corner, the scholars wanted complete silence when they stayed here, so they had an extra layer of material put in to protect it from the sounds of the outside world.

The only interaction we have with the outside world are the three pulleys that raise and lower what we need and what we no longer need to the ground. (And yes, Book. I've considered openings as a means for escape as well. But as neither Jalyna nor I am the size of a bucket, I'm afraid we won't be leaving that way either.)

What would I have heard? Would Rob have found his tongue and challenged my uncle? Would the rest of the military have arrived and stood by him? Unfortunately, I'm afraid I'll not know until we escape. I can't hear a single peep from the other side of the wall, and the door is nearly as bad. Not the soldiers practicing their marching or the children laughing or sheep bleating or anything of the normal day-to-day sounds.

And yet I must believe he will hold to his promise to make me his. And I will hold to mine.

Can Maleen escape her tower? Does Prince Roburts keep his word? Find out in The Seven Years Princess: A Clean Fantasy Fairy Tale Retelling of Maid Maleen:

Dear Reader,

Thank you so much for coming along with Sabra and George in their fight for freedom and a happily-ever-after. I hope you had fun! If you'd like more stories about them and other fairy tale characters, you can get them by becoming one of Brit's Bookish Mages by joining my newsletter team. You'll get free bonus content, sneak peaks, book coupons, and more!

Also, if you enjoyed The Sentinel's Song, it would be a huge help if you could leave a rating or review on your favorite ebook retailer or Goodreads to help other readers discover new books.
As always, thanks!

ABOUT THE AUTHOR

Brittany lives with her Prince Charming, their little fairy, and their little prince in a ~~sparkling~~ (decently clean) castle in whatever kingdom the Air Force has most recently placed them. When she's not writing, Brittany can be found chasing her kids down with her DSLR, obsessively organizing, or belting it in the church choir.

<u>Connect with Me:</u>

Subscribe to my website: BrittanyFichterFiction.com
Facebook: Facebook.com/BFichterFiction
Email: BrittanyFichterFiction@gmail.com
Instagram: BrittanyFichterFiction